Josephine looked absolutely striking this evening.

Her pale skin only heightened the dramatic jump from dark hair and blue eyes to pale cheek and finally to dark collar that almost matched her hair.

Derek rushed to her side like an affection-starved puppy. She turned to smile at him, and it may have been his sudden embarrassment or the sight her berry-red lips and absolutely perfect teeth that made him stammer and stutter like a schoolboy of ten.

She must have greeted his mother and father, although he had not really heard her because of the noise in his ears. Others may have been tempted to attribute the noise to bells ringing or angels singing, but even in his present state Derek recognized it for what it was:

Blood coursing through his veins and to his head, sent by a heart that was acting no more sensibly than his eyes.

Dear Reader:

Harlequin offers you historical romances with a difference. Harlequin Historicals have all the passion and excitement of a five-hundred-page historical in three hundred pages, and stories that focus on people—a hero and heroine you really care about, who take you back to and make you part of their time.

We have some great books for you this fall. I've highlighted a few, and I'm sure you'll want to look for these and our other exciting selections. Here's what you can look forward to in coming months: *Rose Red, Rose White* by Marianne Willman is a passionate romance set in medieval England. *Texas Heart* by Ruth Langan is the story of a young woman who goes in search of her father and finds love along the way. *Apache Summer* is the third and final book in Heather Graham Pozzessere's miniseries, and it features Jamie Slater. Lastly, in December, look for *Chase the Thunder* by Patricia Potter, which is an exciting Western romance and a sequel to *Between the Thunder*.

We appreciate your comments and suggestions; our goal is to publish the kinds of books you want to read. So please keep your letters coming. You can write to us at the address below.

Karen Solem
Editorial Director
Harlequin Historicals
P.O. Box 7372
Grand Central Station
New York, New York 10017

Game of Hearts
Sally Cheney

Harlequin Books

TORONTO • NEW YORK • LONDON
AMSTERDAM • PARIS • SYDNEY • HAMBURG
STOCKHOLM • ATHENS • TOKYO • MILAN

Harlequin Historical first edition December 1989

ISBN 0-373-28636-8

Printed in the U.S.A.

SALLY CHENEY

was a bookstore owner before returning to her first love—writing. She has traveled extensively in the United States, but is happiest with the peaceful rural life in her home state of Idaho. When she is not writing, she is active in community affairs and enjoys cooking and gardening.

Because of Shanan

Chapter One

The Manor at Ettington, which was a small town about twenty miles from the famed Stratford-upon-Avon, was quite average as manor houses go, but due to the fact that it was the only manor house in Ettington, the townsfolk looked upon it as their personal Buckingham Palace. It had three stories and countless rooms (actually, Broderick, the butler, had counted them and knew exactly how many there were—including all of the rooms off rooms at the back of rooms. But he was the only one who knew. The servants didn't dare ask Broderick, and the master never thought to) but none of the rooms, excepting the formal dining hall and the main drawing room, were very large, and put alongside the other great houses of the county, it would have been completely unremarkable. It wasn't, though. Put alongside the other houses of the county, that is. It was in the middle of farms and woods and consequently dominated the surrounding countryside.

The house belonged to Squire Westover and had belonged to a Squire Westover for more than five hundred years. The present Squire Westover, Perseus Westover, was nothing like his namesake, the son of Zeus who slew Medusa in Greek mythology. But he was very like his own father: not too tall, not too slender and not too clever. But he had been clever enough to marry Catherine Bainbridge when he was a young man, and since then sparkling wit had not been required of him.

Catherine Bainbridge had been a brilliant success when she burst upon the social scene at Stratford over thirty years before. She had danced with every young swain and had flirted furiously with most of them. Although not from a rich family, with no dowry to speak of, she had been showered with proposals from gallant young men who swore to her that their hearts would surely break in two without her. Catherine may have been just a young girl and in society for the first time in her life, but she had an alert mind under her cinnamon curls and was not easily swayed by these tumultuous declarations of love.

It was then that the young Perseus Westover arrived on the scene and played his trump card.

"Dear Catherine," he had told her one night, when the moon was a silver gold and the heady odor of the lilac bushes surrounded the garden walk. "I do not have a massive golden mane of hair like Matthew Randolf. In fact, judging from my father and his father before him, in a few years I shall have very little hair of any color. Nor do I have a slender figure like Frederick Darrington."

"That is true," Catherine had said in agreement, and young Perseus had blushed.

"But Catherine, I love you with all of my heart, and I assure you I always will. And though I may not have the physical attributes of your other suitors, I do have more money than they do."

Perseus could tell he had struck a telling blow, and, in fact, Catherine married him just three months later. Neither had ever regretted their partnership. Squire Westover only grew to love his wife more with the passing years, as she proved herself canny in her household affairs, and, in a few years, his business dealings, as well. She had made him the proud father of first a daughter, Emily, then three years later a son, Derek. Thirteen years after Derek was born, and to their mutual astonishment, Catherine had one more daughter, Rebecca.

Though Catherine didn't love her husband with wild passionate abandon and never had, she was truly fond of him, and he *was* rich. By relinquishing, for the most part, the reins of his farm and lands into her hands, he only became more so in the succeeding years.

Emily had grown to young womanhood with the early blossom that so often foretells a quick fading of the bloom. Her father thought she was beautiful, had always been beautiful and would always be beautiful. Her mother, though, recognized the hothouse flower her daughter was and brought Emily out early, allowed her two short seasons of social life and then insisted she accept the proposal of Samuel Addison, pointing out to Emily his comfortable station, a home just forty miles from London, and remarking herself on Mr. Addison's severe squint and evident poor eyesight.

Her daughter's marriage was not as convenient or as successful as her own. Emily was not as bright, Mr. Addison was not as rich, Emily didn't like the London traffic or crowds, and Mr. Addison got glasses.

"An unfortunate invention," Mrs. Westover had said with a sigh. "They could have been almost happy."

Having arranged her daughter's life, Catherine next turned her attention to her son, Derek.

Perseus Westover had been named for a famous Greek hero, perhaps in the hopes that he would emulate that Perseus in some ways. He had not.

Derek Westover, on the other hand, had been named for no one: no one famous, no one in history, nor anyone the Westovers or Bainbridges were related to or even knew. He had been given that name solely because his mother liked it, and it was just as well that he wasn't named for anyone against whose memory he had to compete, because very early in life he would have totally eclipsed the original.

He was taller than the Westovers, even better looking than the Bainbridges, as pleasant as his father and as intelligent as his mother. He had Catherine's full chestnut hair and showed every indication that he would keep it. His eyes were the flashing sparkling brown that often go with reddish hair and always go with a quick mind. His father had given him a rather prominent, not completely straight, nose, but his mother had passed along a square firm jaw that made one forget, or at least forgive, the nose.

Neither of his parents were musical in the least, but Derek had taken quite naturally to the piano. His father thought it clever and cute, but his mother thought it more than that and saw to it that he had lessons commensurate with his talent. By the time he was ten, he was quite accomplished, and by the time he was eighteen, he showed so much virtuosity as to cause the young ladies in his audiences to swoon and the sophisticated gentlemen to nod their approval (granted, the young ladies would have swooned regardless of Derek's ability, for he cut a slender and unspeakably romantic figure at the piano; but the sophisticated gentlemen frequented the London music halls and were not willing to give their approval to anything less than excellence). As he reached his middle twenties, however, the rascality of prolonged bachelorhood seized him, and he refused to play in public any longer, although he never ceased to play for his own enjoyment in the privacy of his home.

His parents were not readers; he had read every book in his father's library and had extended it considerably. His mother was certainly diligent and could, by applying herself, oversee the Westover accounts, which his father could not do with any amount of application, but numbers had always been a struggle even for her. Derek took to the mathematical sciences as naturally as he had the piano, and before most of the other boys his age were called upon to reckon their own allowances, Mrs. Westover gratefully handed over the books to her young son, which he had ever since managed with greater ease and more finesse than she ever had.

No one in either of his ancestral lines, as far back as they could trace (and as all the landed gentry did, they took great pride in their genealogy and could both go back several generations in their records) had ever shown any artistic ability. In this, at least, Derek conformed. He could not draw a recognizable circle, and his eye for color would have him combining golden yellow with navy blue and hoping for a pale mint green. But he did, at least, recognize this as a shortcoming, and was a great admirer of those more skilled than himself in the visual arts.

Derek was fond of both of his parents and had always endeavored to conform to their wishes. He had attended the reputable school in which they enrolled him and had excelled in all of his classes. They had suggested he spend a season abroad, so he spent one summer in Paris, the next in Venice, and soon was hopping about the continent enough to satisfy the most demanding of parents. His mother had wanted him to meet and be personable to a fair number of respectable young ladies, so he had, leaving acres of broken hearts in his wake. His father had winked, nudged him in the ribs and hinted that he "sow a few wild oats." Being the dutiful son that he was, he had complied with that suggestion, as well, shattering still more dreams and fond hearts. But the years passed, and his own heart remained whole, unscarred, unmarked in any way and exclusively in his possession. His mother became concerned.

"Give the boy time, m'dear," Squire Westover had murmured around a smoking pipe and a full stomach.

"'Boy' indeed!" Mrs. Westover had fumed. She was ignored by her husband, so she decided she would take matters into her own hands.

But in this Derek refused to be manipulated. No one else could fall in love for him, nor was he going to fall in love just because he was told to do so.

"What is so vital about love, Derek?" his mother had demanded. "Look at your father and me. I didn't love Perseus at all when I married him...."

At that Squire Westover looked up at his wife with such a hurt expression she was compelled to hurriedly add, "But I soon came to love him dearly," which undermined her entire argument. She decided next time to talk to Derek about this when his father was not in the room.

"Your father's name must be carried on," she said.

"A man needs to be married."

"The house and farm would not be hurt by a little dowry money."

"Miss Whatsit would take you in a minute, you know."

"The Whosit girl confessed to her mother, and she to me, that you are quite the catch of the county."

And so on and so on from the time he turned twenty-four. Derek Westover was a mere mortal. His twenty-sixth birthday was commemorated with a quiet little family gathering.

"How much gayer this would have been with my little grandchildren around my knee," Catherine had said with a sigh.

Emily, who had come with her husband and family for the week, pointed out to her mother that she had four of Emily's rosy-cheeked, flaxen-haired, brassy-voiced children around her even then.

"I am talking about Derek's children," Mrs. Westover had hissed.

Emily shot her brother a shocked look.

"Derek!" she gasped. "Have you some little bastards sprinkled about the countryside?"

Derek assured his sister that to his knowledge he was completely childless, that their mother was only hinting that he get married and raise a family.

"Oh," Emily said, and Catherine sadly shook her head. Not only had Emily's looks faded, but her mind seemed to be getting dimmer with each passing year.

It was three months later that Mrs. Catherine Westover looked up from a letter she had just received.

"From the Forresters, dear," she said. "Ulanda says the cutlery manufacturing is still going well there in Sheffield. Gregory's holdings have skyrocketed, if one can trust her business sense."

"Mmm. Yes, I suppose they have. Old Forrester got in on the ground level of that one. I imagine his stocks have at least tripled, possibly quadrupled. Beastly good luck, the chap has. Beastly good." The squire didn't sound quite as congratulatory as his words seemed to merit. A listener might have been tempted to suspect it was not the fulfillment of his life's dream to have this acquaintance of his raised to heights of phenomenal wealth.

Catherine Westover might have thought that herself, but she wasn't paying enough attention to her husband's familiar mumblings. Instead she continued to peruse the missive, from which she looked up in another few moments to pointedly address her son, seated by the window, reading his own mail.

"It seems the Forresters are making all the money they could possibly want—" the squire quietly snorted "—but as far as finding a husband for Phyllis, they have had no luck at all. There is no one but rude workmen and wealthy, old, *married* industrialists in the area. Ulanda says she wishes Phyllis could come to the country long enough to meet someone more suitable. She hints that the dowry they are willing to settle on the girl will be—handsome, to say the least."

"I never thought Phyllis, would grow up to be such a hard looker that they'd have to buy the girl a man," her husband said, grinning.

"Don't you listen to him," Mrs. Westover said, darting a stern look at her husband. "Phyllis is lovely. Quite lovely. That is, I assume she's lovely. Admittedly, it's been years since we've seen her, but she was a darling little girl, if I remember correctly."

"Years since you've seen her?" Derek asked.

His mother was encouraged. At least it proved he was listening. "Well, yes, some years. She is, perhaps, not in the pink freshness of sixteen-year-old childhood, but I am sure she's a beautiful woman. It's just that her parents don't want her to marry beneath her position and are willing to make a marriage more than worth any man's while. Any *gentleman*, that is."

"Invite her down to stay with us, Mother," Derek said carelessly, barely looking up from the London newspaper he had just received by post.

"Now Derek, m'boy," his father said gravely. "This Forrester lass isn't like some of the other young things you've...." his voice faded uncomfortably with the recollection that his wife was sitting on the other side of the desk.

"I am aware of that, Father," his son said. "Perhaps I'm ready to accept my responsibilities."

He left the room then, with his parents looking after him. The expressions on their faces were just the opposite of what one would have expected considering the conversations between them on this subject during the past several years. Perseus Westover was smiling as if his fondest desire had just been granted him. His wife, on the other hand, watched her son leave with a worried, discontented look.

"I do believe the boy is contemplating matrimony," Westover said.

"I believe you are right," his wife said in a considerably more subdued tone of voice.

"I say, Catherine. What are those other letters you have there?"

"A report on the wool sales," she said carelessly.

"And how did we do?"

"Not as well as we had expected," she said. Catherine Westover had said the same of the sale of anything on their farm at any price for as long as Perseus could remember. Quite often the figure was actually far above anything he had expected, and he wondered sometimes what his wife's expectations were.

"And that other one you have there?"

"It says Rebecca has been requested to leave Miss Moreling's school, too. Really, Perseus, you must speak to your daughter. We are rapidly running out of schools that will accept her." She stopped and Westover made suitably gruff noises into his double chin. She sighed and started composing her next speech to her somewhat wayward daughter. "I am afraid we will have to engage a tutor until we can reenroll her someplace else. Don't you think so?"

"Of course, of course, m'dear. You do what you think best."

"I always do," Mrs. Westover murmured as she reached into the desk for her pen and enough writing paper for the two letters she had to write.

Chapter Two

Mama, it will do you no good to fuss and fume any longer. I have made up my mind—I am going to take the position. In a private home. You are not to worry, it is perfectly respectable, and you know there is nothing demeaning about being a governess."

Josephine had talked long and soothingly to calm her mother's first horrified reaction to her news, but at Josephine's latest mention of "governess," Mary Foster embarked once again on a tirade of guilt and grief.

"Oh, that we should have been brought to this. That my daughter, my own daughter, should find it necessary to seek employment, to leave her home and hearth."

Mary Foster had never been a professional actress, of course, but she had studied acting on an amateur scale, both at school and since her marriage in friendly gatherings. She had a remarkable natural flair and was now pacing up and down the length of the parlor, gesticulating wildly, on one sentence her voice rising fearfully and on the next dropping to soft dramatic levels.

Josephine was impressed, but only with her mother's acting ability. The grief expressed, she knew, was largely assumed for the desired effect. If Josephine had suddenly sunk to her knees, begged her mother's pardon and assured her that she would never leave her side and would banish all thoughts of gainful employment, no one would have been more nonplussed than Mary Foster.

"That your father could have brought us to this level," Mary continued mournfully, perfectly secure that her daughter knew this was only for show.

What Josephine's father had done to "bring them to this level," was to have invested heavily in the linen industry in Sheffield months before the introduction of electroplating cutlery manufacturing really put Sheffield on the map, brought international recognition to the city and sudden unimpeachable wealth to stockholders in that industry. The linen industry was left choking in the dust. From the very finest girls' schools and private tutors, Josephine had progressed steadily downward through the good, the mediocre and finally to the extremely economical. Actually, Josephine had soon discovered that all these institutions taught essentially the same things, but the status Josephine's first school had conferred had been immense, and as long as the money was available, neither Josephine nor her father begrudged Mary the thrill she got from announcing that "*her* daughter was enrolled at the Eastonian Lyceum."

When the flow of money was reduced to a trickle in the Foster home, however, both Josephine and her father had insisted she attend someplace less expensive, and then someplace less expensive than that. The complete depletion of educational funds coincided with Josephine's graduation. She had been quite contented to return home, and now as the final bottom dropped from the Sheffield linen industry and the factories were preparing to close their doors, she was equally content to seek employment to aid her father in his current financial struggles.

And her mother, despite her present antics, was just as content as her husband and daughter at the contemplated step.

Josephine allowed her mother another lamentation or two and then produced the letter.

"In fact, Mama, I received word today. I have been engaged to tutor a young lady in a small town called Ettington, about a hundred miles south of us."

"A hundred miles!" her mother shrieked, throwing her arms over her head.

As she started to fall, Josephine ran to catch her. One of Mary Foster's finest theatrical accomplishments was her ability to swoon on cue. She was admired for it all around Sheffield and was often called upon to perform at even the most informal of gatherings. But as acknowledged an expert as she was, she still took her own family by surprise occasionally. Josephine just barely made it to her mother's side to catch her before she hit the floor.

"Oh, my darling daughter," Mrs. Foster whispered weakly as she opened her eyes. "Is it definite, then?" Josephine nodded and her mother smiled wanly. "Then Godspeed, my dear. You know you have my love and support."

The letter had been crisp and concise.

Your school was recommended to me by an acquaintance of mine who has had satisfactory dealings with Miss Crawford's pupils before. Upon inquiry, Miss Crawford spoke highly of your accomplishments and has persuaded me that you would make an excellent teacher for my youngest daughter, Rebecca.

Rebecca is thirteen, has spent some time in various schools, is bright and, I believe, teachable.

If the position is acceptable to you, you may write to me at . . .

There followed a name and address. Josephine had written. Further letters had been exchanged as to salary, education, living arrangements and particular interests. After all that, final negotiations were made for place and time of meeting and then, and only then, had Josephine revealed her plans to her mother.

The letter she now read to Mrs. Foster was from a Mrs. Westover: Josephine was to be met at the Ettington railway station on the seventeenth of July, and from there she would be taken to Westover Manor. Josephine was mildly surprised by the closing of Mrs. Westover's letter.

I am looking forward to meeting you, my dear. We are hoping you will love Ettington as much as we are sure all of Ettington will love you.

That was a good deal warmer and more effusive than Mrs. Westover had sounded in any of her previous epistles, and Josephine was puzzled as to how she should respond.

What she did not know, what Mrs. Westover did not know, and what took the very self-assured Phyllis Forrester back a pace, was that Mrs. Westover had mistakenly switched the last page of the two letters she mailed that day. Josephine was slightly flattered. Phyllis Forrester was more than slightly offended by the condescending officious tone to the final instructions she received, topped off by a brusque statement.

Will Trolley will be in town on the eighteenth of July delivering eggs to market and has agreed to meet you and carry you and your luggage to the manor in his cart.

Mrs. Westover was expecting to receive one lovely young lady of good breeding into her home, and one of not so fine quality. Mrs. Westover, at least, was not in error.

Chapter Three

Broderick was not accustomed to being sent on errands. He had clawed and grappled his way to the highest echelon of his profession and was considered by all, himself most particularly, as "being above this sort of thing." He sniffed and raised his nose another fraction of an inch. Mrs. Westover had explained carefully, in fact a little fearfully, that the young lady arriving today was a Miss Forrester from a family of good blood and excellent money. The Westovers hoped to be joined by marriage to the Forresters through the expected Miss Forrester and the young Mr. Westover. It was vital, therefore, that they make a very flattering first impression upon the young lady.

And how better could they impress Miss Forrester than to have her escorted from the train to the manor by the very impressive Westover butler?

Broderick sniffed again. Despite his mistress's solicitous attempt at justification, an errand was an errand, and when one held the position of butler in a prominent household, one did not run errands.

He stood at stiff attention as the train pulled in and supposed he would, in time, be able to forgive Mrs. Westover. The promised monetary bonus and free weekend starting a month from Friday next would aid the healing process.

The steam and stench swirled around the passenger carriage, and Broderick backed stiff-leggedly away. There were farmers and merchants meeting passengers or goods and some very low riffraff milling about.

Pickpockets, Broderick thought grimly, clutching the handle of his umbrella in a murderous grip.

The passengers descended the steps of the train one by one to be instantly enveloped and lost in the cloud of smoke and people waiting on the platform. If Broderick was expecting the air to clear and bells to ring when the young Forrester woman stepped off the train, he was sadly mistaken. Three or four quite nice-looking young, and perhaps not-quite-so-young, ladies (Broderick had been waiting in the passage to clear away the tea service when Mrs. Westover had commented that "she may not be in the pink freshness of sixteen-year-old childhood") had come off the train, but they either had been met or had returned to the carriage when it became evident that the fresh air they were seeking was not to be found at Ettington station.

All of the passengers who were disembarking from the first-class carriage seemed to have done so, and Broderick was preparing to leave and tell Mrs. Westover that Miss Forrester had not been on the train. Let her worry about locating the errant guest—that was not part of his instructions. Though, of course, the bonus and the weekend would still be expected; *that* went without saying.

He was turning away when his step was stayed by a polite, "Sir? Excuse me, sir. Are you from Westover Manor?"

He turned to face the pleasant-voiced speaker and was somewhat relieved to see that while she was definitely no longer sixteen, neither could she be called middle-aged. She was not tall, but then next to Broderick, most people were not tall. She had light brown hair, wide eyes and a neat but unremarkable figure.

"Miss?" With guarded haughtiness. This could very well be Miss Forrester, but it could as easily be a mere nobody seeking directions. He would wait until he was sure before he displayed too much grace. No one would ever have accused Broderick of being promiscuously polite.

"I was to be met by someone from Westover Manor. Am I mistaken or are you my escort?"

Broderick approved of her choice of words. "Servant" would have been so much more condescending than "escort," and yet would have been used by many people of both higher and lower caliber than this young lady. He was not sure, however, that he approved of her approaching him at a train station, gullibly willing to believe that he or anyone else was going to take her to her desired destination. As he glanced around the station, though, he realized there was no one else there who could have possibly come from Westover Manor and forgave her her slip in decorum. Broderick conveniently forgot that he had been in the act of leaving this sweet young thing alone here just before she had stopped him.

"Miss Forrester?" he asked.

Ettington is south of Sheffield, and there was more nasality to the pronunciation here. Also, Broderick was several inches above her and added his own clipped nasality to the native speech. He was obviously mispronouncing "Foster," but Josephine was far too awed to correct him, so she merely answered in the affirmative.

It was, of course, Josephine Foster whom Broderick had met here at the Ettington station, as arranged in Mrs. Westover's confused letters. But it was "Miss Forrester" he subsequently introduced to Mrs. Westover, and the "My dear! How delighted we are that you could come," was meant for Phyllis Forrester, though it would not have been as heartfelt if Phyllis had been the young woman standing there.

"Why, thank you very much," Josephine said, favorably impressed by the great geniality shown by gentlefolk to their governesses here in southern England.

"Broderick, have Alex take our guest's trunks up to the Green Room."

"Trunks, ma'am?"

"Yes, her trunks," Mrs. Westover said, but careful to keep the impatience out of her voice. One did not get impatient with Broderick.

"Trunks?" the girl asked stupidly, and Mrs. Westover hoped she wouldn't have to revise her initial favorable impression of the girl.

"Yes, my dear. Your trunks. Your luggage. Your valises."

"This...this is all I brought," Josephine said, feeling somehow inadequate.

"All?" Mrs. Westover gasped, amazed until the explanation occurred to her. "Oh, of course, you were planning on doing some shopping here, no doubt. I'm sorry. I certainly should have explained to you that Ettington is a very small community whose dress shops are hardly up to Sheffield standards. But I make most of my purchases from an accomplished little woman in the village, and perhaps you wouldn't be wholly disappointed in her work. And, of course, you're right, it is so much trouble to travel with large quantities of luggage.''

Mrs. Westover indicated Josephine's one bag to Broderick, who in turn indicated it to little Matty Clark, who had been passing in the hall, and then she led the young woman into the front drawing room.

The front drawing room was used only on state occasions: Sunday teas; the introduction of a new pastor to a select few in his congregation; visiting relatives who were as well- or better-off than the Perseus Westovers (poor relations took lukewarm tea in the back sitting room and could consider themselves lucky to get that). The chairs were uncomfortable, the paneling gloomy and the small fire never warm enough in winter. Fortunately it was midsummer, so the room was merely stifling. It was such an uncomfortable room that it demanded one to be impressed if one was invited within its doors.

The ladies had settled, as much as possible, onto the high-backed chairs and were about to begin a stilted conversation, when the quiet air exploded with a rather rude expletive.

''The front drawing room!'' the voice said. ''Surely I'm not expected to sit in that hellhole again to take my afternoon tea?''

''Excuse me, my dear,'' Mrs. Westover said with a tight-lipped smile, her cheeks blazing. It might have been from embarrassment, but judging from Mrs. Westover's determined stride as she left the room and the infuriated whisperings heard in the corridor immediately following her departure, Josephine decided the red was caused by anger. Great anger. Mrs. Westover was certainly concerned about the impression being made on the new governess. Unduly so, to Josephine's thinking. In fact, the longer she sat on this chair, the more she agreed with the speaker in the hall.

The lady of the house was suddenly at the door again. Behind her and considerably below her was a balding little gentleman with the satisfied paunch of a prosperous country squire.

''Pardon us, my dear,'' Mrs. Westover said. ''I would like you to meet my husband, Perseus Westover.''

Mr. Westover came into the room appearing justly chastised from the argument, but holding out his hand in friendly greeting. "Delighted that you could join us. And how long do you think you'll be staying?"

"Mr. Westover!" his wife hissed.

The gentleman looked around in surprise. "What?" he asked.

Mrs. Westover fixed a pleasant smile over the scowl she was directing toward her husband, which made the resulting expression somewhat alarming. "We are all in great hopes that the young lady is here to stay quite some time," she said meaningfully.

There seemed to be some sly message conveyed in her words, which Josephine must have missed.

Evidently the squire was aware of the meaning, though, for suddenly his face broke into beams of joviality. "Of course. Of course. Quite some time, what?" he crowed.

Josephine looked on at the antics of the two elder Westovers in utter confusion. She shook her head slightly and then sat again, since Mrs. Westover was politely indicating her chair.

Mrs. Westover picked up the bell on the small side table and rang it sharply. Before the echo had died, Broderick was standing at the door.

"Ma'am?" he inquired.

"Hasn't Derek...I mean, young Mr. Westover, come in yet? He knows we were taking early tea today, and I especially wanted him to meet our guest."

"I shall inquire, ma'am," was the butler's cold reply. He turned and left, leaving Mrs. Westover to look nervously around the room.

"Warm for this time of year, wouldn't you say?" Squire Westover interjected pleasantly.

Josephine smiled and nodded, though she wondered what other climate Mr. Westover expected in July.

"I think this is Derek now," Mrs. Westover said, suddenly interrupting their sparkling conversation. "Derek, we're in here," she called gaily.

A dark form appeared at the threshold of the room. Josephine was still exchanging quiet comments with the senior Mr. Westover when Mrs. Westover kicked his foot and directed all their attentions to the door. "My dear, this is my son, Derek, about whom you have no doubt heard much already."

Looking at the man standing at the door, Josephine was quite sure she had never heard anything about him and was only sorry that she had not. He was very tall and very debonair and very handsome, without appearing to be very aware of his physical attributes.

He approached her chair.

"A pleasure to meet you, Miss . . ."

"Foster," she said softly, feeling suddenly very shy.

So this was the girl his mother had chosen for him, Derek thought. Not bad, all things considered, but a shy little thing. He bowed gravely over her hand. Perhaps it was just as well that she had a self-effacing manner and a voice he could barely hear. The less she would intrude herself upon his life the better. He was trying to accept this development philosophically, but he was not going to let a necessary marriage interfere with his enjoyment of life. It was not going to add to it, he was sure, so not letting it detract was the best he could hope for.

When he was a young man, he supposed he had been as dreamy eyed as the youths who frequented the stage performances and taverns today, although he could not remember it. Once he had believed he would meet a woman who was beautiful, intelligent, exciting, amusing and entertaining. One by one he had abandoned the qualities he was insisting upon. Now he thought he was simply asking for a nice-looking woman who was mildly witty and satisfyingly intelligent, who would make him happy. At least, he told himself he would be happy, but every year he stayed single he became harder to please. The attractive women he knew were not intelligent; the intelligent women were usually not in the least attractive, and if they were, they were not at all entertaining. When both he and the women he knew were younger, he had believed appearances superceded all other considerations. But one thing he had learned in his twenty-six years of observation, was that women tended to lose their looks, and there needed to be some attribute left that would make the relationship worthwhile.

He was dissatisfied, but he didn't know it was bachelorhood with which he was dissatisfied. He would have been happier if he had been married, even though it was marriage that he seemed to be fighting.

All of which explained, in part, the attitude he had upon meeting the young woman with whom his mother had informed him he *would* fall in love and to whom he would be married. She was a pretty little thing. The startling blue eyes she lifted to meet his were bright and intense and seemed to bespeak a mind working behind them. The lines around her lips and the tilt to her eyebrows indicated humor, but Derek, meeting her, reminded himself that though he must marry her, he surely was not going to love her.

Josephine, meanwhile, was still completely confused. The butler, Broderick, had afforded her much more respect than she would have expected the head of the staff to pay a young governess. Mrs. Westover was positively effusive; Squire Westover was a dear, and she knew they would have hit it off regardless of the time and place of their meeting, regardless of their individual stations. But now this young Mr. Westover, this Derek about whom she was supposed to have heard so much, had taken her hand and looked into her eyes with such welcome and surprised warmth it took her breath away. Then suddenly a veil was dropped behind his eyes, and his expression came close to raising goose bumps on her arms.

"I assure you that the pleasure is all mine, Mr. Westover," Josephine said.

He straightened, and though his mother impatiently indicated the empty chair next to Josephine, he walked across the room to sit in a chair almost hidden behind the door.

Of course, Josephine thought. It must be more comfortable. But the almost defiant look she caught him directing toward her seemed to put a different meaning on his choice of seats.

"And when will I meet Rebecca?" she asked, purposefully choosing to direct her thoughts away from the puzzlingly angry gentleman across from her.

"Oh, how lovely of you to remember my youngest daughter," Mrs. Westover gushed. "I wasn't even sure you knew about my other children. What a dear you are. Perseus, isn't she a dear? Derek, don't you think the young lady is a perfect dear?"

Josephine looked in amazement from Mrs. Westover to Squire Westover and finally at the younger Mr. Westover. This family was very odd, she thought a bit nervously. To think it remarkable that she should be aware of the young lady as whose governess she had been employed, Josephine found to be as utterly ridiculous as some of the antics of the "Family of Sillies" one read about in one's school primer. The expression on her face when her eyes finally met Derek's was such a study in comic bewilderment it forced him to smile at her sympathetically.

"Yes, yes, Catherine. The girl is a dear. Yes, indeed," Squire Westover was saying.

"But don't you think she must be an exhausted dear, Mother?" said Derek. "I am sure Miss Forrester would love to rest for an hour or two and get settled into her room now."

The younger Mr. Westover had mispronounced her name, but Josephine was in such a state of confusion, she let it slip by. And, too, she was awfully grateful to him for reminding her hostess that she had been on a long and wearying train ride today.

"I apologize to you," Mrs. Westover said, rising. "It quite slipped my mind that you might like to relax for a bit—we were enjoying your company so much. I'll have Sophie come help you unpack."

Josephine rose also, but before abandoning the effort, she thought she would make one more attempt to meet her charge.

"What about Rebecca?"

"How precious," Mrs. Westover cooed, patting her cheek affectionately. "Rebecca is visiting some friends this afternoon, but as soon as she returns, I shall certainly tell her you were asking after her. She will be very flattered, I'm sure."

"Mrs. Westover, I don't—"

"Now, now, now. Not another word until dinnertime. We don't want to completely bowl you over on your first afternoon with us, now do we?"

Josephine looked helplessly at the men standing in front of their chairs. Squire Westover was smiling broadly, thumbs under his black belt, supporting his protruding stomach, his head nodding and bobbing in approval. The younger Mr. Westover was watching her carefully with a slight smile on his lips. Neither seemed to be willing to offer an explanation for the family's very odd behavior, so Josephine left the room with the twittering Mrs. Westover. She was, despite that lady's best intentions, completely "bowled over."

Chapter Four

At eleven o'clock that evening, Josephine was still completely bowled over. Everything was so different from what she had expected her introduction to the working world to be. She was treated graciously, shown to what must have been, and indeed was, one of the finest rooms in the entire house. Mrs. Westover would not allow even a mention of business all evening long and included Josephine in the evening meal and after-dinner conversation as if she were a member of the family, or even an honored guest.

The squire had been too busy eating at the supper table to talk and had fallen asleep in what was obviously his easy chair almost before he could get his feet up onto the ottoman. Broderick had appeared noiselessly now and again throughout the evening to serve the coffee or brandy to the gentlemen. Mrs. Westover had talked hurriedly, almost nervously, it seemed to Josephine, telling her local stories and gossip. She had launched once into a panegyric of her son and his attributes and accomplishments, but a low and distinctly ominous "Mother" from that young man had immediately silenced her on that subject.

Derek enjoyed the evening immensely. He had seldom seen his mother try to make a good impression before. Generally she cared nothing about what other people thought of her, and generally she made a favorable impression. People did not always *like* Mrs. Westover, but they were always willing to admit her accomplishments, her talents, her wit and her intelligence.

Now, tonight, as she set about the unaccustomed task of presenting that image, she was failing miserably. From the looks of puzzlement, boredom and even sometimes pity on

Miss Forrester's face, one could see that Catherine Westover was not awing her young guest. At least, she was not filled with the kind of awe that Derek's mother would have found flattering.

At last, unwilling to let his mother sink any lower in her future daughter-in-law's estimation, Derek volunteered to play the piano.

"Oh, would you? My dear—" Mrs. Westover turned excitedly toward Josephine "—you will love this. My son is a marvelous pianist. And this is something of an honor, you know. He hardly deigns to play for anyone anymore!"

Josephine smiled and endeavored to appear as properly impressed as Mrs. Westover's tone seemed to prompt. When she felt that she could not, in good conscience, meet Mrs. Westover's gaze any longer, she murmured and ducked her head. She hoped it looked as if she were shy and embarrassed, instead of merely at a loss for words. Mrs. Westover was convinced. Josephine stole a glance at the young Mr. Westover and saw that he was not.

"Derek, dear, do play something by that nice Mr. Haydn. He wrote such amusing little tunes," Mrs. Westover continued.

Derek winced and seated himself at the keyboard. "Certainly not, Mother. I shall play a nocturne by the brilliant and refreshingly hedonistic Frédéric Chopin."

Josephine's little gasp was completely overshadowed by Mrs. Westover's shriek of outrage. Squire Westover jerked awake, looked around in alarm and finally settled on his son as being the most likely cause of whatever was the current uproar.

"Wh-what is going on, Derek?" he was finally able to ask, but his somewhat breathless question was also covered by his wife's considerably more vociferous protest.

"I forbid it, sir! I will not allow that man's music to become an influence in my home. They say," she said in a shocked and confidential undertone to Josephine, "that he lived with that shameless woman. Without the benefit of marriage." The last words were carried on a rising note of injured sentiment.

Josephine looked coolly at her employer with wide and innocent eyes. "The years Chopin and George Sand were together saw the composition of some of his most brilliant pieces, Mrs. Westover. Evidently they found their relationship satisfying and stimulating.'' The girl looked down at her hands and murmured softly, though quite audibly, ''Perhaps we are not in a position to judge them.''

Mrs. Westover choked on the sip of after-dinner coffee she had allowed herself, and Derek snorted loudly from the piano bench, nearly choking himself. The squire reopened his drooping eyelids and glared at his son.

''Derek, I will have no more of that kind of talk here,'' he said sternly. Derek tried to redirect the squire's attention to Miss Forrester, but his father, having delivered his warning, already had his eyes closed again.

''Derek,'' his mother began.

''I shall leave it to the young lady, Mother. What shall it be? The charming but insipid Mr. Haydn or the passionate Frédéric Chopin?''

Josephine looked uncertainly at Mrs. Westover. She didn't want to antagonize her employer this early in their relationship.

''I would hardly call Joseph Haydn's music 'insipid,' Mr. Westover. He wrote some magnificent pieces.'' Mrs. Westover was obviously pleased. Regretfully, Josephine continued. ''But for the piano, there really has been no one since Bach himself who was the master of the keyboard that Mr. Chopin has proved himself to be. I only hope you can do him justice, Mr. Westover.'' She couldn't resist the last little jab, seeing the light of gloating in his eyes. She expected him to look away petulantly, with an artist's annoying temperament. Instead his expression was one of delighted surprise.

''I shall do my best, Miss Forrester. My very best.''

''Miss Foster,'' Josephine automatically corrected, but Mr. Westover had already turned to face the row of ivory keys and obviously did not hear her over his concentration.

Josephine knew something about music, and like Mrs. Westover and most of the rest of the European continent, quite a bit about international scandal, so she was well acquainted with Frédéric Chopin's reputation, his genius, his talent, his music and his mistress. But she had never heard the particular nocturne Derek played. He had announced it as the Nocturne in C-sharp minor, but it wasn't the sweet sentimental little melody with simple accompaniment that the term *night music* seemed to suggest. It was filled with passion and drama and a poetic grandeur that dazzled Josephine. But the pianist dazzled her even more. Mr. Westover played as if he were part of the piano. His eyes seemed to absorb the notes, and the music flowed through him and out of his fingertips as he caressed the keys before him.

He finished the last plaintive notes and then sat motionless, as if regaining his strength. Josephine found herself somewhat drained, as well, even shaken.

"Well?" Derek said, turning, with one eyebrow raised and a challenging smile playing at the corners of his mouth.

Josephine looked into his dancing brown eyes and nodded. He seemed to want a vocal admission, but before she could open her mouth to speak, Mrs. Westover broke the spell.

"I am sure that was very nice, Derek, but you know how much I adore Mr. Haydn, who, by the by, was always a perfect model of decorum."

Derek tore his eyes away from Josephine's glowing blue ones, and concentrated, or at least tried to, on his mother's words.

"Next time, Mother," he said vaguely. "I promise next time it shall be Joseph Haydn. For you."

"But Mr. Chopin and myself thank you for tonight," Josephine said softly, and Derek had to be quite stern in reminding himself that he might be going to marry this girl, but he would be damned if he was going to love her.

As the sun filled her room the next morning, Josephine opened her eyes, and smiling, a bit in wonder, she looked about her. It was a large room, which only seemed to expand as the sunbeams bounced off the glowing brass bedposts and ricocheted around the room, across the silk dressing screen and around the rims of the sparkling porcelain pitcher and basin on the stand next to the armoire. It was not the sort of room she had come expecting to inhabit for the next several months.

When she had made her decision and told Miss Crawford she would be accepting the post as proposed in Mrs. Westover's letter, Josephine had been invited to a rather solemn tea at which Miss Crawford presided, feeling it her duty to burst any foolish bubbles of expectation her pupil may have been fostering concerning employment as a governess.

"Josephine, my dear," she had begun mournfully, handing her a cup of tea that seemed to have joined in the spirit of the occasion and was an uninviting watery lukewarm. "Yours is a noble ambition—the desire to aid your parents in their hour of financial ruin—"

"Miss Crawford, my parents are hardly in a state of financial ruin," Josephine interrupted.

Her teacher covered the girl's hand with her own and smiled in commiseration. "Let me finish, dear. I know that perhaps this will be difficult for you to hear, but it is only for your own good.

"Now, while I laud your motives, and certainly the post of governess is a respectable and honorable one, my conscience directs that I warn you as to what to expect, for I have been a governess myself, you know." Miss Crawford's last sentence was spoken in an undertone, as if she were revealing a personal secret to Josephine, and Josephine alone. But since her teacher had come to this school for young ladies directly from a post of governess, and spoke often of her former position and pupils in her classroom, Josephine knew quite well that Miss Crawford had been a governess. However, having been so admonished, she said nothing and allowed her well-meaning teacher to continue.

"The governess is in an awkward position in the household. She is not a member of the family, of course, but because she is, in theory (and certainly in fact as far as you are concerned) well educated and often from a good family, she is also not really a part of the serving staff. You—or rather, *she*—may therefore be subject to loneliness, a feeling of estrangement." Josephine nodded and started to tell her dear teacher that she was aware of the distinction she would face and hoped she was prepared for it. But Miss Crawford stopped her again with another pitying smile and pat on the hand.

"Nor is that everything," she continued. "Your student or students will be the children of wealthy parents, probably indulged since birth, sometimes stupid, always lazy, and yet you will be expected to teach the young ones to their parents' admiration. You will be fought and criticized by parents and students alike." This notion Josephine was not going to adopt and allow to color her first meeting and subsequent experience with her employers and charge, but she also believed she was prepared for whatever personal confrontations she would encounter.

And lastly, Miss Crawford had warned her what to expect as far as living arrangements.

"For some strange inexplicable reason, governesses are always relegated to the smallest, coldest, dankest, draftiest room in the house. The appointments, if any, are old and timeworn, the bed lumpy, the blankets thin. In short, I hope, my dear, that you have not chosen this avenue with misplaced faith in Currer Bell's romantic tale. Do not expect to find the love and intrigue Jane Eyre found. Be prepared for the worst, and you will not be disappointed."

Josephine nodded dutifully and finished her cold tea. As she stood to leave, Miss Crawford delivered a parting warning. "You mustn't begin this venture with any romantic notions, Josephine, because I can assure you that there is nothing romantic about being a governess."

Now, as Josephine folded the thick quilt back and rose from her truly luxurious bed, she looked around the room and smiled at her teacher's warnings. She had been wrong about one aspect of being governess. In this house, certainly. The appointments were hardly timeworn, and the house was not big enough to hold all the rooms if this was the smallest. No, though Miss Crawford's advice had been sincere, she was wrong about the room.

And then upon the canvas of her mind appeared the wavy-haired image of Mr. Derek Westover and his teasing brown eyes. She shook her head resolutely, but the image remained, and she sighed. She had taken Miss Crawford's talk to heart and had come here prepared for a life of dreariness and solitude. Was it her fault, then, that after the first night nothing her teacher had told her seemed to be true? Romance might never have been a part of Martha Crawford's teaching experience, but unless Josephine was very careful, it could become a troublesome and intrusive part of hers.

Mrs. Westover expressed a desire to speak to Josephine shortly after the family had breakfasted on nothing less than royal bounty. Mrs. Westover had told Bertha that she wanted their young guest to be favorably impressed with the Westover home, including, perhaps especially, the meals. Bertha, of course, was offended.

"What? The missus don't think my cookin's good enough for the likes of that hoity-toity Sheffield lassie, don't she? Well, we'll see about that!"

She had promptly, in a huff, used up half of the week's provisions concocting a breakfast that would have impressed the queen herself, and would have been sufficient for the entire royal household plus a fair meal for a few London families, as well. Of course, Josephine was impressed; Mrs. Westover was more than that. She immediately dispatched Will to pick up more supplies before he met Rebecca's incoming governess this morning, and sent Sophie to the kitchen lauding the meal, the service, the flavors, the colors, and anything else Sophie could see to laud that would mollify Bertha. Mrs. Westover recognized a cook's huff when she saw one. For a very strong-willed woman who ruled her friends and family with an iron hand, she often found she had met her match in her serving staff.

Now, having pulled Josephine aside, she announced with decision, "The first item of business this morning is, I believe, something of a wardrobe for you. Derek and his father will be busy about the estate for most of the morning, perhaps the entire day. And Rebecca is not expected back until late this afternoon," Mrs. Westover began as Josephine sat down, having expected her instructions to concern the lessons she would be required to give her new student. Much to her surprise, the conversation had taken a totally unexpected direction.

"Wardrobe?" she asked, bewildered.

"Well, of course, we can't have you being seen in the same three dresses—"

"Two," Josephine corrected.

"—at all of the teas, socials, visits, parties and balls that are planned for your stay."

Socials? Parties? Balls? Josephine was in a daze and made some weak protest about having no money....

"Well, I wouldn't expect you to have any ready cash with you, my dear. I am sure you were assuming that your father's credit would be as good in Ettington as in Sheffield. You couldn't have known that our little community is not able to handle credit transactions. But you mustn't worry about that— allow me to do this one little thing for you. Mr. Westover and myself would consider it a privilege to be allowed to purchase a few attractive little frocks for your stay with us," Mrs. Westover gushed, and felt she could well afford to. She was expecting a good deal more than the price of a few dresses in the promised Forrester marriage settlement. And the girl was an only child, with doting parents, so in time . . .

With a gay laugh, Mrs. Westover was off to the dressmaker's and the milliner's, her still-protesting guest in tow.

Shortly thereafter Messrs. Westover set out to visit some complaining tenants situated on the outskirts of the Westover property.

Which accounts for the fact that there was no one of the host family present when Will Trolley returned with a nice-looking but frosty new governess.

Chapter Five

Phyllis Forrester had been somewhat placated by her mother.

"Now dear," her mother had said. "I am sure Catherine— that is, Mrs. Westover—didn't mean to sound short in her letter. She no doubt had other things on her mind, what with the details of the estate I understand she is largely responsible for herself. I know she would be devastated to think she had offended you. She has made some rather broad hints that she hopes you and her son will be attracted to each other. And I don't have to tell you our hopes on that subject."

Phyllis tossed her head slightly, not fuming any longer, it was true, but not as willing as her mother to forgive what she considered a very decided slight.

"She no doubt meant the farm carriage," Mrs. Forrester continued. "Not the farm 'cart.' So promise me you will go and be your most charming self for just a fortnight. Will you do that for your mother? You know I am only concerned for your welfare. This would be a most advantageous marriage..." Mrs. Forrester continued, and would continue for at least another quarter of an hour. Phyllis had heard these remarks from her mother, father, paternal grandmother and a great aunt on her mother's side repeated any number of times with any number of variations since her mother's first letter was inspired and sent more than two months before.

The Westovers were a fine old family: an unattached and reputedly well-favored older son, landowners of some degree, impressive house, well connected. Oh yes, she knew it all, and she was willing to admit it did present an inviting prospect. So, while she was not going to swallow her pride (for which her well-proportioned frame simply did not have the capacity) she would attempt to overlook Mrs. Westover's deplorable lack of manners and would spend a few weeks in Ettington, trusting that this Derek Westover was as well-favored and as well-heeled as her mother avowed him to be.

According to the final page of that last letter she had received from Mrs. Westover, the date for her expected arrival had been set on the eighteenth of July. It was just another sample of Mrs. Westover's poor form that she had *informed* the young lady what day she would be expected and at what hour they would receive her at the manor.

For a solid week prior to that day, the Forrester house was in a constant uproar getting Phyllis packed. She had expensive tastes, true enough, but all that glitters is not necessarily gold, and Phyllis didn't seem to understand that.

"These are country landowners, my dear. Your taffeta gowns and emerald earrings would look out of place there."

"Or anywhere else," Phyllis's father had mumbled to himself.

"The dark red ensemble is very nice. You will make a striking impression coming off the train."

"But don't let her take the yellow, Ulanda," Mr. Forrester groaned.

Mrs. Forrester agreed with him. "You really shouldn't wear yellow, Phyllis."

"Tell her she nearly caused a jaundice panic the last time she appeared in public in that dress."

Mrs. Forrester did not tell her daughter that, but she did stay to oversee all the packing, coming back later in the day to remove some things Phyllis had insisted on, including several absolutely horrendous outfits that Phyllis loved. Mrs. Forrester was thus able to go to bed that last night assured that her daughter would at least present an enticing aspect.

Phyllis was roused a good deal earlier than her usual time; earlier, in fact, than she could ever remember rising before, though she had gone to bed later than this on a number of occasions.

"The train is scheduled to depart at 8:07 this morning, and we must take all your trunks with us. Come now. Don't dawdle."

Despite the cajoling of both of her parents, Phyllis refused to be hurried, refused to be happy, and the fact that they made the train at all could only be attributed to the train's standard refusal to be on time.

Ulanda Forrester watched her daughter board the train with a twinge of fondness and a mist of dew springing to her eyes. The next time she saw her daughter, she would have taken that final step toward marriage. Who knew, she might even have fallen in love. Ulanda brushed delicately at the tear in her eye and decided that a mother's heart was indeed a foolish thing. What more could she ask for her daughter than that she make a profitable match?

The hundred-mile trip from Sheffield to Ettington took Phyllis through a part of the English countryside she had never seen before, but she was much too wrapped up in personal concerns to notice the new sights slipping by the coach windows on either side of her.

She was not going to like Ettington; she already didn't like Mrs. Westover, despite her mother's assurances as to that lady's worth; and Mr. Derek Westover was going to find it difficult to gain Miss Forrester's approval.

The train pulled into Ettington at a quarter to one. The young lady was tired, rumpled, hot and hungry. And in no mood to receive any but the most delicate kid-glove handling. To her immense irritation, there was no one waiting on the platform for her. She scanned the well-dressed people waiting behind the boisterous rabble that crowded around the descending passengers. No one seemed to be looking for anyone; they all seemed to have found who they came to meet. One fine-looking older gentleman had appeared a trifle anxious for a moment, and Phyllis was sincerely hoping she would be the one to ease his mind, when his expression suddenly gladdened as a plump pretty young lady ran into his arms. Even across the station and above the hubbub Phyllis heard the delighted, "Grandpapa!" She turned from the happy reunion with a sour look on her face. The crowd was thinning, which increased her bad temper even more. The very idea! To allow her, Phyllis Forrester, to languish—yes, languish!—at this bumpkinish train station! Suddenly she heard a voice behind her call out, "Foster! I'm lookin' for a Miss Foster here." Even the pronunciation of her name was incorrect here, and it was unspeakably gauche for a man to call out any lady's name in a public place. But what more, really, could one expect of these country dolts?

"Here, my good man," she cried in her highest-pitched, most haughty tones. "Are you looking for me?"

"I am if you're Miss Foster come for Westover Manor." The speaker was a rough-looking young man of the rustic variety: coarse uncombed black hair; grimed and gnarled work-worn hands; smudges on cheek and forehead and several layers of clothing that seemed to have been donned one at a time, each to cover a hole in the article beneath it. His teeth were, surprisingly, white and strong looking as one sometimes saw in the peasant classes who ate many fresh fruits and vegetables and few of those delightful sweets and dainties that simply wrought havoc with one's complexion and dental well-being. He flashed his teeth often in smiles directed to friends, acquaintances, pretty girls and, finally, at Phyllis. His eyes were very dark, and, while attractive, still a good deal too bold for one of his station to be directing at her.

"Yes, I am Miss Forrester." She stressed the pronunciation and hoped it would sink into his thick, though admittedly good-looking, skull. "I have just come down from Sheffield to spend some time with the Westovers. I had no idea that I would be forced to wait at this station until everyone else was gone, but now that you are here, I suggest we leave."

The young man laughed loudly in real amusement, directly into her startled face. "Well, Miss Forr-es-ter," he separated all three syllables distinctly this time, but just the way he said the name in a slightly falsetto voice and with a mocking lilt, made her suddenly feel foolish for insisting on the change. "I suppose as long as we have your permission, we had better get going." He laughed again, but this time the laugh seemed to invite her to join.

She forced herself to be offended instead and turned with pursed lips to face the baggage platform where they were only now bringing out her last trunk. "There are my things."

He turned to look at which luggage she was indicating. There were five massive trunks lined up like squat soldiers on the platform.

"Gar!" He whistled in amazement. "Are all those yours?" Phyllis smiled in satisfaction; the young man finally seemed to be properly impressed with her. "The last time I saw that much luggage was when my Aunt Matilda came down from London to spend the year with us. And my Aunt Matilda weighs in at twenty stone!"

Phyllis gasped, slightly taken aback to be compared to a lady who weighed about 280 pounds.

"I wouldn't have thought a good-lookin' young lass like yourself would have need of that much covering," the young man continued. There was a burst of laughter around the two, and only then did Phyllis notice the group of rowdies standing about them, with lewd grins on their faces and expectant looks in their eyes, as if the fellow before her was a welcome and regular local wit.

"Ho, Will Trolley," one of the smirking audience called. "How many trunks d'ya think the lass needs, then?"

"Waaal…" Will drawled slowly, enjoying the spotlight and the girl's embarrassment. "To my way of thinking, she don't need no trunks of clothes at all. I was just about to decide she was wearing more than enough right now."

"You're just the fellow to right that wrong, Will!" came the rejoinder from the group, followed by loud guffaws. Scarlet mounted Phyllis's cheeks and enflamed even her eyes. Will could see that they had overstepped the bounds and was immediately sorry.

"Here now, what are you all just standing around for? Mike! Paulie! Load those things for me, why don't you boys? Come on now. Miss Foster—er, Forrester—has had a long ride and would like to get to the manor." Mention of Miss Forrester's destination worked like a charm on the rough young men. Cheerfully they tackled the trunks, and laughing and calling to each other, soon had them on the cart.

And it was just that: a rude farm cart, the sort of conveyance used to bring eggs and produce to market and carry milk jugs and beer barrels around to farm tenants.

Mr. Trolley lifted Phyllis up onto the uncomfortable bench with a gentleness and gallantry that surprised her. But as the last trunk was hoisted onto the back of the cart and the horses started down the road with a sullen clop-clop, the young lady was having serious misgivings. Things were not going at all the way her mother had assured her they would. Not at all.

Her eyes met Will's momentarily, and he gave her a gay encouraging grin.

Of course, she had to admit, she *had* discovered in twenty-four years that her mother's way was not always the most pleasant.

Chapter Six

Will Trolley stole a glance at the firmly molded profile beside him in the farm cart and mentally shrugged. Trouble there, he said to himself, for that icy profile promised fireworks to come. He grinned, for he always enjoyed a little trouble. Pity the girl won't be around long, he thought.

The household staff enjoyed the occasional struggle of wills with the mistress. The outcome was usually a toss-up, but they had learned long ago to allow Mrs. Westover the first victory. It gave her the impression of superiority necessary to her peace of mind and the staff's positions. Will could tell just by the set of the girl's jaw that this one wasn't going to back down, first time or last time, and they were probably going to be the same time.

Upon their arrival at the Westover Manor, however, they were informed that the family was not in. Sophie explained their various whereabouts, but it was obvious to Phyllis that the maid's attention was not directed at the important Miss Forrester, but rather at the bumpkin beside her. That the bumpkin was not entirely oblivious to the maid's coquetry was evidenced by his grin, his wink, his offensively familiar manner and, finally, by the gentle tap he deposited on her very ample derriere as she turned back toward the kitchen with a giggle.

Of course, it was the sort of demeanor this class of people displayed all the time to each other, but until now Phyllis had been entirely above, or anyway apart, from this sort of friendly camaraderie. She was determined to be scathingly superior to the young man the next time he deigned to notice her. But the grin and wink with which he turned to her undermined a great deal of her scathe.

"Looks like the cat's away, eh?" he whispered loudly to her, and she was inexplicably pleased to see an added flounce in Sophie's retreating figure, signifying that the wench had heard Will, as he had no doubt intended. Still, she was able to infuse her response with enough chilled scorn to back Will away a step or two.

"I beg your pardon, my good man? 'The cat's away,' you say?" The raised eyebrows and slight curl to her upper lip were additional touches she thought of at the last minute.

" 'The mice can play,' don't you know?" he said, and then called loudly down to the kitchen before Phyllis had a chance to register her shock and disapproval at his unseemly intimation. "Hey! Soph! Where's this lass to settle?"

"Ask Gwen," the maid shrieked back, and with no further explanation, Will turned toward the stairs.

The back stairs, Phyllis noted, narrowing her eyes as she added this to the list of slights to her dignity that was getting longer with every passing moment. If she hadn't wanted the chance to give Mrs. Westover and the whole despicable Westover family a piece of her mind that would wither the flesh on their bones and root them to the floor, where they would stand as a timeless warning to other thoughtless hosts, she would have instructed this Will Trolley person to take her belongings right back out to the wagon this instant and return her to the train station, where she would catch the next train back to Sheffield.

"Gwen, m'darling, where're you at?" Will was calling down the hall.

"What do you want, Will Trolley?" an exasperated-sounding voice called from one of the rooms, to be directly followed by an exasperated-looking woman. Gwendolyn smoothed a lock of the blondish-going-to-gray hair out of her eyes and looked the two of them over carefully, the young lady in particular. "And there's no reason to knock the plaster off the walls with that bellow of yours."

"Now don't be frettin', sweet Gwen. Just tell me where the missus wanted to put this young lady, and I'll leave you to your leisure. Sorry if we woke you from your nap." He grinned roguishly, and at his insulting imputation, the older woman directed one of her work-worn hands at Will's cheek, but he playfully ducked and, finally, Gwen smiled herself.

"You've got the devil in you today, Willie, that you do, indeed. Come on, then, I'll take you to the room, then I'll thank you both not to bother me again today. I'm tryin' to get things straightened up for the miss what's visiting." Her voice was friendlier, but the gleam in her eyes when she looked at Phyllis made it plain that she was very serious. Phyllis would not have believed it in any other house, and even in this veritable Bedlam, she could scarcely credit the cheek of this servant to a visitor of quality. As soon as she got to her room, she was going to write all these instances down; she was no longer certain she could remember them all, and at the planned dressing-down she was going to deliver, she wanted to be able to recite them *all.*

"Here. Put her things in here, Will. There's the room Mrs. Westover thought you could use for a classroom, and Becky'll be back tonight, so if I was you, I'd be ready to start lessons t'morrow, though I'm sure the mistress will want to talk to you when she gets back with the young lady. She'll let you know. Dinner's at six in the kitchen...."

"The kitchen!" Phyllis cried.

"Aye, the kitchen, missy. And you can take that look off your face. In this house you get paid with the rest of us, so you'll eat with the rest of us. Where did you expect to eat? In the dining room with the family and Mr. Derek's bride-to-be? Don't be stupid, girl. Will, when you finish up here, I need some help moving a bureau in the Green Room."

Will put the small suitcase on the bed and looked around at Phyllis for approval and some sort of indication as to where she wanted her trunks. "No governess I ever saw before had more 'n one dress with a different color sash for Sunday!" he muttered under his breath. But her back was to the young man, and when she didn't respond to his several pointed "Ahem's!" he piled the rest of the boxes he had been able to carry in this load noisily on the floor at the foot of the bed.

Phyllis simply could not respond. At first she had been furious at Gwen's treatment of her and then hard at work arriving at a conclusion. Miss Forrester was not actually stupid, but not much thinking had ever been required of her, so being called upon suddenly to do some deductive reasoning found her totally unprepared. It took a few moments for all of the facts to assemble themselves and parade before her in orderly fashion.

She had been met at the station and escorted here with a blatant lack of hospitality. Since arriving she had not met her hosts, nor did they seem at all worried about her creature comforts. Then something had been said about being paid with the rest of them so she could eat with the rest of them. A Becky had been mentioned, a classroom, Mrs. Westover wanting to speak to her....

Eureka!

She had been mistaken for Becky's new governess. But what was that Gwendolyn had said about Mr. Derek and his bride-to-be? From a number of rather broad hints her mother had dropped, she had been led to believe that *she* was the younger Mr. Westover's intended. What, then, could Gwendolyn have meant?

Again her thoughts assembled themselves for review. Now that the machinery was oiled, so to speak, the process did not take nearly as long this time.

The governess, the real governess, had arrived before Phyllis and had been taken for the visiting fiancée. After all, while the families corresponded more or less regularly, she herself had not seen the Westovers since she was a child. She had been a very small child and barely remembered the occasion, and the people not at all. It did bespeak a deplorable lack of regularity for such a mistake to have occurred, but she could forgive that much easier than the serving staff's earlier treatment of a guest in this house.

Well! They would be apprised of their mistake soon enough, and by a fiery impassioned diatribe—Phyllis could assure them of that!

She was, in fact, deciding a course of action, and Miss Forrester was the type of woman who, having set her mind on one idea, was next to impossible to channel in another direction. But just before the gears locked, young Will Trolley approached and stood close enough to her for her to smell the hay on his clothing, and another scent about him that she found strangely exciting.

"Your Miss Becky won't be back till tonight, and I wouldn't think even the mistress would expect you to set up class before tomorrow. What say we meet after supper down by the hayloft and get to know a little bit about each other?" He had slipped his arm around her waist and gave her a quick squeeze and a sly wink of the eye.

The Westovers might not return for a while—they would no doubt be horribly embarrassed—and her mother had implored her to make a good impression with the family. Perhaps it would be best if she waited just a little while. If she allowed herself a night's sleep first, she would be able to view the whole thing with a cool eye and explain the mistake to the Westovers without any of the parties involved being mortified beyond recuperation. It would save face and feelings for everyone.

It sounded wonderfully noble, and Phyllis herself believed that such was her reasoning for deciding to put off the confrontation until the next morning. But Phyllis Forrester had never before been motivated by concern for others, so her belief in her own charitable spirit was wholly unfounded. The simple truth, simply put, could be stated in two simple phrases: coal-black hair and dark sultry eyes. Will Trolley's coal-black hair and dark sultry eyes, to be specific. And not being Phyllis Forrester until tomorrow morning would allow her to be a simple serving girl for the rest of the evening.

Chapter Seven

Unlike Phyllis Forrester, Josephine Foster was very quick-witted, had always used her mind remarkably well, and the thinking process came quite naturally to her. In fact, although it would never have been admitted anywhere where Miss Forrester's money was esteemed, Josephine was considerably brighter than Phyllis. Nevertheless, through diligent effort Phyllis had arrived at the truth before Josephine had even stopped to wonder about the situation. One reason for that was, of course, that Phyllis wanted the situation to change, and Josephine was being treated like a fairy-tale princess. Another reason was that Phyllis had nothing to do but think, while Mrs. Westover barely allowed her young guest a chance to breathe in their madcap race to and about Stratford; thinking was positively out of the question.

"Now, Mrs. Neeman, the young lady needs these dresses as soon as possible."

Mrs. Neeman looked up at Mrs. Westover with the quick nervous movement of the sort of grayish little bird one sees hopping about fretfully on a cold winter afternoon. She had no time for Mrs. Westover and her endless admonitions today. The good Lord, in all His wisdom, had given Mrs. Westover considerable business insight, so that with her guidance, the Westover property had doubled in value since her marriage to Squire Westover; unfortunately He hadn't left well enough alone. He had also given her an officious manner, an air of superiority that was irritating even when warranted, and a deplorable ignorance as to when it was not. Mrs. Westover could barely thread a needle, and yet she insisted upon instructing, criticizing and commenting on every stitch her dressmaker attempted to put into the cloth. For good reason Mrs. Neeman's motions became even quicker and more nervous whenever she looked up to see this particular client come through the door.

But, in what appeared to be an attempt at compensation, Mrs. Westover was also generous, which made her servants, friends and regular merchants enduring and long-suffering on her behalf. Usually Mrs. Neeman allowed her to advise and direct for as long as she wanted, while the dressmaker went right ahead and sewed or snipped or whatever it was she was involved in. Today, though, besides the two dresses and the ball gown for Miss Foster, or Miss Forrester (she was never able to get it right; first Mrs. Westover would pronounce it one way, and then the girl would pronounce it the other way, until Mrs. Neeman was thoroughly confused) she also had an order for a ruffled bouffant afternoon tea dress for old Mrs. Halverson that she must somehow redesign to appear, if not actually becoming on the old dowager, at least not mawkish. She did not have time for Mrs. Westover today.

"Certainly, Mrs. Westover. I understand that, but surely you understand that for me to be able to do that, I must have some time to work." There was a hopeful rising note to Mrs. Neeman's sentence, a note of which Mrs. Westover was completely unaware, as unaware as she was of the chirping and twittering of the little December sparrows.

Josephine, however, heard the plea and answered it. "Come, come, madam. We have burdened this good woman quite long enough. I wish I could convince you that all of this is unnecessary, but if you insist on ordering something, one dress is quite sufficient."

"Oh, aren't you a dear!" Mrs. Westover beamed, patting her cheek fondly with two gloved fingers. "Isn't she a dear, Mrs.

Neeman?'' The dressmaker nodded quickly, then immediately returned her attention to the cloth in front of her.

"The green chiffon or the mauve satin, did you say?'' she asked around a number of pins she was holding between her lips.

"Oh, really, I don't—''

"The mauve, I think.''

"I look terrible in mauve,'' Josephine protested.

"The green, then?'' Mrs. Neeman asked, eyeing the girl sharply. She was right; she would have looked like a bruised plum in the purple-red material. The girl had a true eye and was not influenced by the fact that the mauve material was twice as expensive as the light green. So many girls would have made their choice according to price, trusting that people would believe a woman could not possibly look atrocious in something that cost as much as the crown jewels. Mrs. Neeman approved. Mrs. Neeman disapproved of a great many things and people, though never once in twenty-five years of dressmaking had she given voice to her opinion. The ladies of Ettington and Stratford who could afford her assumed her high prices bespoke her phenomenal talent. Mrs. Neeman was indeed extremely talented, but her prices were the only expression of disapproval she allowed herself. The ghastly dress for Mrs. Halverson, for instance, would cost Mr. Halverson many a trip to his broker or banker, and his wife would believe the money well spent. It would be horrible, of course, but like the mauve material, no one would dare believe that, because it was so expensive.

Ah, but for this girl! Such a trim figure, such lovely eyes, such a nice manner. The wealthy Mrs. Westover was fawning over her and was obviously willing to buy anything she wanted, and still the girl chose not the most expensive, but the most tasteful. For this girl she would make the clothes for half the usual price. Mrs. Westover would be pleased and would try not to wonder why a favored guest in her house was not considered worthy of Mrs. Neeman's best. And Josephine, if she ever saw the bill for the dresses, would be absolutely appalled that the law-abiding citizens of this village allowed such blatant highway robbery to go on right under their noses.

They left Mrs. Neeman's, with a parting, "One dress, Mrs. Neeman. Just the green one," from Josephine. And a, "Certainly not, dear girl. *Both* the afternoon frocks, and the ball gown, as well, Mrs. Neeman. You can send the bill to the squire," from Mrs. Westover as they went out the door.

The next stop was the milliner's, and it was possible that this visit would have gone on indefinitely if Josephine had not reached the end of her rope. They had spent what she believed to be three, maybe four, grueling hours (but was in fact only one and a half) while she posed and they arranged, studied and cooed, until she had felt like a china doll belonging to a very hard-to-satisfy five-year-old.

"Oh, please!" she finally cried, loudly enough to make herself heard above the two taller and much louder females standing over her. "Please, Mrs. Westover, Miss Franken. Really, it is fine. The hat with the yellow daisies is lovely, Miss Franken. And it is quite sufficient, Mrs. Westover. Just allow me to... I mean, Mrs. Westover, please, let us return to the manor." The eyes she turned on Mrs. Westover were brimming with appeal.

"She's tired," said Miss Franken, the milliner, sympathetically.

Mrs. Westover looked surprised.

"Are you tired, my dear?" she asked.

"Exhausted."

Mrs. Westover smiled weakly at Miss Franken.

"We have been at this rather a long time. Do assemble the one little bonnet the way we discussed."

"Did we decide on the small porcelain canary with that?" Miss Franken asked, eager for all the details to be exact. Mrs. Westover had been quite fond of the little bird, but Josephine shook her head firmly.

"It appears not, Miss Franken," Catherine Westover said sadly. "If it looks like we do need another of your lovely creations, we will return next week." Josephine groaned. The ladies decided not to pursue that topic any further. "Come along, my dear. I believe if we urge Alex a trifle, we can be back to Meadowview by teatime."

"Meadowview" was what Mrs. Westover had been striving to convince her husband to call his home for almost thirty-five years, since they had been married. Perseus Westover had allowed his wife to name the children, to hire and fire the servants, to decorate their home, choose their clothes and, finally, to handle most of his business dealings. He allowed those things because his wife was thrifty, industrious, manipulating and intelligent, and by giving the woman her ''head,'' his home was well run, and his business prospered. In every other case he could see a good reason to allow her to have her way. But as for the name of his house, he would not follow her lead. It was the one thing in which he defied her (which, of course, frustrated her all the more) and he was sorry to be forced to put his foot down on such a seemingly trivial point, but the fact remained that there was no meadow around his house. There was the lawn, the drive, the orchard, the farm buildings, the cultivated fields, a small wood, and if one shaded one's eyes and looked carefully, on a clear day one could see two tenant houses to the east and one to the south of them. But there was simply no meadow to view from his home, so for thirty-five years, his wife, who simply happened to adore the name Meadowview, had so called his house, while the squire and everyone else who ever referred to it, called it the manor. It was, after all, the only manor house most of those who referred to it ever referred to, so there had never been any confusion, except when Mrs. Westover called it Meadowview, and no one knew what she was talking about.

''Where?'' Josephine asked now.

''Back to the manor,'' Mrs. Westover said with a sigh, pulling the girl behind her as they left Miss Franken's establishment.

Chapter Eight

The carriage rolled up the drive and stopped in front of the house just as the large imposing grandfather clock in the front entranceway started to chime four o'clock. Broderick was peering out the narrow window beside the door, trying to decide about tea. Of course, he would set the tea things out whether anyone was there or not. His dilemma was deciding between fresh hot tea and crisp sandwich greens, or the left-over lukewarm tea in the kitchen and the wilted lettuce and watercress from the staff's informal luncheon. Broderick was not worried about the expense; he was even less an economist than he was an errand boy. Besides, he firmly maintained that a household that employs a butler is not called upon to pinch pennies.

So the idea that the Westovers would actually prefer *not* to have tea prepared and put out if no one was there never occurred to him; his concern was the work he might be able to save himself. Broderick was a prince among butlers, meeting fully the constant demand on his services, but he was, nevertheless, perfectly willing to save himself labor when he could. He was a prince, not a saint.

The question was decided for him with the arrival of the carriage, however. By the time the ladies entered the front door, the teakettle was on, the sandwiches were being hurriedly assembled, the cakes and sweetmeats were being arranged, and Broderick was standing statuesquely at the parlor doorway as if he had been standing there, expecting them, all day.

"Have the squire and young Mr. Westover returned?" Mrs. Westover asked as she handed him her gloves and removed her hat.

"No, ma'am the gentlemen are not here. The governess has arrived, however. I was informed that she arrived with Trolley this forenoon."

"You haven't met with her, then, yourself?"

"No, ma'am."

"Well, I will see to that after tea. Please serve as soon as Miss Forrester returns from freshening up. For a young lady coming straight from the whirl of social life in Sheffield, she certainly does tire easily. One brief day at the dressmaker's, and she is come back quite ready to collapse." As Mrs. Westover made that comment while turning into the parlor, she wasn't actually discussing one of her guests with her butler, but in fact both Mrs. Westover and Broderick felt gratified by the disclosure. It was a discreet form of gossip, and for shocking or important news, it was the quickest and surest way to spread a story to the other houses in the neighborhood. Mrs. Westover might not see any of the other ladies from the parish for a month or more, particularly in the winter, and as far as she knew, her staff didn't intermingle if she didn't, but nevertheless, if the tale was scandalous enough, the servants of the families for miles around could have their entire households apprised of it in one day, two at the very most.

The fact that Miss Forrester was exhausted after shopping would not make it to any of the other houses. Broderick doubted that this particular tidbit would traverse from upstairs to downstairs in this house.

The men did not return in time for tea, and directly after finishing the meal, Mrs. Westover suggested that the young lady retreat to her room for a rest. Josephine had been unable to make even a pretense at witty repartee as they sipped their tea, and try as she might to prevent it, her eyelids were drooping comically by the time the tea things were removed. As she laid her head on her pillow, before she sank into a much-needed sleep, she was able to congratulate herself once again on finding such a thoughtful, generous, undemanding employer.

Phyllis was not anywhere near as impressed with Mrs. Westover as an employer. The only thing that enabled her to tolerate the treatment she received was the vision of how mortified and grief stricken Mrs. Westover would be when Phyllis rectified the mistaken impression tomorrow and returned to her home in Sheffield with her fortune intact. Which put to the lie her professions of charity in waiting the day before making the announcement.

"Now then, Miss Foster," Mrs. Westover had begun after rapping peremptorily at the door to her room (which really was meant for the governess and still was not the smallest, coldest, dankest or draftiest room in the house, though it was a good deal nearer the mark on those counts than Miss Forrester was accustomed to or expecting) and entering without invitation. "As I explained in our correspondence, you will be instructing my youngest daughter, Rebecca. Rebecca is a precocious, flamboyant, exuberant girl. A number of her instructors have found her to be excessively so, though I am sure you will simply find her lighthearted and high-spirited.'' Mrs. Westover's firm tone encouraged even Phyllis, who was not in fact dependent upon the lady for her wages and position, to so find her daughter. "Rebecca will be returning tonight,'' Mrs. Westover continued. "So you may meet her then, though, of course, she will spend the evening with the family. However, tomorrow morning, directly after breakfast, I will expect you to begin your lessons according to an outlined plan I would like to see tomorrow morning directly *before* breakfast.

"Now Rebecca has studied both foreign languages and geography in several of the institutions in which she has been enrolled, and has shown little aptitude for those subjects. I would suggest that before you delve into either, you first try to pique her interest and develop your study of them slowly.''

Phyllis looked down and noticed that her fists were clenched and her knuckles were turning white. This charade was not going to last long enough for her to actually be called upon to teach anything, but the very mention of foreign languages and geography made her ill at ease, if not actually nauseous.

"She is also not interested in cooking, fashion, sewing, painting, art or literature. She is, unfortunately, very interested in horses. And dogs. But horses more than dogs. I allowed her to associate more than I should have with Alex, the head groom, during her younger impressionable years. And last time she was home, I fear she developed a schoolgirl's crush on one of the younger farmhands. Will . . . something or other. I forget his surname.''

"Trolley,'' Phyllis volunteered with a slight breathless quality to her voice. Mrs. Westover glanced at her sharply. She didn't approve of that sort of thing. The whole idea of pounding hearts and tragic sighs and mindless passion was utterly ridiculous to her. She had certainly survived well enough without it in her own life and saw no reason why everyone would not be as sensible.

No, she certainly did not approve of romance. In fact, she disapproved of it heartily. She disapproved of it in her serving staff, in her acquaintances and in her family. It caused servants to act thoughtlessly, her friends to act foolishly, and her son had so far refused to act at all until he found the elusive dream. The notion of romance was foolish, and she would not begin this new mistress/employee relationship by hiring a young lady who came to her already starry-eyed. Mrs. Westover studied the girl suspiciously. If there was one young man in her employ who was likely to incite infatuation, it was that good-looking rascal Will, whom Mrs. Westover herself had noticed. Not with any whimsical middle-aged longing, but rather with an eye for trouble spots. The young man was a good worker, however, and she had found it simpler to discharge one flighty maid and send her daughter away to yet another school, than to find another young man who worked as well and who, so far, seemed satisfied with his none-too-generous wage.

But Phyllis was a healthy young English girl of the florid persuasion, and try as she might, Mrs. Westover could not determine if the young woman was blushing or was instead in high color because of her day's exertions and her natural complexion.

She was, in fact, both.

Mrs. Westover decided to dismiss the matter for now, but she would keep her eye on this one.

"Well, the origin of my daughter's equine fascination is of no importance and can be of no possible interest to you." It was spoken as a warning; Phyllis recognized the tone, if she wasn't completely aware of the reasoning behind it, although she had a fair idea as to that, too. "What you must be interested in, is instructing Rebecca in those feminine arts for which she has shown no affinity, and dampening, if possible, her obsession with horses, which is reaching unhealthy proportions."

Phyllis liked Rebecca already. She felt an unfamiliar tug of genuine fondness at her heartstrings as she realized that the very pointed instructions she had just received were very similar to, if not identical with, the ones certain of her own schoolmistresses and governesses had received. When Phyllis was ten, her father had uncharacteristically taken her with him to the races one day. It was only a local race and relatively unglamorous as far as that went, but to a young girl the horses had seemed fast and strong and beautiful, the riders skilled and clever and daring. And her father had spent the entire day with her alone.

From that time, Phyllis had become obsessed with horseflesh: riding, breeding, caring for, racing, hunting, talking about. Anything at all to do with horses fascinated her. She ate, drank and lived horses. She talked of nothing else when awake and dreamed of nothing else when asleep. Her mother thought it rather odd to begin with, and finally after more than a year, it disturbed even her father.

She had been sent to schools that had been told the same thing she had just been told. Horses became a taboo subject. Her teachers introduced no conversations that might be digressed to a discussion of horses (although Phyllis had with great ingenuity managed to slip horses into the most innocuous of subjects), was refused racing notes, and was absolutely banned from the stables. Finding herself fighting an undauntable tide, Phyllis had surrendered and allowed her passion to be quelled. She developed into the cosseted petulant young lady she was, making demands on her parents that may have seemed unreasonable, but were in truth only a poor substitute for her abandonment of her one true love.

Phyllis was not aware of her reasoning; she only knew that if Rebecca loved horses, she would do all she could to help the girl. She didn't even stop to consider that she was barely going to meet Rebecca tonight, and that tomorrow she was planning on exposing the several layers of fraud, mistaken identity and impersonation that were going on in this house.

"You indicated the wage was entirely acceptable.... Miss Foster? The wage?"

Phyllis marshaled her attention back to Mrs. Westover, who was still talking.

"I trust we are not going to have any lack of cooperation concerning your pay?" Mrs. Westover asked again, and Phyllis shook her head, although she was quite certain that if she was really assuming this post, there would be a good deal of salary negotiation. Mrs. Westover had not elevated her husband's lands and business dealings to their unquestioned profitable status by being a spendthrift.

"You will usually eat with Rebecca. Proper etiquette is one of the areas of her education I find sadly lacking. We are expecting you to instruct her carefully in that, as well. However, we are entertaining a guest for a few weeks, and while she is here, you will usually eat with the other servants." Again Mrs. Westover studied the young woman carefully to detect any sparks of rebellion. Yes! They were in her eyes, though she silently nodded her acquiescence. Mrs. Westover hoped for Miss Foster's sake that she was competent at her post. She only allowed her servants to show a little spirit because they were outstanding in their duties.

"Now I believe I can allow you to finish unpacking. You will find your room quite comfortable." She smiled benignly, demonstrating now her finest mistress-of-the-manor manner. "Gwen may wish to speak to you later about the time of your meals, and your laundry, et cetera. But you will not hear from me again until after Rebecca arrives, which will be sometime this evening." She nodded, turned and left.

So far, so good; the girl appeared suitable for the job. Perhaps with a bit too much initial spunk, and obviously of the plebeian, working class, but clean and reasonably tidy for all that.

Chapter Nine

Derek found himself looking forward to getting back to the manor and spending a quiet evening at home. He was fond of his younger sister and would be happy to see her again, but he knew that Rebecca was not his main motivation to completing their business as quickly as possible and returning. Normally, if he and his father finished early enough, it was their custom to stop at The Lone Hunter for a round of ale or whiskey and soda. The wine cellar at the manor was one of the finest and most extensive in the shire, but stopping at the pub had become a pleasant finish to a day of fast talking and hard riding, and it gave the father and son a time to be alone together, man-to-man. It was an enjoyable interlude they had both come to anticipate with pleasure.

The squire had an earthy sense of humor, which, out from under Catherine's restraining hand, kept the crowd at The Lone Hunter laughing and nudging their neighbors throughout their whole stay. Or if the talk was quiet, on a more serious note, Derek was often surprised by his father's occasional flash of keen insight. His mother was the acknowledged brains in the family, with an analytical mind that could work through a problem, carefully turning over every bit of information, until she arrived at a solution. She was energetic, conscientious and undauntable in both her physical and mental labors. His father was much more relaxed in his efforts, unable or unwilling to put forth the time and energy himself. And yet he could occasionally arrive instantly at a solution to a problem or a true estimation of a person that it took his wife days of contemplation at which to arrive. Of course, Catherine Westover usually did not realize that, and the good squire was careful not to let her know. He wanted no rifts in their relationship, nor did he really want his wife to know he was more capable than she believed him to be.

Despite Derek's appreciation of his father and their time together, tonight he suggested they skip their usual stopover and get right home. Perseus Westover smiled to himself. Characteristically, he intuitively knew what his wife would spend the next several weeks prying at their son to discover: Derek was falling in love. The squire approved. He approved of most things his son did, but he was especially delighted by this turn of events, because he was very much delighted by the girl.

Dusk had swept its long black cape across the sky and was now gathering it about its shoulders as, with a scowl, it turned to night. The two men turned their horses into the long lane that led to the house, almost colliding with the neat little figure that was just emerging from the tree-encased gloom.

"Oh!" came the faint feminine squeak. Derek drew his horse up sharply.

"Who? What?" Squire Westover said in confusion, still unsure of what had happened in the time that it took his son to respond to the start, recognize the figure and dismount to apologize.

"Miss Forrester, are you all right? We weren't expecting to meet anyone here. Yourself least of all. You are not injured, I hope?"

Josephine pushed a strand of hair out of her eyes that had flown loose as she jumped back. The early summer moon, which had been up even before dusk, shone on her face and in her eyes as she looked reassuringly at the young man. Derek assumed the rapid beating of his heart was caused by the near mishap and did not notice that it actually increased when the girl smiled and shook her head.

"It was my fault, Mr. Westover. I thought I would like to take a little walk this evening before it got dark, but it would appear that I waited too long. And then I was so intent on the owl I thought I saw there through the trees, that I was not aware of approaching riders." She laughed a little uneasily, perhaps unduly awed by the man before her.

The truth of the matter was that the owl had not been engaging all of her concentration, but had disturbed her reverie. She had been thinking about Derek Westover. If the sun had not set, she would have had to call it daydreaming. But its being eventide, she allowed herself to pass it off lightly as "thinking about him."

When she had awakened in her room after a brief nap, it had taken her several minutes to orient herself to her surroundings. She could hear, through the muffle of a long hallway, several flights of stairs and a number of doors between, sounds from the kitchen. Probably the tea things were just being cleared away. The noises were very indistinct, until she heard a squawking female laugh that carried clearly through the whole house. Having just joined the staff of this house, Josephine was relieved to note that the servants were allowed to be individuals complete with a sense of humor.

She stood up and straightened her rumpled dress and hair, smiling as she did so and shaking her head. She was allowed considerably more leeway in this house than a simple laugh-filled afternoon in the kitchen. This was not at all what she had expected of full-time employment. Escorted to the home by the head of the staff, treated to an evening of food, conversation, music, taken on a shopping expedition by her new mistress and at that good woman's expense. Altogether different from the

lot of a governess to which Miss Crawford had tried to steel her.
Not to mention the young man.

That was easier said than done. Having introduced him as a
subject in her mental conversation, he very soon became the
exclusive topic.

What depths there were in his brown eyes. What varied and
exciting layers to his character and personality they seemed to
promise. He looked the part of the well-to-do heir of a landed
gentleman, with his broad shoulders, narrow hips and pur-
poseful stride. But already she had been surprised by him, by
his wit and his sensitivity at the piano. His hands were suited
not only to the reins of a horse or the barrel of a hunting rifle,
but could glide swiftly over the keyboard, gently, lovingly,
passionately, conjuring up magic in the notes that filled the
room. Very skillful hands.

She shook her head again and left the quiet room. She must
clear her head; it would not do to waste her time contemplating Derek Westover's brown eyes or long fingers or thick waving hair. She wouldn't think another thing about that hint of a
dimple in his cheek or the rapt attention with which he carried
on a conversation. The air of amusement, and at the same time
pent-up energy, that swirled around him, that ebbed and flowed
with his varying moods.

She just simply would not think about him.

"Broderick!" she called. The loud shout was startling in the
quiet of this wing. She hadn't meant it to sound much louder
than her regular speaking voice, but that part of the house
where she was standing—at the head of the second-floor balcony, with the domed ceiling two stories above her head and the
tiled floor two stories below her feet—had the excellent acous-
tics of a Grecian coliseum. It seized the sound and amplified it
before she had a chance to modify it.

"Miss?" Broderick's quiet bass voice sounded at her elbow
while the echoes of her call were still bouncing off the walls. It
was Josephine's turn to be surprised, which surprise she did not
conceal well.

"Excuse me, miss," Broderick murmured as Josephine
gasped, jumped and paled slightly. There were certainly occasions when being probably the finest butler in this county had
its rewarding moments. Broderick smiled slightly, which was as

much as he ever smiled. Though, as usual, he managed to hide it behind the gloved hand he raised to his lips as he cleared his throat.

"Broderick! I am sure you just robbed me of a year's growth!" she exclaimed involuntarily, but managed to end with a smile. Josephine's smile was charming, candid, always seemed genuine and almost always was. Broderick had a keen eye and could have detected the difference; fortunately, this time it was completely genuine, and the butler found himself being precipitately "won over" by the girl, without the customary ten-year waiting period on his approval.

Perhaps I am getting old, he thought. But as he watched the girl's delicate fingers smooth her skirt, he knew his approval had nothing to do with his changing age.

"Broderick," Josephine began, having regained her composure. "Where is Mrs. Westover?"

"It is Mrs. Westover's habit to see to household affairs in the afternoons. If possible, she prefers not to be disturbed during this time." She preferred not to be disturbed because, in recent years, since Derek had taken over so much of their business dealings, including domestic concerns, she was less in the habit of seeing to household affairs than taking a nap in the afternoon. But she and Broderick kept up the pretense; it was one of the butler's sacred duties to maintain the image of his mistress.

Catherine Westover would have denied it, but through the years, as many married couples seem to do, she and the squire had become very much alike. They'd started their lives together with totally different, sometimes completely opposite character traits. But during over thirty years of marriage, they had grown closer and closer together, until now the squire was much more conscious of social pressures and made a studied effort to make a good impression on the people he met, something he never would have considered worrying about before his marriage. And Mrs. Westover, for her part, was learning from her husband the art of napping.

Josephine felt mildly chastised and added a modicum of meekness to her manner, of which Broderick also approved.

"I see," she said. Then more to herself, "And I suppose Miss Rebecca hasn't arrived yet, or I would have been informed."

The butler didn't flicker so much as an eyelash, which Josephine took to mean she was correct. "Can you tell me, then, something I can do to keep myself busy until the young lady—or the gentlemen—return?" She mentioned the gentlemen with a break in her voice and a slight coloring of her cheeks.

Broderick's eyelashes did flicker then, in puzzlement. Like Mrs. Westover, he wondered what the young lady's extraordinary interest in Miss Becky was. He didn't need to inquire about the blush.

"Would the young lady like to change her apparel or have her hair redone? I could send for Sophie."

Josephine shook her head.

"Why would I want to do that?" she asked, touching her hand to her hair to make sure it was smooth and brushing at her skirt to flatten any wrinkles that might be offending the butler.

"Reading? Music? Needlework?" Even after serving in this house for almost thirty-five years himself, it was still something of a mystery to Broderick how a gentlewoman filled the hours of her day, and he was being hard put to think of any more suggestions for the young lady.

"I would prefer something outside—I feel I must get some fresh air."

"It is later than usual for an afternoon ride, but if you would like, I can have Alex or Will saddle one of the horses for you...."

"Oh, no, nothing like that. Really. You mustn't bother." The girl seemed almost embarrassed by his proposal, and his eyelashes flickered again. Unknowingly, Josephine had set a new record; she had surprised Broderick twice in one conversation into nearly revealing emotion.

"Certainly not, miss. Whatever you would like, then."

This was turning out to be a good deal more embarrassing and uncomfortable than it needed to be, Josephine felt.

"I would just like to go for a little walk. Is that possible?" she asked with something like desperation in her voice.

"Entirely possible, ma'am."

"Is there a path or lane I could follow? This is only my second day here, and I wouldn't want to lose my way. You understand."

"Of course. You could simply follow the lane that leads to the front gate. That is almost a quarter of a mile, but you will find it tree-shaded, and with the low afternoon sun, I do not believe the young lady would find it too warm."

Josephine had no patience for the girls she knew who pampered and protected themselves against every breath of fresh healthful air that came their way or any invigorating exercise they might undertake. Even her mother would be able to walk a quarter of a mile without fainting. Silently Josephine pooh-poohed Broderick's solicitation.

"That sounds lovely, Broderick. Please inform Mrs. Westover I am just out for a brief stroll, if she should ask."

So that was how Josephine came to be in the lane and almost run over by the returning Westover men.

"Here, Father," Derek said, handing the reins of his horse to the good squire, who had finally become aware of what was transpiring. "Take Verity with you back to the stable. I am afraid we have given our guest a start, and I had better see that she makes it back to the manor without further mishap." This short speech could have sounded like duty-bound resignation, but there was a lilt to Derek's voice and a tilt to his lips and eyes that fairly shouted this would be a privilege and a pleasure.

"Tell me, Miss Forrester, how are you finding our little hamlet?" he asked, turning to the young lady. "You and my mother went into the village today, I believe? That is something of a trip. I only hope you are not too exhausted. Should you be out walking now?"

"Mr. Westover, first of all, let me assure you that while your concern is well-taken, I am a woman of sound mind and body, and a few miles in the luxury of your very elegant carriage was hardly a test of my physical endurance. Although, strictly between the two of us, the fitting and flitting around the shops in town almost was."

Derek laughed appreciatively. Here was that which he had never thought to find: a female who thought the shopping rigmarole as unpleasant an experience as he did.

"But this brief little walk," Josephine continued, "was just the bit of invigoration I needed. I have thoroughly enjoyed it, up to, and yes, even including, the brushing collision with your horse. And finally, my name is—"

"Mr. Westover!" a voice hailed the gentleman loudly from the direction of the stables, interrupting Josephine's valiant attempt to rectify the mispronunciation of her name, which everyone here seemed to be laboring under. Looking up, they both saw a handsome, though roughly clad, young man standing at the doorway to the spacious building that lodged the Westover horses. "It looks like Verity has picked up a pebble in her hoof. Did you want to check it before I do anything with it?"

"Will Trolley," Derek said to Josephine. "He looks to the horses and fiddles a bit with the farm machinery. He is not as good with either as Alex, but under that man's capable tutelage, I expect him to become quite expert." Then, turning to the young man, Derek shouted, "I'll be right there, Will. Have Alex wait for me." He apologized briefly to Josephine before he left her. "This is hardly the sort of penitent action you deserve after my heedless horsemanship, but do you mind awfully if I allow you to return to the manor alone?" Derek's voice sounded unduly anxious as he tried to see her face through the gloom that surrounded them completely by now. "Oh, it is dark and you don't know the property. Perhaps I had better..."

Josephine put her hand on his arm and smiled.

"A woman learns at a very early age that gallantry must be dismissed in the face of a man's favorite horse. Please tend to your pretty little mare, and I shall heroically traverse the hundred steps, so fraught with peril, to the front door and the safety of Broderick's protecting arms." And with a parting pressure on his sleeve, she was gone. The hand had reminded him of a lily as it rested against his coat sleeve, and he was sorry when the slight weight was lifted and the slight figure had retreated into the evening gloom.

"Damn the rock!" he mumbled as he shuffled sullenly toward the waiting Will Trolley. He cursed several other objects and people on his way to the stable, barely stopping himself from damning his beloved Verity. The evening was warm, it would still be some time before dinner was served, and it would have been completely natural for him to have suggested a turn or two about the rose garden before they went in. Now, of course, Miss Forrester would go into the house, close herself in her own room until supper, after which his mother would, as she always did, dominate the conversation and would never hear of allowing them a few minutes alone.

He was still mumbling when he reached the stable. Will almost asked Mr. Derek to repeat himself, but he distinctly heard a rumbling, "...be damned!" as the young master entered the doors, so he decided not to pry.

"I thought you were returning with my son," Mrs. Westover said in surprise as she greeted Josephine inside the house.

"I am afraid his horse picked up a pebble, and he has gone to see to it," she explained.

"I see. Well, his precious little horse is hardly as important as yourself. The squire told me what happened and I hope you are all right. I have had Gwendolyn take some hot water up to your room, and you are certainly excused from the dinner table if you feel light-headed at all or, heaven forbid, you are injured."

The good squire must have embellished his recounting with some highly dramatic, though largely fictitious, details. Josephine assured the lady that she was quite, quite all right, and only felt that she needed a change of clothing.

"That horse barely nudged me off balance, and my skirts became entangled in the underbrush at the roadside. I will utilize the hot water before supper, if I may, though."

"Oh, my dear!" Mrs. Westover exclaimed as she took the young woman's arm under her own and led her to the staircase up to her room. "You cannot imagine how relieved I am to hear you say that. I was thrown into a dither when Mr. Westover told me of the mishap—an absolute dither!" This was the same Mrs. Westover who had personally overseen the dressing of a ghastly wound sustained by young Brian Pentlock when he had caught his clothing in their beastly new harvesting machine and been unable to extricate himself before his hand and right leg were very nearly torn off. Brian still limped, it was true, and had been forced to abandon the cold and heavy exercise of outdoor labor and join his father in their modest cabinet-making business, but that he was alive at all could only be attributed to Mrs. Westover's calm leadership in the crisis.

The little community of Ettington all agreed that the change had been nothing but beneficial for Brian, as he had learned the skill of cabinetmaking at the knees of the best craftsman in the area—his own father. He combined that skill with a sort of sixth sense he had about wood and space and color and design and was fast overtaking his father in local renown. Business was already increasing, and Brian's work would go on to be recognized and appreciated throughout the entire kingdom, and in time Pentlock cabinets would be collector's pieces, sold for exorbitant prices at auction. All owing to Mrs. Westover's cool, clear thinking in a time of emergency.

But as she led the young girl to the stairs, simpering and cooing the whole way, Josephine could only judge her employer to be one of those women who twittered and screamed and fainted when they pierced themselves with an embroidery needle. Charitably put, she thought Mrs. Westover was an extremely sensitive lady; what she was, was a scheming mother.

Chapter Ten

Rebecca Westover seemed to have liked the idea of her mother's young cinnamon tresses and her brother's auburn mane, but had evidently considered their efforts halfhearted. Becky had blazing red hair that curled wildly at the merest hint of moisture, darting off at odd angles and wrapping itself around any stray protuberance. For years she had humored her mother and worn it long and straggling. Being thick hair, it could have looked quite nice with a great deal of care and solicitation, but Becky could not be bothered with something so totally inconsequential—especially when it would rob her of precious time in the stables.

Joseph Baxter owned the farm nearest to the Westover property. Though he was not "gentry" as the Westovers were, he owned his farm and managed to realize a modest profit on it three out of every five years, which is the best that any small farmer can possibly hope for.

He and his wife, Barbara, lived in a modest home, but while it was nowhere near as imposing as the manor, it was considerably more cozy. They had—which is the whole purpose for introducing the Baxters into our narrative—a number of children, one of whom was a thirteen-year-old daughter they had christened Titia and who had been called nothing but Tilly since the day she was born.

Because the Baxters were independent farmers, had attended school themselves and insisted their children all complete several years of school, and because they honestly endeavored to better themselves and their lives, Mrs. Westover allowed, and even encouraged, her youngest daughter to associate with Tilly. That reasoning was perfectly truthful, but in her heart Mrs. Westover knew Becky would not have required her mother's consent, that the permission was given for Mrs. Westover's sake, and not her daughter's.

Besides Tilly, the Baxter household included an assortment of younger and older brothers and sisters. Tilly herself fell approximately in the middle of the brood and was a happy, relaxed, unpressured girl. Children who arrive neither first nor last in a family often are that way. They can see that all is not left up to them, that their parents' success at child rearing does not rest solely with them, so they are able to enjoy their journey through life, free to do what they can, but not expected to do everything. If child number three is good at painting, how marvelous! If not, number four is coming and very well may be.

Tilly had that attitude, which made her a wonderfully soothing childhood companion to Rebecca, who was not only the youngest child of the Westovers, but was widely separated in age from her brother and sister, and was thus in a rather ambiguous position. Understandably, then, she was temperamentally more intense and self-demanding than her friend. They had exchanged confidences since their first meeting as children, had shared the same attitudes and gone through the same stages that little girls go through. During the past two years, while Rebecca had been in and out of boarding schools, the girls hadn't seen much of each other, but they spent as much time as possible together whenever Becky was in Ettington.

The Baxter home had been Rebecca's first stop in her latest vacation—as she liked to refer to her frequent dismissals from schools. Since the Baxters lived between Miss Moreling's school and Westover Manor, it was perfectly logical that Rebecca break her journey there.

When last the girls were together, Rebecca had noticed an alarming preoccupation her friend was developing with boys. She had started alternately dreaming of them, talking about them and parading before them twenty-four hours a day. Becky was willing to admit that the male of the species probably had his place, after all, she knew a bit about horse breeding, but she considered Tilly's fascination bordering on excessive and a complete waste of time, especially when it kept her from the stables, of which, ironically, she had free run. There did not seem to be the least amount of justice in this world!

Now it was quite true that Rebecca was madly in love with Will Trolley, but that was a deep and sincere love, fostered by the fact that Will dealt better with horses and knew more about them than almost any other person Rebecca knew. Except Alex, that is. Will was an older man, true. But it gave one—especially if that one was a thirteen-year-old schoolgirl—a rather heady feeling to be in love with a mature man of twenty-three. And Rebecca was sure that her love for Will was based on mutual interests and respect; it had a sound foundation.

Tilly, on the other hand, was completely indiscriminate with her affections, and as far as Rebecca could see, she either was now or had been madly in love with every male person in the parish, including Will Trolley. She only based that last affection on the fact that Will was "a dream come true"—to use her own words—so Rebecca knew she could not possibly love him as much as she did, but it gave the girls at least one common source of conversation and giggling, where their interests differed in other areas, for the time being, anyway.

Now to return to the discussion of Rebecca's hair, which, if the Dear Reader will remember, was the topic that introduced this chapter. Rebecca arrived at the Baxter home in something of a foul temper. While she tried to pass her dismissals off lightly, rejection is always painful, especially to an adolescent girl, who has not lived long enough to realize that a person's worth need not be measured by the opinion of others. Her mother had informed her that a governess had been engaged for her, so she was not to expect a slothful holiday when she arrived home. The governess, Rebecca was sure, would be polite, extremely proper and have been instructed not to ever mention or allow Becky to mention, horses. She would be a girl just slightly older than Becky and yet would put on unbearably superior airs just because she could discourse in Greek or compute sums or something equally useless.

So Rebecca was already irritated, and when she was finally deposited in the Baxter home and had embraced Tilly's mother and then run up the stairs with Tilly, her hair, which had been hot and irritating the whole ride, became hopelessly tangled in her bonnet ribbons.

"I hate this!" she wailed. "I'd like to just cut it all off!"

"Becky!" Tilly was shocked. "Here, let me help," and together they fussed with the ribbons for several minutes. Finally, triumphantly, Tilly untied the last knot. "There!" she announced. "I knew we could get it. And now don't you feel silly for talking about cutting it off?"

"I certainly do not. Look at it, Till. All curling and fizzing and going any which way. It would be much more practical for a horsewoman to be allowed to have short hair."

"I don't think your mother wants you to be a horsewoman," Tilly said.

"But I am, whether she wants it or not. I won't always be stuck under her rules, you know. But look...." Rebecca held the sagging bush of her hair away from her face and up off her neck. "I wouldn't look so bad."

The other girl came behind to inspect the mirrored image with her friend.

"No, I guess you wouldn't. As a matter of fact, that's quite becoming." Tilly went from behind her to sit on the bed. "You know," she said, curling one leg under her in a position that would have horrified both of their mothers and every teacher Rebecca had ever had. "I happened to be walking behind Will" (she didn't need to identify which Will she was talking about) "on my way to the church last Sunday." Rebecca also didn't need to have witnessed the race from the Baxter door almost into Ettington to catch up with Will, to know how Tilly had just "happened to be walking behind" him. She only envied her the opportunity. Having been away from home for several months out of the past year, and banned from the stable most of the time she did spend at the manor, it had been quite some time since she had been able to maneuver a chance encounter with her father's farmhand.

"He and Ed Colter were talking, and I know Ed said something about short hair. I heard Will very well—you know what a strong deep voice he has." Rebecca nodded. The girls had listed and categorized every one of Will Trolley's adorable characteristics time and time again, and had quite often noted his fine baritone voice. "And he said he liked the idea of shorter hair on the girls."

Later that afternoon there had been a number of furtive trips up and down the stairs by Tilly, and at suppertime she asked her mother if Becky could stay the night.

"She's really very tired, I think. What with the ride here and . . . well, everything." Her mother had made vague sympathetic noises and said that if Tilly would ask the girl who helped with the housework to drop a message off at the manor on her way home then Becky could certainly stay.

Mrs. Baxter wondered a little where she would put Becky at dinner, as it always took some juggling to fit one more person around their crowded dinner table, and this week her oldest son, Merrill, was home, doing some work for another farmer in the neighborhood. So she was quite relieved when Tilly said that all Becky wanted was a tray in her room.

"She's really very tired, you see," Tilly explained earnestly.

So Rebecca had a bowl of Mrs. Baxter's very delicious lamb stew on a tray, but she didn't eat very much of it. She was actually sick to her stomach when she looked in the mirror and saw what Tilly had done to her hair.

One doesn't really like to imagine how she would have felt if she had known that the girls with shorter hair Will Trolley admired were a new breed of short-hair cattle.

Chapter Eleven

The room in which Phyllis found herself stationed was considerably smaller and less elegantly appointed than the sumptuous guest room Mrs. Westover had specifically prepared for her—the room in which Josephine was now gingerly washing a scrape on her knee while Gwendolyn hovered over her with enough ointment and bandages to wrap and mummify the girl's entire body.

Phyllis's room was on the other side of the house at the back, so that her single window looked out over the cattle pasture, with a view of the stable. The furnishings and bedding were all fresh and clean enough, but were pared down to a bare minimum. Phyllis considered it all very Spartan, and thought herself quite put upon to have only one thin towel with the bowl and pitcher, one quilt on the bed and that bed without even a canopy.

Shabby, she thought as she scornfully turned her back on the room to look out the window. She was on the point of turning away just as disdainfully from that pastoral scene, when she saw Will Trolley's black head and broad-shouldered figure emerge from the stable door.

He really was a very nice-looking fellow, Phyllis realized with something like surprise. She supposed she had always known that men of any class could be handsome, but since she had been carefully trained from her childhood to consider only a man's pocketbook and station, she seldom gave men without those a first glance, let alone a second. Was he from a good family? Was there a title anywhere in his line? Was he well-to-do, preferably rich? Then it doesn't matter, Phyllis, what the man looks like; he would certainly be an acceptable husband.

"He's a stupid oaf."

"That doesn't matter."

"He's a womanizing roustabout."

"That's neither here nor there."

"I understand he beat his last wife to death."

"Pooh-pooh, my dear. You place too much credence on the word of others."

"But—"

"And too much importance on trivial quirks of character. He has considerable wealth, and his cousin's uncle is Lord Pemblton."

Was it any wonder that Phyllis should emerge from such intense schooling wearing blinders that permitted her only to see money and position? It was, in fact, to her credit that she had allowed Will Trolley's forcible intrusion into her limited range of vision to awaken her suddenly to the realization that a man's worth could not always be measured by his balance in the bank and his ridicule of gainful employment.

As she lingered at the window, watching the skillful way Will handled the horse he led out of the stable, he turned his head to the manor house and raised his eyes.

He saw her! Their eyes met and Phyllis was surprised to feel her heart skip a beat. He smiled and waved a casual friendly greeting. That, too, surprised Phyllis, who could not remember the last casual friendly greeting she had received. The men with whom she socialized had been trained the same way she had been. Was her father wealthy? Did her family have political or financial ties that could prove beneficial? Was she apt to inherit any holdings from either the patriarchal or matriarchal lines?

They did not see or even consider her. If she favorably satisfied an inspector's checklist, and he her mother's, then the match was favorable. So far, fortunately, they had been unable to reach any mutual agreements, and until now Phyllis had been spared a frigid union that would have linked two uncaring people.

Because of that, because she was unattached, still free for a brief space of time—or at least until she met the young Mr. Westover, whom Phyllis had come as prepared to despise as Derek had been to despise her—she could admire the handsome figure of the Westover's hired man, and yes, as he motioned her to raise her window, she could even flirt with him, if she liked. And, raising the window far enough to get her head out, she realized that she would very much like to flirt with this young man.

"Coming?" he said.

"Coming where?" she asked.

"Now, I know from Alex that little Becky—Miss West-over—won't be back until tomorrow. Why sit up in that room by yourself tonight? The night is warm. I'm finished here, or I will be in a few minutes, anyway, as soon as Mr. Derek has taken care of Verity. We could meet at the barn."

"I don't know..." Phyllis started. She meant to say that she didn't know where the barn was and ask for directions. Will, though, assumed his character had been described to her by Sophie or Nell already. Both Sophie and Nell could have told the new governess stories about him that would not have been to his credit, as well as a girl or two from every farm in a twenty-mile radius of the manor. So naturally Will assumed that Phyllis's protests were stemming from distrustful maid-enly honor.

"All right, then, how about a little stroll down a country lane? The moon's up tonight, and I promise my best behavior."

Phyllis smiled. The soft moonlight reflected off her face, making her appear very young and trusting. As Will looked up into the window, he reluctantly repented of his plan to lure the girl to a dark and quiet spot off the lane into the woods. He had the unfamiliar urge to actually assume the role of gallant country swain, which his clean-shaved chin and candid eye so often belied.

"When?" she called softly.

"I still have to get Mr. Derek's mare rubbed down and put to stall, but meet me at the kitchen entrance in about a half hour."

"I'll be there." He smiled and nodded and then turned back into the stable doorway.

As Phyllis closed the window, her mind was aswirl with the foolish romantic thoughts that young girls of Rebecca's age usually get out of their systems to assume a more realistic view of the world by the time they reached Phyllis's age. But her romance had never been given vent; it had been dammed into a tiny chamber of her heart and conveniently forgotten. Until now, until Will Trolley's smile put a crack in the dike, releasing the schoolgirl fancies she had held in check for so long.

At any other time, on perhaps any other night of the year, that would have been perilous for Phyllis's virtue, she who knew so little of passion and who was crediting Will with noble traits he did not usually possess. But the moonlight had set her face alight with such trustful expectation that Will knew, glancing over his shoulder as he entered the farm building again, that he could and would fulfill his image, this once, for her.

The problem facing Phyllis now was to meet her usurper, warn her, enter into a pact with her that, if she would continue with her deception one more night and then peacefully depart (Phyllis didn't suppose the girl would be allowed to stay on as governess, not after hoodwinking the entire Westover household, a feat Phyllis was forced to admire), she would see that no avenging party or letters would follow her, destroying any hopes of future employment, certainly in this end of the kingdom. After the monumental humiliation Phyllis was planning to heap on these people, she did not suppose they would feel in the least inclined for outraged revenge. But if they did, Phyllis held an ace: after meeting Will Trolley, she wasn't viewing this mistake as quite the disaster she had at first, so if they would be willing to let the other girl go, she would be willing not to make the whole embarrassing story quite so public.

Phyllis quietly opened the door to her room and stealthily looked up and down the length of the hall. It was dark and narrow, lighted by a single lamp. She shut the door behind her and started toward the stairs, stopping herself from actually tiptoeing, so that if she was unfortunate enough to meet someone here, she would not have to explain her actions. She would definitely have been expected to explain tiptoeing. So she straightened her posture and walked with firm, albeit soft, tread to the stairs.

A guest room, she rightly assumed, would not be positioned at the back of the house, overlooking the stable and outbuildings. At least in the houses where she had formerly been the guest, that had hardly been the practice. If she was not mistaken, that was a rose garden on the other side of the house, and surely the room meant for herself would overlook that pleasant view.

She made her way down the stairs and crossed the open gallery that overlooked the entranceway and ran the width of the house without being seen.

I shall easily reach the room, she was thinking when she heard a soft, but extremely penetrating, cough behind her.

"Is there anything I can do for the young lady?" the dark-clad Broderick asked as he emerged from the shadows of one of the adjoining halls. He spoke the words perfectly solicitously but somehow managed to instill the message into them that he was the head servant in this house, and it was not actually his duty to help other members of the staff. And Broderick adhered religiously to his duty, seldom straying beyond those precise limits.

"I . . . I have a message for the young woman who is staying as a guest here," Phyllis stammered, startled by his sudden appearance.

"I would be happy to convey any message to Miss Forrester for you."

"No . . . no, thank you. I mean, Miss, er, Forrester asked to see me personally."

"I do not recall Miss Forrester leaving that message," Broderick said icily, assuring her with his tones that no messages were forwarded in this house without his knowledge.

"Actually, you see, I was formerly employed in Miss Forrester's home. . . ."

"Oh, really? I thought I was acquainted with the entire Forrester serving staff. And it must have been some time since they employed a governess for their only daughter. Certainly long before you could have assumed that post."

"That is, I mean, I was employed in a home where Miss Forrester was staying."

"I understood from Mrs. Westover that this was your first position since your graduation from a Miss Crawford's school for young women."

"Well, it is officially. It was while I was still attending Miss Crawford's school that I met the young lady."

"Ah," Broderick said, nodding understanding and acceptance of her last explanation. He did understand and accept it, but, of course, he did not believe it. The girl was lying through her teeth, as any idiot could see, but anyone who could maintain her calm and manufacture lie after blatant lie earned the butler's respect. The girl obviously wanted very much to see Miss Forrester, and since she did not appear to be carrying any concealed weapons, Broderick deemed it permissible.

"You will find Miss Forrester's room at the end of that passage," he said, pointing out the corridor in question. "But I am sure you already knew that, since Miss Forrester sent for you." There was irony in his voice, and Phyllis cleared her throat to try again.

"Miss Forrester—that is to say, the young lady—merely invited me to call on her if we should ever be in the same house, or village, or...place, again." Oh dear, she thought in despair, this is terribly awkward. She felt like falling on her knees and crying, "Oh, it isn't true. Take me away," and offering her wrists for the manacles.

But Broderick's only response was, "Certainly, miss." Then he turned and disappeared just as noiselessly and just as completely as he had appeared.

Shaken, but still firm in her resolve, Phyllis continued on her perilous quest. Moments later she was at a very broad, heavy, rich-looking door, tapping lightly. The wood absorbed the sound, and she was compelled to exert more force to make herself heard.

"Come in," were the muffled words that finally filtered back through to her, and she turned the ornate knob and entered the room—her room.

Chapter Twelve

Josephine stood at the foot of her bed, awash in the voluminous folds of one of Mrs. Westover's dressing gowns. The chiffon ruffles and laces billowed about her face and around her slender figure restlessly, reminding one of a tiny tugboat battling a stormy sea.

Phyllis entered the room prepared to detest the intriguer who had taken her place. She was instinctively certain that the girl must be a conniving scheming female, indeed, to have maneuvered Mrs. Westover so neatly into believing she was Miss Phyllis Forrester, and that she must therefore be on her guard against the young lady's wiles herself.

The figure before her was not what she had been girding herself to face, and the warm open smile Josephine turned in her direction took the wind from her indignant sails.

"Yes? Did you want to speak to me or to Gwendolyn?" Josephine asked. She was alone in the room at the moment, but she thought perhaps this young woman had come looking for the maid, who, a short time before had left the room, taking Josephine's rumpled and torn skirt with her.

"Nell can have these things mended, washed and pressed by tomorrow morning, so don't you worry a thing about it if your trunks don't get here by then," she had said.

Josephine had said nothing; nothing about there not being any trunks in transit, nothing about having only this one change of clothing until the dresses Mrs. Westover had so graciously ordered for her arrived, nothing about how, having been engaged as a governess, she had come totally unprepared for the social demands that were being made upon her. She had gone over her protestations, objections and explanations countless times to countless people in this house. So far they had gone unnoticed, and she had no reason to believe that Gwen would give any more attention to her words than anyone else.

She was still waiting for Rebecca to arrive. She was sure that as soon as she was immersed in the actual business of teaching, her career (if one could call a first and only post of governess a career) would then be seen as important to her. Perhaps when she proved she was an able teacher, she would be treated like one. That was not to suggest that she had any objections to the way she had been treated up to now. How could she, when she had been afforded the treatment of a royal visitor and taken into the bosom of this warm and generous, though very strange, family? But no one appeared to be taking her seriously as a governess, and though she did not object to the familiarity being shown her, as if she were a close personal friend of the family, her main fear was that she would forget to take *herself* seriously as a governess.

But until Becky arrived and helped put her position back into perspective, she would allow herself to enjoy the luxury being offered her. She was a naturally pleasant person, and her present mood only made her feel more so. Therefore, the face she turned toward the caller at her door fairly beamed, and her voice welcomed the young lady sincerely.

"Miss . . . Forrester?" her visitor said.

Josephine thought she might give it one more try.

"No, actually my name is Foster. Josephine Foster. I am afraid there has been some sort of mix-up with my name, and people here have been insisting on adding another syllable to it. But it is simply *F-o-s-t-e-r*, Foster." And she smiled again, a little timidly, as if she were not sure how her strong stand on the subject would be taken.

"I was under the impression that you were Miss Phyllis Forrester, a guest of the Westovers."

"Phyllis Forrester? A guest?" She laughed a tinkling little laugh. "Oh, my, no," she said as she turned back toward the bed and began to straighten the coverlet. "I am the new governess here. I don't know how on earth you could confuse me with this Miss Forrester. We are probably not at all alike."

"Well, as a matter of fact, Miss Foster, we are not."

"I beg your pardon?" Josephine stopped fussing with the bed and turned a puzzled look at the other young woman.

"And though others may be confused, I can assure you that I would never mistake you for Miss Forrester." She paused for dramatic effect. "Because, *I* am Miss Forrester—Miss Phyllis Forrester. And I believe you have assumed my identity and usurped my position in this house."

Chapter Thirteen

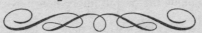

Oh, Tilly, what will my mother say?"

Tilly sat with her friend in commiserating silence. She did not know exactly what Mrs. Westover would say when she saw her daughter's shorn head, but she knew the lady well enough to know that her reaction would be clamorous and impassioned. She prayed fervently that Becky would not describe in too lurid detail her own part in the fiasco. Granted, Tilly's hand had held the shears and had even done the snipping, but only at Becky's insistence and under her direction.

"My mother has an old curling iron. If I can find that, we could use it and maybe it wouldn't look quite so. . ." Rebecca's stricken eyes met hers, and she couldn't bring herself to say "terrible." "So startling," she finished lamely.

Rebecca nodded, too heartsick to stop and ask herself if her friend knew any more about a curling iron than she did about cutting shears. Tilly did not, but luckily Mrs. Baxter knew that and stopped her daughter on her way back up the stairs with the iron.

"What are you doing with that?" she asked.

Tilly's vow of silence evaporated with her mother's first question. She tearfully confessed what had happened, then led Mrs. Baxter to the scene of the crime—for surely, the way Rebecca's hair looked *was* a crime—where Rebecca proved as malleable as her friend and retold the whole gruesome story from start to finish.

The shears had been big and awkward, much better suited to cutting canvas or hedges than a young girl's glowing tresses. And Tilly was inexperienced and easily startled by cries of outrage from her friend or suspicious stirrings outside the door, and had, more than once, taken an unplanned gouge in the tuft of hair she had been holding. So while most of Rebecca's hair was chin length, or perhaps a bit shorter, there were scattered areas that measured no more than an inch and seemed to poke out defiantly. It was these patches that drew the eye like a magnet and made the overall impression much worse than it actually was.

Mrs. Baxter, viewing it with a more or less disinterested eye (being neither the victim nor the perpetrator) saw, after some study, that all was not lost and reprieve was possible.

"Tilly dear, now stop that crying and fetch me the small scissors in my sewing drawer downstairs," she said coolly, taking the reins of the situation into her capable hands, reins that the two distraught girls eagerly relinquished. Mrs. Baxter saw that the girls were quite penitent enough, and, being the exceptional woman who felt no need to express personal views that would deepen guilt, refrained from making useless comments and even from asking pointless questions. The deed was done, could not be immediately undone and could only be mitigated now. Heated words would not help. Besides, it was not her hair or even her daughter's. Mrs. Baxter was always able to view things in perspective.

The scissors Tilly brought from downstairs were much smaller, and Mrs. Baxter had kept her husband and sons shaved and shorn for enough years not to be intimidated by either the blades or her task. Heartlessly she snipped off the longer hair, which Rebecca had looked upon as the only saving grace on her scalp. But the scissors continued to consume what was left, and the poor girl hardly felt in a position to tell Tilly's mother how to proceed. Surprisingly, when she was finished, the overall effect was not bad, though all of her hair was now shockingly short.

"Is that iron hot enough?" she asked her daughter, who had calmed down considerably; after all, it was not her hair, either, and she had inherited her mother's clear vision. Between the two of them, they captured and curled every stubborn strand, framing Rebecca's pert nose and, despite her mother's most frantic safeguards, determinedly freckled face in a bouncing cloud of red-gold curls. The effect was charming, and Rebecca recovered quickly from the deep depression into which she had been plunged by Tilly's doomed attempt at hairdressing. She was all for riding home right then, even as late as it was, sure that her mother would be charmed by her new carefree look. Mrs. Baxter could have told her that her mother was not going to be convinced by either the practicality or the attractiveness of her daughter's shorter hair and very well might lock the girl in her room until the curls had grown several inches, but Rebecca was so much more cheerful and hopeful than when Mrs. Baxter had entered the room that she did not have the heart to dash the girl's hopes.

"Why don't you just spend the night here, dear? We've already sent word you're staying; your mother won't be expecting you. We'll fix your hair again first thing in the morning and get you on your way then."

The plan sounded perfectly reasonable to Rebecca, who, with a final approving look in the mirror, went downstairs to join the family for the evening. The Baxters had all been warned what to expect, so they received Rebecca's altered appearance with good grace. Startled looks were exchanged only behind her back and out of her sight. Though thoughtful of them and certainly reassuring to the girl, it did leave her completely unprepared for the reception with which she would be met in her own home.

Chapter Fourteen

I ... don't know what you mean," Josephine said slowly, but not truthfully. In the time it took her to inhale and get her mouth open, she had grasped Phyllis's idea, and by the time her one sentence was afloat on the air, all of the questions she should have been constantly asking herself (and to do her justice, ones which she had occasionally asked herself, even in the middle of the flattering attention she had been afforded, and despite Derek's unsettling brown eyes and touching solicitation) were answered. She had been mistaken for someone else. According to the young lady before her, for this very person. Broderick had been sent to meet a visitor to the manor;

Squire and Mrs. Westover had greeted someone they thought was to be a guest in their home. And Derek Westover... whom did he believe he was meeting?

Josephine lived close enough to polite society to be aware of how romance was orchestrated in their world. Had young Mr. Westover been informed he was meeting a matrimonial candidate? That he was to treat her with that possibility in mind? That he should talk, walk and laugh with her, set out to win her heart? She flushed furiously as the thought raced through her mind.

Phyllis assumed the sudden reddening of the girl's complexion was due to humiliation, fear of retribution, perhaps even, incredibly, anger. She would have been amazed to learn that the rush of blood to Josephine's face was from a heart that had been touched in a single day by a truer shaft than any that had assaulted her in all of her preceding twenty-three years.

"I mean," Phyllis began coolly, but with less venom than she had expected to inject into the words, "that *I* am the Phyllis Forrester as whom you have been masquerading. I was invited to spend a fortnight or so with the Westovers, with a view to making the acquaintance of an eligible young man or two in this part of the country. My father is very wealthy."

Contrary to what was perhaps the Reader's first impression, that last statement was not a non sequitur. In very few words, it established Miss Forrester's position and authority and cut through speech after speech of explanation as to how she was to meet these young men, why the meetings and what she could expect to develop from them. With that one sentence, Josephine understood the young lady's stand and motives and why, if she had been mistaken for her, she had been welcomed so royally.

One thing this sentence did not do, which was one of the effects Phyllis was most desirous to produce, was to impress and intimidate Josephine. For Josephine had, somewhere in her climb to maturity, divested herself of the unnecessary luggage of prejudice, bigotry, timidity and lack of self-esteem that allows another's titles or possessions to overwhelm one.

"I assure you, I have not been masquerading as you or anyone else," she replied with some dignity. "At least," she added, "not intentionally."

"That may be true, Miss Foster. We will let it pass for now."
The words surprised Phyllis even as they issued from her
mouth. This was not the direction she had planned for this interview to take. As she had proceeded step by stealthy step to
this room to confront the young woman, she had imagined
storms and hot language and even hotter tempers here. Instead, she and Miss Foster were speaking calmly and with genuine courtesy. It occurred to Phyllis, for probably the first time
in her life, that quiet reasoning could accomplish one's goals at
least as quickly and efficiently as loud demands and tantrums.

"We must rectify this mistake immediately," Josephine said
desperately, beginning to gather up her things as she spoke. The
sooner, the better—the sooner, the better, she repeated resolutely to herself, relieved that she had only spent one evening in
the company of Mr. Derek Westover, had only taken one brief
moonlight stroll with him. She barely noticed that her hands,
reaching across the bedclothes, were shaking a bit.

"Perhaps not immediately," Phyllis crossed the room and sat
conspiratorially on the edge of the bed, leaning close to Josephine and stopping her in midflutter. "Perhaps tomorrow
would be just as well."

Josephine stopped to look at the other woman in surprise.
She could not imagine what this Forrester woman was thinking. And not even her wildest dreams would have led her to
imagine that this very proper-looking young woman and the
equally improper-looking farmhand she had briefly glimpsed
were romantically involved. One invitation to view the hayloft
does not perhaps constitute romantic involvement, but it is
certainly a step in that direction.

"Oh, no," she finally said. "I would not think of taking your
place a moment longer. It is completely improper."

"It is rather late, though, don't you think? Surely we
wouldn't want the servants to be forced to relocate us and our
considerable luggage so late at night?" Consideration of the
serving class was also totally foreign to Phyllis and not actually the motivating reasoning behind her argument.

"No, I would not want to prove an unnecessary bother to the
staff," Josephine agreed uncertainly, and, while she was much
more apt to be aware of the convenience of others, that was not
her motivating force in this instance, either.

"Now, Miss Foster," Phyllis began reasonably. "I will admit that I was somewhat indignant when I realized the mistake that had been made. I naturally assumed you had some part in the deception, but after meeting you, I can see that you are taken as much by surprise as I was. I realize now that it was an innocent case of mistaken identity by all the parties concerned, and it occurs to me that the revelation will be as startling, no doubt even painful, to Mrs. Westover." It had also occurred to Phyllis that she could mold this situation to her best interests; she would be able to explain her actions and motives completely by concern for others, instead of making up some other excuse for her desire to pose as a governess until tomorrow.

Josephine's emotions during Phyllis's speech had fluctuated between injured defense and sympathetic camaraderie. A sensitive young woman, she naturally was tenderly affected by Phyllis's plea for compassion in Mrs. Westover's defense, and demonstrated by nodding and murmuring the proper words of agreement that she was perfectly willing to fall in with any plan that might save face for dear Mrs. Westover—though after meeting her, not even Josephine would ever really think of referring to her as "dear Mrs. Westover." The phrase was too small and weak to describe that very imposing lady.

"Then why don't we continue as we have been?" Phyllis asked. "For tonight, anyway. Then perhaps tomorrow you and I can approach the squire and Mrs. Westover and explain things to them." Phyllis could not have told how that word "perhaps" sneaked into her plan. It had been her definite design all along that she would, bright and early the next morning—at least bright and early for Phyllis, which would have put the event somewhere in the middle-to-late forenoon—have the pleasure of humiliating the Westovers. It must be for this girl that she was being so careful, she thought; for some strange reason she seemed almost to like her.

Josephine honestly saw no need to carry on the charade further and was very uncomfortable with the idea of posing as Miss Forrester for even one night. But since she was not the injured party in the confusion, had been, in fact, treated to luxury and good-fellowship while Miss Forrester had been hailed as and accorded the meager civility due a hired servant, she hardly felt in a position to dictate their next moves.

"Yes. All right. If that is what you want to do," she said. "But I really don't think—"

"Tut, tut," Phyllis stopped her impatiently. "We have agreed to avoid what embarrassment we can, and at the beginning of a fresh day, with the sun shining and the birds singing, perhaps it will not seem distasteful at all and will be laughed away. Come, humor me in this."

Josephine nodded again. What a truly thoughtful person Miss Forrester was. It made her feel ashamed of her selfish desire to free herself from the situation, regardless of the other people involved.

"Certainly," she murmured. "If you think that is best?"

"Of course it is," Phyllis responded heartily, rising as she prepared to leave. "Now remember—not a word, not a single word to anyone about this. And then tomorrow morning, you and I shall talk again."

She left and Josephine was alone in her room, her room that had been filled with blazing color just ten short minutes before. That color now seemed tinged with gray.

Chapter Fifteen

Derek Westover had been impatiently waiting in the drawing room for thirty minutes, which is to say, "an eternity." Infatuation is one of those forces in nature that grotesquely warps one's perception of time. Half a day spent in the company of the object of one's admiration flits by on the wings of a hummingbird, while an hour out of his or her sight lengthens and grows, stretching and expanding, but never ending.

"Hasn't Miss Forrester come down yet?" Mrs. Westover asked. She had just entered the room quite grandly, in an effort to instill in the girl she had assumed would be there the proper awe and respect, and was peeved to find her effort wasted on the two men who had witnessed her arrival, since her husband had always been impressed and her son never would be.

"No, not yet," Derek said glumly, taking a gulp of cognac from his father's excellent stock. Mrs. Westover disapproved of her son's drinking before dinner, and while the squire usually did not mind, he could not help but join his wife in her disapproval tonight, because the very fine brandy was hardly being tasted, let alone appreciated, by his son as he callously threw it down his throat.

"I will instruct Broderick to have Nell check on her," the lady said, but as she reached for the bell, Josephine herself came through the doorway.

She was wearing the nicer of the two dresses she had brought with her, which was a quiet modest little fawn-colored muslin. By itself it was plain and unremarkable, completely appropriate for a governess. She was wearing with it, however, a swatch of mahogany chiffon that Miss Franken had insisted she take with her as she left that lady's establishment.

"Now you just take that with you. I can't do a thing with it— it's too small for a veil or a drape and too large for a bow. But I think it would be just perfect for you—a scarf or a kerchief or something."

"I am not able to pay—"

"Did I say anything about being paid? Just take that and not another word."

Miss Franken had appeared so offended by the suggestion of remuneration that Josephine did not dare raise any further objections.

Tonight that scrap of material was tucked here and there around the neckline of the dress she wore, setting her eyes and hair off beautifully. She looked a little paler this evening, but the Westovers attributed that to the various adventures of the day and night in which they had severally involved her. They all had to admit that her pale skin only heightened the dramatic jump from dark hair to blue eyes to pale cheek and finally to the darker collar that almost exactly matched her hair. Derek especially was willing to admit that she looked absolutely striking this evening as he rushed to her side like a lonely af-fection-starved puppy.

It was just the sort of action for which he would have been the first and most witheringly sarcastic to belittle any other man. He realized that just as she turned to smile at him, and it may have been his sudden embarrassment, or it may have been her berry-red lips and absolutely perfect teeth that made him stammer and stutter like a schoolboy of ten. (Derek himself al-ways maintained that it was the latter and that he had a clear flash of himself acting like a simpleton over Josephine's glo-rious smile, but the truth was that Josephine's lips were pale, just as was her face, and she had a left incisor that was a trifle longer than the other and slightly crooked, so her smile was not perfect, and if Derek saw it as such he must have been blinded by . . . well, if not love at that time, so soon after their meeting, surely something more than mere appreciation.)

She must have greeted his mother and father, although he had not really heard her because of the noise in his ears. Oth-ers may have been tempted to attribute the noise to bells ring-ing or angels singing, but even in his present state, Derek recognized it for what it was: blood coursing through his veins and to his head, sent by a heart that was acting no more sensi-bly than his eyes.

Finally, though, she turned her head to him.

"Good evening, Mr. Westover," she said quietly, almost whispered.

"Good—humph." He cleared his throat. "Good after-noon...that is, evening, to you." He took her hand, which she was not actually offering, and raised it to his lips. That, at least, he carried off with some savoir faire.

If possible, the girl grew paler as his lips brushed her knuck-les. She thought his kiss was like a restless butterfly that touches the petals of one flower ever so lightly and then trembles off to set another blossom aquiver, and imagined that the next flower the butterfly passed was her heart, as she felt it flutter and bump to the nervous beating of satiny wings.

He continued to hold her hand long after the polite social amenities had been exchanged, putting Josephine in an agony of emotional turmoil.

Mrs. Westover beamed at the two young people, delighted that things were going so exactly as planned. Better, in fact. Derek—as even she, who could decipher very little else about her enigmatic son, could tell—was falling in love with the girl. It was being reported from Gwendolyn's room on the third floor to Bertha's quarters across from the kitchen that the young man already was head over heels in love, but Mrs. Westover, if she had learned nothing else from her son, had learned not to jump to conclusions and was willing to reserve final judgment. Whether he had actually arrived at his destination or not, though, his mother could tell that he was well on his way.

The squire, though certainly as pleased as his wife by the turn of events, got the distinct impression that the girl was uncomfortable this evening. He did not think he was wrong in believing she was very fond of his son, so was at somewhat of a loss to know why she should be ill at ease. But he knew she was, and more than ill at ease, she was almost to the point of physical suffering.

"How pretty you look, dear girl," the squire boomed jovially, grabbing her hand away from Derek's, which had seemed like a bed of burning coals to her, and placing it securely under his own arm as he turned toward the dining room.

"I understand you and Mrs. Westover went into town to order some dresses today," he continued, "but damme if I can see how you could be in anything prettier. What say ye, m'boy?"

"Oh, no...I mean, oh, yes," Derek stammered. "That is, I agree wholeheartedly with you, Father. Miss Forrester looks glorious this evening." Derek smiled in her direction, making a rare display of his dimples. Unfortunately, Josephine was still wincing over the "Miss Forrester" and was unable to appreciate how really adorable his smile was.

"Now don't you two be ridiculous." Mrs. Westover scowled reprovingly. "Why, the dresses we ordered from Mrs. Neeman today will put this plain little outfit to shame." Tactless, as usual, the remark did at least manage to finally put some color in Josephine's cheeks. The squire patted the hand resting tremulously in the crook of his elbow.

"They can add all the silk and satins and buttons and bows they want, but to this simple farmer's eye, it will be but gilding on the lily. Gilding on the lily, and nothin' more."

Dinner was late and long and awkward. Derek was able to act like a man of reason most of the time, only slipping into imbecility on a few occasions: when Josephine looked in his direction, and once when he asked her for the salt cellar and their fingertips met. Mrs. Westover was much too busy watching and interpreting every word, glance and sigh of the young people to supply the much-needed intelligent conversation, and though the good squire was happy, concerned and jovial, it had been more than thirty years since he had been called upon to carry the dinner table repartee solely on his shoulders, or rather his feeble tongue. Even in his youthful days, he had hardly possessed what could be called an eloquent manner, and he was now so pitiably out of practice that Derek's request for the salt cellar was very nearly the cleverest remark made all evening.

As for Josephine, the meal was pure torture. She had been much taken with this young man in the one evening spent in his company, willing to believe his every flattering remark, trusting implicitly the show he made of enjoying her presence. Tonight, though, after the shattering revelation made to her, she saw through his feeble attempts at charm to the hidden motive of fortune hunting that spurred his every suave word. The extent of Josephine's budding love for this young man could be clearly demonstrated by the fact that, just as he believed her lips to be cherry red and her teeth to be pearls of perfection, she believed his awkward tongue-tied utterances to be suave words.

In fact, while she was trying gallantly to despise him, all she could manage was to become more and more miserable, cursing (well, not actually cursing; Josephine Foster would as soon consider cursing as she would wearing her misleadingly frail lace-and-whalebone corset over the top of her blouse and skirt) the glaring light of truth that revealed everything to her and prevented her from being charmed and delighted for even one more evening. She had to confess to herself, though with great mortification, that if she had the money, if she were the heiress he believed he was wooing, and knowing what she knew, or thought she knew, about the ulterior motive of his pleasantness, she would have, even then, allowed herself to be courted. Courted, and yes, since truth was intruding itself upon her, she would be viciously truthful in return: in short, she would have allowed herself to be courted and then married to this attractive, witty, knowledgeable, brown-eyed, dimple-cheeked...*cad*!

"If I remember correctly, you sing, do you not?" Mrs. Westover was asking as the company took their places in the drawing room once again. At the end of the strained meal, which had made everyone nervous and uncomfortable, the lady of the manor had herded her clumsy lot into this room, to be nervous and uncomfortable there. "I seem to remember that your mother made some references to your voice lessons?"

What Ulanda Forrester had been doing was acting the part of diplomat. She knew of young Mr. Westover's accomplishments on the piano (from earlier years when he had played more and his reputation traveled from house to house, spread by weekend visitors at the Bentleys', who had just heard him play last month at a house party of the Maxfields') and did not want to dampen his hoped-for ardor by telling him that her daughter had a tin ear and the voice of a jackdaw. In point of fact, Phyllis had taken singing lessons until neither she nor her instructor could bear it any longer, which was shortly after they were begun.

Josephine, on the other hand, had a pleasing little voice, and while it would never get her to the operatic stage, it could delight a small gathering of friends willing to give her the benefit of the doubt. When her family had been a little better situated, she had taken a few voice lessons herself, until the funding ran out, which was shortly after her lessons started, too.

Therefore, she naturally responded to Mrs. Westover's question by saying, "Why yes, I did take lessons for a short while some years ago." She then blushed prettily; all of the Westovers assumed it was because she was guilelessly modest, and they were charmed all around. Actually, her blushing had nothing to do with her modesty (of which she did have her share, but not an undue amount). She had realized suddenly that Mrs. Westover had been addressing her question to Phyllis Forrester, with reference to Mrs. Forrester, her mother, not herself, her mother, or any singing she might have done.

However, the words were in the air and of public domain, as it were, by now, and Mrs. Westover leaped on them like a fox terrier puppy who has suddenly discovered his supremacy over a pile of loose stockings.

"Wonderful!" Mrs. Westover cried. "Do sing for us! Derek, won't you accompany Miss Forrester while she favors us with a song?"

Derek smiled as if that were perhaps the finest suggestion ever made; in fact, he was chiding himself for leaving all the brilliantly romantic ideas for his mother to produce, while he sat mute as a marble statue. He smiled encouragingly at Josephine, very anxious to hear her sing and secure in the knowledge that her voice would be as perfect as her lips and teeth. Which, in the glaring light of reality, was a pretty fair comparison.

Josephine looked at Mrs. Westover and saw that she was prepared to fight to see this scheme carried out, and being too fatigued by the events and emotions of the day to involve herself in an unsightly squabble that she would lose regardless, she silently rose and went to stand beside the piano like an early Christian facing a pride of Roman lions.

Derek sprang from his seat and was at the piano almost before Josephine got herself turned around to consult with him.

"What would you like to sing?" he asked.

"My repertoire is somewhat limited, I am afraid."

"'Piangerò la sorte mia,' from Handel's *Giulio Cesare*? Or perhaps Verdi's 'Addio del Passato,' from his recent triumph, *La Traviata*?" Derek suggested helpfully.

"Oh, nothing so grand as that." At last she was forced to smile at him; the idea of her singing "Addio del Passato" was simply ludicrous. "I am sure you are acquainted with 'Greensleeves'? Let us try that before we proceed to anything more ambitious."

Derek played a dazzling cadenza, struck a comfortable E-natural and sat waiting for her to begin. His keyboard dexterity had taken her breath away, and she paused to compose herself before she began. Just as the silence was becoming uncomfortable, she started to sing.

"Alas, my love, you do me wrong,
To cast me off so discourteously,
When I have loved you, oh, so long,
Delighting in your company."

The tones rang clear, with just the merest trace of tremolo revealing her nervousness. As her voice rose to the higher notes of the chorus, she was relieved to hear that her singing had never sounded better. It was almost as good as Derek believed it to be.

"Oh, wonderful, my dear! That was lovely! Wasn't that lovely, Perseus? Perseus!" cried Mrs. Westover enthusiastically.

"What-ho, m'love!" the squire exclaimed as his wife savagely kicked his shins to rouse him from a very comfortable catnap. He had reached that period of his life when music not only soothed his savage breast, it positively anesthetized him.

"I said, was not Miss Forrester's song lovely? Although I cannot expect you to know, after having heard only her opening note," she added in an accusing undertone.

"Of course it was. It truly was, m'girl. Can't say as when I've enjoyed a song more. Give us another, won't you?"

Kindly Squire Westover had, with those flattering words, locked Josephine into an evening of song, an evening to which she did not feel equal.

Chapter Sixteen

While Josephine was struggling to maintain her composure and quality of voice, Phyllis Forrester spent an evening that, quite simply, changed her life.

She had hurried from the guest room where Josephine was so comfortably installed, made her way across the balcony and back up the stairs to her room to fetch a shawl to take with her on the "little stroll down a country lane" Will had promised her. She had taken the back stairs and passageways almost to the kitchen before she stopped to consider that she was well within the scheduled meeting time, and if she was waiting at the kitchen entrance long before Mr. Trolley came for her, would she not look awfully anxious? After a moment's pause, she admitted to herself that the trouble was, she *was* awfully anxious, and for one evening she would let maidenly reserve be hanged.

Will Trolley solved the dilemma admirably by being at the entranceway when she arrived. That was as it should be, Phyllis thought complacently as she wrapped the shawl around her shoulders and stepped out into the evening with Will. At least that was what she had always been taught.

The "country lane" that Will led her along was not the tree-lined carriage drive leading to the front entrance of the manor that Josephine had traversed earlier that evening. Will was more familiar with the back of the house—the fields, the farm buildings, the vegetable garden instead of the rose garden. He took her with him into his world.

"So," he started, to break the ice between them. "How long have you been a governess?"

"I have never been a governess," she said with some surprise in her voice, and then caught herself. "That is to say, this will be my first position."

"Your first time, eh?" He smiled at her suggestively.

"As a governess, yes." They were silent for a few moments, and Will moved a step nearer to her so that their shoulders brushed as they walked.

"Why did you start? A girl like you don't look like she would need to get money that bad."

"Looks can be deceiving," Phyllis said with irony. She couldn't help but think of her mission in being sent here to the Westovers. It was to meet and marry the young Mr. Westover because, as her mother had said, they could certainly use the money. They, the Gregory Forresters, who could buy and sell more goods and livestock in a single afternoon of trading on the market floor than this rough young man would see in an entire lifetime of working on farms. And in that same vein, they were auctioning off their only daughter to the highest bidder, because "they could use the money."

For the first time, Phyllis winced at the indignity of the phrase. It was true, and she supposed she had always realized it, but she had never formed the phrase "auctioned off" in her mind before.

Will's fingers brushed her hand and then grasped it firmly. More than companionably. Romantically.

"Your fam's money's none of my business, and I'm sorry for any trouble you may be having at home, but I can't help but be a little glad for it, too."

She looked at him, surprised. Then he smiled and squeezed her hand.

"It brought you here tonight, didn't it?"

Will Trolley was a coarse roughened farmhand from the skin out, but inside he had the natural finesse and style of a count, a duke. At times he displayed courtliness as if born to royal blood.

Phyllis looked at him in something of confusion and felt herself blushing. She already had a florid complexion, and a blush usually brought her facial tone to the quite unbecoming hue of a raw beef heart. But she knew, even as the flush mounted her cheeks, that tonight, under this moon, with this man, she was beautiful. It is a wonderful feeling when a woman knows that so assuredly.

She returned the pressure of his hand. Will felt a genuine warmth in his heart and was pleased to realize that he was doubtlessly going to fall in love with this girl. He tried to fall in love with at least one girl every month or two, and so far, since his adolescence, had been able to meet his quota. He never questioned whether the women returned his love, which they almost always did. But in his thoughtless self-absorption, he never doubted either that the women fell out of love as rapidly as he did.

So Will noticed nothing unusual about the sensation in his heart and loins when Phyllis squeezed his hand. He assumed this love would be like the countless others in his life: intense, passionate, and brief.

Nevertheless, he decided to make one change in this romance. He decided to forego the well-used hayloft tonight and remain true to his earlier chivalric impulse. Tonight, anyway. But Will, with his best intentions, wasn't reckoning with Phyllis's rebellion, desperation and discovery in the situation. Phyllis herself was more than a little unprepared for the excitement she felt flowing through her. She had been raised a lady, taught and warned continually against the temptations of the flesh (which, until this instant, she had never understood). She should have shown maidenly shock at Will's familiar manner and felt virginal relief as he tried to steer them to a more populated section of the farm. But, truth to tell, Phyllis was in no mood for Mr. Trolley to suddenly become conscience stricken.

Now Phyllis, though a proper young lady, was not wholly ignorant of the more enjoyable functions of a hayloft. She herself had never indulged, but the other girls who attended the Eastonian Lyceum, while from prestigious families, had been no better than they needed to be. Finding themselves sequestered in an all-girls' school, those who had no actual experience felt justified in allowing their imaginations to run wild. The result was that for six years, Phyllis had first received instructions and then given them as to the possibilities a moonlit night and a cozy hayloft presented.

"Oh, Will, what is that building?" she asked about the structure that could never, by any stretch of the imagination, be anything but a barn.

"It's a barn, miss," he said, attempting to veer away from it, while Phyllis forcefully guided their steps toward it.

"A barn, you say? Do you milk cows and things in here?" she asked, peering inside the darkened doorway.

"We milk a few cows, sure, but it's used mainly to store things."

"What things?" she asked as she disappeared through the doorway, and Will was forced to follow to answer her question. This scene gave him the feeling of déjà vu, but from a distorted angle. He had planned almost this exact scene, before his nobler instincts got the better of him, only with him leading the way and expansively explaining things to the young woman's timid inquiries, as, less and less sure of herself, she would follow him through the barn and finally up the stairs to the loft. Instead, here he found himself meekly following the girl, suddenly shy to be alone with her in this dark echoing building and made uncomfortable by the direction her steps were leading them.

"What is up there?"

"It's the hayloft, I suppose."

"You suppose? You mean you have never been up there? Well come, let us see what it's like!" She put her foot on the first rung of the ladder, but Will grasped her arm and stopped her.

"I mean, yes, I've been there. It's just a hayloft."

"Well, even if you have seen it, I have not. I think I should experience something tonight I never have before." She climbed the first step and was now above him.

"I don't think you'd want to go up there," Will said with something like desperation in his voice. "There's nasty things up there—spiders and bugs and—*mice*!" He produced that last triumphantly, sure now that she would be dissuaded. That was something he had spent his entire life since he discovered women denying: mice in the hayloft. He had always been sure that no girl he had ever taken with him up there would have gone if she had known about the mice.

And one potential night of romance had indeed ended in chaos when Becky Tuttle closed her hand in ecstasy and submission around what she thought would be a pile of straw and was startled, instead, to find herself suddenly holding a squeaking wriggling little rodent. She had screamed loudly enough to bring Alex running from his shed. Being taken unawares, Will had gouged the young lady painfully in the ribs, and she had drawn her knee up sharply. At any other time that would not have concerned him, but being in the positions they were at the time, that particular nervous reaction of hers made him see stars and brought tears to his eyes. The mouse, he was sure, was killed in the ensuing scuffle. For many minutes afterward he had wished he had been, as well.

Since then Will had conscientiously cleaned the loft at least once a month; more often than that if he was involved in one of his "grande amours," and since Miss Tuttle, none of his lady friends had come in contact with a mouse. But Will was careful never to mention the possibility of such a meeting, however remote, and was sure that when he did now, Miss Foster would retreat with a shriek, and thereafter for any future liaison with her, he would have to use his alternate romantic retreat: the family carriage.

To his utter astonishment, Phyllis only climbed a step higher and laughed down into his face.

"Then you will have to come and protect me, Mr. Trolley. Surely you would not allow a lady to venture up here alone?"

What more could he do? Saint Peter himself would have been hard put to further deny this young woman, and Will Trolley was *not* Saint Peter. Though later that night he could have sworn he was in heaven.

Chapter Seventeen

Rebecca rose early the next morning, before anyone at Westover Manor would be awake, except Broderick and Alex. In the Baxter home she was the last one up. Mrs. Baxter had already prepared three shifts of porridge, with bacon for some and thick slices of bread for others, with two gallons of milk gone by now. Baxter men, boys and girls had been getting up, washing, dressing, eating and leaving for work for two hours by the time Becky carefully made her way down the steep stairs.

"Good morning, Rebecca," Mrs. Baxter greeted her over her shoulder. "As soon as you're ready, Ned will drive you over to the manor."

After she had breakfasted, Becky hurriedly gathered her things together. She was dreading the confrontation with her mother she knew would ensue upon her arrival, but she was nevertheless anxious to be home. Her father would be there, and Rebecca could not remember her father ever being cross with her. Derek would be there, teasing her, as usual. And Will Trolley would be there, whether she got a chance to see him or not. The light of his presence would somehow illuminate the air, she was sure.

But the one she was most eager to see at Meadowview manor was Gallant Rider.

Rebecca believed (and was close to being correct) that Gallant Rider was the world's most handsome stallion. He was out of Derek's own Verity and a fine stud from up-country twenty or thirty miles. He had still been a frisky young colt when Becky left for Miss Moreling's school last fall. She hadn't had a chance to see him during her brief Christmas holiday, which her mother had kept packed and busy with social engagements. Even her father had refused to side with her on the matter, which was not like him. When she had not been compelled to accompany her parents to gathering after gathering, they had both insisted she stay in the house with their guests.

It had been pleasurable enough, she had to admit. She had made the acquaintance of the Rawley boy, who knew more about racing and the better London tracks than a young man his age should legally have been aware of. Becky didn't care much about betting and odds and handicaps, in which Terence Rawley was fast becoming a bona fide expert, but the boy also knew stories about fantastic equine feats that simply left Becky agog. The stories may or may not have been true (Terence was just repeating what he had heard or what he had seen through a very narrow crack in a stable door) but Rebecca accepted all of his stories as Holy Writ. So no, her Christmas break had not been a total waste of time.

But she had not seen Gallant Rider since last fall, and she now could hardly wait to find out how he had been growing. She had left strict instructions with Alex to see to his care and his training, and if she could not be there herself, she knew that Alex was the next best thing. What he might have lacked in soul-wrenching passionate adoration of the animal, he made up for in unparalleled knowledge.

Rebecca threw her things together feverishly now, as the prospect of finally getting to see her Gallant Rider came forcefully to her. Absorbed in her daydreams about the horse, she was taken off guard when she raised her eyes to the mirror and the reflection of her hair. Sleeping on her hair had disarrayed the curls, and Mrs. Baxter would not be able to make any repairs on them this morning. In the cold light of day, Rebecca had the good sense not to ask Tilly to curl it, but decided instead to brush it as best she could and go home with it the way it was.

Mrs. Baxter and Tilly stood at the doorway of their house, waving after the cart as it jolted out of sight. Depending upon the reaction of the Westover family to Rebecca's daring new hairstyle, it might be quite some time before they would see their little neighbor again.

"Brodey!" The familiar call rang once again through the manor halls, which for too long had been silent. Nell and Sophie, who were cleaning crystal and shining silver in the morning room, giggled behind their hands as the butler made his stately passage through the room in answer to the call. He gave the two women a stern reproving look as he passed them, but the truth of the matter was that little Becky, with her blatant refusal to abide by any rules of decorum, simply delighted Broderick. Broderick, that prince of propriety, allowed Miss Becky to take liberties and make demands as if she were a favorite niece or an indulged granddaughter. Indeed, if "Brodey" had ever stopped to make the analysis, he would have found that that was exactly what she was to him. He was not married, and while he did have a married sister, she did not have any children. The fondness he felt for Rebecca was that which would have gone to nieces, nephews, children and grandchildren, and was all concentrated on one young girl. Behavior that would have shocked and horrified him from anyone else was looked upon with a sort of amused exasperation when committed by her.

And while Becky did not take advantage of Broderick's indulgent sentiment, that she was aware of it could easily be demonstrated by the fact that she shouted the shortened version of his name so that it was heard from one end of the manor to the other. Any other person—whether staff, guest or member of the Westover family, if they had dared such flippancy, would have committed it only in low undertones in the farthest recesses of the house.

"Brodey!" she called again, impatiently tearing off her bonnet and tossing it and her gloves aside in the general direction of the umbrella stand.

"Miss?" Broderick said quietly, gliding into the entrance-way. As Becky turned her riotous head of shortened curls in his direction, the butler was so shocked by the alteration that he raised his eyebrows and coughed softly behind his gloved fist. Such demonstrative behavior from such an impeccably restrained man proved, beyond a shadow of a doubt, that Becky's action had been radical in the extreme and would be so viewed by her mother.

"Brodey, have Matt carry my things up to my room, will you? And where is my mother? I suppose I must report to her—the sooner we get this over, the better."

By this time Nell had come into the front hall. As the butler moved his shoulder a bit, she got a full front view of Miss Becky and gasped quite audibly. Broderick's shoulders stiffened even more, warning the little maid to silence without ever turning in her direction.

"Your parents are both now in the upstairs library," he said. "But perhaps you would like to take a brief moment to freshen up before going to them?" He was thinking that perhaps Gwendolyn, who, despite their silent but never-ending struggle for power, he had to admit was remarkably clever with her ladies and their toilets, would be able to disguise, repair or hide the girl's haircut. He would talk with her as soon as Rebecca went up the stairs, and between the two of them they might be able to quell the monstrous eruption that would surely result if Mrs. Westover greeted her prodigal daughter now.

But the finest, most selfless of intentions, oft go awry, as the poet said. In this instance it was Becky herself who was to blame, with her unmistakable "Brodey!" Mrs. Westover had heard the cry, even from the upstairs library.

"Becky is home," she announced to the squire, who was reading his paper with a pair of reading glasses perched precariously on the tip of his nose.

"Hmm," he said. "Have Nellie bring her up here."

"Never mind. I will go get her myself. We need to speak with her."

By that, Mrs. Westover meant that she would speak and he could scowl in agreement with her firm words. She did not mean that he was to nod, wink, smile and shake his head sympathetically, but he would do that, as well.

So Catherine Westover was descending the stairs to the front hall just as Broderick was finishing his suggestion that Becky "freshen up."

"Rebecca? Are you home?" she asked in a calm reasonable voice, before she saw her daughter clearly.

"Yes, Mother. It's me."

"Rebecca, your father and I would like to speak to... *Rebecca*!" Unlike Mrs. Foster, Mrs. Westover had never fainted in her entire life. But she afterward hoped that the few moments when she saw her daughter's hair for the first time since it was cut, would be the closest she ever came. In later years she was able to admit that, after a few weeks, when the style had molded more to Becky's head and personality, and had been properly curled and recut here and there, it was not really too bad. It was, in fact, although she was never able to admit this, actually quite becoming. But Mrs. Westover's shock of that morning could be attributed to the effect of badly disheveled curls and absolutely no prior warning.

The peculiar hysterical ring that marked Mrs. Westover's cry brought Sophie running from the kitchen and Gwendolyn and the squire to the balcony that looked down onto the entrance hall.

"What is it, m'dear?" the squire asked with some concern in his voice. Then, seeing his daughter for the first time, he said, "Why, Becky, it looks like you've got your hair cut."

Broderick had served in this house since shortly after the squire and his lady were married. He had learned to accommodate, satisfy and occasionally sidestep the very officious mistress of the manor. He knew her as a capable, industrious, demanding woman and employer, and rightly held her responsible for most, if not all, of her husband's very good financial fortune. But until the moment Squire Westover greeted his newly shorn daughter with such perfect aplomb, he had never really afforded the squire the respect that was his due.

Becky greeted her father warmly and moved away from the doorway so the light was no longer shining through her hair.

Mrs. Westover took a deep breath, which seemed to clear her head. Broderick motioned to Nell, who went for Becky's handbag, and went himself to instruct Matthew, the odd-jobs boy, to carry the rest of Miss Becky's things up to her room.

The crisis was passed, although all the words that were to be spoken on the subject would be issuing forth for quite some time. But for now, Becky was home and welcomed into the bosom of her family once again.

Chapter Eighteen

Miss Foster, this is my daughter Rebecca. Rebecca, Miss Foster will be your governess while you are home this time. And I suppose you will be staying through the summertime, anyway. Now I have spoken with Miss Foster concerning your curriculum and what I would like you to be studying. I have also spoken to her about what I would *not* like you to be studying. I believe we are all clear on that subject." Mrs. Westover paused while she rested a stern glance on the young woman and the girl in front of her. "I will be busy consulting with Bertha for most of the morning, as I have asked the Winfields to come for supper this evening."

Becky made an expression of distaste (to a young girl interested in horses first and young men second, this elderly couple seemed doddering, feeble and—to be blunt—uninteresting) but Mrs. Westover ignored her daughter's grimace and continued.

"Therefore, I will leave you two together to get acquainted and begin your lessons today. Miss Foster, dinner will be served at seven-thirty, so please dismiss Rebecca in plenty of time to get changed and dressed."

Phyllis bit down on her tongue to prevent the rude reply she longed to make. The nerve of the woman! She was to dismiss Rebecca early, was she? So the girl could eat in the dining hall with the family and guests. And what was she, Phyllis, supposed to do? Eat here? Or in the kitchen? She was the daughter of one of the leading stockholders in the Sheffield cutlery industry, an heiress and woman of considerable fortune. And *she* was not to eat at the same table as the Westover family.

Mrs. Westover thought she heard something that could almost have been a derisive snort from the girl, but decided that it had been a sneeze, instead.

"Pardon me, madam," Phyllis said, wiping delicately at her nose with the handkerchief she pulled from under her belt. She was—in actual fact—rather pleased by this news once she recovered from her brief snit. Will had left her with an open invitation to the hayloft if she were free of an evening, and as she contemplated being with the handsome and charming Mr. Trolley again, she was certain she would enjoy his company more than dinner with the Westovers and their guests, however brilliant those guests might be.

Mrs. Westover left her daughter with the new governess, wondering vaguely why the young woman's parting smile reminded her of the cat that swallowed the canary.

"I suppose you will want to know what I've been studying and how far I have progressed?" Rebecca said glumly as she prepared to recite the sketchy course of her education for yet another disapproving instructress.

Phyllis smiled. "I don't think that will be necessary," she said. "Why don't we discuss, instead, the respective strengths and weaknesses of the Thoroughbred and the Arabian breeds of horses?"

Rebecca was taken aback and looked at her new teacher in dumbfounded surprise. She was quite certain that Miss Foster had received the standard instructions about avoiding the mention of horses and anything to do, be it ever so obliquely related, with horses, and she was not sure that she approved of such flagrant disregard of her mother's wishes. On the other hand, Gallant Rider was half Thoroughbred. So she was curious to discover what Miss Foster could tell her. When she had been very young, she had been allowed the freedom of the stables, and Alex had talked with her, some, about the different breeds. But she had been too young and ignorant to pose the right questions, and Alex had never been garrulous. Alex himself considered speech a very low form of communication, as he was a strong advocate of the grunts, coughs and nods that made up his most eloquent expressions.

It must not be assumed, however, that Alex was uncommunicative; he actually was very expressive in his monosyllabic conversations, infusing into a single "mmph" paragraphs of explanation, innuendo, opinion and considered judgment. What would take another man five minutes to express, Alex could completely dispose of with a raise of the eyebrow, a shake of the head and a gravelly clearing of his throat.

By those very means of communication, Rebecca was aware that, while Alex thought a Thoroughbred to be a very handsome horse, there was nothing to beat an honest Suffolk Punch for practical on-the-farm purposes. But Alex was never long on justification, and while he had left Rebecca with the impression that "he had his reasons," he didn't offer any facts or figures to support his verdict.

Therefore, the carrot Phyllis was dangling before her eyes, the chance to express nearly five years of pent-up opinions, was overwhelmingly tempting to Rebecca. So even as she was thinking, Mama wouldn't like this, she was saying, "Oh! What do you know about Thoroughbreds? Aren't they the most beautiful animal you've ever seen? Gallant Rider—that's my horse, my very own horse, although they don't let me see him much, but Papa said I could have him when he was born—well, Gallant Rider is a Thoroughbred stallion, partly. And you should see him!"

For the next four hours the new governess and her young pupil remained in eager consultation behind the schoolroom door. Broderick glanced in once to inquire about tea, but was dismissed summarily when Phyllis informed him that Miss Becky would be eating early with the family and she herself had early plans for this evening, so neither of them would be taking tea that afternoon, thank you very much. Broderick's departure was absolutely frigid. He was more convinced than ever that he did not care for the new governess at all. But he did have to admit that he was impressed with the way she handled Miss Becky. The girl had seemed to be thoroughly engrossed by Miss Foster's lessons, and since Broderick had never known Miss Becky to be that interested in her schoolwork before, he would, for her sake, allow the young teacher a good deal more leeway than he usually granted new staff members.

Mrs. Westover may have been under the impression that she did the hiring and firing in this household, but her decisions invariably coincided with her butler's wishes. There was no doubt in the upstairs or the downstairs regions of the house that Broderick was the very real power behind the throne.

Chapter Nineteen

To return to Josephine, who, as the most miserable, nervous and uncertain of any of the characters in this little drama, should not have been abandoned for so long. But, unfortunately, while Phyllis was involved in her romantic tryst, Rebecca was returning to her reluctantly accepting family, and the girl and her supposed governess were engaged in blatant rebellion, all Josephine had done was worry. That was all. And as occupying as it was for her, it does not constitute riveting literary fare.

But now we should turn our attention to Josephine once again.

She had risen late that morning anyway. As she had not known how she could face another day of unbearable suspense regarding her sure and certain discovery, her mind made the task easy for her by shrouding itself in the comforts of sleep for two extra hours. Her true feelings for Mr. Westover could plainly be shown in the fact that she was most troubled by wondering what his reaction would be when her fraud was disclosed. She told herself that he was despicable, pursuing her for her imagined wealth, careless of emotional involvement, flagrant in his plays for her favor. But like the mother before King Solomon who agreed to relinquish her child rather than see him harmed, Josephine's almost involuntary response to the predicament revealed the truth in her heart.

After finally rising, she then spent at least twice as long in getting dressed as was really necessary, to be certain that when she went down to the breakfast room, she would not meet him. Her care was needless, as Mr. Derek had left before even Alex was up, to ride to Ettington and discuss a sale of livestock with Wilbur Greene.

The two men were both sharp businessmen, and each had made it a practice in the past few years to attempt to gain an advantage over the other. Any advantage. Derek was young and strong, but Wilbur was mature and knowledgeable. The Westover land was better, but the Greene stock was excellent. They had both found it difficult, if not impossible, to establish a telling superiority in any field, and after several years were reduced to making the attempt toward superiority by having a better-looking saddle or being on speaking terms with higher-ranked nobility. If pinned down and questioned, no doubt both would have admitted that their behavior was juvenile. But they had never been pinned down, and their contest continued with unabated fury.

A point of real concern to them was the fear that the other might arrive first at an appointment, with the result that each found himself setting out for their meetings at ungodly hours somewhat preceding dawn. But at least this rivalry had sparked a mutual discovery of the serenity to be found in the predawn English countryside.

So the only results of Josephine's late arrival at the breakfast board were congealed eggs and cold muffins. She hardly noticed this fact, however, since the only food she took was the strawberries and cream, and that she barely tasted. Nell and Sophie were disgusted when they were finally allowed to clean up the breakfast things. It was long past the accustomed hour, and their work schedule was seriously in arrears.

"She struck me as the sort what'd be up with the chickens. Never took her for a laze-abed," Nell muttered to Sophie as they traversed the hall from the morning room to the kitchen with heavily laden trays.

"Me neither," Sophie said, shaking her head carefully so as not to disturb her painstakingly balanced load. "But you never can tell. I guess she thinks that if she wants to be picture pretty in the afternoon, she can't waste it all on the morning."

"If she wants to be picture pretty by *this* afternoon she'd better hurry," Nell said. "Her face is white enough to shock a ghost." The women giggled companionably as they backed into the kitchen and deposited the dishes on the board.

Back in the morning room, Mrs. Westover peeped in to find Josephine listlessly gazing out the window at the wide expanse of garden and fields around the manor.

"I am afraid Derek is not expected back until late this evening, if that is for whom you are watching," Mrs. Westover said.

Josephine jumped. "What?" she asked guiltily.

"I said, there is no use looking out the window, Derek won't be riding up the lane for quite some time. He left before sunup this morning, and we are not expecting him until after dark tonight."

If Mrs. Westover had been more keenly attuned to the nuances of facial expressions, she would have recognized that which registered on Josephine's face at her announcement as one of relief. As it was, she was gratified by the change, mistaking it for disappointment.

"I was not looking for Mr. Westover," Josephine said quietly. "But I do hope that whatever has called him away was not an emergency."

"Oh dear, no. He is convinced that he must give every matter about the estate his personal attention, and at ridiculously early hours, too. But I don't know what I should be complaining about. His handling of the estate has proved beneficial to us all, and I am sure he would argue that these early risings contribute to that prosperity." As she said this, Mrs. Westover had been fussing about the room, straightening a cushion here, relocating an objet d'art there. Now, though, she sank onto the sofa and appeared to be settling in for a stay of considerable duration. Josephine groaned inwardly as she recognized the look of "intimate chat" on her hostess's face. She really did not believe she was up to this.

"Well, this is the first real chance we have had to talk since you arrived, Phyllis, my dear," Mrs. Westover said, smoothing her skirts around her and carefully infusing her voice with pleased and casual surprise. Even the real Phyllis would have been able to see through this careful maneuvering. Mrs. Westover had quite obviously planned this private meeting with an eye to grilling the girl, and Josephine could easily imagine the kind of questions that would follow. How much money did the Forresters actually have? How much, exactly, would be settled on their daughter? Would she allow Derek and his family to control these assets? Josephine shuddered at the cold-blooded bartering of human lives and hearts that passed for marriage among the wealthy.

In Mrs. Westover's defense, however, it should be stated that, although the lady was extremely practical and not averse to welcoming new money into her home, she was not totally motivated by scheming avarice. She had glanced in the morning room as she passed the doorway, seen Josephine and had honestly been pleased to think that the girl was fond of and missed her son. Realizing that Josephine was alone and unoccupied, she had come in to keep her company and perhaps get to know her future daughter-in-law a little better. Things had gone swimmingly that first evening and the next day, but today Miss Forrester seemed a little withdrawn, and Mrs. Westover wondered if there was anything troubling the girl.

"Won't you sit here beside me and tell me about Sheffield? Is it very different from this part of the country? And how is your mother? You know, although we have corresponded regularly since she married your father and moved with him to Sheffield, I don't suppose I have seen her a dozen times in the years since then."

"My mother is doing well," Josephine said, following Mrs. Westover's suggestion and sitting next to the lady. "She sends her love," she added as an afterthought.

"Does her lumbago still bother her? In one of her letters, she was complaining about it."

"Only when it rains," Josephine returned the standard response, but hoped for Mrs. Forrester's sake she was not completely accurate, because it seemed to rain almost every day in Sheffield, especially during the cold months.

Mrs. Westover was shaking her head sympathetically but was watching Josephine with an expectant eye. The young woman realized she had only answered one of the questions put to her.

She was better prepared to talk about Sheffield, however, and only hoped that she would be discussing the places Mrs. Forrester had mentioned in her letters to Mrs. Westover. She kept the descriptions on safe ground, speaking in generalities: the city's buildings and spots of interest, operas and concerts that had played in the area, the little bit about society that she knew or could intelligently invent. She mentioned once the Sheffield mayor and a certain councilman whose policies and personality she had no use for, but caught the surprised look in her hostess's eye and realized that city politics was hardly a recognized area of interest for a young woman of her supposed station and situation. She wisely directed her comments back to the meringues and crèmes of society and pretended, like numberless women before and since, that she had no appetite for the heartier entrées of social affairs.

Mrs. Westover listened to Josephine's recital with great interest. She had decided years ago, shortly after her marriage to Perseus Westover, that a woman in her circumstances had two paths she could follow. Her accommodating squire would have cheerfully moved her, if she had insisted, to a larger town, even London itself. He could have returned to Ettington two or three times a year for hunting and to take care of the minimum of estate business that would have required his personal attention. In time, she would probably have weaned him entirely of the hunting.

And there would have been endless cultural and social opportunities in a larger city. In London, or even Birmingham or Sheffield, she would never, as she did here, sometimes suffer weeks of boredom and ennui. There would have been something to discuss besides the price of wool and the danger of the weather to the crops. Her tea parties would have been sparkling affairs, with gay and witty people engaging in amusing repartee, instead of the Winfields, whose closest approach to amusing repartee had been Gladys Winfield's scathing denunciation of the county fair board. In London she would have been discussing royalty or political scandal. If they discussed the crops, it would be in relationship to the national economy. Society in a larger community would, without doubt, have offered more variety.

But instead, Mrs. Westover had elected to stay in Ettington on her husband's estate after her marriage, learning to share his interests, rather than the other way round. In some way, she had dimly realized how unhappy Perseus would have been if she had forced him to abandon his quiet country home. And in making that sacrifice, she had found that while the society was more brilliant in London, in Ettington, Catherine Bainbridge Westover *was* society.

She was like the cock that crows regally from atop the dung pile, instead of scratching for the scattered corn with the rest of the chickens. She was now completely satisfied with the decision she had made and would not change her position of unquestioned authority in this small community for any cosmopolitan center. But she did love big-city gossip when she could get it. She wanted to know who had worn what to which event, and who was there in a similar gown, and what had been said, and whose husband was reported as being a very near and dear friend—if you understand my meaning—with what stage actress of questionable moral repute. She could not see the plays and hear the concerts presented, but now, with a source of this information before her, she could hear all about them. Mrs. Westover's thirst for information far exceeded Josephine's retrievable lore, but much to the younger woman's relief, Broderick entered the room as she neared the finish of the royal-party-at-the-theater-story, which she was relating as an eyewitness report. Actually, the story had been told to her by Daphne Miller, who had heard it from an aunt whose neighbor actually knew a man who had been there.

"Ahem," Broderick began. Josephine had noticed that a great many of Broderick's communications began that way, and quite correctly she assumed that was how well-trained butlers introduced themselves into a conversation.

"Yes, Broderick?"

"Bertha has asked if it is possible to speak to you."

Bertha's actual impatient words had been, "I can't do another thing here till I talk to the missus. Not another thing. Broderick, do you hear me?" This last had been snapped savagely as he opened the kitchen door and started down the hall.

"What about, Broderick?"

"I believe she has a question as to the menu for this evening."

A verbatim translation would be: "Perch and mashed potato and parsnips—in one meal? I won't do it. These hands just couldn't fix a meal like that and serve it up to people. Maybe throw it out in the trough. Is that what the missus wants me to make? A meal for the pigs? Well, you can tell her..."

"I thought we had that all decided upon. You will remember special arrangements had to be made for the Winfields, who will be dining with us this evening."

"I remember, madam, but Bertha is unclear as to what will be served to whom and sincerely wishes to speak with you."

Bertha had said in her usual colorful way, "Cookin' for a woman with a sick stomach and a man with no teeth is like servin' mush to mummies. But the missus likes to be neighborly, and if anybody can make this slop taste good, I guess that body is me. But I'm not goin' to do a thing till I talk to the lady, so get 'er down here, Mr. B."

Reluctantly, Mrs. Westover excused herself and left to confer with, and pacify, her excitable cook.

"Broderick?" Josephine asked as he turned to follow the mistress.

"Yes?" he said, pivoting grandly on his heel and standing majestically in the doorway.

"I... I had a question I needed to ask you," she began uncertainly. In that particular pose, the normally aloof butler seemed absolutely Olympian, and Josephine was feeling more than a little nervous to begin with.

But unbeknownst to all of his associates, Broderick had a soft spot in his heart, which Josephine's uncertain tone and look pierced like a hot poker. He melted on the spot. To the naked eye he might be still as severely correct, demanding and unforgiving as ever. But inside, for this girl, he became her stalwart champion. Not another derogatory word about her, her wardrobe, her juvenile literary taste (as evidenced by the strange collection of books she had brought with her that would seem to appeal more to a child than a woman of society) or her excessive sleeping habits, would ever be uttered in his presence without swift and decisive retribution. He would defend, aid, abet and harbor her without any, or at least very little, thought for himself.

He stepped almost companionably into the room, and in the softer light that came through the windows, Josephine seemed to see, or rather to sense, his warmer sentiments.

She took a calming breath. "Do you perhaps have a railway timetable?"

"The young lady is thinking of leaving us so soon?" Broderick asked, allowing a note of real regret to creep into his voice.

"It may be necessary," she said softly.

"I am sure the master and his lady will regret to hear that. It was my understanding that you would be staying at least a fortnight."

Hedging, Josephine said, "If I am welcome for a fortnight, I shall surely stay. But for my own information, could you please secure me a timetable?"

"Of course, ma'am," was Broderick's courteous, if confused, reply.

"Oh, my," Josephine murmured after the butler had left the room. "However did I get into this predicament?"

She turned disconsolately toward the window again, and so we leave her at the end of this chapter as we found her at the beginning: worrying.

Chapter Twenty

The meeting with Mr. Greene had been profitable. *Eminently* profitable. Derek had bought twenty-five head of Mr. Greene's excellent cattle and had managed to sell him those blasted sheep that had been doing him no good but shearing his pastures. The two men had parted with the understanding that another meeting later this fall would also be mutually advantageous.

Mr. Greene left the meeting as satisfied as Mr. Westover. Several generations of Greenes had raised the finest Hereford beef in quite a large area of central England. But his cattle were big, tended to be mean, seemed to have a wayfaring spirit bred into them, and after raising, tending, nursing and herding the creatures, they were sold and slaughtered for all your trouble. Sheep, on the other hand, were too stupid to be adventurous, and they just kept growing wool year after year.

So the sale had been satisfying to both men. But the day, for all its agreeableness, had been a long one. Important negotiations could not be rushed, for neither man wished to seem in too much of a hurry or too eager to make a sale. As a young man, Derek had often thought that everyone's time could have been far better employed if the negotiations were less protracted. But the local farmers were strong adherents of the old adage, slow and steady wins the race, and they refused to be hurried. So through the years, Derek had been forced to perfect the skill of doing the least amount of business in the greatest amount of time.

But it was some of the hardest work he ever did. A full day of working, sunrise to sunset, with the men harvesting a field, didn't tire him the way that a day of struggling to keep his natural impulses to be hasty in check did. So when he returned that evening, several hours after dark had fallen (having stayed at the pub where the negotiations took place long enough for both men to toast their triumphs a number of times) he was exhausted, pleased with himself and drunk.

He had been humming a tune someone had been singing at The Lone Hunter. The lyrics had been lewd and hilarious, but all he could remember now was, ''Dora, sweet lady, a tried and true friend, Dora, my darlin', my own in the end,'' which did not convey the hilarity he had found in the song at all. So he hummed and smiled to himself in vanishing recollection as he rode up to the stable.

''Alex, my good man!'' he thought he called, but the sound that came from his mouth was actually an unintelligible mumble.

''Guess they've all gone to sleep, ol' Verity, ol' gal. But 'ere, I s'pose I can put my own horsey to bed, what?''

He slid from his horse, but when his feet hit the ground, he found it amazingly slick and was unable to establish a firm footing. Ever so gently he continued sliding from his saddle to the floor to his knees, until he finally lay huddled and insensible next to the patient mare.

He stayed there, drifting in and out of an uncomfortable unconsciousness, for more than an hour. Several times he was roused by some sound that seemed to be coming from over his head, and finally was awakened completely by the sound of the trapdoor to the hayloft opening and a ray of lantern light appearing. A distinctly feminine giggle sounded.

"I have to go now, you naughty boy!" a woman's voice said.

Peering blearily into the darkness, Derek could dimly see the lower parts of a female form through the trapdoor to the hayloft. A man's laugh floated down through the opening, and a pair of trousered legs came to stand next to the skirt. "See what you've done to me," the man said. "You wouldn't leave a poor fellow in this condition, now would you?"

"Will, I'd better..."

"I'll tell you what you'd better," said the man, dropping his hand to run it caressingly down over the girl's hip and around to cup her buttocks.

"Don't you ever get enough?" the girl asked.

"Do you want me to?"

"Never!" There was a pause in the conversation, followed by some heavy breathing. Finally the girl pulled away with apparent reluctance.

"I need to get back," she said. Will must have whispered something that Derek did not hear. The girl did, though, and it obviously pleased her.

"Of course I do," she said sweetly. And then, "Yes, tomorrow if I can. If not, Friday night, for certain."

The girl closed the loft door and groped her way down the ladder. It was pitch-dark in the barn, and not surprisingly, she stumbled over the mass of arms and legs lying where she had thought the way to be clear.

"Oof!" The air was forced out of her lungs as she landed heavily on the gentleman.

"Well, hullo, there," a voice said, exhaling an alcohol-laden breath next to her ear.

"Who are you?" the girl demanded.

"I might ask you the same question, my dear. But to answer yours, I am Derek Westover." There was a gasp, and he chuckled. "And now may I ask who it is I find leaving my groom's obviously very pleasant company?" Again, that is what Derek meant to say, and again his actual verbalism fell quite wide of the mark. But the young lady lying on top of him evidently grasped enough of his meaning to be startled and confused.

"Phyllis Forrester," she said without thinking.

It was now Derek's turn to be startled. He froze, and Phyllis, the *real* Phyllis, escaped his grasp and ran through the stable door to disappear into the dark. At the same instant the loft door opened again, and Will Trolley appeared with the lamp.

"What's goin' on down here?" he demanded suspiciously. He held the lamp high, saw the man on the floor, and after a moment more, recognized him. "Mr. Derek!" he exclaimed, hurrying to his young employer's side. "What's the matter?" Rough hands quickly ran over Derek's arms and legs, checking for breaks. Will detected none and as soon as the other man spoke, his contorted position was explained, not by his words so much as the smell of alcohol that filled the air around him.

"Will, 'sat chu?" Derek said, grabbing his stable hand.

"Yes, sir, it's me, Will. Come on now, we need to get you to the manor."

"Will, you were with the girl from the house?" Derek was showing no interest in rising, which was making Will's attempts to help him almost impossible.

"I was, sir," he said impatiently. "She's my newest lady friend."

Derek laughed hoarsely. "You picked yourself a real lady there," he said, but by that time Will was supporting him on his feet and couldn't spare the breath to answer him.

Taking him up the back stairs, Will got the master to his room and pulled his boots off after he had dropped him face-down onto his bed.

"Did you get some good breeding stock today, sir?" Will asked.

"Yes. V'ry good," Derek muttered into the coverlet.

Will had turned to leave and didn't catch Derek's last bitter words.

"But not as good as you did."

Chapter Twenty-one

Derek could always tell by how miserable he felt the next morning how successful he had been the day before. The local farmers were not only deliberate deliberators, but they one and all considered a person's drinking ability to be the true test of a man. And, of course, if that was their rod of measure, then Derek felt it incumbent upon himself to meet that measure. So while quite often Derek could not remember what had transpired the day before until he read the signed documents, he always knew that if he was sick in the morning, then the previous day must have gone well.

This morning he felt as if the entire Tallyho Hunt Club, twenty-three members strong, with twenty-three horses, thirteen couple of hounds, and one bushy-tailed very-frightened fox were all galloping hell-bent inside his head from the left ear to the right ear, where they all pulled up sharply, spun and raced back to the other side of his head.

He should have been jubilant.

But unaccountably he was not. He was sure the deal had gone through. He could almost remember that. It was something else that had happened last night that had him depressed, but he could not remember what it was. He tried to think hard, to bring it to mind, but the memory was lost in an alcoholic haze, and the effort made him want to regurgitate.

There was a careful tap on the door as Derek finally was able to win the battle and sit up.

"Sir? Mr. Derek? Are you awake?" Matt barely whispered as his curly head poked around the door. Broderick had sent him to inquire, but made it plain to the boy that his master probably did not feel well, was quite possibly in a great deal of pain, and if Matt did or said anything any louder than the falling of a feather, he would be paying for it at the kitchen sink for the next week and a half.

"Yes, I'm up, Matty. It's all right. You may come in. Got any warm water with you?"

"No sir. Mr. Broderick just sent me up to look in on you, but I can fetch some warm water in a flash." The boy turned eagerly to the door, but Derek stopped him.

"Oh, never mind. Cold water will help to clear my head. Then maybe I will remember," he mumbled that last sentence thoughtfully to himself.

"What, sir?"

"Nothing. Nothing, Matt. Why don't you lay out some clean clothes for me, and then you can go tell Gwen she had better fumigate my rooms. Mr. Greene demands a great deal of the people with whom he does business. It stinks of liquor in here."

Matt grinned as he laid out the trousers, white shirt, cravat and waistcoat. He reached for the frock coat, but Derek stopped him.

"Not the entire wardrobe, Matty. I can assure you I won't be going anywhere formal this morning—possibly never again. The way I feel today, you had better save the best things to bury me in."

Matt chuckled and Derek felt his own face break into a smile, which quickly faded as he realized that his face had not been prepared for such activity. He should have allowed it a wash, a shave and several hot cups of tea before he demanded anything so strenuous of it. The hounds in his head had chased the fox to ground, and all twenty-three horses were stamping impatiently at his forehead.

"Agh!" he said, putting his hand to his head and sitting down abruptly on his bed again.

"Sir?" Matt asked in alarm.

"It's all right. I am going to be fine," Derek said, waving his free hand vaguely while he kept the right one clamped firmly on his forehead in what he was sure would be a vain attempt to keep the horses, riders, hounds, fox and his brains from spilling out of it.

"Can I get you something?"

"Tea," Derek groaned. "Hot. And strong enough to tan leather. Tell Bertha I want her very worst." By then Matt was gone, leaving the young master to either sink or swim as best he could.

In other regions of the house things had been humming for several hours before the pounding in his skull woke Derek.

Nell and Sophie had followed Mrs. Westover's usual instructions not to wait breakfast for Mr. Westover. The young master's hangovers were legendary in the servant's quarters, and they did not need to be told that the only thing Mr. Westover would want until late afternoon would be Bertha's tea.

Becky had breakfasted alone in the schoolroom. It was Mrs. Westover's understanding that the new governess would eat breakfast with her daughter in the schoolroom and begin lessons shortly thereafter just as every other governess had done before. But Phyllis had quickly made it clear that she could not be expected to breakfast with the girl quite so early in the morning, that lessons begun at ten o'clock taught the same things as those begun at eight, and that Rebecca's mother did not really need to be told all that.

About the time Derek was assaulting his face with fistfuls of cold water, Phyllis appeared in the schoolroom. The downstairs maids were not around the new governess enough to notice, and the upstairs staff hadn't paid her enough attention, but Becky noticed a change in her teacher, even in the short time she had known her. Phyllis had become easier to get along with, simpler to please, more willing to smile and less willing to scold. She had, in short, mellowed.

For this change Will Trolley was responsible. He might not be quite what her mother considered "our class, dear," with his crude manners and his risqué humor, but he brought out a side of Phyllis her mother scarcely knew she had. For the first time in Phyllis's life, she was concerned about someone else's happiness. She loved to be with Will, and she loved to see him happy. He had simple tastes, but Phyllis was not even surprised to find that they exactly coincided with her own. They laughed at the same things, were interested in the same things and found pleasure in the same things. In some of those same things a great deal of pleasure. And suddenly knowing him, both intellectually and biblically speaking, her life was much easier. She no longer felt driven to prove herself superior to others; was no longer under a stress of which she had not even been completely aware, but which had kept her trying to balance on a razor's edge for years now. And whatever else Mrs. Forrester may have thought of Will, her daughter needed him.

Another thing Rebecca noticed was that the lessons she was receiving from the new governess were completely haphazard. Heaven knew she had been in enough institutions of learning to have a fair idea of how things were supposed to be taught. Even considering the scant attention she had paid to the learning process, she was quite intelligent enough to realize that her lessons were not proceeding in an orthodox manner. One hour Miss Foster would discuss music, and Rebecca would be asked to identify different instruments as pictured in a book her mother kept in the library. But no mention was made of the distinctive sounds the instruments produced or the mode of playing them. The next hour they would drift into songbirds and birds in general, though Miss Foster did not seem to know the difference between a goldfinch and a bullfinch. Rebecca wondered if she knew the difference between a goldfinch and a buzzard. They occasionally touched on a little science and some basic mathematics, with Becky doing most of the instructing in those two subjects, which delighted the girl.

In fact, skipping ahead of our story a little, it was to Phyllis Forrester and her complete lack of qualifications as a teacher that Rebecca's further education could be directly attributed. For the first time in her life, Becky found she knew more than someone else. It surprised her, certainly, but she also found the sensation very gratifying. Suddenly she discovered she had a genuine desire to know more about finches and arithmetic and what exactly made the steam engine such a wonderfully powerful contraption. In time she would return to boarding school, and when she turned eighteen, she would take the unprecedented step within her family of entering a women's academy in Coventry, thus achieving a higher education than any Westover woman before her. For the rest of her life, she would be endowed with an alert questioning mind and a love of knowledge.

Thanks to Phyllis's ineptitude.

Will and Alex, along with the rest of the farmhands, had been doing chores since the cock's first crow this morning, although Will seemed a little fatigued.

"The boy needs to spend a little more time in bed," Alex said to himself. Which only goes to prove that even the most sensible experienced diagnostician cannot always be correct; it was the time Will had been spending in bed lately that was exhausting him.

Mrs. Westover was answering correspondence in her study. It was her firm belief that national and international crises could be averted if enough letters were exchanged. Certainly it was the rule by which she managed her husband's estate, and in thirty-four years her letter writing had proven only beneficial to their business affairs. Whether or not it was *the* cause of their financial success, as she averred, was problematical.

The squire himself had arisen not much earlier than Derek's first brush with consciousness, but he woke a good deal more alert to begin with than his son and was up and bustling about while Derek was still debating whether to try to get up or just go ahead and die and get it over with. The squire had informed Alex last night that he would like to look at some of the fields today. That was not altogether true; he actually had no more desire to do that than to promenade in his undershirt at Buckingham Palace, but he considered it his bounden duty and one he would not shirk, regardless of how loudly The Lone Hunter called to him or how tightly the steel bands on his easy chair in the library held him. He, like most of the rest of the household, was aware that his son would be out of commission for the early part of the day, anyway, and as reward for the many hours of service and sacrifice Derek devoted to the estate, the squire was occasionally willing to make this effort.

So only Josephine is still left unaccounted for. Despite her grave misgivings, the meal the night before had been very pleasant. For the first time she met the girl on whose account she was in this house. She liked Rebecca immediately but seemed to sense there was a part of her she never could have touched as a teacher. Josephine would have been an excellent tutor for the girl, explaining, helping, lecturing, and informing in the very best manner. In fact, she would have been just as fine an instructor as the ones who had preceded her. And she would have left Rebecca as rebellious and recalcitrant as all the rest of them.

Fortunately for Becky, she had been snatched from Josephine's very capable hands. She was introduced to her, instead, as "the young lady from Sheffield come to visit us for a few weeks."

"How do you do, Miss Forrester? I am afraid my mother did not tell me you would be joining us, so I have come home for my—vacation—a little unprepared and informally."

"Oh, please, don't feel obligated to awe me," Josephine protested, smiling her charming smile and taking the girl's hand in her own. "Let us not try so hard to impress each other that we find it impossible to be friends."

Rebecca's mother may not have given her any prior warning about their visitor, but since the shock of Becky's haircut had worn off a little, her mother had spent some considerable time in conversation with her younger daughter, informing her about Miss Forrester, who she was and who they hoped she would become. Therefore, Rebecca assumed that Josephine's candid request for friendship was spurred by the likelihood that they would be sisters-in-law. The truth was that Josephine was desperate for an ally in the house, and she was, honestly, a very friendly person.

"I understand you have just spent a few months at Miss Moreling's school. I have heard of Miss Moreling. What did you think of her school?" Josephine asked as Broderick served the soup. It was the only thing Josephine could remember distinctly from Mrs. Westover's letters about the girl, and it seemed like a safe starting point for conversation.

A cloud passed over Rebecca's brow, and Josephine suspected that perhaps this was not a safe subject. Miss Moreling's was evidently not a happy memory for the girl.

"Oh, it was all right, I suppose. Herbert—he was the gardener—had a big brute of a mastiff dog he called Curly." Becky smiled at this one happy memory that lighted the months of misery, loneliness and feelings of abandonment she had suffered from. "He was an old dog, and what hair he had left was short and absolutely straight. I will never understand what possessed Herbert to call him Curly."

Mrs. Westover looked up sharply. Certainly she had nothing against members of the Canidae family, had even once in days past been the only slightly reluctant guardian of a rather gorgeous spaniel, but dogs were animals, and a discussion of dogs specifically could so easily be led to animals in general, and from hence it was but a hop, skip and a jump to horses. Anything could do it, as Josephine immediately demonstrated.

"Oh, you are fond of dogs?" Josephine asked. "Do you like other animals, as well?"

"I am rather fond of horses," Rebecca said shyly, ducking her head and tasting the consommé in front of her.

"Oh, really?" Josephine said, unaware of the ripples of anxiety floating across the table from Mrs. Westover's direction. Catherine Westover knew that Rebecca, having been given the opening, would dominate the conversation for the rest of the evening, and that conversation would deal exclusively with horseflesh. Rebecca would be aware, after their talk this afternoon, that her mother was particularly desirous of favorably impressing this young lady and would be unwilling to create the unpleasant scene that would be necessary to shut Rebecca up.

"I am afraid I know very little about horses myself. Perhaps you could tell me something about them?" Josephine said, smiling encouragingly at the girl.

Mrs. Westover very nearly clapped her hand to her forehead at that, and as it was, had to disguise the gesture as a smoothing back of her already painstakingly arranged hair. Broderick raised his eyes to the ceiling in a "Lord help us now" expression that sent Nell to kitchen with a fit of giggles.

But to everyone's surprise, Rebecca simply returned Josephine's smile.

"Perhaps we could discuss horses sometime. I imagine I know an anecdote or two you might find amusing." Her new governess had suggested that she not try to intrude horses upon the family's conversation quite so often. Phyllis had pointed out that it made Mrs. Westover uncomfortable, and surely between the two of them they could exchange enough information to satisfy the girl. Rebecca had promised to try to restrain herself, although she knew the task would not be an easy one, and was now intent on keeping that promise.

Mrs. Westover was extremely surprised, but could only be relieved that the evening would apparently pass without reference to members of the equine species.

Squire Westover, having finished his soup and several biscuits, and being far enough into his lamb chops and vegetables to allow his reassociation with polite society, took Josephine's entertainment in hand at that point and kept the young lady comfortable and amused for the rest of the evening.

After they had retired to the back parlor, the squire told story after story about the people he knew and the places he had been. They were harmless little stories that more often made fun of himself than anyone else, and displayed no rancor even when the fun was aimed at the other person. As he finished his last story, having to do with a stray goat, an appetizing basket of laundry and a certain cleaning woman in the neighborhood who, until then, had had a fondness for her employer's liquor, Josephine laughed appreciatively and thought, How peaceful it would be if it were always like this, without *him* here. And she truly thought she believed that.

Paradoxically, however, she found her eyes straying wistfully several times during the evening to the chair Derek usually occupied. Once she thought she heard a horse approaching the house, and her heart started to race uncontrollably, but it was either a farmhand headed to the stable or her overeager imagination inventing the sound. However, it is entirely possible that she did find the evening easier in his absence.

Love can be an exhausting experience. One must fret and ponder, gaze and wonder, spend a great deal of time and energy and accomplish very little. Preparation for a rendezvous can take hours, and even when that has been accomplished, much of the time together is spent worrying about the success of one's labors. When one is in the same room with the object of one's affection, even when talking with someone else or doing something apart, at least half of one's attention must be directed to one's lover and the other half to oneself, which leaves very little attention left over to devote to the conversation or the activity.

Is it any wonder, then, that when Josephine retired to her chamber that evening she really believed she had no desire to see Derek Westover ever again? She had thoroughly enjoyed a relaxed charming evening, as compared to the previous evening she had spent in his company, when she had performed song after song while being agonizingly aware of her own inadequacy. He had listened with an enraptured gaze that to anyone else might have been quite convincing. She, of course, was not taken in for a moment—well, perhaps for a moment. At the end of that evening she had been exhausted; her nerves were frayed and she had fallen into bed like a rag doll, unable to stand for another moment and then unable to sleep for more than an hour.

Last night, on the other hand, after spending the evening with the squire, Mrs. Westover, Rebecca and the omniaccommodating Broderick, she had gone to bed feeling drowsy and serene and had fallen asleep immediately. Almost immediately.

It was plain to her that Mr. Derek Westover's presence was not conducive to her peace of mind, and that therefore she must dislike him intensely. Josephine, however, did not have any previous training in love. Will Trolley could have told her from his vast experience that nothing is worse for one's peace of mind than love.

This morning she awoke feeling quite refreshed and a little less fearful of Phyllis and the terrible Pandora's box they held between them that was only loosely latched. Evidently that young woman was in no rush to expose the deception. Perhaps there would actually be time to extricate herself from this misadventure before she was discovered.

As she entered the breakfast room, Mrs. Westover was just finishing. "Phyllis, my dear! How bright and cheerful you look this morning. You bring the sunshine right into the room with you," said Mrs. Westover with her usual intimidating goodfellowship. Taking Josephine by the arm, she led her to the sideboard. "I do believe Bertha has quite outdone herself this morning," she said. Spread before Josephine's gaze were kidneys, sausages, rolls, cakes, fresh fruits, preserves and everything else good for breakfast she could imagine, plus one or two items she would never have thought of and did not even recognize. Josephine was more used to porridge or milk toast of a morning and was finding breakfast with the Westovers a greater adventure every day.

As Josephine selected the dishes that looked especially appealing to her this morning (and as a matter of fact, she was feeling little short of ravenous) Mrs. Westover kept up her steady stream of chatter. It would have amazed Josephine to have learned that Mrs. Westover was normally an intelligent sober woman whose utterances were usually well thought-out. And acquaintances of Mrs. Westover's who saw and heard her now around her guest would have been just as amazed. Mrs. Westover herself was a little amazed.

"Where is..." Josephine managed to slip into the conversation when Mrs. Westover paused to sample one more of Bertha's rolls, though she had already breakfasted and was not really hungry at all.

"Derek? That is, Mr. Westover?" she finished for the girl, helpfully. "I am afraid Mr. Westover is feeling a little under the weather this morning. I know this is two mornings he has missed breakfast, but it was unavoidable. He will probably be able to join us this evening, though."

Josephine had been going to ask for the salt cellar, but all thought of food in general and condiments in particular vanished at the mention of Derek's indisposition.

"Oh, I am sorry," she said with a good deal of warmth in her voice. "I do hope he is not too ill."

"No, no, my dear," Mrs. Westover assured her, gratified by her alarm. "Actually, Mr. Westover is not precisely 'ill' at all. He is...he is, well, feeling the effects of a successful business deal." Mrs. Westover left her unenlightening explanation hanging but appeared to be reluctant to expand upon it. Josephine was feeling a little foolish for her display of emotion and decided to let the matter drop. Obviously Derek was in no danger, or Mrs. Westover would not be sitting here exchanging inanities with her, so she would trust that all would be well with him whatever his present ailment.

This was shortly after the pounding in his head and the nausea in his stomach had first slapped Derek into bleary wakefulness, and he himself was not at all sure that all would be well with him. But then, it is so much easier for one not suffering to be optimistic.

Mrs. Westover excused herself as the young woman was finishing her breakfast.

"I do hope you can find something with which to amuse yourself for the rest of the morning. This is my regular correspondence day, and I have a number of letters to write and post today."

Josephine might be pardoned for assuming from this remark that Thursday was the one day a week Mrs. Westover set aside for correspondence, and by devoting an entire day to that express purpose, she was able to finish the necessary letter writing and not bother with correspondence for the rest of the week.

To the contrary, Thursday was her "regular correspondence" day, the day on which she answered letters from friends, relations and casual acquaintances. Letters of no pressing urgency or even slight importance. Letters that she could think of no earthly reason why she should respond to immediately and some letters she allowed herself time to justify responding to at all. The other six days of the week could all be considered correspondence days for the composition of "important" letters.

At Mrs. Westover's apology, Josephine smiled quite understandingly.

"Certainly, I will be able to fend for myself," she said. "Please attend to your letters, and do not think another thing about it." Mrs. Westover continued to chat and comment on this and that, but she was at least standing up and eventually made her way to the door.

"Now, you will send word with Sophie if there is anything you need or if you want to see me? Please, consider this house your own," she said as she shut the door behind her. Josephine sighed. Mrs. Westover was a pleasant enough woman, almost to excess, and normally Josephine would not have found that taxing. But now that she knew *why* the lady of the manor was being so very gracious, her every kind word seemed to grate on Josephine's nerves.

At last she was alone, though, and had the opportunity to make a few personal arrangements. She reached for the bell rope and hesitatingly pulled it. Somehow she hoped if she pulled it very gently, the ringing in the servants hall would be softened. It obviously was not, because she heard echoes of it even here in the morning room with the door closed.

It did, however, produce the desired effect.

"The young lady wishes something?" Broderick asked as he opened the heavy door soundlessly, appearing to glide into the room.

"Yes, I do, Broderick. I was just wondering if you were able to secure the railway timetable for me that I requested?"

"I brought it with me, miss," he said as he handed her a folded sheet of paper, a trifle reluctantly, it appeared.

"Oh, thank you!" she exclaimed as she snatched the paper from him. She turned toward the window to examine it and skimmed over the tiny confusing listings while the butler remained by the door, motionless.

"Ahem." He finally cleared his throat, and Josephine jumped. In her concentration and effort to interpret the encoded messages on the paper, she had forgotten she was not alone in the room.

"Yes?" she asked.

"Will that be everything?"

"Yes, I am sure it will be. And thank you for getting this for me so quickly."

"Certainly, miss. But I believe I speak for the household when I say I hope this does not mean you will be leaving us soon."

She almost blurted out, "Just as soon as I possibly can!" But the sincerity in Broderick's voice penetrated before she could do so.

She smiled, instead. "This is only for future reference," she said, casually folding the paper again and slipping it under the belt at her waist.

Broderick nodded silently, but was not deceived. When a paper is grabbed so eagerly from a proffering hand and then scrutinized to the exclusion of one's immediate surroundings, it is not of little importance to that person. Even as Josephine stood smiling calmly at him, her nervous fingers never lost contact with the paper at her waist.

This was troubling. Obviously the girl was planning on leaving precipitately. Not only would Broderick be sorry to see the pleasant young woman leave, but he suspected it would dash Mrs. Westover's hopes. She had been a lenient, patient mistress since the girl's arrival, partly to maintain an idyllic impression of Ettington, the manor and the Westovers. But her more appealing demeanor was not all assumed. Broderick knew that the young lady's presence had actually soothed Mrs. Westover. The girl was charming and seemed to bring other people's best qualities to the fore as well. He did not want to think what Miss Forrester's sudden and unexplained departure would mean to the rest of the family and the staff.

Something had to be done to ensure that the young lady stayed, or at least took a more leisurely departure than Broderick suspected she was planning. He did not suppose tying her to her bed and locking the door would accomplish the desired effect of an engagement between Miss Forrester and Mr. Westover. But perhaps Mr. Westover himself could restrain her with silken threads, as it were.

Broderick had not become a feared and respected name in his profession by allowing things to go unnoticed. Miss Forrester's every flush and sigh, Mr. Derek's avid gaze and puppyish expressions, even Miss Forrester's eyes on the young master's chair when he was not in the room and Derek's recent swilling of expensive alcoholic beverages had all been noted and interpreted by the butler. He knew these two young people were in the headlong process of falling in love with each other and so was confused by the girl's decision to leave. What was needed here was for the two of them to be together, to become so caught up in their romance that they would find themselves suddenly married, and Mrs. Westover and her servants could then live happily ever after.

Having determined the end that he wished to achieve, he lost no time in putting his line of action into effect. It was at this point he sent Matt up to help the master face the world again. If he understood the girl's transparent plans, and he was quite sure he did, there was no time to lose. He also instructed the boy to make sure the master was presentable when he came down. He didn't think the young lady was a prude, but he could see no gain to be made by Mr. Derek presenting himself as a drunken sot, either.

Thirty minutes later Matt rushed into the kitchen with a breathless demand for hot tea, though he carefully refrained from requesting "Bertha's worst." He did not want to offend the very flammable cook, and besides, Bertha's every pot of tea already had the reputation of being the worst in the United

Kingdom; she was a superb cook and yet the maker of such tea as to bring tears to the eyes of a brave man.

"Is the young master up then, Matthew?" Broderick asked, even with such an innocent inquiry maintaining his lordly dominance.

"Yes, sir," Matt murmured, properly dominated.

"Will he be joining us for lunch?" the butler asked.

"I think that's highly unlikely, sir," the boy said. Despite the older man's overbearing presence, he grinned. "Mr. Derek is still feeling like he's been run over by a meat wagon and isn't sure he's ever going to eat again. But I'm pretty sure you can plan on him for supper."

"Humph," Broderick said with exactly the right inflection that told Matt that in most instances more respect ought to be shown one's employers, but that Mr. Derek was not most employers, and perhaps this instance warranted a little looser rein on one's amusement. It was not a chastisement, only a reminder for Matt's future benefit.

Broderick and Alex could have had a well-matched head-to-head contest on loquacious monosyllabic communications.

With Mr. Derek having joined the world of the living again and Miss Forrester at loose ends in the morning room, the only problem remaining for Broderick was to maneuver the two into the proper romantic setting, guard against interruptions and allow their very willing natures to take their course.

"Matt, suggest to Mr. Westover that fresh air might do him some good, and there are some ailing bushes at the end of the rose garden he ought to look to."

As Matt scampered back up the stairs (Broderick watched with approval; the butler liked page boys who scampered) Broderick went himself to the morning room.

"Ahem."

Josephine, who could not remember ever having been a nervous person before, jumped violently as he cleared his throat. She supposed it was because the man moved like a wraith, making his entrances and exits on winged shoes that never seemed to touch the floor.

"Yes, Broderick?" she asked, secure in the knowledge that if she ignored her high-strung nerves, he would, too.

''The mistress sent me to tell you that the rose garden is lovely in the early afternoon and has requested that you join her briefly there.''

No, the roses did not need to be looked to, and no, Mrs. Westover had not invited the young lady to join her in the rose garden. Mrs. Westover had never invited a guest to join her in the rose garden and probably never would.

The mistress realized that rose gardens are recognized essentials of a country manor, and if she believed in nothing else, she believed in conforming to the established mores of a distinguished class. But Mrs. Westover did not like rose gardens herself. She found the aroma cloying, the thorns and branches grasping and the possibility of bugs much too threatening. On a summer afternoon the scent alone would have been unbearable to her, and she didn't dislike anyone badly enough to inflict that punishment on herself.

However, one of the advantages of being an absolutely flawless butler was that people tended to assume one was also flawlessly truthful. All of Broderick's statements, which, to do him justice, were nearly always perfectly true, were accepted as gospel.

Without a second thought, Josephine donned Miss Franken's becoming bonnet, which had arrived that morning, and made her way to the rose garden.

Derek had gratefully received the tea Matt had brought, and after gulping the first half of the cup down quickly enough to bypass his enraged taste buds, he was able to hear the boy's suggestion about the fresh air and the ailing roses without so much ringing in his ears. He supposed Broderick was right, and a walk in the air would go a long way to clearing his head. They had a gardener, but evidently Broderick thought the roses needed his personal attention. Derek never thought to question the butler any more than Josephine had.

''Sir, would you like the frock coat now?'' Matt offered helpfully as Derek stood.

''No, thank you, Matty. A little sun on my arms and breeze in my face will be good for me. And if it isn't, it will serve me right.'' He smiled and winked at the grinning youngster. His face wasn't surprised by the smile this time, and Matt was relieved to see the young master was feeling better.

Broderick watched Mr. Derek leave for the garden. The timing was perfect as Miss Forrester must have just reached the garden. The day was perfect. The sun shone brightly, but there was a cooling breeze. The roses, he knew, would be glorious this time of year, even if midday was not the ideal hour for them. Miss Forrester, he had noted, looked heartbreakingly beautiful in her new frock and bonnet, and Derek, he hoped, would no longer have bloodshot eyes. He nodded to himself in great satisfaction. Once again he had averted calamity and in this instance had also set to rights the course of true love. He had a great deal for which to congratulate himself. The Westovers, he was sure, felt themselves lucky to have him in their service, but they couldn't possibly feel as lucky as they truly were.

Twenty minutes later, as he stood near the side door instructing Nell as to the order and means of cleaning the heavy draperies in those windows, he was surprised to hear the sound of a woman's feet running up the gravel walk from the garden. He moved away from the door, and not a moment too soon. Josephine threw it open and stumbled into the hall. She did not see the butler and maid, but ran blindly to the stairs and up to her room. Both Broderick and Nell heard her sob woefully as she passed and had noted that tears were streaming down her cheeks.

She had barely shut the door to her room behind her, and Nell was still looking in amazement at Broderick for an explanation he was not able to provide, when the front door was flung open with enough force to shake the windows where the butler and maid were standing. Heavy footsteps stomped the length of the receiving hall and then the air was shattered by the sound of Derek's bellow. Nell dropped the jar she was holding. It had been a semivaluable dynastic china jar, and it shattered when it struck the tiles, but the butler's look assured her that the cause had been sufficient and she would receive no reprimand. He was not able to say anything, because by then he was hurrying away in answer to Mr. Derek's furious call.

"BRODERICK!"

The call brought everyone, save Josephine, to the front hall: Gwendolyn, Sophie, Bertha, Nell trailing behind Broderick, and Mrs. Westover from her study. The steel in Derek's eyes sent everyone scurrying back to their retreats. The young man had called for Broderick; let Broderick deal with it.

"The master called?" he asked blandly, but not as blandly as always. Broderick was, after all, a man, and not only was the look in Derek's eyes enough to freeze the blood of any man born of woman, but Broderick was also forced to admit that one of his finest orchestrations had somehow gone badly awry.

Chapter Twenty-two

The disintegration of Broderick's brilliant plan had come about in the following manner....

Derek had checked all the roses in the general direction Matt had pointed out to him, but could see nothing wrong with any of the bushes, and it suddenly occurred to him that even if there *was* something wrong with the roses, he was not qualified to rectify it or possibly even detect it. He became first irritated with Broderick for sending him on this meaningless errand and then annoyed with himself for blindly doing the bidding of one who was paid—handsomely—to do his bidding. And from there his annoyance grew. The sun was hot; the breeze didn't reach this part of the garden; his head ached and many parts of his body were sore—he believed he had fallen off his horse at one point in the night before. He was annoyed at Wilbur Greene for putting him in the immature position of trying to prove himself, and he was annoyed at his father for leaving all the business transactions of the estate to him (which was not something that had ever annoyed him before). He had the further feeling that there was one more thing he should be annoyed about. Something that had happened last night. And it especially annoyed him that he couldn't remember what it was he was so angry about.

Meanwhile, Josephine was at the far end of the rose garden. She was in good spirits, or at least she kept telling herself she was in good spirits. The timetable Broderick had provided her showed there was a train leaving Ettington station tomorrow evening for Worcester, Birmingham, Derby and points north.

She didn't suppose she would be able to clarify the situation to Mrs. Westover personally before that time, but she was already composing in her mind the letter of explanation. She was not sure how to account for Phyllis's part in the deception, and she would like to have the chance to discuss it with the other young woman. After all, she had not exposed the fraud and pointed an accusing finger at Josephine, which she was certainly in a position to do. But if they could not speak before tomorrow night, Josephine would simply tell her side of the story and trust that Phyllis would be excused in the name of youthful and wealthy high spirits.

Derek Westover was a very handsome man, and she was sure that he and the real Phyllis Forrester would make a very attractive and monied couple. Phyllis would be the monied one.

Josephine despised herself for thinking it the moment the thought entered her head. She did not enjoy being catty, and she blamed the detestable Mr. Westover for bringing her to that now. She had nothing against Miss Forrester and a good deal against Mr. Westover, and yet here she was making hateful mental comments about the young woman and remembering only his brown eyes and occasional dimples. Well, she would have no more of that! If Mr. Westover was here right now, she would certainly give him a piece of her mind and tell him exactly what she thought of his behavior.

It was at this point in their respective soliloquies that Josephine came around the bend in the path that exposed the other end of the rose garden to her uninterrupted view, and Derek turned to confront whatever was this new annoyance he heard coming toward him.

Josephine gave a little cry of alarm.

Standing there in her new bonnet with the flush mounting her cheeks as he looked at her, she was indeed heartbreakingly appealing, but she was also, Derek remembered with a start, the young lady who had been trysting last night with Will Trolley in the hayloft. He could not remember seeing her face, but he could now definitely remember her identifying herself as Phyllis Forrester.

No wonder he was feeling so out of sorts today. This was the kind of young lady his mother had selected for him, a loose woman who obviously took her pleasures where and when she could. A young woman whose morals did not bear investigation and whose face was a good deal lovelier than was warranted by her behavior. Well, it would be quite some time before he knuckled under to Catherine Westover's importuning again.

As these thoughts whirled in his head, he refused to focus on the real source of his dismay: that he had been falling in love with this young woman, deeply and quite permanently. He had believed her to be intelligent, witty, thoughtful yet not maudlin. He knew she was beautiful (even now he believed she was more beautiful than she actually was) and he saw the pedestal on which he had placed her crumbling before his eyes.

"You will have to forgive me if I startled you, Miss Forrester," he said with such bitter disdain in his voice it sent a chill over Josephine.

But two could play at that game. Here before her was the very fortune-hunting scoundrel whose various and sundry flaws of character she had spent the past two days listing and memorizing. Mr. Westover apparently thought that just by being charming and personable, he could wed any young woman he pleased, take her money and then, no doubt, pursue the same delights she was sure he enjoyed now as a bachelor. She certainly was not going to be naive enough to succumb to his considerable charms again, and if she could sour the betrothal between him and the real Phyllis Forrester, the girl would have cause to heartily thank her.

"Mr. Westover, I admit I am surprised to see you here," she said just as coldly.

"I daresay you are, Miss Forrester. Though I can think of no better place to meet with one's lover." He, of course, suspected that Miss Forrester and Will Trolley had arranged to meet here this afternoon, but she thought he was referring to himself in all of his insufferable masculine vainglory.

"I came here to enjoy the beauty of the garden," she replied. "Unfortunately, I see that enjoyment cannot be complete."

"You mean, I suppose, as long as I am here?"

"You may interpret my remark as your conscience directs, Mr. Westover."

She's a fine one to speak of one's conscience! he thought, but he merely said, "Then perhaps you were planning on meeting someone else here?"

"And if I were, what possible concern is it of yours?"

"None whatsoever, I assure you. You are perfectly free to meet with whomever you wish, for whatever purpose you choose. Though I caution you to consider the consequences of your actions. You should remember your place in society." Derek was only offering her a bit of advice, even yet with some genuine concern for her and her reputation.

Josephine interpreted it as the gauchest, most blatant bid for a woman's fortune she had ever heard of. He was advising her to consider the consequences of losing his favor, cautioning her that without her fortune and imagined social prominence she certainly could not expect anyone as grand as himself to offer marriage. She was appalled! Stunned! Outraged!

"Mr. Westover!" she cried indignantly. "I do not need your patronizing guidance, and I would appreciate it if in the future you would kindly not concern yourself with my affairs."

"Miss Forrester, your affairs are of no interest to me. I only hope they will not become of interest to the general public."

"Mr. Westover, I find the air here has suddenly become unbearable. Please forgive me if I return to the manor, and if the person I was expecting to meet comes while you are here, please inform that person that I am indisposed for at least the evening and that I will most probably be leaving on tomorrow night's train." She turned sharply on her heel then and strode rapidly away, but not rapidly enough to miss Derek's parting words.

"That will be for the best for all concerned, I am sure. And I imagine the person you were planning to meet here can find someone else even better suited for their purpose!"

* * *

Josephine hurried up the path toward the house, going faster and faster as she neared the side door in a vain attempt to outrun Mr. Westover's hateful words. No doubt he and his mother could, between the two of them, turn up some wealthy prospect soon, but even in her anger, Josephine found herself thinking that nobody could be as perfectly suited to Derek Westover as herself. Before the truth had come out and she realized his motives, they had discovered several mutual interests, had exchanged witticisms that had amused and delighted them both, and had shared, she was sure, an admiration for each other. An honest admiration, fortune or lack of same notwithstanding.

How dare he say his mother could find someone better for him! Did the man have no backbone? No say in the matter himself? One thing she would have done for him if she had been his wife, would have been to teach him to stand on his own two feet! Why, if she was to be here for just a short while longer, she would make him see that there was no one who could make him happier, and happy or not, she was convinced in her own mind that no one could possibly be better for him.

By now she was in her room, pacing the floor and wringing her hands. She had passed Broderick and Nell while the thoughts of him looking for someone else with a larger fortune were still running through her head, but now as she walked back and forth, the tears stopped and a grand determination was forming in her mind.

What better revenge could she ask for than to make the foolish Mr. Derek Westover fall madly in love with her and then dash his hopes by revealing her penniless state? Phyllis seemed to be in no hurry to expose the fraud, and now that she had her own emotions firmly in check (that was what Josephine truly thought) she could cunningly and coldheartedly pursue and ensnare the avaricious Mr. Westover with the final goal of breaking his heart!

Nothing so quickly puts the roses back in the cheeks of a woman who thinks there is no further purpose for living than the hope of revenge. Josephine's cheeks fairly glowed.

Derek had turned in disgust and left the garden by the east gate as Josephine hurried up the path toward the house. He had a considerably longer distance to cover than she did, but she was stumbling up a gravel path in satin shoes, blinded, in addition, by her tears for part of the way. Derek was striding along the well-packed carriageway with the long and determined strides that are a fuming man's equivalent to tears.

What a little piece of baggage! How could his mother think of bringing her to this house with matrimony in mind? And worse yet, though it brought a blush to his tanned cheek, how could he have found her so bewitching? Charming? Alluring? He thought they had been on something of the same intellectual plane. What, then, did she find so attractive about Will Trolley? Derek himself liked Will because he was a hard worker, he didn't shirk, he could hold his liquor and knew the words to all the popular off-color ballads. He also was a good friend, was interested in the world around him and could be counted on to help a fellow in need. Will Trolley was a good man, but Derek did not believe that the attractions he saw in Will were the things that would captivate the genteel little Miss Forrester.

Derek also knew that Mr. Trolley's dark good looks held a kind of fascination for a certain type of woman, as did his willingness to ignore convention, decorum and maidenly protests. But Derek had not thought his Miss Forrester was that kind of woman. Indeed, she gave him the distinct impression that when she voiced maidenly protests she would expect them to be taken very seriously, and when she did not voice any protests, a man could consider his ship to have come in.

But what did he care about Mr. Trolley, Miss Forrester, her protests or his own floundering ship? The young woman was leaving tomorrow night, wasn't she? And good riddance to her. Derek, for one, would be glad to see the last of her. He was delighted. Absolutely delighted.

"BRODERICK!" he bellowed. Other heads and bodies came in summons to his call, but as he looked at each of them, they seemed to melt into the woodwork. They evidently failed to recognize how joyful he was.

"The master called?"

"Broderick, I checked all of the roses at the end of the garden. I could see nothing wrong. But then, I'm not a gardener.

If you want some professional advice, then by all means talk to the gardener.''

''Oh, no sir. If you found nothing that required your attention in the garden, then it must have been my imagination. I must say, though, that I am relieved to hear you say you found nothing wrong. From your tone of voice, I was afraid you had encountered some sort of trouble in the garden.''

''No trouble there at all,'' Derek snarled.

Chapter Twenty-three

Dinner that evening was readied carefully, as the whole staff felt as if they were walking on eggshells. Mr. Derek and the young lady had not been seen all afternoon, though garbled versions of what had transpired earlier and several ingenious inventions as to the cause of the uproar were circulated around the house, upstairs and down.

Gwen, who usually kept herself aloof from household gossip, deigned to pass along the intelligence that Miss Forrester had asked for her bags immediately upon her return to her room, but had later sent them back unpacked. That she was contemplating leaving was by then obvious to most of the servants, though only Broderick knew she had been planning her departure even before whatever had occurred in the rose garden had occurred.

Mr. Westover's employees could not believe that he had been the offending party in the fracas, but they found it equally difficult to think that the very delightful Miss Forrester had been the cause of the uproar. The stories were therefore highly imaginative in their attempts to explain the situation. Nell, who was a true romantic and had only the year before seen a local production of Mr. Shakespeare's *Romeo and Juliet*, was convinced the two had discovered that their families had fought on different sides in the War of the Roses, and knowing that, they could not possibly be married. Miss Forrester's tears, as she confidently told Bertha, must have been tears of heartbreak and desolation, while Mr. Westover's fury was obviously at a cruel fate that had so arbitrarily prevented their happiness.

Matt informed Sophie that Will had brought Mr. Derek in drunk the night before and he, himself, had had to help him to get dressed this morning. Matt had deduced from all that that Miss Forrester's family could not allow her to marry a man who imbibed, though Mr. Derek must have passionately tried to convince her that his drinking was only occasional.

Everyone had a different explanation, which they whispered to each other in hurried conversations all afternoon long. Phyllis had heard something of what had happened from Gwendolyn and Sophie, and later Nell had expounded her own theory to the new governess. Phyllis said nothing, but she suspected Nell's version hit very widely off the mark. Phyllis herself never offered an opinion, though later that afternoon, Rebecca seemed eager to discuss it with her. Of all the people in the house, Phyllis was the only one who suspected the difficulty arose from a certain switch of identities and the contingent misunderstandings, though not even she knew the whole story. She hoped that Josephine had not confessed everything to Derek, because she knew that would shorten her relationship with Will considerably. Phyllis, like Will, was at this point still under the impression that the attraction they felt for each other was temporary and that each had the ability to end it at any time.

But as the afternoon wore on and she received no summons, Phyllis was relieved to assume that Josephine had at least not implicated her in whatever had passed between the girl and Mr. Derek in the rose garden.

Will Trolley, who did not know he was one of the principal characters in the steamy and tumultuous drama being enacted in the main house, also knew nothing about Derek's explosion earlier that day and his very touchy humor since then. As far as Will knew, he and Mr. D. were still the same old drinking buddies they had always been.

In the middle of the afternoon, Will was surprised to find Derek in the stable saddling Verity.

"Mr. Derek," he said. "What are you doing here? With your dad out seeing the fields, I thought you'd be taking it easy today. Especially after the night you had last night." He grinned and winked at the other young man with a look in his eye that said if he had been standing any closer he would have dug Derek slyly in the ribs.

"I hope it's all right with my field hands if I take a ride of an afternoon," Derek said with undue roughness. "And I think the less said about last night the better—don't you, Will?"

He swung stiffly into the saddle and cantered painfully away, though he kept his back straight, refusing to appear at a disadvantage to the rascal who watched him leave.

Though Will could, in truth, be called a hot-blooded rascal, at the moment he was simply confused. He and the young master were on excellent terms. They were great friends, as a matter of fact. Mr. Derek was something of a hotblood himself, and the two of them had shared more than one ungentlemanly exploit. Will was understandably at a loss to account for Mr. Derek's narrow-minded attitude concerning Miss Foster. If he wanted to have some fun with his little Josey, and she certainly wasn't protesting, why should Mr. Derek get on his high horse about it?

Shaking his head, he left the stable in something of a study. You just couldn't tell. Rich folk, he had decided, must have a touch of lunacy bred into them from the beginning. Nothing else could account for Mr. Derek's random insanity. Thank heavens his bouts with it were usually few and far between, though Will was forced to admit they had been alarmingly regular for the past week.

Mrs. Westover had been on the verge of abandoning her correspondence when she hurried to the front hall to see whatever was the matter with her son. Catherine Westover considered herself equal to practically any situation with which she might be faced, but after meeting her son's eye this afternoon, she, like the serving staff, saw no need for her presence when Derek had specifically called for Broderick. It was probably something to do with the farm or the house anyway, and by suppertime he might be calmed down enough to tell her about it with a less savage ring to his voice.

She therefore hurried just as quickly back to the study and wrote three more of her "regular correspondence" letters. Finally, well into the afternoon, about the same time her son was leaving Will in a muddle in the stable, she put her writing implements away and stood slowly, carefully realigning her statuesque frame after a day spent bent over her writing table.

A job well-done, she thought in satisfaction. She had written to Elizabeth Ashleigh, chairman of the local Waifs and Widows Saints-Day Food Baskets committee, expressing her willingness to donate her considerable skills to the project. Though Mrs. Westover had not met her equal in Mrs. Ashleigh, that woman would give her a run for her money to gain ultimate control of that prestigious committee.

She had also written to Lucien van de Meir, late of Oxford University, where he had been Professor of classical literature. Professor van de Meir had relocated near Stratford "to inhale the same atmosphere that inspired the immortal Bard," and was the darling of women's teas and social gatherings for a fifty-mile radius.

Mrs. Westover had written to inquire if he would be available to speak to a number of the ladies of Ettington in about two months' time. Naturally, she would welcome him to Meadowview for at least a fortnight. Mrs. Westover was not as easily charmed as many of her acquaintances by van de Meir's condescending erudition and did not look forward to acting as his hostess for two weeks, but her friends had been imploring her to have him speak to them, and she knew from certain sources in Stratford that the surest way to secure Mr. Van de Meir's services was to offer a period of free and luxurious room and board.

She had also written to Parson Moniff to compliment him on his acquisition of new hymnals, and while she was at it, to make a suggestion as to the theme and content of his next sermon. Mrs. Westover often wrote to the parson letters of fabricated importance and always included a number of suggestions. The parson, though a small man who looked as though he would be easy to intimidate, was a sincere man of God and did not act on Mrs. Westover's suggestions unless he felt moved upon by the Spirit to do so. Such inspiration came just often enough to convince the good woman that she was a valuable aid to the preacher, and she felt it her Christian duty to continue her advice.

The rest of her long day at the writing table had been filled with a number of (even) less important letters and a perusal of her son's meticulous account books. In good conscience she could leave the desk now. Looking at the clock, she was surprised to see how late it was.

"A person ought not to stay indoors all day on a beautiful day like this," she thought guiltily. Perhaps a stroll in the garden, even the rose garden, would be pleasant. She would ask the sweet little Miss Forrester if she cared to join her.

Gwen brought back the rather strange report that the young lady had declined the invitation, saying that she had already been to the rose garden once today at madam's invitation, and she had found one visit more than sufficient.

Mrs. Westover took her stroll in solitude, and between her and Will Trolley, a good deal of puzzlement was expended that afternoon.

As evening approached, Mrs. Westover decided to have Rebecca and her governess join them for dinner. Though thirteen and no longer a child really (indeed, some parents would have been seriously investigating the marriage market by the time their daughters reached thirteen) Rebecca usually preferred to eat in the schoolroom or with Bertha and Sophie in the kitchen. However Mrs. Westover felt that it was high time Becky started facing the grimmer realities of life, including the fact that dinnertime was not a time of laughter, loud talk, wild stories and blatant gluttony. She must bow to convention and, like it or not, accept the fact that in polite society diners engaged in banal conversation, made bored inquiries and indulged in only refined gluttony. One must be careful never to enjoy one's associates or food too much when dining in public.

And, besides, his younger sister usually delighted Derek, and perhaps Becky could dispel the shocking case of bad temper he seemed to have acquired. So Mrs. Westover sent instructions with Nell that she would expect Rebecca and Miss Foster in the dining hall at seven o'clock on the dot.

Phyllis was the sort of person who was easily influenced by her surroundings. A kind person would say she adapted well.

Others, however, might accuse her of being without definite character or personality. Practically speaking, her pliability had allowed her parents and home life to shape her into a demanding, haughty, vain young woman who had been told she was superior and therefore assumed she must be so. Then she had come into this household with that personality stripped from her, had been placed in a subservient position, had fallen into bed, and probably in love, with a farm laborer. She was in the process of losing her old snobbery, but had not as yet gained a new confidence to replace it. So when Mrs. Westover's summons came, Phyllis flew into a dither.

"Oh, my goodness!" she cried. "Dinner with the family! Do they dress? Should I dress for dinner? Well, of course I should. What do you think, Becky? How formal? Too gay, do you think? Perhaps a little more sedate?"

All her life Phyllis had had definite ideas as to clothing and fashion. They had usually been foolish, occasionally garish, but at least they had been her own. Now she could not decide what to wear for dinner, what color was right or the style she should choose, and she was asking the advice of a girl more than ten years younger than herself, with almost as bad an eye.

"I don't know, Miss Foster," Rebecca was saying. "I like the lavender with the gold sash...."

Finally someone with a modicum of fashion sense stepped in.

"Miss Foster, it really is not planned as a formal evening. Perhaps the quiet blue with that pretty little collar would be best." Nell had never seen a member of the staff with as flamboyant a wardrobe as Miss Foster's. Her first impulse had been to be coldly jealous, but so many of the dresses were hopelessly showy—and some, despite Ulanda Forrester's best efforts, were simply ghastly—that Nell decided that the young woman needed a clear head guiding her rather than a cold shoulder shunning her.

In relief Phyllis excused herself to put on the blue dress and the collar, and Nell went with Becky to help her get ready.

Preparations were taking place in other parts of the house, as well. Squire Westover had returned from a tiring day and was struggling to divest himself of his horsey aura and yet change as few clothes as possible.

Mrs. Westover merely put a fresh scarf around her shoulders and tucked a crisp handkerchief under her belt. Being mistress of the house, she was allowed more leeway in the rules, due largely to the fact that she dictated those rules. She had Gwen reshape her hair and then, being ready herself, she tapped gently at the squire's door.

"In a moment, m'dear," he called with as much impatience in his voice as he ever allowed when speaking to his wife.

For his part, Matt was tapping discreetly at the young Mr. Westover's door.

"Did you need any help, sir?" Matt asked timidly. Derek's anger earlier in the day had been unsettling.

Now, however, though Mr. Derek was still solemn, little Matty was relieved to see that he no longer appeared to be furious.

"No, thank you, Matt. Is dinner ready so soon?"

"Broderick will be ringing shortly, sir."

"And I suppose my dear mother expects the whole gay party to be there, cordial and civilized?"

"Well . . . yes, I guess so, sir," was Matt's bemused reply.

"Never mind. You may report me ready, and rest assured I will be one of the first out of the starting gate when I hear the bell."

Matt was evidently dismissed, so he backed carefully out of the room, keeping a watchful eye on Mr. Derek until he closed the door. If the choice was between a prostrating hangover and whatever was ailing the master now, Matt would prefer to deal with the hangover.

So would Derek.

And Josephine. Poor Josephine; she always seems to be last in the chronicling of our characters, the one who is the pivotal element in our little drama. Perhaps it is not fair that she should be mentioned last so often, but her actions and motives require more explanation than the rest of our cast, so it is most convenient to save her until the end.

Josephine had determined to charm and win the heart of that scoundrel, Mr. Derek Westover, with the intention of crushing it cruelly. She had told herself she would be heartless, as cold-bloodedly calculating as Mr. Westover had been regarding her supposed fortune. What better time to start than at dinner that very evening? Provided the rogue dare show his face after his vile comments that afternoon.

Just thinking about it brought a high color to Josephine's cheeks that was extremely becoming. She recognized that fact as she glanced at the mirror above the dressing table and smiled wickedly. If she could just continue to contemplate the error of Derek Westover's ways—as indeed, how could she help if she were to be in the same room with him all evening?—it would bring his capture and defeat one step nearer.

Josephine's wardrobe was nowhere near as extensive as Phyllis's, but then, the queen would have been hard-pressed to match Phyllis's wardrobe in scope. But Josephine had chosen her new frocks and gowns with a much truer eye, and she wore them with a quiet natural grace that added a charm to her clothes that any number of ribbons and baubles could not.

Alex had returned from Ettington that morning with the bonnets and dresses from Miss Franken and Mrs. Neeman. The dressmaker had sent two afternoon dresses and the promise that her ball gown would be arriving shortly. Josephine had at first intended to return them, now that she understood the illusion under which Mrs. Westover had been suffering. But the dresses themselves changed her mind. Not only was there a pale green one with yards of flowing chiffon, there was also a trim little rust-colored dress with copper accents that brought out the gold lights in Josephine's brown hair and made her blue eyes glow. The dresses were irresistible.

All right. She would keep them, but she would, absolutely, recompense Mrs. and Squire Westover as soon as she secured another position somewhere. How much could two simple dresses cost? (It would have taken Josephine at least two years to repay the price of the gowns on her meager wage as a teacher. And only then if she had been willing to give up little conveniences such as food.)

She allowed her hair to flow languidly to her shoulders and took time in front of the mirror to make sure the candlelight brought out those surprising gold highlights.

By then she was hearing Broderick's authoritative ring, so she hurriedly dabbed on the merest hint of her mother's eau de cologne.

"Now, you take this with you, Josephine," Mary Foster had told her before she left. "And if you meet an attractive eligible schoolmaster or curate in Ettington, use it. What could it hurt? I know this scent was the reason your father married me."

Josephine had enough respect for her father's judgment to be quite certain that his heart was not won with the smell of perfume, but as her mother had said, what could it hurt?

She was on the verge of rushing breathlessly from her room and down the stairs, but she stopped with her hand on the door handle. That was not the sort of demeanor expected of an heiress, who could afford to have people wait for her. She must act and think like a wealthy, beautiful, desirable woman if she hoped to convince Mr. Westover she was. And then, when he was so very sure of his victory in love, she would . . .

With a toss of her head that sent sparkles of light darting through her hair, she calmly opened her door and stepped out into the hall.

"Oh, my dear!" Mrs. Westover cried. "How lovely you look this evening. That dress certainly *looks* as if it were one of Mrs. Neeman's finest creations, regardless of how inexpensive it was." Mrs. Westover really did not make a studied effort to be tactless, but she had been fretting ever since she saw Mrs. Neeman's considerably less-than-usual bill that the workmanship or material would be blatantly inferior. As a matter of fact, this dress that the little dressmaker had sent *was* one of her finest creations, to be outshone only by the ball gown that would follow shortly.

"Doesn't she look lovely, Perseus?"

"Indeed she does. That she does, Mrs. Westover. But with or without the dress, the girl's as pretty as a picture." Mrs. Westover gasped and dug her husband in the ribs. The squire looked in surprise at his wife, trying to figure out what it was he had said, and there came something that sounded very like a strangled titter from Broderick's general direction.

"Miss Forrester, my daughter and her new governess will be joining us this evening. I would like you to meet Miss Foster. Miss Foster, Miss Forrester. Forrester and Foster? Isn't that interesting how alike your names are?"

The two young women were regarding each other suspiciously across the short space that separated them. The ice would be thin this evening, and not only must they both watch their footing, but each prayed that the other would tread carefully, as well.

"Interesting," Phyllis said.

"Very," Josephine agreed with a tight little smile.

"Well, where is the boy?" the squire boomed through the strange stillness that had settled on the room.

"Here, father. Ready when you are."

Josephine turned to watch Derek come down the stairway. She had been hoping to enthrall him with her appearance this evening, but she had not prepared herself for his. He was devilishly handsome in his evening coat and cravat, with his hair tousled just a bit and his dark brown eyes flashing.

"Derek, why don't you lead Miss Forrester in," said the squire, "while I give your mother my arm? Becky and Miss Foster won't mind being together, I suppose. Broderick, if you please?"

Chapter Twenty-four

Derek would have arranged the procession into the dining hall rather differently. He would have given his mother his arm, insisted his father escort the uncomfortable Miss Foster (it always seemed awkward for these young women who are suddenly placed in so new and grand a situation) and left Miss Forrester and his sister to come in how they could. But his father's was the reigning voice here tonight, so Derek would don his most civilized armor and escort the woman his father instructed him to escort, regardless of the moral integrity she might or might not possess.

To his chagrin his armor was not impenetrable, and the creaminess of her neck against the dark brown and surprising gold of her hair did not go unnoticed. Nor did the shadow of an elusive fragrance that seemed to be playing at hide-and-seek around her form. (Mary Foster was not as completely foolish, David Foster as stolidly levelheaded, nor the fragrance as wholly negligible as Josephine believed.)

Derek would also have arranged the seating differently, as would Phyllis and Josephine, because after the confusion of holding Miss Forrester's chair—she took an unnecessarily long time to seat herself; Josephine was practicing her regalness—and answering a question Broderick had about the wine, which was also unnecessary and only done for form, because Broderick was, without question, the finest authority on wine south of Birmingham and north of London, he found himself between Miss Foster and Miss Forrester and seated directly across from his mother.

The young ladies were shaken, and several times during the meal each one responded to a remark addressed to the other.

Mrs. Westover was quite calm herself, and so was able to sustain the wobbling conversation.

"Miss Foster, I understand that you come from the same part of the country as our Miss Forrester."

"Sheffield," they said together.

"Miss Forrester has told me a little about your city, but I don't suppose you have shared many of the same activities."

"I don't suppose we have," Phyllis said. She darted a look at Josephine and hoped whatever she had been reported doing was at least something she would not be ashamed of.

"You were with Miss Crawford...how long did you say?"

Josephine coughed softly twice into her napkin.

"Two years, madam," Phyllis said.

"I have never met Martha Crawford personally, but I have corresponded with her on a number of occasions," Mrs. Westover said, but then she could have made the same claim concerning half the population of the United Kingdom. "She is certainly well-thought-of. I trust her school is conducted admirably?"

"Oh, yes!" Josephine said with spontaneous enthusiasm. Mrs. Westover looked at her in surprise.

"Why, Miss Forrester, I understood you attended the East-onian Lyceum."

"Yes, of course I did," Josephine said, by now able to lie glibly without missing a beat. "But Miss Crawford's reputation as a teacher is widely known."

"And if it isn't, it certainly should be," Phyllis added. The girls were gaining considerable respect for each other.

The conversation remained completely superficial, however, and Derek wondered why his mother didn't say something to Miss Forrester about her plans to leave. He hadn't known until this afternoon that she was contemplating an immediate departure, and he was quite sure his mother had not expected her stay to be so brief. He came to the conclusion as the meal continued with no evident unease—that is, no *evident* unease; there were a number of people sitting at the table who were very, though not visibly, uncomfortable—that Mrs. Westover was not aware that Miss Forrester was going to leave.

For a moment he seriously considered making some tactless comment about her designs, but realized that if his mother knew the younger woman was thinking of departing, she would surely try to dissuade her. And that he did not want her to do. The sooner the young lady left, the better to his liking it would be. Looking at her now, he was glad he could no longer be taken in by her innocent appearance.

But he had to keep reminding himself of her deplorable behavior all through the meal, because looking at the clear brow, the direct eyes, the candid smile, hearing her cool voice and honest laughter, it was difficult to believe she was anything but the sweet guileless woman she appeared to be.

Josephine was having the same difficulty maintaining her belief in Derek's underhandedness, but she was having better success than he was, having practiced it longer.

Besides, tonight she was concentrating on being as charming, as delightful as she possibly could be, and men the world over will testify that there is nothing more lethal than a beautiful woman who sets out to charm.

"Mr. Westover," she said, turning to him and smiling in a way that reminded Derek of a rose opening its petals to the sun. "Why should we be discussing our poor little city of Sheffield, when I understand that you have been to Paris, and to Brussels and Rome, as well.''

''I have traveled a bit,'' he admitted.

''How exciting. Do you know,'' she turned back to Mrs. Westover and spoke as if sharing a guarded confidence with her, ''I have never been abroad myself.'' She glanced quickly at Phyllis, who gave a slight nod of agreement.

Having received a sort of confirmation, she decided that a lie worth telling is worth telling well.

''I have traveled a little around our corner of the country and met some delightful people in Manchester, Nottingham, Stoke-on-Trent, even as far south as Derby—''

''I have a widowed sister living in Derby,'' the squire interrupted cheerfully. ''Perhaps you know a Minerva Twitchell?''

Josephine smiled nervously and shook her head. Just when she was beginning to enjoy fictional embellishment, up stepped someone who wanted documentation. She supposed she ought to keep it simple in the future.

''That is more or less what I understand from your mother, my dear,'' Mrs. Westover said. She had a puzzled look on her face and seemed to be studying the girl. Josephine thought she would definitely keep it simple.

''Your mother mentioned you hadn't traveled much,'' Mrs. Westover continued. ''I was surprised to learn that a young woman of your station has not traveled more.''

''Well, Mother, traveling is not the same undertaking for a woman as it is for a man,'' Derek interjected. ''Not only are the preparations more extensive, but the safeguards that must surround a young woman as she travels aren't necessary for a male.''

''Of course, dear. I am not suggesting that Miss Forrester dart about the globe with your same abandon. But perhaps in the company of friends of your family?''

''Capital idea, m'dear,'' the squire said, his fork halting midway to his mouth. Perseus was not insensible to his wife's broad hints, and the idea of taking the girl with them on some of their excursions did strike him as a capital idea. ''Didn't you say something about the South of France this winter? You'll join us, won't you, Miss Forrester?''

The squire's spontaneous generosity took Josephine by surprise.

"Squire Westover," she protested prettily. "This is not the direction I expected my inquiry to take. I thought only to have your son tell us something of his travels. Let us do that first before we make any more elaborate plans."

"Of course, but do think about France this winter. We'd love to have you with our happy little family," he said, smiling and patting her hand.

So Derek told about his travels, at least the parts that would interest the ladies and that would bear repeating in mixed company. Both young women listened with rapt attention, because in truth, the journey from Sheffield to Ettington was the farthest either had been alone, although Phyllis did accompany her parents on their occasional modest jaunts to Dublin, where her father had some small holdings. With two attractive women hanging on his every word, Derek found himself enjoying the evening immensely, despite his best intentions to the contrary.

And the questions Miss Forrester (that is, Josephine) asked were intelligent and searching. He couldn't help admiring her quick mind and insight. What fun she would be to travel with. As he recounted a few of his adventures, even in a secondhand retelling, she made him see aspects of the episodes he had missed. Imagine what he could show her in Vienna or Milan or Venice, and what she could show him by being with him!

Becky had heard all these stories before, and had also overheard a few others Derek had shared with Will Trolley or his father that he was leaving out tonight.

She was bored.

She supposed she understood why Miss Forrester and even her Miss Foster seemed to be enjoying the stories. Derek could describe the people and the countryside so that his listeners thought they were seeing them right before their very eyes. But the wonder had worn off the scenes for Becky, and the really good stories weren't being told. For example, Derek had attended a horse race in Monte Carlo in which she knew her governess would have been more interested than a detailed description of the Swiss countryside. Unfortunately, Derek had lost a great deal of money on that particular race and wisely decided not ever to mention it to his parents, who had simply been disappointed by the evident failure of the corn sale they had been expecting that year.

At the mention of horses, even to herself, Becky turned her attention to the much more enjoyable pastime of contemplating the world of horses and her special favorite in that rather populous species: Gallant Rider. But she wasn't particularly pleased by even that prospect this evening. She had been home for days now and still had not been able to sneak out to the pasture to greet him. She and her governess had discussed it a number of times, but so far they hadn't found a propitious time to make the attempt.

Becky preferred the freedom of home to the structured atmosphere at a boarding school, but even here she sometimes felt like a prisoner. Her mother had deputized the entire staff, from Broderick to Alex, to guard against her fascination with horses.

So Becky was feeling frustrated and dissatisfied and—bored.

Finally the long meal was ended, and Rebecca and her father, the only members of the party who had not been dreading it, were the only ones relieved to see it finished. Not that the squire had found anything objectionable in the food or the company; it would just be much more comfortable to doze in an easy chair than here at the dining table, although that was by no means impossible, as he was busy demonstrating.

Mrs. Westover had been nervous about Derek's mood, but whatever had vexed him so alarmingly this afternoon had evidently been either resolved or forgotten. It was neither, but the sincere flattering of the male ego is the sauce that makes even the bitterest herbs palatable to a man, and whatever the real or imagined characters of the young ladies at his sides, neither could be called bitter herbs.

Despite Phyllis's flurry and distress at the summons, she had enjoyed the meal and the conversation. She was starting to gain a new self-assurance—one that would rely on her own developing charm, rather than on the artificial prop of her fortune.

Josephine would have admitted that she found the meal tolerable and that she was gratified by the initial success of her flirtatious behavior. She would not have been as willing to admit that the places Derek Westover had talked about sounded thrilling and the thought of how happy she would be sharing some of those adventures with him crept into her mind more than once during the meal. Despite their very best efforts, Josephine and Derek found themselves drawn to each other, however much they might deny it, ignore it and protest it.

The last four persons mentioned were therefore sorry when Broderick had overseen the removal of their dessert plates, and there was no earthly reason for them to remain seated at the table any longer.

Becky claimed her governess immediately and insisted they retire. Phyllis was willing to do so, as the sooner she could see her young charge safely deposited in her chambers for the night, the better chance she had of meeting with Will later on. Accordingly the two excused themselves and left with no further ado.

As Josephine and Derek stood up from the table, their heads seemed to encounter the fog of mistrust and latent anger that had been hanging above them but not actually intruding itself for the whole meal.

"I believe I shall retire early, too," Josephine heard herself saying, which was not the way she had planned to end this first evening of her campaign. Derek merely nodded coolly at her announcement, which was also not the way she had planned for him to bid her good-night. But she paid her compliments to her host and hostess and left the room with as much dignity and allure as she could put into what she couldn't help but consider a setback and a retreat from this evening's battlefield.

"I am sorry the young ladies left us so early," the squire said regretfully. "I'd hoped for a game of cribbage or whist after such a pleasant meal." He sighed and sank into his favorite chair.

Mrs. Westover glanced at him ruefully from her needlework. Her good husband, she knew, hoped for nothing more than two or three hours of uninterrupted sleep before he went to bed. But she joined him in his regret. She had hoped for some more conversation or singing, possibly a quiet game of cards, with or without the squire's participation. The meal had been so pleasant that she had expected her pet marital project to make some significant advances tonight.

After the young ladies' departure, Derek seated himself near the reading lamp with a copy of *Robinson Crusoe*. He had read it before, of course, which was just as well, since it was not receiving his full attention tonight. For a woman who had left the field of battle in disgrace and temporary defeat, Josephine had certainly wrought havoc in her wake.

Chapter Twenty-five

D espite her original intentions, Josephine did not leave the next evening. Dinner the night before in the close company of the real Miss Forrester had firmly convinced her that the young lady was as desirous as herself to continue the deception they were perpetrating. Josephine, who was an extremely honest person, tried not to think of it as living a lie. She could not really call it anything else, so she tried not to think about it at all.

Instead she concentrated on the challenge before her. Derek Westover remained very cool toward her, try as she might to captivate him. She had never practiced feminine wiles before, considering them silly and meaningless and, yes, deceptive. But having thrown her hat into the ring and her strict code of honor to the wind, she found that she, like every other daughter of Eve, had a wellspring of innate talents that only needed to be tapped before gushing forth in tinkling laughter, fluttering eyelashes and shows of womanly weakness.

She was a perfectly capable girl, and though not large, she had a wiry strength she had developed through years of managing most problems for herself. Yet now, when young Mr. Westover or the squire or even Alex or Will was around, she wasn't able to lift a flowerpot or tie a knot. The least exertion tired her, and the slightest shock was apt to give her the vapors or make her faint. But more effective perhaps than those ploys was the way she clung to every word Derek said and brightened whenever he came into the room (which actions were not as artificial as she believed).

So for more than a week, matters stood as they were, or rather, moved forward at an almost imperceptible rate. Josephine felt ever more sincere in her efforts to gain Derek's regard, and Derek felt more and more inclined to overlook Josephine's indiscretion and a willingness to explain away what he knew he had seen. Will and Phyllis spent as much time as possible together in a state of bliss, but as neither one was aware of how permanent their relationship was becoming, who knows how long it would have taken for them to reach that realization?

This Author could not write, nor the patient Reader read, of the agonizing weeks, perhaps months, it would have taken to have reached a denouement in the different dramas being enacted on the Meadowview stage. Perhaps it is therefore fortunate that two powerful catalysts presented themselves to hurry this story along and put our actors and audience out of the misery of indecision.

The first of these occurrences was Rebecca's visit to Gallant Rider, and the second came in the form of a telegram delivered to Mrs. Westover that same afternoon.

"I don't feel well today, Miss Foster," Rebecca said on the morning in question. Phyllis could see she was grumpy and restless, but could detect no sign of illness in her charge.

"Oh? What is the matter?" Phyllis asked. It should have been of no concern to her that the girl was lying to her with some ulterior motive for avoiding her lessons today. After all, Phyllis was not really her teacher, did not have to hold this position to keep food on her table, and certainly had enough interests of her own to occupy her attention if the girl refused to study today. But her position had started to generate true feelings of guardianship. She actually cared about the girl and her problems. She wanted to know what was troubling her and would have been willing to help her if she could. It was a marked departure from her previous twenty-four selfish years.

"I don't know—I just think I had better stay in my room today. Perhaps we could skip today's lessons?"

"Well, if you really don't feel up to it, I suppose that would be the best course," Phyllis said, eyeing the girl carefully. "Is there anything I can do for you? Should I notify your mother?"

"No!" was Rebecca's alarmed outburst, but she tried to cover her mistake. "I mean, let us not alarm Mama. I am sure this is nothing serious, and I will be fully recovered by tomorrow and ready to get back to Australia and long division." It was a bribe, and Phyllis recognized it as such. If she would allow her student this one free day, Rebecca was willing to study two of the subjects she found most distasteful.

Phyllis hesitated for just a moment and then decided to cede the point. Since she was not strong herself in geography or mathematics, she would arrange some time with Josephine today to refresh her memory and develop a lesson plan.

Josephine was greatly admired by the staff for the way she befriended the new governess. They spent an hour or two together almost every afternoon, although the other women on the serving staff were unable to see what they had in common, other than their birthplace. But perhaps to two newcomers in a strange place, that was enough. A bit of home can form the basis of a beautiful friendship.

Actually, the girls were not close and would never become great friends, as there were basic differences in their personalities. But they did share a certain amount of admiration for each other. No, the hours they spent together were not for the sake of friendship, but rather as a means to the continuance of their sham. Every day Josephine outlined a simple lesson plan and drilled Phyllis on the facts she would be teaching. It was a clever ploy and worked well enough, although there were some lessons the young ladies thought it wiser to delete altogether.

"I am, you are, he is. We are, we were, you are, you were..."

"I don't understand," Phyllis said.

"We are conjugating verbs. These are present singulars, to be followed by present plurals. We are, you are, they are. Then, of course, the past and future tenses, singular and plural, and their perfect cases..."

By that time Phyllis's eyes were glazed, and one could see the struggling cogwheels of her mind grinding to a halt.

"Josephine?" she asked dreamily. "How vital is this lesson?"

Josephine stopped her recitation and studied the young woman across the table from her.

"Every student must study the conjugation of the verbs," she explained carefully.

"Then don't you think Rebecca has studied this before in some of the other institutions of learning she has attended?"

"Oh, certainly. But . . ."

"And when Mrs. Westover finds another boarding school willing to accept the girl, either from foolhardiness or ignorance, they would most likely present this same lesson, would they not?"

"Any reputable school would," Josephine felt herself being worn down.

"Rebecca already has, and will again, receive instruction on conjugating verbs, then. I really cannot think that it is absolutely essential for me to try and teach this."

"It will appear strange if you do not."

"To whom? Rebecca? I think I know our student well enough to say that she will overlook any strangeness she may notice. Mrs. Westover? She is not present for the lessons, and anytime she looks in, we will simply be studying something else. The rest of the family? I see less of them than I do of Mrs. Westover."

"Phyllis," Josephine began, in one final attempt. "Any *real* governess would teach the conjugation of verbs."

"Any *real* governess would have some idea of what she was talking about. What you have said about them so far makes no modicum of sense to me whatsoever, and I suspect you can never make it clearer to me than any of the instructors I had when *I* was traveling the circuit of boarding schools."

She looked at the other woman with a set and impenetrable expression on her face, and Josephine felt that she had hit a solid brick wall. The conjugation of verbs was a basic element of education, but perhaps in this one unusual instance it could be omitted from the curriculum.

But today, since Becky had volunteered the subjects, Phyllis felt more or less compelled to apply herself to at least the basics of Australian geography (which, to her delight, Rebecca had loudly complained against when it was first mentioned in the book on world geography Josephine had provided) and mathematics.

"All right, if you do not feel well today, I don't suppose one free morning will appreciably mar your education. I will busy myself in another part of the house, in fact, to assure you of uninterrupted peace."

Rebecca watched the door close behind her governess with bated breath. She could hardly believe her good fortune. Miss Foster was, without question, the most gullible instructor she had ever had. And Rebecca had, in her thirteen long and trying years, come under the tutelage of a great many instructors.

There went a fine educator. The world of learning would be a much more pleasant place if all the educators in it were more like her. Becky was living proof that Miss Foster's lessons were every bit as efficacious as those of all her other sundry instructors. Miss Foster inspired the student's interest, not just the student's fear of discipline.

Being at last alone and having an entire morning of assured solitude, it was time for Rebecca to put her long-thought-out plan into action. She finally had decided to take matters into her own hands where Gallant Rider was concerned. She had been thwarted on every front in her efforts to see her glorious stallion and to spend some time with him. He had been a spirited colt, and Becky spent hours picturing the noble figure he must present now. She could see him grazing in a meadow, alerted by some sound or scent and raising his handsome head to better listen to the wind. She knew exactly how he would look galloping to the top of Ember Knoll and the power and complete understanding that would be necessary to control him. And soon, very soon now, he would be ready to sire young colts of his own. She smiled as she thought how the collective horse-owning eye of the vicinity must be on her Gallant Rider and their mares and fillies.

Rebecca had a very good imagination, which had carried her through her separation from the light of her life, her fiery stallion, but she could not rely exclusively on dreams, especially now when she was within two pastures, a stable, outbuildings, a garden path and the downstairs rooms of him. She had hoped, when she first got to know her new governess, that Miss Foster would aid and abet her in her quest, but lately even she had seemed unwilling to listen to stories and plans involving Gallant Rider and always changed the subject when Becky tried to pin her down as to when they could go see him and what help she could be called upon to supply.

It was solely up to her, Becky decided. The first step in her campaign was to be alone for some period of time. She had been trying to arrange that for days now, but all morning long there were lessons, then lunch. After lunch and an hour or two more of studies, Rebecca should then have had some time alone, but Nell was always around, or Sophie, and if not them, Gwendolyn was more companionable than Becky had ever known her to be. If she did manage to make it downstairs, there were Bertha and Broderick, and if those lines of defense failed, little Matty Clark was *always* at the door like some damned goalkeeper. The game of football she seemed to be playing with the staff might have been amusing if she had not felt so much like the ball.

She had decided that the only time she could make it out to the pastures was during the time she was supposed to be in school, provided she could make it out the back door before the opposing team had a chance to regroup and firm up their defenses. Therefore, with no further delay, waiting just long enough to hear Miss Foster's footsteps fade completely away, Rebecca opened her bedroom door quietly and glanced up and down the hallway. The coast was clear.

As she tiptoed down the hall toward the back stairs, it occurred to her how demeaning it was to be forced to sneak around her own home like some thief in the night. Like many thirteen-year-olds before and after her, she was laboring under a strong persecution complex. It was a hard burden to bear, but she was at an age that made the whole world seem united in an effort to thwart her every whim and desire. Adults always assure such young people that he or she will grow out of it, but just occasionally, even they wonder if the thirteen-year-old doesn't have the clearest view of the world.

This morning, however, Rebecca had taken the world unawares, and made it all the way to the path leading to the pasture without meeting anybody.

At last! After such a long time she was going to get to see her Gallant Rider again! She had gone over this scene as it was to be enacted hundreds—no, thousands—of times: sleepless nights at Miss Moreling's, during lessons, while eating. Since she had been home she had thought of very little else, and it had seemed especially real here because she was so close to the real flesh-and-blood horse.

She would call softly to him. Perhaps he would even re-member her, but she was not depending on that because it had been so long, and he had still been but a colt when she'd seen him last. Whether he recognized her or not, she would speak to him and approach him, but very carefully because stallions, she knew, were nervous and high-strung. It wouldn't take her long, though, to establish a rapport with the horse. She had heard amazing tales of animal sensitivity to caring, to trust, to com-plete fearlessness. It was almost as if they could see adoration. And Rebecca *did* adore her Gallant Rider. He would know that; she had no doubt.

Then when she had his confidence, she would jump on his bare back, and together they would go galloping off over hills with the wind blowing through her short saucy curls. In her daydreams she and Gallant Rider rode away into the sunset, and the scene faded.

The smile that danced about her lips was delightful. It told what words never could, of how excited and happy and thrilled by the prospect she was. She saw the picture of herself and her horse before her eyes, tempting her and pulling her toward the pasture.

Finally, after endless months of waiting and dreaming, she stood at the pasture fence, separated by only the boards and fifty yards of grass from her very own Prince Charming. He was nibbling at the tender blades around his feet; he was larger, of course (though perhaps not as large as she had been imag-ining him) but the chestnut coloring with the white markings on his forehead and front left fetlock were the same (the chestnut was not as rich looking nor the white markings as dazzling as in her dreams, but perhaps that was the effect of the light).

Any moment now he would hear her, sense her presence, sense her love. Then he would raise that proud head, shake his mane—which she was sure would ripple in the breeze—and neigh questioningly, perhaps challengingly, at her.

She stood at the fence railing a minute or more without him ever looking up. She was surprised when he did not respond and then she grew impatient.

"Gallant Rider?" she called softly.

He took a lazy sidelong glance at her.

"Gallant, it's me, Becky. Don't you recognize me?"

With utter indifference he went back to his grazing. Rebecca climbed through the fence with the grace and ease that only a very young girl could manage in a long dress and totally unsuitable shoes. But Rebecca was not concerned with the picture she might be presenting. Something was wrong here. Gallant Rider was acting very strangely. Even now, when she, a relative stranger, was inside his pasture and on his turf, he continued to eat, only taking a few careless steps away.

"Ho, Gallant. What's wrong?" She half smiled and asked jokingly, "Since when did you become so tame?" Then it was no longer a joke. She was afraid she understood.

Chapter Twenty-six

Perseus Westover met a friend as he and his son rode into town that morning. It was wholly accidental, but the good squire was more than willing to admit he would rather drain a cool ale in The Lone Hunter with Joseph Hacker than engage in a long discussion of crop prices and a final agreement that would most probably leave him dissatisfied, if not angry.

Derek did not even need to be told his father's preference.

"If you trust me to handle things," he said. The fact that he had been handling most everything on the Westover estate for almost ten years now was proof enough that his father did trust him, but Derek paid his father his respect with the comment. He then went on to the business meeting alone, and Perseus and Joseph went to attend to their particular business.

Once ensconced in his favorite chair at The Lone Hunter, the squire gratefully took two tankards of the heavy beer he fancied, but drew up short now that he had reached the limit of what his wife would tolerate.

"Come on, Perse," Joseph Hacker said as the squire drained his second mug and then pushed back from the table as a signal that he was finished. "One more for each of us, Pete."

"No, Pete. That's enough for me," the squire called over his shoulder to the proprietor, who was standing uncertainly with two clean tankards in his hand.

"Now, Perse, how long's it been since we downed a few together? One more won't make any difference."

"Not to you, maybe, but you don't know my wife. Later, Pete," he called again as he stood to leave. Pete was by then putting one of the mugs he was holding away. Joseph Hacker may not have known Mrs. Westover, but Pete did. "Another time, Joseph. My best to your family." The squire shook his friend's hand and left him alone to nurse another mug of beer and mutter to himself about "how some people let themselves be pushed and pulled any which way by some damnable harridan and it'd be a cold day in hell before he'd let his life be run by any puppet master in petticoats!"

Let it be mentioned, however, that Perseus Westover was extremely happy being controlled by Mrs. Westover, while Joseph Hacker and his wife could not stand each other's company.

Because Squire Westover wisely left The Lone Hunter after his short two ales, he arrived back at the manor before his son, in the late morning.

"Is that you, Perseus?" Mrs. Westover asked in surprise as he noisily entered the house through the front doors. He had left Charlemagne, his horse, in Matty's hands.

"Yes, m'dear."

"Home already?" Catherine Westover entered the hall and looked around her. "Is Derek with you? I expected your business to take longer."

"I left Derek to finish it alone. I met a friend..." He casually left the sentence hanging, but his wife was able to supply the rest of the explanation. The Westovers had been married long enough for her to know her husband's habits and predilections. She no longer faulted him for them, if, in fact, she ever had. And it was obvious, anyway, that he had heeded her strictures on the quantity consumed.

So she nodded her understanding and retreated to her study once more. She was to the postscript of a pressing piece of correspondence and wanted to finish it and have Sophie post it for her. In a few minutes the squire followed his wife into the room and settled down with a newspaper into a comfortable chair near her desk to catch a bit of a nap. He was not, after all, totally insensible to the effects of two full tankards of the very respectable local brew.

It was upon this peaceful and domestic scene that the back door burst open twenty minutes later, to prove how precarious is man's grasp upon serenity.

The squire jerked to consciousness at the loud clatter of the door slamming into the wall and looked up to see his younger daughter's slight frame in the doorway. He let out a gasp. He might be only half-awake yet, but he was able to see the expression on Rebecca's face.

"You have emasculated my horse!" she cried in a very loud and penetrating voice, further advancing the image of avenging angel she presented.

"Rebecca Westover!" her mother exclaimed, and the squire was amazed and admired her for the tone of outrage with which she managed to infuse her voice. Rebecca and her mother were very much alike.

"Mother, how could you? You have reduced him from the magnificent animal he might have been to a lumbering spiritless mass of flesh!"

"Rebecca, I do not think this is the time or place—"

"You weren't planning on there *ever* being a time or place. Did you hope to keep me from Gallant Rider until he or I died?"

"I would appreciate it if you would allow me to finish my sentences without thoughtlessly interrupting," Mrs. Westover said icily, and Mrs. Westover could put enough ice into her words to keep their summer icehouse stocked until mid-June. "As I was about to say, your father thought it would be in the best course not to have another...virile male horse in our paddock. Better for the stock, and certainly better as the riding animal of a young lady."

The squire was not actually afraid of his thirteen-year-old daughter, but he regretted deeply his name's introduction into this discussion as the instigator of what Rebecca obviously felt was a heinous crime. Truth to tell, neither the squire nor his wife deserved the full weight of Rebecca's wrath. It was kindly, dear-hearted, clear-headed Alex who had first suggested they geld Gallant Rider. He was very fond of young Miss Westover and shared to the fullest her fascination with horses. If she had been a boy, he would have taken the lad under his wing and taught him things about horses that not fifty men in England knew. Master Derek had been a bright and willing student, but he did not have the necessary equine fever that would have loosed the strings on Alex's almost boundless hold of knowledge. Derek was taught, instead, what he needed to know about horses to be a fine gentleman, which indeed was considerable, but he was not given the full benefit of Alex's expertise. It was a testament to Alex's insight and judgment that Derek was not even aware that there was more to learn.

Rebecca would have known and delved, and Alex could have opened unlimited horizons for her—if she had been of an only slightly different gender. But she was a blossoming young daughter of the landed gentry, and whether anyone else knew it or acknowledged it, Alex knew that it would not do to have a girl of Rebecca's age and station spending all of her time and interest with such a spirited, fiery and very male animal. It would be entirely proper for her to have a docile, mild, presentable mount that would show off her considerable horsewomanship without threatening the self-esteem of any male companion with whom she might ride. Gallant Rider, as a gelding, would be a handsome enough animal and would be, though perhaps not all the horse Rebecca could handle, all the horse she should have been able to handle.

When Alex made the proposal to Squire Westover, he clothed it in phrases like: "not as much uproar in the stables," "safer, longer-lived animal," and "not as valuable a stud as Abednego appears to be."

The squire agreed and suggested the alteration to his wife for final approval. Mrs. Westover agreed on the grounds that Rebecca's attachment to such a large male horse would tend to be extremely embarrassing in front of her friends.

Castration seems a harsh punishment for causing Mrs. Westover embarrassment, and if that had been the only consideration behind the decision, Rebecca would perhaps have been justified in her fury. But tracing the reasoning back to Alex, its instigator, one can see the wisdom in it.

Derek was, in this instance, not consulted on the matter, which was strange. But Alex knew he would never be able to explain to Derek the delicacy of the situation. While if he went directly to the squire, such a demanding explanation would not be required of him. He could, in fact, use a completely different line of reasoning to accomplish the same end.

The operation was already completed when Derek learned of it. He was a little puzzled by what appeared to him to be such an arbitrary decision. He knew that his sister would not be pleased, but he and Rebecca were usually separated by several hundred miles of boarding school attendance, and always by a difference of gender and a thirteen-year difference in their ages. They certainly liked each other well enough, but they had never been so close that Derek would appreciate the full impact this would have on his younger sister.

Therefore, having questioned Alex, he was directed to his father and finally referred to his mother.

"Derek, my dear boy, as your father pointed out to me, Gallant Rider will be a much more manageable horse, more suited for a young lady. And more—oh, how can I put this?— more *discreet*. I am sure you understand."

Derek was amused to see his mother blush slightly over her rather awkward explanation. His amusement took the edge from his irritation, and he dropped the matter, saying merely, "I would appreciate it, though, if being in charge of the livestock, I were at least informed of their disposition in the future," which speech was delivered with only slightly accusing accents.

Slightly accusing, on the other hand, was hardly the way Catherine Westover would have described her youngest daughter now standing before her. Mrs. Westover was in the uncomfortable position of believing herself to be only partially in the right (which, in itself, was a startling departure for her; Mrs. Westover lived her life with the dogged determination to make correct decisions for herself and her family whether they liked it or not, and to think herself only partially right weakened her position considerably) and had the added handicap of being totally unable to justify to her daughter what motives she did have.

Gentlewomen, after all, were theoretically completely unaware of the male reproductive system, starting with the stamen in flowers and proceeding throughout the entire flora and the fauna kingdoms. Mrs. Westover could hardly discuss with her daughter the removal of a part of Gallant Rider she refused to acknowledge he possessed. In time her daughter would join the ranks of her ignorance-professing sisters and understand that enjoyment unconfessed was better than no enjoyment at all. But that would be after many more uncommunicative years between mother and daughter.

At that moment, however, with Rebecca standing over her, all Mrs. Westover could do was put forth a great show of sputtering bravado, which may have awed and impressed her very impressible husband, but which Rebecca hardly saw at all through the mist of red before her eyes.

"I cannot forgive this, Mother," Rebecca said, infusing a good deal of her own ice into the words.

"Oh, come now, Rebecca. Do not let us have a show of thirteen-year-old dramatics," Mrs. Westover said with a sigh. Thirteen-year-old dramatics was exactly what Rebecca was indulging in, but in this one instance it would have been better for Catherine Westover to have backed down just a step and perhaps played along with her very volatile daughter, if only for a few minutes. Instead, her sigh had been tinged with enough belittlement to change Rebecca's dramatics from words into actions.

She swung about in a great flurry of incongruous ruffles and frills (many of which had been snagged and torn during her expedition to the pasture) and rushed from the room.

The squire and his wife sat in dazed silence for a few minutes, both of them gazing at the door frame as if their daughter still stood there.

"Harrumph." Perseus Westover cleared his throat finally in a way that conveyed both disapproval and uncertainty.

"Well, really," Mrs. Westover said with the same quality to her voice.

"My dear, do you suppose . . ." the squire began.

"We might have been a little precipitate," Mrs. Westover finished.

"Harrumph," the squire said again, shaking the papers that had fallen across his knees. This time the noise was one of near disbelief; it was the closest to an admission that she may have been wrong he had ever heard his wife make. Unfortunately there were no witnesses, Squire Westover thought regretfully. No one would ever believe it. "What shall we do about . . . ?" He flicked the paper in Rebecca's general direction.

"Perhaps I can speak to her later. If necessary," Mrs. Westover replied. To outward appearances the elder Westovers returned to their letter and paper respectively. But it was several minutes before they could clear their minds enough to make sense out of either.

Chapter Twenty-seven

Two hours later the second catalyst was introduced into the brew fermenting at the manor. Mrs. Westover had finished her correspondence and had left the room unremarked by the squire, who was enjoying a well-earned nap. Thirty minutes later he woke and quit the room also, making his way to the pantry, where he hoped Bertha had put the rest of the very delicious apple dumplings she had produced for breakfast. He did not find the dumplings, but he did come across a pan of tarts that were evidently for dinner that evening. They were small and he ate one as he looked through the rest of the shelves. Not surprisingly, it was also delicious, and the dumplings having joined the ranks of the ghostly legion of surplus goods that seemed to march out of his home regularly, he took several more tarts, arranging what remained to camouflage his pilfering. His efforts were not entirely successful, and hearing what sounded like a step in the next room, he beat a hasty retreat.

A man, if he is careful, need never lose all of the little boy in him as he grows older. Joseph Hacker would have strode into his own pantry or kitchen and demanded a dumpling or some tarts from his cook, and being in his employ, she would have given them to him. Bertha would know as assuredly as Hacker's cook that the master of the house had taken the tarts, but his naive furtiveness was so endearing that Bertha would, as she had done many times in the past, forgive him with a smile and a shake of her head. Whereas she would have given Joseph Hacker his pan full of tarts as she was reaching for her coat and hat preparatory to leaving his employ.

The squire...well, sneaked *was* what he did, up the back stairs and into the second-floor library. He sat behind the large oak desk in the plush and imposing chair eating the jam tarts he had brought with him while he kept a careful eye out on the doorway. He had just finished the last one and had brushed the crumbs from his mouth, his hands, his cravat, and his lap, and had progressed down to brushing them off the chair, when the door opened.

It was Mrs. Westover.

"Hullo, m'dear," the squire said. Mrs. Westover murmured something about "needing to find a reference," and went to the bookshelves to look over the volumes. Finding the book she was looking for, she sat in the chair next to the window and began lazily leafing through its pages. The squire had not chosen this room at random. It was used to a great extent by Derek as an office for managing the affairs of the Westover estate. There were, therefore, ledgers and books and letters and accounts to be looked over, providing a ready excuse for his presence in the room. As his wife opened her book, he, too, opened a record book before him and started looking over the figures.

Squire Westover and his wife were very comfortable with each other—more comfortable than they were in any other setting. After thirty-four years together, they no longer consciously sought each other out. But they seemed to gravitate to each other as if they were magnetized, so that by design or not, if they were in the same house, they were usually in the same room.

Josephine and Phyllis had also spent much of the day together. They were not as wholly compatible as the squire and Mrs. Westover, but intrigue makes for very cozy bedfellows, as well.

"Australia is bounded on the east by the Pacific Ocean and on the west by the Indian Ocean. Discovered by the Dutch in 1606 and known to us until the end of the last century as Botany Bay..." Josephine spoke slowly, watching Phyllis take down her dictation. She tried to present the lesson simply and concisely, hoping the other young woman would deliver it verbatim. She suspected, and rightly so, that if Phyllis did any ad-lib teaching, Rebecca would come away with some rather bizarre ideas about Australia.

But this was easier than the long division had been, as it required only a regurgitation of facts. Long division necessitated an inkling of understanding on Phyllis's part. It was a testament to Josephine's skill as a teacher that after only three grim hours, with the brunette and blond heads bowed together over the study book and work sheet, Phyllis finally did understand some of the machinations of long division, though the theories and logic behind it were still well beyond her grasp. Nevertheless, she would be able to teach a girl eleven years younger than herself, with absolutely no practical knowledge of mathematics (after her teachers had moved beyond "If you have three horses and one runs away, how many do you have left?" Rebecca lost interest in the subject) a few basic steps without leading her completely astray.

"The aborigines are the natives of Australia and are a very ceremonial people. We will discuss at another time their ceremonial dances, elaborate initiation rights, their mythology and native religion."

"Shall I write that down?" Phyllis asked.

"You might mention something about it. It will tease Rebecca and entice her to learn something more about the continent."

"'...about the continent,'" Phyllis repeated haltingly as her pencil moved slowly across the paper.

"No, no, you don't need to write that," Josephine said with a laugh.

"Just a note to myself," Phyllis assured her, as with a final dot of an *i* she sat back to survey the results. "Is that everything?"

"I believe that is all you will need for a day or two." Josephine tried to keep the weariness out of her voice, but she certainly hoped the information Phyllis had would last for at least two days, and longer than that, if possible. Miss Crawford had told her something of the rewards and frustrations of teaching when Josephine confided her decision to gain employment as a governess. She had said that her spirits would be raised to mountain peaks as she saw a student master a concept or accomplish a goal, while perhaps the very next day she would be plunged into an abyss as a carefully prepared lesson was completely rejected. But Miss Crawford had said nothing about this bone-grinding fatigue. Josephine's back ached, her eyes hurt, her legs were sore, and there was a throbbing in her head that made everything else seem inconsequential.

"What a relief." Phyllis sighed. And to her credit it should be noted that she had maintained more or less strict concentration on her books for an unprecedented length of time.

Wearily the young women parted company: Phyllis with the stable as her ultimate destination; Josephine to relax on the feather mattress and luxurious softness of an eiderdown quilt, for once not questioning the playful Providence who had placed her in this precarious predicament.

"Telegram for Squire Perseus Westover," a young boy's voice piped at the back entrance.

Begrudgingly, and with something of an effort, Bertha signed the paper held up to her, ignoring the boy's expectantly outstretched hand completely. The boy turned, disgruntled, and so did Bertha.

"Where is that little jackanapes Matty when he's needed?" she muttered. "Always underfoot, pestering a body for a taste of this or a pinch of that. But come an errand to do and he's gone like a will-o'-the-wisp. Nell!"

Her call sounded short-tempered, and Nell put her head around the door frame cautiously.

"Telegram for himself," the cook said, putting the envelope into the younger maid's reluctant hand. Nell held it suspiciously away from her body and eyed it with distrust.

"Can't Matty take it up?" she asked. Nine times out of ten, the message in a telegram is unwelcome, as everyone knows. No one on the staff was gambler enough to willingly buck the odds and be the deliverer of such a message, as the Westover family had never been noted for their placid acceptance of bad news, and such ire was often taken out on the bearer.

"Matt's not about. You'll have to take it up," was Bertha's short reply.

"Matt's *always* about," Nell grumbled to herself as she made her way to the front hall. There she met, as she had hoped she would, the butler. "Broderick," she said, endeavoring to keep the triumph out of her voice. "A telegram for the squire." She dropped the envelope onto the small silver service tray at the entranceway.

In this game of Pass the Bad News in which the servants were engaged, Broderick played a rather ambiguous position. Generally, the passing of unpleasant duties would follow the pecking order of the staff, and having come "down" to Nell, she could not usually pass it back "up" to Broderick. But telegrams were of such importance that it was entirely proper for the head of the staff to look after them personally. Of course, it was also entirely fair for him to pass it on to one of the other servants, but having once transferred something, one was considered off the playing field for the remainder of that period. Nell was therefore safe.

"Matt?" the butler asked as he picked up the tray with the air of a regal martyr.

"Not to be found," Nell called carelessly over her shoulder as she disappeared around the hallway intersection.

It was as Broderick stood holding the tray at the foot of the stairs that Phyllis appeared at their head.

"Miss Foster." His tone was peremptory. "A telegram has just arrived for Squire Westover. Deliver it to him, if you please." There was, however, never really any question as to her pleasure.

She took the proffered envelope, and with none of the trepidation that anyone else on the staff might have felt, returned to the library she had just passed, having noted both the squire and his wife in that room.

"A telegram for the squire," Phyllis said after tapping discreetly at the open door. Phyllis was becoming a very well-mannered young lady. While the upper and moneyed classes may or may not be genteel, depending upon their mood or length of establishment, their serving staffs must never be anything less than meticulously correct. If she had joined the family as a guest, it would not have been necessary for Phyllis to have changed her rather shoddy self-centered manners at all. But as a member of the household staff, her deportment had to be flawless.

"Thank you," the squire said as he took the envelope Phyllis handed him and opened it. Phyllis nodded slightly and was nearly out of the door before the squire's next words brought her up short. "Oh, this is from Gregory Forrester, m'dear," he said. "He and his wife received your letter and are delighted that the young people are getting along so famously." He finished reading the few lines on the paper and looked up with a slight frown furrowing his brow. "Says he and Mrs. Forrester are coming down to complete the arrangements. Should be here, let's see, that will be tomorrow sometime."

Chapter Twenty-eight

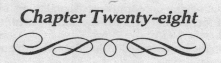

Young Matt Clark had made a terrible mistake. He knew that now and, with the pessimism of youth, saw it as the end of his professional life.

It had begun so innocently.

"Matty, will you fetch Mama's old carpetbag for me?"

"Yes, miss."

"Oh, and Matt, bring it up the back stairs, if you would."

"All right, Miss Becky."

How is a boy of nine supposed to see through all the wicked machinations of the female mind? he asked himself wildly now. At the time he had merely carried the bag up the back stairs.

He had been somewhat taken aback when Becky opened the door to his gentle tap. When he had gone down the stairs he had left a frilly young woman in the recognized apparel of femininity: petticoats, skirts, laces and bows. Standing before him now was either a smallish delicate-looking boy or a girl in most unorthodox dress. She was wearing brown flannel trousers that looked a bit small through the hips, with a white shirt that was a little baggy (though only thirteen and certainly not amply endowed with feminine curves, Rebecca had wisely chosen a shirt that would hang loose and be unrevealing of what form she did have). She also had on a waistcoat and a little violet bow tie. When she opened the door she was holding a pair of spats in her hand.

"Miss Becky!" Matt cried, greatly surprised.

In alarm she grabbed his arm and pulled him into the room. Hastily she thrust her head out the door and looked carefully up and down the hall. Evidently satisfied, she softly closed the door and turned to face the boy. "I'll take the bag, Matt," she said, reaching for the carpetbag he had forgotten he was holding.

"Miss Becky, what have you done?"

"It's just a little joke, Matt. But I want it to be a surprise. You won't tell anyone how I'm dressed, will you?" Wordlessly he shook his head, still trying to make sense out of what he saw before him. "Good," Rebecca continued. "Now Matt, I need you to do something else for me. I want you to saddle a horse for us."

"Oh, no, miss. I'm sorry, but we have strict instructions—"

"Not Gallant Rider. You needn't worry."

"I don't know..."

"My mother told you not to allow me near Gallant Rider, isn't that correct?"

"Yes, it is."

"Fine. I don't want to go near Gallant Rider. I just thought I would go out for a little canter on a gentle mare out of our paddocks. Young ladies are allowed that, aren't they?" Matt looked pointedly at her outfit, and she saw the inconsistency of her argument. "Well, my mother didn't say I was not to go near any horse at all, did she?" Matt looked as though he were trying to make up his mind as to that question, but Rebecca plowed ahead before he could reach a decision. "No, she did not. Gallant Rider was the only horse she specifically said I was not to go near, so you will not be disobeying her by saddling another horse for me." She hurried him out the door, again without giving him a chance to think anything through.

In the stable Matty was relieved to find Belle Rose patiently munching from her feed trough, and he promptly slipped a saddle on her back. If he had been forced to choose another horse, perhaps he would have stopped to reason out his actions then, but Belle Rose was the only horse the Westovers owned that Matt was absolutely positively sure would not kick him. She was as mild and as gentle as a creature could get on this side of the grave. She seemed, in fact, to be just precariously balanced on the line separating the living and the dead.

Returning to the house, he called softly through her door. "Miss Becky, I have Belle Rose saddled for you."

"Saddled for *us*, Matty," Rebecca said, opening the door a few inches and suspiciously looking out.

" 'For us,' miss?"

"You didn't take her around front, did you?" Becky asked with something of alarm in her voice. She had opened the door wider by now, and Matt saw that her outfit was complete, from the spats on her shoes to the small flat hat perched jauntily atop her head, anchored in position by a red curl or two that were clutching at its rim.

"No, miss. She's at the service entrance at the rear. 'For us'?"

"Oh, come along, Matty. We're just going to take a little ride."

Once again the boy was caught up in events, hurried along by a more forceful will, and before he knew what was happening, he found himself behind Miss Becky riding Belle Rose out the gate and into the lane.

As he bounced around on the horse's rump, holding the carpetbag with one hand and wondering what to do with the other hand, he diverted his attention from his immediate uncomfortable surroundings by contemplating an overall view of the afternoon's activities. What he saw appalled him. He was very fond of Miss Becky (she was a lot like his older brother, whom Matt adored, except she knew more about horses and he had longer hair) but neither of those considerations could blind him to the fact that the girl was definitely running away. At any time that would have been catastrophic in the Westover house, but worse and worse, she had pressed him into service as her accomplice.

A moan escaped his lips.

"What did you say?" Rebecca asked over her shoulder. It was not necessary to maintain watchful control over her mount, just as it was not necessary for the skipper of a barge to exclusively man the tiller: neither the barge nor Belle Rose were going anywhere fast.

"I was just thinking that I would surely like to get off this horse, Miss Becky."

"How would you get back to the manor?"

"I would be more than willing to walk back, miss."

"But Matty, how would Belle Rose get back?"

"Why, miss, you would bring her back, surely." Matt said it without conviction. He meant it as, and it sounded like, a plea.

Rebecca was quiet for a moment. Finally, in a conciliatory tone, she said, "Hang on for just a few more minutes, Matty. We're almost there."

Matt assumed "there" was Ettington, since they were at the outskirts of that small community already. Poultry and other domestic animals were continually darting out into the street. Rebecca thought fondly what a test of her horsewomanship it would have been to have ridden Gallant Rider through this and kept him under control. Then the muscle at the base of her jaw locked.

The *old* Gallant Rider, was her fierce thought, and just as fierce was her determination not to cry over this. But even as she made that resolution, a tear slipped down her cheek. "All right, you can cry, but not now!" she whispered to herself, and with the promise her tears retreated for the present.

"Where are we going, miss?" Matt asked timidly.

Rebecca started; she had almost forgotten the boy was behind her.

"We are going to Ettington station, Matty," she answered him grimly.

By now they were in the middle of the hubbub of town. Shoppers and merchants haggled in the shops, at the doorways, sometimes bringing their dickering out into the streets. Though not large, Ettington did boast a nice little eating establishment and even in the midafternoon a few elegantly appointed couples were carefully making their way toward the place over the rough boardwalk. Carriages, barouches and broughams were more the order here than large clumsy riding mares, and at any other time, Rebecca would have been mortified. But just now she was much too caught up in the designs of her grand revenge to give more than a fleeting thought to her present regrettable mode of transportation.

The station was abustle with men and an endless stream of baggage all performing an intricate ballet around one another.

Rebecca slipped from Belle Rose's back and reached up to Matty for her valise.

"It looks like the 3:15 is going to be right on time today," she said with forced cheerfulness. If Matt hadn't been so deafened by the pounding of his own heart he would have heard the uncertainty creeping into her voice. Being here, at the station, in the center of an uncaring crowd that was threatening to heedlessly gobble her up and then just as casually spew her out again, shook her in her spiteful intent.

Her Aunt Minerva Twitchell (who has already been mentioned) lived in Derby. It was her plan to flee to Mrs. Twitchell and throw herself on that good woman's mercy. The two were not particularly close. In fact, Rebecca only saw her Aunt Minerva once every other year, when it was the Westovers' turn to host her and her entourage for the Christmas or Easter holidays. But if she remembered correctly (it had been almost two years since she had seen her aunt by this time) her Aunt Minerva was a kind and sympathetic woman. And even if she were not the most compassionate being in the world, surely anyone with a human heart beating in their bosom could see the injustice that had been done to Rebecca.

With that thought uppermost in mind, the girl squared her shoulders and entered the small wooden structure where tickets could be purchased.

Matty watched the retreating figure until it disappeared through the doorway. He himself sat motionless astride Belle Rose, where Rebecca had left him, watching that door, scanning every face and form that emerged. Waiting. The ground started to tremble under Belle Rose, and the horse under the boy. With much screeching and smoking, a huge black dragon-looking thing drew into the station on the other side of the ticket building. Matt had seen plenty of trains before, but none had ever seemed so hungry, so grasping, so malevolent as this one did. Dimly through the smoke, he could see people getting on and off. Once his heart leaped into his throat when he saw a fluffy red head bobbing up and down in the milling crowd. He tried to determine whether it was approaching or departing when, first, he was relieved to see that person was definitely getting closer, and seconds later was bitterly disappointed to see that the person was a shop girl wearing a perky little hat with red flowers scattered over the crown.

After a while the activity around the gasping engine waned, and Matty saw a man in black stand at the passenger opening.

"BOARD!" Matt heard the man bellow, and two stragglers hurried up the steps. There was a flurry of noise and smoke around the track, and like some black beast out of hell, departing amid fire and brimstone, the train pulled away from the station. Turning on Belle Rose and straining his neck, Matt watched the last car for as long as he could see it, and then the smoke for two minutes longer than that.

Finally he sank back into the saddle and looked around him. There were still a few people moving about, but compared with the recent activity, the area seemed absolutely still and deserted. He nudged Belle Rose forward a few steps until he could see right into the doorway of the station house. Except for a porter and the lady who sold tickets sitting behind her window, that room seemed to be empty, too.

He didn't dare dismount Belle Rose. What would he do with her if he did? But he knew it was no use to go into the station, anyway. Rebecca was gone. He didn't know where, but he knew considerably more than anyone else at the manor. The only trouble was, did he dare tell anyone?

He turned his quiet horse, who had been snatching forty winks while she had the chance, and headed back through Ettington in the direction from which they had come such a short time before. His mind kept circling around the idea of what to do when he got back to the manor like a dog pack happening upon a covered parcel, warily investigating it, trying to discover if it would be good to eat, but never forgetting that it could be lodging something dangerous.

He ruled out Mrs. Westover immediately as a confidante; the very thought of admitting the duplicity to her made his blood run cold. The squire was the second name to be checked off his mental roll call. Like everyone else in the family, household and all of Ettington, Matt knew the squire was easier to please and get along with than his very demanding wife, but in a case of aiding and abetting his youngest daughter in running away, Matt sensed that the squire would in the end be the most unforgiving of the two. No, neither the squire nor Mrs. Westover would learn of Rebecca's departure from him, and if he could possibly manipulate the story, they would never learn of his part in that departure from anyone.

Broderick? One did not manipulate Broderick. Gwendolyn? Matty didn't have enough to do with her to justify approaching her with this. But now he was moving down the totem pole to Bertha and Sophie and Nell, with all of whom he shared a mutual liking. The trouble was they were not in any position of authority to do anything, and they would immediately send him with his bad news (they all liked Matty, but not well enough to offer their own heads for his) to Broderick or one of the Westovers.

Like the first dog who sniffs at the parcel and then rejoins the circling pack, he backed away from the problem to regroup and started from the beginning again.

Not Squire and Mrs. Westover, not the staff. Mr. Derek? Last resort. He would be easier to talk to than the other Westovers, but the girl was still his sister, and Matty thought it best to avoid personal involvement with all members of the family if at all possible.

Miss Foster! The governess. A logical choice. Not a part of the family, in daily contact with the girl, her friend, often her overseer. But wait, that woman would probably wish to avoid complicity for that very reason and might be one of the first to pass him along to Broderick or the family. He just couldn't be sure about her.

What about the other young woman? Miss Forrester? Now there was an interesting idea.

Not being a member of the serving staff, it would never occur to her to insist he, a mere page boy, speak to the Westovers himself. Not being a member of the family, she would not be as grief stricken at Becky's departure and less inclined to blame him for her disappearance. It seemed the perfect solution.

By now he was back at the manor and had unsaddled and put up the mare. All that remained was to find Miss Forrester and relieve himself of this heavy burden.

Chapter Twenty-nine

Josephine was swathed in veils and silky fabrics, cushioned on downy pillows with a bowl of grapes and pomegranates, papayas and mangoes at her elbow. She felt a cool shifting of the air above her head, and looking up she saw a fan of peacock feathers, as large as Broderick's two-man serving tray, slowly being drawn back and forth. Her eyes followed the line of the fan's long handle, and without surprise she saw Derek Westover acting as wafter. He was half-nude, but it was nevertheless definitely Derek. His muscles rippled with the effort of moving the fan, and Josephine smiled sensuously.

"Here, slave!" she said in a throaty voice she hardly recognized as her own.

He rested the fan on the floor and came to her side with an effort to appear dignified, but unable to hide his eagerness.

"Yes, O mistress?"

"I hunger, slave," she said.

He picked up the cluster of grapes and pulled one of the plump fruits free.

"For a grape, mistress?"

"A grape will not satisfy this hunger," she said as she guided his hand to her lips.

"Is it, perhaps, for fruit more precious than these that you crave?" he whispered next to her ear so that his warm breath stirred the feathery strands of hair on her neck.

"More precious, indeed, thou slave to my will." She snaked her hand up the warm firm flesh of his bare arm and smiled wickedly to hear his sharp intake of breath. "Sit thou beside your mistress and give to her that which she desires," she commanded.

Derek sank to the voluptuous folds of the materials covering her couch and sat gazing ardently at her scantily covered form, yet obviously fearful of her power and authority.

"Do you not find me beautiful?" she asked him, to which he was able only to nod as he watched her breasts rise and fall to the rhythm of her breathing. Unable to restrain himself longer, he pulled her roughly to him as his lips sought and found her willing mouth.

Their limbs followed the example of their searching tongues, and soon the feel of silks and satins against her skin was replaced by the more tantalizing touch of Derek's skin.

But just at that moment a distant knock sounded, and Josephine clutched wildly at his form, which now eluded her grasp and was suddenly far away.

"Derek!" she cried desperately.

"Mistress?" came the faint reply.

"Come back, my own, my love! I am yours!"

"Miss Forrester?"

"Wha-what?" Josephine's eyes blinked open, and the volume of *Arabian Nights* dropped from her hands onto the floor.

"Miss Forrester, it's me, Matty. Matt Clark. Can I speak with you for just a minute?"

Flustered, Josephine pushed a stray strand of hair back to join its fellows and stood up.

"Certainly, Matt. I'll be right there," she sounded a little breathless, which surprised Matt since he assumed she had been just resting. Josephine opened the door and confirmed the assumption with her sleep-puffed eyes.

"What is it, Matt?"

"May I come in please, miss? I would prefer it if we could keep this between the two of us."

Somewhat at a loss, Josephine moved back from the door to allow the boy to enter.

"Yes, Matt?" she said.

The boy looked around him, very ill at ease. He saw the fallen book at her bedside and picked it up to hand to her.

"I think you must have been reading this before you fell asleep, miss," he said.

Josephine blushed as she took the book from him and placed it on her bureau. She cleared her throat to cover her embarrassment, but when she again looked at Matt, she could see he was not at all concerned with her and what her dreams might have been about.

"What is the matter, Matt?" she asked.

"Oh, Miss Forrester, I think I've done something terribly wrong." His young voice was shaking, and tears sprang to his eyes. Immediately Josephine was at his side on her knees, her book and dreams forgotten—for the moment.

"What is it you think you have done, Matt? It can't be as bad as all that." She put her arm comfortingly around his waist.

"Well, miss, it's not what *I've* done, exactly. But I knew it was going to happen, don't you see? I just didn't know how to stop her. It's not my fault." There was such a pleading tone in the boy's voice that Josephine quelled her impatience at his so far totally unenlightening story and gently urged him once again to tell her what happened.

"It's Miss Becky, ma'am," he said.

"What about Becky—Miss Rebecca?" Josephine cried. Was it something serious? Was she injured? Even dead? Was it some tragedy Josephine could have averted if she had been doing her duty?

"She's run away, Miss Forrester."

"Run away?" Josephine sounded almost relieved. Compared to the possibilities that had sprung to mind, Rebecca's running away was a very minor problem, indeed. "Where is she, Matt?" she asked. It was probably just a matter of catching up with her on foot, perhaps even having the gig made ready, if she had ridden a horse, and reasoning with her to convince her to return.

"Where is she?" the boy repeated her question stupidly.

"Yes, Matt. Where can I find her?"

"Well, on the 3:15 train out of Ettington, but I don't know where that is now, ma'am."

Josephine dropped back onto her heels, stunned.

"A train?" This time it was her turn to sound stupid.

"Yes, ma'am. You see..." And so, bit by bit, Matt somehow got the whole dreadful story told to Josephine.

In his recounting of the events, he wasn't able to explain Rebecca's anger, hurt or feelings of betrayal that had led to her flight. Those were motives Josephine would have to sort out at another time. Right now she was much too concerned with the effect of Rebecca's action to worry about its cause. She was standing by now, and since the point in Matt's story where the girl had gotten off Belle Rose at the station, she had been pacing up and down in front of the chair from which the boy was delivering his narration.

"And you do not know where she was going? She did not tell you any of her plans?"

"No, Miss Forrester. She didn't say anything but that it was a little joke. But I don't think it's a very funny joke. Do you, Miss Forrester?"

"No, Matty. I do not think it's funny at all."

They lapsed into silence, with Josephine continuing her pacing and Matt nervously watching her.

"She didn't say what train?"

"The only thing she said about a train at all was that the 3:15 was on time."

"Three-fifteen? The 3:15," Josephine mused. "Ettington cannot have that many trains. Chances are someone will remember a girl with red hair and perhaps be able to tell us where she was going."

"Only they'd think it was a boy with red hair," Matt reminded her.

"What? Oh yes, of course. A small boy with red hair."

"Are you going to tell Mrs. Westover?" Matt asked, trying to make the question sound casual. The Westover parents needed to be told; his task now was to convince Miss Forrester to keep his name out of the story.

To his surprise, though, Josephine's answer was a definite negative.

"No! No, I don't think I had better go to the mistress with this." Matt was surprised to hear her speak of Mrs. Westover as would a servant addressing the lady of the house, but Josephine was thinking much too hard and fast to guard against every slip of the tongue. If Mrs. Westover was to discover that Rebecca had run away while Josephine was impersonating a guest in her house, retribution would be swift and sure. And warranted! That the real Miss Forrester would abandon her role of governess the moment blame was laid in that quarter was an absolute. But superseding all other considerations was her realization of what Derek's reaction would be if his cherished little sister were to meet with some mishap while her ostensible guardian was foolishly playing the coquette with him. She shuddered to think about it.

Her one recourse was to find the girl herself and bring her back. She would still be held at fault, and she ought to be, since the fault was surely hers. But no permanent damage would have resulted from her lapse of responsible behavior, and she hoped the Westovers' ire would not be permanent, or too far-reaching, either.

"Matty," she said, coming to a halt in front of the chair he was occupying, where his feet dangled in midair. "Is there a gentle old horse out in the stable you could saddle for us?"

"Yes, there is, ma'am. Belle Rose. I just put her away. 'For us,' ma'am?"

"Go saddle her and bring her around to the servants' entrance. I will meet you there."

Once again little Matty Clark slipped the saddle onto Belle Rose's back. The old mare stood patiently munching, as if it were all perfectly normal for her to be saddled and ridden for two long sessions in one day. The truth was she had not seen this much excitement since that night in her fourth summer, thirteen years ago, when she had run twelve miles, with a younger Alex riding bareback, to fetch Dr. Jones who had warned Catherine Westover that a woman of thirty-six could run into difficulties in delivery.

Matt was trying to convince himself that having been reported to a responsible adult, the problem would now be attended to correctly, and he did not need to worry anymore. But somehow this was not what he had expected to happen when he got his story told. This saddling of the mare and bringing her to the back door smacked suspiciously of certain actions of his earlier in the day, which he was terming as foolish now.

"Are you ready?"

"Me? Ready?"

"You have our horse saddled, I see. Well, she doesn't look too wild, I suppose."

Matt was dumbfounded. First by Miss Forrester's appearance and then by Miss Forrester's words. The young woman looked extremely nervous and was dressed in a bizarre outfit that looked like a blending of styles worn to the hunt, an afternoon tea and a formal ball. Her words surprised him, because the horse she spoke of as not looking "too wild," looked, in fact, to be only semiconscious, and also because when Miss Forrester referred to that horse, she said disconcerting things like "our horse."

"Yes, ma'am. I mean, no ma'am. This is Belle Rose, and she's as gentle as a kitten. Did you ask if *I* was ready?"

"Well, certainly Matthew. However could I locate the station without you?"

"The station is the only train station in Ettington, ma'am."

"Yes, of course. But I want to make sure I ask the right people and am able to give them the correct information, you understand. I could not do that without your help, Matt. And besides—" she exhaled sharply as she drew herself up onto the saddle with a hand from the boy "—how would Belle Rose get back if you did not come along?"

Matt stood frozen; it was happening all over again.

"You'd bring her back yourself," he whispered.

"What? Oh, yes, yes, of course I will. Unless something comes up, that is. Now hurry along, get behind me, I suppose. There, just like that. And I do believe we're off!" was her surprised exclamation as, with Matt's jump onto her rump once more, Belle Rose started down the lane.

Matt's account of his second trip into Ettington could have been stated in one sentence: "We arrived at the Ettington station without incident."

Josephine's story would have been a good deal more verbose, bordering on the hysterical and rife with despair, danger, excitement, tragedy and utter relief. Josephine's narration would comprise an entire chapter, and as seen through her eyes, would very nearly prove the pivotal point in our story. But boiled down, bereft of all subjective drama, it could, in essence, be stated: they arrived at the Ettington station without incident.

In great relief Josephine slid from the saddle and put the reins into the hands of a man standing near the door of the station. After her harrowing ride, she was not particular as to whom she was delivering Belle Rose; fortunately he was a porter, who was paid modestly by the railroad company to perform that and like services, and was usually handsomely tipped by the ladies and gentlemen on whose behalf his services were rendered. He would be receiving no tip from the young lady, he was quite certain, but since there were no paying patrons waiting for him, and she was a fetching little thing—if somewhat oddly dressed—he would hold her old nag. Not that Belle Rose was going to require much holding. One thing she had learned in her seventeen years, was to go to sleep anywhere.

Inside the station it was just as Matt had been telling her: one track into Ettington, one station in town, one ticket seller behind her grille. Josephine knew the boy had been telling her the truth, but what he did not know was that she was very unsure of herself and even frightened. She would have agreed wholeheartedly with Rebecca that the company of a nine-year-old boy can put real steel into one's backbone.

"May I help you, miss?" the woman behind the screen asked in a pleasant voice, just as if she did not sit in that box six days a week assuring frightened farm wives and smoothing ruffled feathers, day in and day out, smiling brightly at everyone the day her daughter had a baby boy, and just as brightly the day after her mother died. Now, at the end of a long summer day, her voice was still cheerful and soothing when she addressed the young woman in the rather remarkable outfit.

"I am inquiring after a passenger who took one of your trains today."

"Incoming or outgoing?"

"I beg your pardon?"

"A passenger coming into the station or going out of it? Incoming or outgoing?"

"Oh, yes. I see. Well then, she would have been outgoing."

"I will do my best to help you, miss, but I must confess that I don't remember all of the faces that come through here." She did not really see most of the faces at all, as a matter of fact. She had cultivated a pleasant attitude of complete detachment.

"You may remember this passenger. A young girl, thirteen years old, with red hair." Matt tugged urgently at her skirt, and Josephine looked inquiringly at him.

"A boy, miss," he reminded her.

"Oh, yes. I mean, a young *boy*. With red hair."

"Was it a girl or a boy you're looking for?"

"A boy. That is, a girl, dressed like a boy. A young man, really. But quite thin and not very tall. With red hair.

"I am sure I would recall a young man with long red hair."

"No, no. She has short red hair. She would have been wearing... What did you say, Matt?"

Matt stood on his tiptoes and peeked into the ticket seller's cage.

"Brown flannel trousers, a coat, a violet bow tie and a round flat hat."

"A skimmer?" the ticket seller asked helpfully, but by that time the boy had dropped down from his toes and had disappeared from her sight and hearing. She repeated her question to the young lady.

"I don't know—I didn't see him, er... her, myself." For the first time in the conversation, and if Josephine had known it, the first time in a long time, a tired exasperated light appeared in the woman's eyes.

"Miss, I really do not believe I can help you. There are so many people through here in a day," which was not altogether true, but she hated to tell the girl that she had trained herself to see only a faceless mob.

"She had short red hair," Josephine said with something like desperation in her voice.

"A lot of people with red hair catch trains, too, miss. I am sorry."

Josephine's shoulders sagged for a moment, and once again Matt tugged on her skirt.

"The 3:15, Miss Forrester."

"Three-fifteen? Oh yes, that's right. She caught the 3:15 out of this station."

"I am afraid I still don't . . ." the seller began, her shoulders sagging a bit, as well.

"Can you just tell me where the 3:15 was bound?" Josephine asked.

"Yes, of course." The woman brightened. "Let us see, the 3:15, that would be Rugby, Nuneaton, Tamworth, Burton-upon-Trent, Derby and Chesterfield."

"If you were running away, which of those towns would you choose?" Josephine asked.

"Running away, miss? I don't know. I suppose, well, yes, I would choose either Derby or Chesterfield. There's really nothing to do at those other stops but milk cows and hoe gardens, now is there, miss?" The woman chuckled appreciatively at her witticism.

"Derby or Chesterfield? Derby . . . hmm. I believe we may have something here. Matt, didn't the squire say he has some family living in Derby? A cousin or an aunt—"

"I think that's where his sister lives, Miss Forrester."

"Sister! That's it. Turnstile, or was it Twinstile? Twitchell! I am sure he said Twitchell." There was a victorious note in her voice as she was able to summon the name from her memory. Decisively she turned back to the teller. "How much is a ticket to Derby?" she asked, sending little Matty's heart down into his shoes.

The woman quoted the price, and Josephine dug frantically through her string purse, which was also a part of her outfit. "I think I have . . . yes, I do have enough." She was panting from her exertions as she handed the money through the opening in the cage. "Now Matt, I want you to take Belle Rose back to the manor."

"What shall I tell them, miss?" He was trying to be very brave about this, but despite his best efforts his young voice shook slightly.

Josephine smiled encouragingly at him. "I will probably be back to the manor with Rebecca before anyone misses us." It may have heartened her, but Matt did not believe it for one minute. It was a rude awakening for one so young to discover that the wise adult world is just as fraught with foibles as a child's world, and that grown-up foolishness differs from childhood foolishness only in its grander scope and more lasting consequences.

The next train into Derby would be passing through Ettington at about six o'clock, which meant it would pull into Derby shortly after eight. There would not be time to get to the manor and back again (at least not on Belle Rose). But Josephine had foreseen just such a development, which explains the oddity of her ensemble and the impression she gave of being ready for anything. She was, in fact, congratulating herself on her forethought and ingenuity, but to a boy of nine it appeared as if the young woman were going off half-cocked on a railway journey of fifty miles, to arrive, in the middle of the night, in a strange town, looking for a girl dressed as a boy, whom she was only half sure would be there in a woman's home whose last name she hoped she remembered correctly.

And, as a point in fact, that is precisely what she was doing.

Chapter Thirty

Despite Mrs. Westover's deep-seated disapproval of romances among her staff, Phyllis and Will Trolley had found it simple to sidestep her vigilance and rendezvous undetected whenever they wished. They had devised a system of signals between them so that whenever Phyllis was free and able to slip away, she placed a vase of flowers at her open window, which faced the stable. If Will was in from the fields and able to meet her, he closed the window in the hayloft on a red bandanna he owned, leaving it to flutter provocatively in the breeze. Phyllis would watch the hayloft, and when she saw the bandanna appear, would hurry breathlessly to the arms of her lover. If she did not see the bandanna, she fretted, fumed and became very short-tempered. Mrs. Westover may not have been aware of the affair, but Phyllis's fellow servants certainly knew when Miss Foster and Mr. Trolley had enjoyed each other's company, and they heartily approved.

Today there was no time for the complicated signaling that would ensure Mrs. Westover's ignorance. After overhearing her parents' wire to the Westovers, Phyllis knew that secrecy would only be possible for one more day. So she realized that she must take decisive action.

"Nell! Come here," she urgently called to the maid hurrying by.

"Yes, Miss Foster?" Although the governess, like Nell, was a paid member of the Westover household staff, she was respectfully addressed as "Miss Foster" by the other servants; further evidence of the unclassifiable position held by the governess in the house.

"Nell, quick, I need to speak to Mr. Trolley."

"Now, miss?" There was surprise in Nell's voice. Miss Foster's relations with Mr. Trolley were a familiar topic of conversation among other members of the staff, and their discretion was always favorably mentioned. Nell had never known either one of them to be so impetuous.

"Yes, now!" There was no question about Miss Foster's urgency. "Do you know where he is?"

"Not exactly, miss," Nell said timidly, a little nervous by now.

"Well, where is he *usually* at this time of day?"

"Midafternoons, miss, he is usually working in the cattle pens."

"Cattle pens?" Phyllis said uncertainly. Here was another part of the real world not readily acknowledged by women of society. She was not at all sure where they were or if she could get to them.

"They're out beyond the stable, miss. I could send Matty out to find him, if you'd like."

"That won't be necessary. I shall look for him myself."

Nell nodded, mystified, and turned to go.

But she was stopped once again. "In fact, Nell," Phyllis said, striving to make her voice sound offhand and casual, thereby alerting the maid to the importance of the next statement. "I would rather you didn't mention my inquiry to anyone else at all."

"Oh, miss," Nell said, opening her eyes wide. "If the mistress were to ask, I would feel it my duty to report our exchange."

Phyllis scrutinized Nell. There was a crafty expression in those innocent eyes. "If I could rely on your discretion in this, I would be happy to present you with that fur collar of mine I couldn't help but notice you admiring the other day."

Nell blushed. She was not above snooping and rummaging through the drawers and wardrobes in the rooms that she cleaned, but she did not like to be caught in the act. Nevertheless, she *was* very fond of the collar in question, and if the price of it were only to keep quiet, perhaps she could do it. She could certainly promise to keep quiet, anyway.

And Phyllis felt easy in offering the fur. She had already owned it three months and worn it twice. She was really rather tired of it.

"Certainly, miss. I will say nothing about your meeting with Mr. Trolley today. I'm sure Mrs. Westover would never ask me, and if she were to, well, I could have a lapse of memory, I suppose."

"It could also be that I may be inquired after later...."

"I don't know where you've gone or who with, ma'am."

"Quite so."

"And the collar?"

"Certainly. You can go get it now."

"Thank you, miss." Nell curtsied and left, feeling rather proud of her dealing, since she couldn't imagine to whom she would have told the very poorly kept secret of Miss Foster's and Mr. Trolley's meetings.

Phyllis watched until the girl disappeared and then walked in the direction of the library and the back stairs. From the servants' entrance, she went across the lawn in full view of the second-story library window, if anyone was looking out. Despite the promise of discretion she had elicited from Nell, she seemed careless of it herself, since by the time she reached the stable and outbuildings she was running and calling loudly.

"Will! Will, where are you? I need to talk to you!" she shouted into the stable door. Several of the horses neighed or whinnied nervously, and Alex came scowling forward to find out what the young woman wanted and what she thought she was doing to spook his horses like that. Phyllis was so relieved to see him, she didn't notice his black look.

"Alex!" she said, making a grab for the older man's hand. He was taken off guard and found his hand in a surprisingly strong grip before he could pull away. "Alex, where is Will? I need to talk to him."

Alex cocked his head toward the back of the stable, which could have meant she was to look either at the other end of the building or outside the door. Alex could never be called ambiguous, though, and a gruff "Out" cleared up any question Phyllis might have had. Without waiting to hear the remonstrances already glinting in Alex's eye (or even really aware that they were there) Phyllis dropped his hand and brushed past him to run the length of the Westover stable.

"Will!" she called again, when she came to the end of the building. She had never been past the stable before, and now she could see why not. The necessary filth and mud of a cattle pen was not conducive to the delicacy of a woman's wardrobe. Stepping back to the relative purity of the stable doorway, Phyllis looked in dismay at the veritable cesspool before her and fervently hoped that she would not have to explore its depths in order to find her Will. With a handful of skirt in either hand, she had almost decided that if she must, she must, when the sweat-streaked farmhand appeared around the corner of the building.

"Willy!"

"Josey?" he asked, surprised. The young lady had never been to the cattle pens before. She didn't even like to come to the stables with him on nights when he had to make a quick stop before they retired to...wherever they could find privacy. It has been said that plague is the great leveler, reducing all men to the same plane, regardless of wealth or position. But Phyllis and Will Trolley had found lust to be the great leveler between them, and anyplace that was free from prying eyes and could boast a reasonably flat surface, six-by-four or larger, could be made to meet their mutual need.

"I said I'd be up to see you later tonight. Couldna wait, lassy?" Will chuckled lasciviously.

"That's not what I came for," Phyllis said regretfully. Even as she said these words, she found herself wondering if a little time could not be found... Then she squared her shoulders resolutely; this was no moment for dalliance, pleasant though it might be.

Will, for his part, was surprised and not entirely convinced by her words. If that was not what Phyllis had come for, it would be the first time since he met her. "What, then, has brought you down to this little corner of the world, my pretty?" he asked as he knocked and scraped his boots against the door frame.

Phyllis smiled. She had not made a mistake, and even if she were completely disowned by her father, she wouldn't lose in the exchange. Will could make sunshine appear and set her heartstrings aquiver by a simple phrase like "my pretty." He was, without question, what she wanted for her life, and she was not about to give him up, having finally found some real happiness.

"Will, we need to talk," she said with a new intensity in her voice.

Will looked up sharply. "What about?"

Phyllis looked around, emphasizing her desire for covert confabulation. "Not here," she whispered.

Will grinned; she was a darling girl, and her games—of which he was still sure this was one—continued to bring surprise and excitement into a sport at which he considered himself a seasoned professional.

"I need to talk to you alone. Would the hayloft be deserted at this time of day?"

"Aye, it would. But Jo, I need to get my chores finished first. You know that. Just hold on for the rest of the day, and then we can...'talk'...in the hayloft as long as you like." He smiled again and gave her a broad wink.

She stamped her foot impatiently.

"This has nothing to do with 'talking' Will. This is important, and we need to discuss it as soon as possible."

At last her urgency penetrated Trolley's skull and diverted his almost relentlessly one-track train of thought. His darling was sincerely worried about something, something she, at least, thought was important. He could afford a few minutes to put her mind at ease; heaven knew she had put him at ease often enough.

"You go on up to the loft, then. I'll be right up as soon as..." His words trailed off, but he held up his begrimed hands, turning them this way and that just in case there was any question as to their present state, and tilted his head toward the water pump.

Not being a total idiot, Phyllis understood his meaning.

"All right," she said as she turned to leave. "But hurry."

"I will, luv. You just hurry yourself." His impulse was to speed her along with a firm but affectionate swat on her generous derriere, but her skirts were a pale peachy color, and he recognized the difficulty she might have explaining away the outline in muck of a man's hand on the nether regions of her dress.

Fifteen minutes later—fifteen minutes spent by Phyllis in clenching hands, murmuring a rehearsal of her explanation and pacing the length of the hay-strewn floor—Trolley's broad shoulders heaved open the trapdoor to the loft. It hadn't taken him fifteen minutes to wash his hands, but his cleansing operations had been more extensive than that, since, despite her words and tone of voice, he suspected this still might be some erotic prelude to a...conversation.

Phyllis hurried to the door and held it open while he climbed into the loft. He took the heavy handle from her and lowered the door gently, then he stood brushing the straw from his clothes, assuming she would notice his efforts on her behalf.

"Will," she began, in distraction turning her back on him even before his tidying was complete. She didn't say anything for a few moments and, finished, he finally looked up.

"What is it that's got you so upset, dearie?" he asked.

"Oh, Will!" she ran to him and clutched him in her arms. But when he responded and started to nibble at her neck, she pulled away. "Not now!" she said impatiently.

"Then what do you want, Josey?" Will demanded.

"Well, for one thing, you could start calling me by my real name."

This was not like the girl he had come to know and please so easily, but Will was willing to play along. "All right, Josephine. I give up. What's the matter?"

Phyllis backed away from him and started pacing the floor again, trying to remember the phrases she had practiced that would explain her present predicament without making it sound as if she had deliberately set out to entrap and deceive him. It was no wonder she was having difficulty finding the words, since that was, more or less, precisely what she had set out to do.

"Will, do you know Miss Forrester?" she began. "The young lady brought here as a prospective bride for young Mr. Westover?"

"Sure. I've seen her."

"Well, I am she." Will merely looked at her. "That is," she continued, "she is me." She couldn't blame his blank look. Somehow, when she had rehearsed this speech, it had made more sense, but the words she had just uttered did sound just as meaningless to her as she was sure they did to him. She stopped her pacing and took a deep breath. She would try again.

"Some time ago, my mother sent a letter to her friend of many years, Mrs. Westover, hinting broadly that her daughter, me, and Mrs. Westover's son, might be mutually attracted to each other, so much so that, in time, after they, that is, we, became better acquainted, we might consider uniting the family fortunes."

Will's blank face showed that he had obviously understood only the occasional word in the foregoing diatribe.

"In short," Phyllis said, and noticed a look of relief on Will's face, "it was hoped we would be married."

"Your mother wanted you to marry me?"

"No, no. Mr. Derek Westover was the husband she had in mind."

"Your mother tried to get you employment here as the governess so you could marry Mr. Derek? A bit cheeky of her, if you ask me."

"The letter my mother sent was not to secure me a position of governess. I am not a governess. *I* am Miss Forrester."

Will seemed to see a glimmer of light as he struggled to make sense of Phyllis's ragged explanation.

"Then what about—"

"Miss Forrester? The other Miss Forrester?"

Will nodded.

"*She* is the governess, the real Miss Foster, not I. Somehow the letters were confused, and our names are so much alike, and when she arrived she didn't understand what was happening, and then when I arrived . . . there you were." She met his eyes at last, and a pretty blush mounted her cheeks.

Will was understandably not crystal clear on several points of her story, but one thing he did know was that he was very fond of the young woman in front of him. And while the discovery that she was the possessor of a great deal of money did not add to his love, it certainly did not detract from it in his practical mind. He opened his arms invitingly.

"Come," he said, and as she cuddled into his enfolding embrace, he murmured magnanimously, "Don't you fret. Why, I'd love you even if you were heir to the throne of England itself."

Once again Phyllis pulled away, remembering she had not finished her tale; that her alarm was not caused by fears of what Will would do when he found out, but what her parents would do when they found out.

"I overheard Squire Westover reading a telegram he received today. It was from my father, congratulating him on the romantic success between Miss Forrester—that is, Miss Foster—and the young gentleman. Evidently those two have hit it off almost as well as you and I."

Will raised his eyebrows in surprise. That young lady had not struck him as being as daringly impetuous as his own little filly.

"Not that well," Phyllis said, grinning. "But Will, the telegram my father sent said that he and my mother are coming to confirm the betrothal and no doubt hurry along the wedding plans. They will be here tomorrow."

At last Trolley comprehended Phyllis's dilemma. And his, too. Will was a bright lad, but tended to be lazy in his thinking. However, one sure way to get his mental faculties into high gear was to throw money into the works.

"So you think some problems will arise when Mr. and Mrs. Forrester arrive," he said with a shrewd note in his voice Phyllis had never heard before, but which she did not find altogether displeasing.

"Don't you?"

"I suppose a farmhand is a considerable step down."

"For my parents, perhaps. I do not mind the step, myself." And she did not. Phyllis had cared about many frivolous and unimportant things in her life, among them money and prestige. But now all she cared about was Will Trolley and her relationship with him.

"Still, that won't help us as long as they hold the purse strings, now will it, love? They do hold the purse strings, I suppose?" It occurred to him that Phyllis might have an inheritance from some rich uncle or an independent settlement of some sort.

Sadly, though, she nodded her head. "But I'm an only child, so I will, in time, be heir to more money than I, or even you *and* I could ever hope to spend. Regardless of whom I marry. If, that is, I don't do anything absolutely unforgivable in the meantime."

They both feared that taking a workingman on a friend's farm as a lover fell into the unforgivable category. But what about as a husband? It might not be the development Mr. and Mrs. Forrester had been hoping for, but if he loved her and she loved him, with honor and honesty, heedless of the worldly obstacles such a romantic union presented...? Perhaps the romance and sacrifice of such a union might have a softening effect on her parents' hearts.

Leaping over all those arguments and explanations, Trolley quickly asked, "Will you marry me?"

And just as quickly, Phyllis replied, "Yes."

The subsequent embrace was ardent but brief. They then sat down on the cushiony piles of hay to coolly make complete plans. They decided they could not be married here in Ettington soon enough to avoid the Forresters; Parson Moniff was sure to insist on the banns being properly called. What they really needed was a little time: time enough to establish themselves as a married couple, time enough to allow her parents' tempers to cool, time enough to make Phyllis's return to her family's bosom a welcome event regardless of any slight differences there may have been between them in the past. A grandchild on the way would help to bridge any gaps in the family relationship, they both thought.

"In a month or two we can go to them," Will said. "And I will do my best to make them like me." He smiled roguishly, and from personal experience Phyllis knew that when Will Trolley set his mind to be irresistible, he was certainly that. She reached over to squeeze his hand, and after an unprecedented forty-five minutes of restrained proximity, the hand squeeze escalated immediately into much more ardent embraces.

"Where shall we go?" Phyllis asked softly over the top of Will's exploratory head.

"Mmph mumr," he said against her bosom. The vibrations of his lips on the soft skin of her breast were tingling and exciting, but his words had not been at all intelligible. Lovingly she put her hands on either side of his face (after all, she did not want to entirely discourage him) and brought his mouth up even with her own.

"Where?" she asked.

"I have a brother near Derby with a small farm of his own." He trailed his fingers tantalizingly across her cheek, over her lips, down her neck, onto her collarbone . . . and, well, the Reader visualizes, no doubt, the general direction he was taking. "We can get married there and stay with Fred until you think it's safe to contact your folks."

"Mmrgh," was what it sounded as if Phyllis said as, tempted beyond bearing, she hungrily lunged for him.

Trolley took that to mean, "All right," but was not at all willing to stop her to make sure.

Chapter Thirty-one

"Going somewhere?"

Will Trolley swung around from his packing to see Alex standing in the doorway of the quarters the two men shared (though Alex spent a good many more nights there than Will). After that initial jump, Will turned back to the cracked and timeworn valise into which he was cramming his modest wardrobe.

"Well, Alex, you've been a decent sort of fellow, so I suppose I owe you some kind of explanation." More than his desire to ease his fellow's mind, Trolley was motivated by a desire to crow. He, Will Trolley, fourth son of a farm laborer sent to an early grave by drink, a harridan of a mistress and the guilt his meek long-suffering wife heaped upon his shoulders by careful design, was about to marry the only child of a very wealthy Sheffield investor. A fine-looking lass with whom, wonder of wonders, he had honestly fallen in love before he had knowledge of her enviable position.

"I've found me a wife," he announced proudly.

"The young miss?"

"Aye, that's the very one," Will admitted, but with an I-know-something-you-don't-know twinkle in his eye.

"Packing?"

It occurs to the author at this point that it is unfair to the reader to report Alex's conversation verbatim; so much of his unspoken message is lost in the translation. That single word, when combined with tone, inflection, hand gesture and facial expression, could more fairly be reported as: "Marrying the governess is all very well and good, and congratulations, Will, my boy. But she's an honest lassie—seems to me a quiet little wedding here at the manor would fill the bill just as neatly, and you wouldn't have to lose more than a couple of days' work between you—though we would certainly allow you a couple of days to yourselves, you old dog. Why, then, are you packing? Where are you going? What are your plans?''

That was what Alex meant, and that was what Will fully understood by Alex's communication. But to maintain perfect integrity as an author, the actual wording must not be editorialized, and what Alex *said* was, ''Packing?''

''Me and my lady thought we might try it up in Derby for a while. My brother lives there, you know, and maybe he'll let us stay over. We suspect that when this little piece of news gets about, all hell will break loose here.''

At this point Alex didn't say anything, but he raised his eyebrows and cocked his head quizzically to encourage Will to elaborate a little on his explanation. He obviously didn't understand why the marriage of a farmhand to a governess would cause the kind of furor Will was hinting.

''Because, Alex, my good man, it is not with Miss Foster, the Westover governess, I am running away, but Miss Forrester, who Mrs. Westover brought here to marry her son. See, she overheard a telegram from her dad saying he'd be here tomorrow to get this wedding on the go. But Miss Forrester—'' Will chuckled at the new name and accompanying fortune he was going to have to get used to ''—Miss Forrester doesn't want to be roped into a marriage with Mr. Derek, though he's a good sort, don't get me wrong there. She'd just rather be married to me, is all.''

Alex stepped back in alarm from the ring of triumph in Will's voice. He did not like to be hasty about anything, particularly forming an opinion, but he sensed immediately the danger in the young man's statement. This would not sit well.

The squire and his lady would not like it, because the young lady in question was their choice for their own son. None of the other servants would like it—the men because it would upset their employers, because it was a brazen attempt by Will to raise himself out of his rightful station, and because none of them had thought of it first. The women wouldn't like it, because they were all in love with Will. Master Derek would not like it at all, because from every indication, he was very fond of the young lady himself. And finally, Alex's chivalry rose in Miss Foster's defense, the young lady Mr. Trolley had so casually, and so recently used, and was now planning to cast callously aside.

Alex, in fact, was upset. He made it a strict policy never to interfere in anything, but if ever he was tempted to do so, this would have been the time. The older man had never been faced with a temptation yet that he could not resist, though. So, instead of grappling with the young man to stop his infernal packing, or better yet, flattening Will with one of the neat deadly jabs for which he had been famous in his younger days (and both alternatives presented themselves attractively to Alex) he merely turned with a gruff, "Harrumph!" and left Trolley to finish his packing, take the damnable trollop and go ahead and bring grief into at least the ten lives here at the manor.

From the length of the several foregoing chapters, it might have been assumed that a great deal of time has passed, but the truth of the matter is that by the time Derek had finished his several errands and calls (both business and social) in Ettington, stopped for one glass at The Lone Hunter, with the necessary accompanying game of darts, and returned to Meadowview manor early in the evening, the six o'clock train out of Ettington to Derby was only just preparing to leave. Indeed, he had seen the billowing clouds of steam announcing its arrival as he mounted Verity in front of the tavern. The house he had left that morning had been filled with a well-ordered family, guest and serving staff. By the time he returned that evening, his sister Rebecca was gone, with Josephine, the woman with whom he found himself reluctantly in love, in pursuit. His intended fiancée had eloped with his best field hand and good friend. And no one remaining at the manor was even aware of all the absences, because they were feverishly attempting to prepare the house for a visit from the Forresters, whom they believed to be Derek's future parents-in-law, who would be arriving the next morning in anticipation of attending a happy and long-anticipated betrothal party.

Having traveled to London and Paris and most of the other great capitals of Europe, little Ettington, England, at times seemed deathly boring and slow to Derek. More than once as he rode around the Westover lands, he thought of those other places and asked himself ruefully, "Why doesn't anything ever happen here?"

It would be a long time before he repeated that complaint.

"Will!" he called, stopping in front of the stable. "Will! Oh, Alex." Alex had appeared silently in the door frame of that structure. Derek noticed with faint surprise that the weathered face looking up at him appeared to be even more grim than usual. "I am a little late tonight," he explained as he slid from the horse's back. "Put Verity up for me, won't you? Or have Will do it. Guess he didn't hear me. Wonder where he is?"

Alex could have told him, but Derek was turned toward the manor by then, and Alex just could not bring himself to break character so radically as to offer information, however much he might disapprove of young Trolley's headlong imprudence.

Derek stomped noisily into the back entrance, endeavoring to shake the dust of his long day off his clothing before he greeted his mother—or Miss Forrester. An unconscious smile appeared at his lips as he thought of that young lady.

"Becky! RE-BEC-CA!" he called through the servants' hall and into the kitchen. He wanted to tell his younger sister he had run into Tilly Baxter's older brother Merrill while in town and that they had exchanged pleasantries concerning their sisters. Derek suspected his sister admired Baxter's blue eyes and undisciplined blond hair, and like older brothers from time immemorial, he wanted to tease Becky about the young man.

He got no response from her, but as he entered the kitchen on his way through to the library, where he hoped to find their guest, he saw little Matty Clark scuttle around the door to the pantry.

"Matt? Come here." The boy's head appeared around the door, and Derek coaxed him into the room. In a colt his behavior would have been called skittish. In the usually carefree and gregarious Matt, Derek didn't know what to call it.

"Where is everybody?" Derek asked. He was surprised to find no one in the kitchen at this hour, for Bertha was considered a permanent fixture there. By now his nostrils should have been assailed by those pungent aromas that cause one's mouth to water and empty stomach to twitch, rumble and churn painfully in anticipation. All his nostrils encountered this evening was the smell of soap and damp dust.

"Getting ready" was the boy's uncharacteristically short reply.

"Ready for what?"

"The Forresters. The mistress says they'll be here tomorrow morning."

Derek noticed that the bright lights bouncing off the copper kettles hanging here and there around the kitchen gave Matt's face a pale sort of greenish tint.

"The Forresters?" he said. "Miss Forrester's parents? Well, I suppose that's all right. Yes. I think that will be just as well. It certainly won't hurt to meet them—only meet them, of course. We won't plan anything else. Oh, Matt, see if you can find Rebecca, will you? I wanted to tell her who I saw in town today. I called but I guess she didn't hear me. I wonder where she is?"

Matt could have answered that question. Unlike Alex, Matt was much more apt to offer, but Derek's eyes were not deceiving him: Matty was a little green. In time it would all have to come out, including his part in it, but the longer he could put off that awful moment of disclosure the better.

Just then Nell entered the kitchen and Matt, with relief, took advantage of Derek's distraction to escape.

Derek was torn between wondering where his sister was (it did seem very odd that she had not appeared by this time, as she usually came running at his call) and contemplating the ramifications of the Forresters' imminent advent. Perhaps this explains why Nell's subsequent remarks failed to make an impression on him at that time.

Nell had found, when she examined the elegant little fur collar in the privacy of her own attic bedroom, that there was a rather unfortunate ink stain on it that she had previously not noticed. She had returned to the governess's room, thinking to make some sort of a surreptitious exchange, only to find that she had gone, taking most of her wardrobe and possessions with her. Nell was therefore out of sorts and rather eager to pass along certain pieces of information regarding Miss Foster.

"I am looking for Rebecca's governess, Nell. Perhaps she can tell me where my sister is, since no one else here seems to be able to do so."

"She's not 'ere, sir. Gone. She left in quite a hurry—traipsing after that Trolley fellow." Besides her ill humor over the promised reward, Nell was also jealous of Miss Foster's more successful hunting endeavors. Miss Foster had not been the only young woman hereabouts to go traipsing after the Trolley fellow, but she was the only one who had caught him.

But instead of making outraged demands of explanation, Master Westover merely nodded absentmindedly and left her to find his mother and learn more about the Forresters' visit.

He assumed he would find his parents in the library, but not only was Squire Westover not dozing in the padded armchair, but even more surprisingly, Mrs. Westover was not there writing letters at her desk.

"Gwendolyn, you do understand that the two east rooms *and* their sitting rooms are to be prepared? Sophie, the silver and the crystal must be dazzling. This is not dazzling. Bertha, we'll just have a light supper tonight—" the squire's heart sank; he had been working up quite an appetite today "—because you will no doubt have to start with next week's baking. This is what I have in mind for breakfast tomorrow.... Rather a late breakfast, I should think, so as to welcome, but not rush, our guests. Now what do you think about melons . . ."

The scene Derek came upon at the front of the house explained where everybody was (or rather, where many people were; enough people to camouflage the absences that in a calmer setting would have been glaring). Servants were scurrying about carting one thing away and bringing back three things to replace it. His mother was endeavoring to direct the chaos around her, and even his father seemed to be in serious consultation with Broderick, which was an extremely unusual departure for the elder Mr. Westover.

"Good evening, Mother," Derek said loudly enough to be heard above the general hubbub. In fact, it would be more accurate to say he shouted his greeting. "Father." He acknowledged the squire's attention, but turned back to his mother for the most succinct explanation of the activity all around him, which was resumed now after the two-second pause his cry had signaled.

"The Forresters are on their way—will be here tomorrow morning," Mrs. Westover said. "Mr. Forrester sent a telegram to your father this morning, expressing his pleasure that you two young people are so . . . compatible. They are coming to—''

"Inspect the merchandise?" Derek asked sardonically.

"Spend a few days, meet the family," his mother continued with a disapproving expression at her son's irreverence. She hoped Derek understood that she was only interested in his happiness, that she had no other motive for introducing him to Miss Forrester. Why, if the girl had been a pauper, as long as her son loved her, it would make no difference to Catherine Westover. Surely he believed that. Why, she almost believed it herself.

"They will be here in the morning, you say?" Derek asked, willing, if she was, to let his remark drop. "Is Miss Forrester ready for their rather portentous arrival?"

"I don't suppose her preparations have had to be quite as extensive as mine," Mrs. Westover said. "After all, it has only been a few weeks since she's seen them. I, on the other hand, must repair the damage of years!"

"What did she say when you told her they were coming?" he asked, anxious to learn the young woman's response when she was informed that her seconds were on their way to confirm all the details of the intended duel.

"What did she say? Oh, I don't know. She wasn't about at the time, so I sent Sophie to tell her when she came in."

By now Derek's curiosity was piqued, so he left his mother and detached Sophie from the endless caravan passing to and fro in front of him.

"Sophie, what was Miss Forrester's reaction when you told her Mr. and Mrs. Forrester would be here tomorrow morning?" There was a half smile on his face, but suddenly it had become very important to him to know if she had been pleased, petulant or panic stricken when she learned of the planned arrival and the decision that would directly follow.

"Lor', Mr. Derek, we've been in such a fuddle here all day, I just haven't had a chance to talk to her. You might ask Nell. . . ."

After talking to one or two other members of the staff (who, as usual, kept passing the ball along) Derek reached the conclusion that Miss Forrester could very well be unaware of the impending visit. If he wanted to know her reaction to the news, what better way to learn of it than to deliver that news himself?

So he set out in search of her. But although he looked carefully through the house, into all the rooms where, even remotely, she might be expected to be, he could not find her. Unbidden but numerous grim possibilities presented themselves to him. She could be injured some place, unable to return to the manor; abducted; lost; killed! Derek was definitely not as indifferent to Josephine as he liked to think.

He was also not a man to worry rather than act. Instead, he was the sort who worried *while* he acted. If she was not in the house—and she was not—the next logical place to check would be with Will or Alex. Maybe she had taken a ride today and had not returned.

Once again Derek made his way out to the stable. He kept a sharp lookout for Will or Alex. Will was nowhere to be found, so Derek, who was by now quite anxious about Josephine, called for Alex. As if he had been watching the younger Mr. Westover in his approach and waiting for his call, Alex appeared almost before the echoes of Derek's voice died away.

"Sir?" he said with gruff courtesy.

"Alex, I have—that is, *we*—have not been able to find Miss Forrester in the house. We were wondering if perhaps she went for a ride this afternoon and has not yet returned?"

"Aye, that she has, sir. And she isn't likely to return soon, either." The statement sounded vindictive and if uttered by a gossipy matron would have been accompanied by arms folded across the bosom, a sharp nod and lips pursed smugly at the end of the sentence. But though it was a voluminous statement from Alex, it conveyed less information than most of his single-syllable grunts.

"What do you mean?" Derek asked in alarm.

"I think I made myself plain, sir. The young lady isn't here now, and won't be for quite some time, I'm thinking."

Derek ached to grab Alex and shake the information out of him, but he merely clenched his fists tightly and infused his voice with as much exasperation as a good shaking would have conveyed. "Alex!"

"Well, the long and short of it is that Mr. Trolley's taken the young lady and run off with her."

Derek was silent for a moment.

So, it was true. Her manner recently, which he had started to think belied the evidence of his intoxicated senses that night he had come upon them together, was a ploy. A sham. She had been covering a shoddy affair with Will Trolley!

But wait. Not so fast. Give the lady a chance, if lady she was and not whore. Will was not scrupulously discreet with several glasses of ale in him, and one afternoon in the Hunter, he had let slip some remarks about the governess and himself that could not be misinterpreted and should not be repeated. What was it Nell had said? Something about Miss Foster and Mr. Trolley having left together. Did she say "run off"? Perhaps his young groom had taken the precipitate step and eloped with the governess. He wouldn't have thought it of Will, but he would rather think it of Will than of his Miss Forrester. In desperation he grabbed for the straw he saw before him. Maybe Alex had misunderstood his inquiry.

"Alex, I was not referring to Miss Foster, the governess. I believe she is the lady Will has been . . . seeing lately."

"Aye, she's the one he's been with."

"Well, now, I do not entirely approve of that sort of thing, of course. Rebecca seems to be fond of Miss Foster, and Trolley did not need to take her away." Derek did not sound disapproving; he sounded greatly relieved. "But I am speaking of our guest, Miss Forrester. . . ."

"That's the very one I'm talking about, sir. Miss Forrester. The young woman invited here by your mother with a view to her becoming a daughter-in-law. To my mind not a good choice, because *she* is the missy what run off with Trolley. Maybe the governess lady took off after 'em. Now that I don't know. But the Forrester lady and Will Trolley left this afternoon for Will's brother's farm outside Derby."

Chapter Thirty-Two

Say what you will about the flighty character of womankind; the claims are as old as time itself and so must be true. But for pure impetuosity, a man in love cannot be outdone.

"Saddle Verity for me, Alex," Derek cried.

"Now? Where you headed?" Alex asked, although he was quite sure he knew the answer already.

"To Derby, of course," Derek said, confirming his groom's suspicions.

"Sir, you've had Verity out all day. Do you think it wise to ride her hard again so soon?" His concern was only half for the horse. Alex recognized the symptoms of hysteria when he saw them. He hoped his young master would take time to think this pursuit through. Even if he was successful and caught the pair, what did he plan to do then? Oh, yes, Alex thought, love is a messy business at best. He counted himself lucky for avoiding that snare. Fervently.

"Oh, of course. You're right." Alex almost had his sigh of relief out before Derek's next words. "Saddle Charlemagne, then."

"Pulled leg muscles."

"Abednego?"

"The squire lent him to Mr. Hacker for the week."

Belle Rose was obviously out of the question and was not mentioned.

"Gallant Rider, then. I am sure my sister won't mind. Well, get moving, man," he said impatiently as Alex clung stubbornly to his forlorn hope of dissuading Derek from his impetuous course.

One reason Gallant Rider seemed so sluggish these days, other than the operation, was that nobody had been riding him. Everyone felt slightly guilty about the horse and his mistress, and they all tended to request a different horse, if possible. But he was still a fine mount, and with the saddle securely strapped on his back, he felt some of the old spirit rising in his loins—his leg muscles, that is.

In the time it took Alex to ready the horse, Derek had thrown a few clothes in a satchel (this might take a few days, and if he was going to have to scorn his former ladylove, he wanted both his manner and his linen to be crisp).

"You may tell the squire and my mother . . ." He paused as he swung onto Gallant Rider.

"Sir?" Alex asked when he failed to continue the thought.

"Oh yes. You may tell my parents... Well, I am sure you will think of something, Alex. I will probably be back before too long, and a detailed explanation may not be necessary." He didn't believe that and neither did Alex, but nevertheless, he dug his heels into the horse's sides and left for the adventure he was pursuing, leaving Alex alone in the stable.

Alex was rather relieved. He had taken part in more adventure than he cared for already, and suspected that even here he would not be secure from further unwelcome excitement.

Gallant Rider took to the road with exhilaration. He had forgotten he knew how to prance, but that was what he found himself doing. A little experimentation showed him that his rider did not seem to be paying much attention to him or this grand evening, and that as long as he kept going in the general direction he was pointed, he could do just about what he wanted. They had left the Westover property at a brisk trot, which he had soon been encouraged to lengthen into a gallop. He galloped hard for a stretch, but then fell back to an easy canter without his passenger objecting. He could drop to a walk, then spring back into a gallop again, all in a celebration of this unbounded world, and all with the hands on his reins held in casual inattention.

Gallant Rider was having a good deal more fun on this trip than Derek.

How could she? he kept thinking. How could he! He had known the truth about her since the third night she had been here at the manor, and yet he had chosen to overlook it, had allowed the girl to seduce his judgment as effortlessly as she had seduced his workman. Her sultry charms had clouded his usually crystalline vision (and that Derek's vision was clouded by something could easily be proved by his perception of Josephine's charms as being sultry; Josephine Foster was about as sultry as an Easter morning).

He had played the goat in her little farce, been led down the garden path by her games and deceptions, teased into love even as she put the horns on his head. Well, maybe it was a little more her fault than his.

Nevertheless, he had been a fool. There was no escaping that fact, or the added fact that that was exactly what he would appear to be. His concern now must be for his father's good name and for his mother's already shaky reputation as a matchmaker. And what of the Forresters? Certainly they had sent their daughter here in good faith, relying upon the Westovers to chaperon her carefully. Could Derek allow their bitter disappointment to go unprotested? Did he not owe them at least an attempted rescue?

Well, no, actually. Even as excitable as was the young man's temper right now, he could not dredge up much sympathy for the Forresters, whom he did not know and whose idea of sending their daughter shopping for a husband he had disapproved of from the beginning.

But with or without that particular coal, he was still able to keep his bad humor well stoked.

A horse never moves as quickly as a train, and Gallant Rider needed to be rested frequently as he had not been exercised much of late. The train ride that took only two hours was a nine-hour undertaking for Derek, so we will leave him for a while. Gallant Rider can keep an eye on him, since his company is not that pleasant right now, anyway.

Besides, events are transpiring with much greater rapidity with some of our other actors, and so more detailed reportage is required elsewhere.

Chapter Thirty-three

Locomotives were not a new experience for Rebecca. She had taken many trips aboard them in the past, going to and coming back from boarding schools. She had even been on this line before and had passed through Derby on her way to Matlock, where she had been enrolled in a school under the horrendous tutelage of a Mrs. Simpson.

Mrs. Simpson had insisted that a young lady's most crying need in education was the Greek language and that pinches in unexposed areas elicited immediate attention and quick responses without producing visible signs of cruelty. Rebecca had returned on this same line a short six weeks later, after she had fomented an uprising among the girls and demonstrated to Mrs. Simpson that if it was painful and unseen on the girls, it was even more so when multiplied fifteen times on Mrs. Simpson. Mrs. Simpson was a healthy woman, with her fair share of strength and endurance. But she was no match for a room full of enraged young girls and a locked door.

But to return to the locomotive and Rebecca's former experience; she had been on other trains, but always before when she had ridden one she had done so with the knowledge and approval of her parents and the help of one of them or a member of the household. This time she was on her own. And it was frightening.

From the moment she had left Matty Clark and Belle Rose outside the station, she had felt minuscule and totally vulnerable, which, she found, was not a pleasant way to feel at all. The woman in the cage selling tickets had seemed completely oblivious to her existence. And the sight of her money disappearing into some dark recess was unnerving, since she knew that whatever safety she could hope to enjoy would be proportionate only to the money she possessed. When it was gone, her self-reliance would be gone, and she had better be in a safe haven by then.

She climbed the short flight of steps and entered the coach. Already seated was a middle-aged gentleman who had seen better days. He was neat and clean and had a jaunty little bowler perched on his head and a brass-handled cane next to him. But the brass was tarnished, and his clothes were gray and worn, and his eyes looked tired enough to give assurance that she was indeed in a third-class compartment.

Not yet seated was an old-looking young mother. Hovering and fluttering about her were a flock of children, who did not even seem to be attached to the ground, much less seated. Rebecca was not sure enough of her position to look for another compartment, but as she squeezed in behind the beleaguered peahen and her raucous brood, she knew this was not going to be a peaceful, pleasant trip. Looking askance at the gentleman on the other end of her bench, she could see the same sentiment in his eyes.

In a few minutes Rebecca heard the "Board!" that Matt heard outside the station. That announcement was followed by an intense flurry of activity on the other side of the carriage in what Rebecca assumed was an attempt to settle things down, which activity in turn was followed by a loud noise and the lurch of the car as it started to roll, which lurch completely undid all of the mother's calming efforts.

Rebecca sat by the door, with her carpetbag guarding her exposed flank, staring straight ahead in the firm determination not to see her fellow passengers or be seen by them. The gentle bouncing of the carriage and the racket of the engines that drowned all other sound and then seemed to decrescendo to an unobtrusive murmur, was having the combined effect on Rebecca that it has had on nearly every passenger on a train before and since. Her eyelids began to close. She was nodding her head when she was startled awake by the unfamiliar feeling of someone tugging at her trouser leg. Jolting into consciousness, she drew her leg back quickly and looked down. One of the children (older than the whimpering infant but younger than the whining brat) was on his hands and knees peering between her feet.

"Mister? Hey, mister, can you reach my ball for me?" the lad queried.

Rebecca didn't respond at once, her drowsy mind taken off guard by being addressed as "mister." After a few moments, the carriage became awfully quiet and, looking around, the girl saw everyone staring at her with puzzled expressions on their faces. Only then did it sink in that the boy had been talking to her, and immediately she reached under her seat for the ball, feeling the embarrassed blush mount her cheeks as she did so.

This is a fine way to remain inconspicuous, she thought as she retrieved the boy's ball and handed it to him. She glanced around the carriage as she sat up again and was relieved to see that no one seemed to be paying her any more attention, except the man at the end of her bench, who smiled slightly and gave her a weak nod.

She vowed to remain wide awake, alert and on her toes after that incident, but the hypnotizing motion of the coach was not to be denied, and in just five minutes she was enjoying a deep sleep.

She slept soundly for the next two hours, or at least as soundly as is possible in a jouncing railroad car occupied aggressively by four loud and quarrelsome children. Finally the train pulled into the Derby station, and though her subconscious had fought off disturbing attacks for almost fifty miles, the screeching of the brakes and the lurching of the carriage roused her at last.

She had not forgotten her recent lesson, however, and the first thing she did was reach for her hat and replace it securely on her head, and the second thing she did was to pull her coat around her, covering up any telltale signs of femininity. She clutched her carpetbag to her, and being nearest the compartment door, she was out of it and onto the disembarking steps before the train had come to a complete rest.

"Cab! Yo!"

"*London Times*—only one day old. Yesterday's paper right 'ere!"

"Flower for your mum, sonny? Some nice violets for her hair. Tuppence a bunch, boy."

"Bread! Hot bread! Getch'er hot bread right here!"

"Shoe shine?"

Rebecca was not an unusually religious young lady who searched for biblical parallels in everyday occurrences, nor did the Derby station have any spiritual significance for her, but the scene that met her senses as she stepped onto the platform brought to her mind vividly the story of Christ and the money changers in the temple. Grasping hands and wrenching voices clutched at her and her slim envelope of money as she stepped away from the protective malevolence of the heaving locomotive behind her.

She believed she was being very circumspect in her dealings with the clamorers, but by the time she was able to break through the living chain that encircled the station, her already skimpy money supply was several shillings lighter, and she found herself in possession of a piece of dried fish, a silk scarf, two periodicals and a dazzling shine to her shoes.

In alarm she counted through the coins in the envelope but consoled herself with the fact that she had enough to get to her Aunt Minerva's, and once there she would throw herself on her relative's mercy with promises of eventual reimbursement from her father, who, she was reasonably certain, would pay to get her back.

"Fifteen-nineteen Beauford Lane," she said to the driver of the hansom cab she had hailed. After giving the address, she was forced to clamber up into the compartment by herself. She was beginning to realize something she never had before: there are definite advantages to being female. Spirit and independence are all very well and good, but on occasion it can be extremely pleasant to receive a little help. This being masculine and strictly on one's own was not all it was cracked up to be.

Once in the cab, though, she rested her head gratefully on the thinly padded cushion. She had made it! At last! She could stop worrying and planning and deliver herself up to an older and wiser rule. With the crystal-clear hindsight of youth, she had about decided this was not the wisest thing she had ever done, and it might have been better to discuss the whole matter with her parents. If her aunt insisted she return immediately to Ettington, she would even do that. She was willing to do almost anything, as long as she did not have to make the decisions and arrangements.

The trip from the station to her aunt's house was taking longer than she could remember it taking before; once she even jarred awake and realized she had dozed off. She had never heard of a cab driver lengthening a passenger's trip in order to pad the fare, but the man holding the lines on his hansom was well aware of the principle. He had noted the youth of his passenger and his sleep-heavy lids and had driven his weary old mare around and through all of Derby before he drew up in front of 1519 Beauford Lane.

"That'll be ten and six, laddie."

"Ten and six! I had no idea Beauford Lane was so far from the station!"

"Street repair—had to make a few detours."

A few detours? If Rebecca had been alert during her ride she could now have qualified as a tour guide for city officials who had lived here all their lives and wanted to see something new in Derby.

"I hope I have that much.... I had no idea.... Perhaps I shouldn't have hailed a cab...." She was taking what coins she had out of the envelope and patting the pockets of her coat.

"Well, how much have you got there?" the driver asked, disgruntled that his plan had backfired.

"One, and that's two, three, five, ten. That's all I have." She looked up with tears of appeal swimming in her eyes, but the lane was dark and the driver was blind to that sort of appeal, anyway.

"Oh, all right," he said gruffly, taking all the money she held in her hand. He stood aside then so she could get out, though he did not, of course, offer any help. A young lad his age could take care of himself.

Rebecca stood, holding her carpetbag, and watched forlornly as the cab drove away with the rest of her money. After it rounded the corner at the end of the lane, she turned around to face number 1519. She had not meant to arrive at her aunt's house destitute, but as matters stood now she was relieved to have arrived at all. Her aunt might scold her, but at least her aunt would help her.

As her eyes found the house they were searching for, however, she realized that her aunt would do neither.

The house was dark and boarded up.

Chapter Thirty-four

Josephine, Phyllis and Will Trolley all arrived in Derby on the same train.

Will and Phyllis enjoyed the ride from the luxurious accommodations of a private first-class coach. The seats were thickly padded and covered with a plush maroon velvet. There was an ingenious little table that folded down between the two couches facing each other, upon which was placed a steaming pot of tea, sandwiches, cakes and crumpets shortly after the train left the terminal. There was a silver drinking cup attached to one wall, and on the other wall was a glorious painting in deep blues and greens, depicting, incongruously, a ship under full sail being pitched about on a stormy sea. It was placed there perhaps with the idea that when passengers saw the dangers to be encountered on the open sea, they would choose again to ride Midland Railway.

The walls of their compartment were covered with a heavy insulating fabric, and by hanging the Do Not Disturb placard outside the door they were able to enjoy two hours of uninterrupted tête-à-tête.

Not surprisingly, neither party was ever aware of the other's presence on the train. Phyllis and Will were just barely aware of the steward as he discreetly removed the tea things. The steward also did not intrude himself upon Josephine and the other passengers in the tightly packed, noisy, smelly fourth-class carriage, which bumped along the tracks, unheeded, at the end of the train. And while Mr. Trolley and his intended begrudged the end of the ride that would necessitate their departure from this very comfortable and convenient retreat, Josephine did not. On one side of her was a farmer smoking something like barnyard manure in a large pipe and holding two chickens on his lap that appeared to have assumed the politics and belligerent attitudes of two opposing sovereign countries. On the other side of Josephine sat a perfectly well-mannered quiet woman, who did nothing more offensive than weigh close to twenty-five stone. After being pounded, punched and bounced around several times by the lady next to her as the train acted the part of a mattress upon which they were all jouncing, Josephine actually preferred her more noxious squawking neighbors and pressed closer to them.

Indeed, she had no choice.

To merely say that Josephine did not begrudge the end of the trip was perhaps an understatement.

In time, though, all things both good and bad must come to an end, and after two hours the end of the journey was signaled to the passengers by the wailing of the brakes and the lurch down the length of the train as each car came to a reluctant halt. The jar to the first-class compartments was subdued but strong enough to alert Phyllis and Will and give them sufficient time to straighten clothes and smooth down hair. The jolt in the fourth-class car at the end of the train left several passengers sprawled on the floor and Josephine perched upon the farmer's lap. Even with a tarry expulsion of smoke hitting her face and the startled fowls pecking her painfully, she looked back at her seat with a great welling of relief. This section of the train had suffered two earthshaking disturbances that rocked the car: the first when the brakes were engaged and the second when Josephine's corpulent traveling companion landed directly on the spot where Josephine had been sitting.

"Derby! All out for Derby!" was the call that filtered down to the passengers here. There was a tired kind of general hubbub as parcels were gathered and family members accounted for. Carried along by the sluggish but irresistible tide that surrounded her, Josephine was swept out of the train and into the damp night air, where she stood, looking around her for a few hesitant moments.

Perhaps the Reader will no longer believe the Author's avowal of Miss Foster's intelligence. Earlier in our narrative, where we were told she was a sensible girl with a good head solidly on her shoulders, the description was no doubt accepted on good faith and a willingness to give her a chance to prove herself. Unfortunately, ever since then she has seldom failed to appear in a bad light.

First, she allowed herself to be carried away by Mrs. Westover's enthusiasm and did not surmise that that good woman was laboring under a mistaken impression until so enlightened by Phyllis (who had contrarily been quick, shrewd and cunning in a further attempt to weaken the author's credibility when it was stated that Phyllis was endowed with less intellectual prowess than her reluctant impersonator).

Josephine, on the other hand, has been hot tempered, shortsighted, and has, on more than one occasion, flown completely off the handle. She was quick to jump to a conclusion about Derek Westover that was totally unfounded and has since doggedly clung to that notion and so has actively labored against this story's happy ending and her own in the process. The Author can only make what feeble excuses for youth and love as are possible, and assure the reader that for the previous twenty-two years, Miss Josephine Foster had been a model of sensible decorum, and who could have known that she would suddenly begin acting like a witless ninny just as this romance started?

Nevertheless, it had not taken Josephine the entire two hours in that crowded railroad car to realize that of the several very stupid things she had done in the recent past, this night trip to Derby without telling anyone was easily the stupidest.

But Josephine was of the logical opinion that mistakes should not even be dwelt upon. She had come here with the laudable intention of retrieving and returning Miss Rebecca; so rather than berate herself unproductively, she would direct her efforts to that end.

Before she could do anything else, she must find out Mrs. Twitchell's address. Mrs. Westover would naturally have had that address, but then, the King of Siam had a hundred wives, too, and both bits of information were equally useful to Josephine.

By now she had a limited supply of money and could not afford to pay for the information.

It is possible that the Reader by this time assumes that Josephine is in fact sunk past redemption, and that she has no more chance of behaving sensibly on this expedition than a pig does of suddenly starting to sing. But she is, in fact, about to mitigate the Author's embarrassment at attributing the young lady with superior intelligence, for Josephine actually has an ingenious plan in mind for acquiring the needed information without resorting to that string purse of hers.

The play at the Dresin Playhouse was a rather tiresome little drama entitled *Faith Hopes for Charity*. It was the sort of production that gentlemen drag their feet about attending and once there wish they had dug in their heels with more determination. The ladies, on the other hand, may not have enjoyed it any more than their escorts, but were able to leave with an enviable feeling of holiness for attending.

The final curtain came down on Faith indeed receiving charity, but only after she had descended from a position of social prominence on a long slide of folly, sin and misspent youth. She had, of course, repented of her legion errors and had determined now to dedicate her remaining years to some good cause or other.

The boxes disgorged their occupants, and the theatergoers were at last freed and allowed to take part in the social discourse that would decide the week's activities and fashions for the ladies and arrange for a number of important business transactions among the gentlemen. Since some of the principle manufactures of Derby were silk and cotton textiles, the information gained and exchanged was often the same and of equal importance to both camps.

Derby was a large enough metropolis that even among this selective social set a new face was not unheard of, or even particularly remarkable. The young lady circulating now through the groups clustered randomly through the lobby was a stranger to many of them. In fact, she was a stranger to all of them, but no one was willing to publicly declare utter unfamiliarity with the girl for fear of committing an embarrassing faux pas by slighting someone's favorite niece. Perhaps she was wearing apparel that was less flashy than some of the women, but that did nothing more than bespeak the girl's modesty and good taste. Besides, such a face and form lent themselves well to simplicity in dress.

No, no, she obviously felt quite at home here, was intelligent and well mannered, therefore she *must* belong to someone.

"And what did you think of Lord and Lady Palmer's ball?"

"The whole affair, I hear, was a crashing bore. You know how ostentatious Lady Palmer tends to be? Well, I was told..."

"I say, Huntley, what's the word from London? Still favoring the West Riding wool, I'll wager."

Scraps of conversation drifted past the young lady as she casually moved from one group to another, smiling and nodding, murmuring a reply to the occasional question directed to her.

"Staying with Minerva Twitchell, did you say? Oh, a friend of her brother's family. I must say, you had me confused for a moment there." The gentleman smiled and nodded in friendly fashion, then turned back to an acquaintance at his elbow and what was evidently a previous discussion on this sweltering heat and possible damage to the incoming cotton crops. The young woman looked at him with a puzzled expression, even raised her hand tentatively, but finally dropped it and wandered away again.

" . . . so I said to her, 'Natalie, darling, that sort of thing simply is not done anymore,' and as innocently as you please, she asked me, 'Why not?' Why not? Did you ever?"

The scandalized recounting of Natalie's social blunder was interrupted as the rather attractive girl attached herself to the group. To the casual, even the careful observer, the girl was simply mingling at random. But the speaker in this group had shared the theater box with the gentleman who had just spoken to her. Logically they were friends, possibly they were married; ideally they shared the same information concerning mutual acquaintances.

"An interesting performance, didn't you think?" The girl dropped the general comment in front of them by way of insinuating herself into the conversation.

"That of the actress or Natalie?" someone asked, and a sprinkling of titters was heard. The girl looked confused, and the speaker at her left shook her head in disapproval at the group.

"I am sure the young lady is referring to tonight's performance, and I must say that was a very diplomatic comment. 'Interesting' is the kindest thing that could be said about it." Another smattering of laughter; the speaker was obviously a recognized wit in the group. "I am sorry, my dear, but I am afraid I did not catch your name."

"Forrester, Miss Josephine Forrester." The girl curtsied demurely. She thought by introducing herself as Josephine Forrester, she would have the best of both worlds. The Forrester name might be her passport into the upper class here in Derby, while keeping her own first name would allow her a little leeway as to her exact relation to the Gregory Forresters.

"Forrester? Forrester? I believe I know some Forresters up in Sheffield. Any relation?" the plump matron to the right of Josephine asked.

"Second or third cousins, I believe. My family hails from Newcastle, actually." Josephine smiled, hoping she had chosen a place far enough north to waylay any further embarrassing questions. This mighty island kingdom sometimes seemed to shrink alarmingly, until not only did everyone know everyone else who lived here, but most had been near neighbors at one time or other.

"Oh? You are new to Derby, then?" The ladies were following the script exactly; Josephine felt completely in control as she expertly guided the conversation.

"Why, yes, I am. I was staying with the Westovers in Ettington before, and thought that while I was here in Derby I should call on Mr. Westover's sister. I had hoped, in fact, that she might be here this evening. I understood she is rather fond of drama. Perhaps some of you may know her? Mrs. Minerva Twitchell?" She smiled beguilingly at the group, giving each a look of frank encouragement, particularly the woman standing next to her.

"If you had found her here that would have been something of a surprise, I must say," that lady said.

"Oh? Was my information faulty? Mrs. Twitchell does not attend the theater, then?" It had only been a guess on Josephine's part.

"On the contrary, she loves it and does not miss a performance, not even one as truly abysmal as tonight's."

"Then I do not understand—"

"If she is in town, that is. But my dear, Minerva Twitchell has been in the south of France since the beginning of the summer. Her house is all closed up. Although," the speaker continued, addressing her attendant audience. "I cannot imagine what she does there for months at a time. The woman speaks deplorable French." This comment drew further smiles and laughter from everyone in the group, except Josephine. She had not really heard anything beyond the woman's "France since the beginning of the summer."

In a daze she almost excused herself from the group before she came to her senses.

"France, you say? Could it be a different Minerva Twitchell? Squire Westover did not mention she was out of the country."

"I really doubt it, miss. There is only one Minerva Twitchell, and only one house at 1519 Beauford Lane. No, I am afraid you will have to miss making the acquaintance of that worthy lady. At least this season."

"No, no, Esne," one of the ladies on the outer rim of the circle piped. "Minerva returned two weeks ago."

"Impossible, my dear Sophia. I sent my card round there Tuesday, and Mitchell brought it back and said the house was still boarded up."

"You must be mistaken, love." There were a few uncomfortable fidgets and a few more eager looks exchanged throughout the gathered flock. This was evidently a long-established rivalry. Sophia's voice was syrupy sweet, and the corners of Esne's mouth turned up deliciously, but all four eyes glittered like chips of ice. "I saw Minerva just a week ago yesterday. We did not speak, but I am sure she saw me."

As if at a tennis match, the heads of the gathered crowd turned in unison for each of the volleys.

"She's out of the country." Thwock! Fifteen-love.

"She was in town Tuesday last." Fifteen-all.

"The door is barred." Thirty-fifteen.

"My cousin spoke to her at Raymond's." Thirty-all.

Smiling weakly, Josephine extracted herself from the hard-fought match. Looking around her she could see that the post-production conversation was the main feature of an evening at the theater and these people would be here for an hour or two longer. It was just as well; a milling crowd would enable her to come and go unremarked. Now that she was in possession of the valuable piece of information she had come for, i.e. the address of the Twitchell residence, the quicker she quitted this establishment, the better. It had occurred to her that even though Rebecca's Aunt Minerva may indeed still be vacationing in France (although that point was certainly not yet decided), Rebecca had been as ignorant of that fact as Josephine when she arrived in Derby, and that the best place to start looking for the girl was still her aunt's home.

At the back of the theater, behind the stage, there were a number of small rooms. Most of them were dressing rooms for the actors and actresses, and none of them were any cleaner or any better smelling than they needed to be. There were also one or two rooms being used to store props and brooms and such like, which were in an even greater state of disrepair than the dressing rooms. As if she were quite familiar with the world of the stage, instead of having been here only once before, and that just two hours earlier, Josephine skirted her way confidently around the strewn boxes, chairs and discarded costumes, arriving at last at the door of one of the storage rooms. There was no one about (the cast members may also have felt that postproduction conversation was the main feature of the evening, but they enjoyed theirs at another, and no doubt more intimate, locale) so Josephine slipped into the room.

In one corner of the room was a pile of clothes that would have appeared to a more fainthearted woman to be a crumpled body. It might even have suggested that idea to Josephine if she had not discarded the clothes herself and put them in that corner when she first entered the theater.

She removed her gloves and put them into her temporarily flat string bag, next the earrings. She had worn this simple evening frock as the foundation to her complete outfit in anticipation of just such an eventuality as being required to appear in a salon or a drawing room or the theater. Once again she carefully drew up the skirt of the evening dress until it rested around her slim hips, where she pinned it securely. (Those pins had given her several moments of discomfort on the train and had also surprised the farmer, his chickens and the rotund woman next to her a time or two.) Next she put the pliable satin slippers in the bag with her gloves, exchanging them for more sturdy footwear. After several attempts, she was able to button her traveling skirt around her waist, over assorted undergarments, the evening dress and a blouse she had put on over the dress.

She slipped into her jacket, reclaimed her umbrella (one can never rely on the English weather) and tied her once-more bulging string bag around her waist. Now, was that everything? She patted the thickness of her hips and remembered her short traveling gloves and scarf. After a moment's search, she found them lurking together behind a box near the corner. There. That was everything. Once more she felt fully prepared to meet the challenges before her. Of course, this preparation in the matter of dress had nearly caused her to pay a dear price of heat exhaustion crowded onto the steaming fourth-class car in the still warm evening of a summer day. Despite what her mother had taught her concerning the difference between ladies and horses, what she had been doing on that train was sweating.

One may accuse Josephine of lack of good sense in this undertaking, but the young woman was meeting the quirks and setbacks that faced her at every turn with amazing aplomb. She found herself now in an unfamiliar city about to start searching for an address, with no money to speak of, in order to help another foolish girl, also with no money. And yet she faced the problem before her head-on, with undaunted courage and a clear mind.

She could not summon a hansom cab and give the driver the address to locate, because her funds were too low. Even if she just made an inquiry, the cabbie would no doubt expect some sort of gratuity before parting with the information. She eliminated the idea of asking the doorman at the theater for the same reason. Who, then, could she feel safe asking, who would not request money from her?

As she mulled the problem before her, she had left the backstage area and made her way to the entrance of the theater through which most of the crowd had already exited. She stepped through the doors asking herself that question and heard the policeman's whistle.

Derby was not so large or so busy that it demanded a bobby on every street directing traffic day and night. The roads were wide and paved, and the drivers and riders of the carriages and horses had not yet adopted the infamously surly manners of their London counterparts. But it had taken no more than one night, several years earlier, of cleanup, quarreling and general cacophony, for the police force to adopt the habit of posting a traffic director at the end of dramatic performances. Hence, the policeman, his whistle and the solution to Josephine's problem.

"Excuse me, sir."

"Miss?" the pleasingly homely law enforcer said, surprised to be hailed by this attractive young lady. Taken off guard as he was, he unconsciously dropped his arm and turned in her direction with a confusing gesture from his other arm. The coachman on the box of the vehicle directly behind him gave a startling "BLAT!" on his disagreeable air horn, which hailed a similar chorus from a number of conveyances surrounding him. The startled bobby presented an amusing picture as he jumped first this way and then that in response to the alarms and catcalls that assailed him from every side. After several piercing blasts on his whistle and a sharp rap on the back of a carriage whose wheels had insulted his already injured toes, order—or a close approximation—was restored.

"Sir?" Josephine ventured again, when she could make herself heard.

"In a moment, miss," he responded, this time not allowing his attention to be distracted.

The crowd from the theater was thinning, and though Josephine waited impatiently on the sidewalk for what seemed like hours, or at the very least several quarters of an hour, in less than fifteen minutes the traffic was flowing smoothly enough to allow its director to join her.

"May I help you?" he asked as he took a handkerchief from a back pocket to wipe his beaded brow.

"Yes, please. I was planning to attend a party at a house in Beauford Lane after the play tonight, but I seem to have become separated from the group, and being a stranger in your city, I was beginning to despair of meeting with my friends again before they moved on...." There was a convincing quiver in her voice, which now ended on an authentic sob.

"Miss, I can't remember seeing a group of young people leaving the theater, but perhaps if you can describe their carriage...?"

"No, no, officer. I am sure they are already at their destination. If you would just be so kind as to direct me to Beauford Lane?"

"Any cab driver will know...."

"I am afraid you do not understand, sir. Being in the company of friends and the party being escorted by our hosts for the evening, I came away without sufficient money with me to hire a cab. If you would give me directions to Beauford Lane, I will walk the distance and may, even yet, be able to catch up with my friends."

"Well, now, miss, I don't think I could do that." Her mouth drooped prettily, and Simmons—for that was the officer's name—continued, "It's much too late for a pretty girl like you to be out alone walking, er, that is, roaming, the streets. I have to stay here until the play crowd has left—and it looks like most of them have—and then I'm off duty. If you can wait just a few moments, I'll escort you to that section of town myself."

Josephine looked into the man's clear blue eyes and nodded.

"Shall I wait here?" she asked.

"Here will be fine. It's best if I can keep an eye on you while you're alone." He smiled and touched his cap before turning to thread his way back through the traffic.

Now bobbies are also men, and Josephine did not make it a habit to go off into the night with strange men, whatever their profession, but the study she had made of Simmons's face and eyes had convinced her. There are some people in this world (regrettably, they seem to be only few and far between) who are as good as they hope they appear to be. This policeman's eyes told Josephine that he was one of them. He said he was concerned for her safety and he could not feel at ease unless he personally escorted her, and she knew he was telling the truth. He meant exactly that, and no more. So patiently she waited on the corner, although she really did not know what she would tell this good honest man if, when they arrived at 1519 Beauford Lane, the house was deserted.

Chapter Thirty-five

With the action simply exploding around our other characters, one begrudges the time and space it would take to bring the Reader up-to-date on Phyllis and Will. It seems especially difficult to justify an entire chapter to the two lovesick honeymooners (albeit slightly before the fact) but the Author does feel a duty to keep the Reader apprised of their circumstances. And, as the somewhat confusing explanation that Will and Phyllis made to Will's brother Fred could not carelessly be tacked on to any other chapter, we must open Chapter Thirty-five with Phyllis and Will in earnest discussion with Fred Trolley.

Fred and Will shared the Trolley cunning, but Fred's had not received the incentive of the young lady's fortune, and it took several times through the telling (by both of them) before he even partially comprehended their situation and understood what they were doing at his farmhouse.

"So you and this fine filly think to be married, eh?" Fred asked with a sly slow wink. That, at least, was clear to him by now. "Then what?"

"We thought maybe you could let us stay here, into the late autumn, anyway. Then about the time Christmas sentiment is making folks think of their family and they get to feelin' charitable, me and Phyll would visit her home."

"But first we'll be married," Phyllis reminded him.

"Yes, yes, dearie. Don't worry. We wouldn't want to compromise your maidenly virtue, now would we?" The two of them laughed a throaty kind of conspiratorial laugh that did not leave Fred completely ignorant. Even in low gear he could tell that, wealthy or not, the young woman before him had very little "maidenly virtue" still in peril.

"Well, that sounds all right to me," he said, nodding deliberately. That he finally understood was clear from his statement. Fred Trolley was a careful man who did not like to miss a point, and even less to have something put over on him. It was his habit to ask questions and to keep asking questions until everything was clear in his mind. "What are you doing here?" "Running away from who?" "Why?" "Married?" The fact that his last sentence had not ended with a question mark and expressed contingent approval was Will's signal that their plan could go ahead.

"Good." The brothers exchanged a quick nod that was the equivalent of a handshake of agreement. Phyllis sensed a change in the atmosphere of the meeting, but she wasn't really sure what had caused it.

"Darcy?" Will asked.

"I said it was all right by me," was Fred's short reply.

"Darcy?" Phyllis repeated.

"Fred's wife," Will explained.

"Oh." If she sounded surprised, it can be excused. So far there had been no mention and no indication of a woman in this house. "You are married, then?"

"Not so's you'd notice," Fred said with a derisive snort.

Phyllis opened her mouth to continue her line of questioning, but before she could say anything else, Will took a backward step and managed to land directly on her toe. Whether he did it on purpose or not (and the fact that he landed heavily and stayed there until all of Phyllis's concentration was diverted tends to indicate that it was on purpose) Phyllis abandoned the subject for the time being.

They had been there for almost an hour by that time, and only then did Fred tell them to sit down and offered Will a cup of ale.

"My own," he said, allowing a note of pride to creep into his voice. Will readily assented and his brother left to pursue his duties as a host. In a few minutes the door reopened, and Phyllis and Will broke off their discussion of immediate plans. They looked up, expecting to see Fred with a bottle or jug in his hand, but instead, a wispy little woman came silently into the room, closing the door quietly and shaking her head with regret at the necessary sound the falling latch had produced. She had her back to them and was carrying a straw basket on one arm. Evidently she had not seen them, because as she turned she jumped violently in alarm when Will saluted her, almost dropping the basket (which held a few eggs) but miraculously saving it at the last moment. Through all of this, she never uttered a word nor made a sound other than her sharp intake of breath, and Phyllis had come to the conclusion that Darcy (she had also determined that this was Darcy) was mute.

"How are you? Didn't mean to scare you," Will said kindly, even rising and offering to take the basket, though he didn't seem surprised when the woman refused to release it. "This is Phyllis Forrester," he said, indicating the girl. "We've come to stay for a while."

"Here?" she said softly, surprising Phyllis. Will nodded. "What did he say?"

"He said it seemed all right with him."

"Oh. Hungry?" Mrs. Trolley was a superior host to her husband, Phyllis was relieved to note. It had taken an hour before Fred had even offered a drink, and that only to Will, but here was his wife tendering a welcome offer of food almost before she was in the house.

"Yes, indeed," Phyllis blurted in her enthusiasm.

The little woman drew back from the sharp sound as if from a physical blow.

"Phyllis and me would thank you heartily for something to eat," Will said soothingly, as if to a small child or a nervous horse.

The woman turned with relief to the kitchen and started to busy herself with the preparation of food. Though Phyllis looked quizzically after her, the memory of Will's foot on her toe was too fresh in her mind to encourage her to question him about his sister-in-law. Instead, they discussed the pending marriage, which interested her more, anyway.

"Fred said he could talk to Parson on Sunday, but I don't think we need to wait that long," Will said.

"We shouldn't wait that long," Phyllis agreed.

"We can tell him that we went through the rigmarole of the banns in the parish we left."

"Will he accept that?"

"I'm sure he will, with a little encouragement." Will looked significantly at her waist, where she kept her purse. Phyllis understood, but hoped the good reverend's demands would not be too exorbitant and that this would be the last. She certainly had enough desire to marry Will, the question now was whether she had enough money.

With no further delay, then, we can now leave Mr. Trolley and Miss Forrester in consultation at his brother's home. Their plans seem to be progressing smoothly, and if all goes well they will be married within the next few days. We will certainly keep the Reader informed of any difficulty that arises in this quarter, but for the time being let us turn our attention from improbable hindrances here to the impending crisis facing Rebecca and Josephine at this very moment.

Chapter Thirty-six

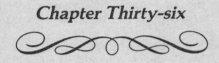

Rebecca was stunned. More than stunned; she was devastated. She had not even considered the possibility that her Aunt Minerva would not be home. It was as if, standing on solid ground, the earth beneath her feet had been suddenly ripped away, plunging her into a bottomless pit. She had absolutely no idea of what she was going to do now. As the utter hopelessness of her situation became apparent, tears sprang to her eyes and rolled down her freckled cheeks. The tears were like the anchor of a mighty ship, and as they fell Rebecca sank to the ground, sitting on the edge of the sidewalk. As a young lady she never would have done it, but as a young man, she drew her knees up in front of her and, wrapping her arms around them, dropped her head to cry in earnest.

Tap...tap...tap.... The approaching sound was right next to her and had stopped before she became aware of it. Taken by surprise, she looked up and through a fog of tears saw the dull glint of a metal cane tip. She raised her head slowly to take in the form standing near to her left shoulder. By the time she reached the head and face, she had recognized her riding companion from the train. It was the gentleman who had been sitting at the other end of the bench on which she had been seated.

How odd, she thought, even then, that being a complete stranger here, in all of Derby, I should meet this man again.

"Difficulties?" the man asked in a sympathetic voice. Rebecca nodded. Using his cane expertly, the man lowered himself to sit companionably at her side. "Was someone supposed to meet you at the station, laddie-buck?"

"N-no," Rebecca burbled, and shook her head to clarify the meaning of her not wholly intelligible word.

"You expected someone to be there, though, didn't you?" the man said, pointing at the darkened house across from them with his cane. The girl nodded again, not trusting her voice to acknowledge the too awful truth. The man reached across the short space between their two bodies and patted one of her drawn-up knees.

"Now, this is no way for a bully young lad to be carrying on, is it? There, haven't you got a handkerchief or cloth in one of those fine pockets? Blow your nose and wipe your eyes, and let's think our way out of this—what do you say?"

Once again Rebecca was reminded of her assumed gender, and though it all seemed so pointless now, she was determined to carry the charade through. The gentleman was right; no self-respecting boy of thirteen—or even ten—would sit here on the sidewalk blubbering like a baby. She may have no idea of what she was going to do, but it occurred to her that although a boy her age wouldn't, either, he wouldn't waste his time crying. Patting the several unfamiliar pockets in her coat, she did happen upon a handkerchief and resolutely dried her eyes.

"That's better," the man said approvingly. "Let's get a look at you now." Rebecca turned to face him, managing a shadow of a smile. "On the train I took you to be twelve or so, but by this light I would put you nearer ten." Since weak behavior is more easily forgiven in the young, Rebecca decided to stifle her wounded pride and indicated to the man that his guess was more or less accurate.

"Where are you from?" he said, stretching his legs and tapping the toe of his dull scuffed shoes with his cane.

"Ettington."

"That's a ways, young man. Quite a ways." The man's voice had a musing, soothing quality to it that encouraged reliance and disclosures. Rebecca could almost feel the hard position in which she found herself softening under his influence. She failed to recognize that softening as perilous quicksand, however. "You left your family there?"

"Yes."

"That's a little unusual, isn't it, to send a lad of your tender years off to a strange city without confirming the destination?" The man peered intently at Becky and, blushing faintly, she turned her head away in what she thought was a nonchalant avoidance of his gaze. "You are running away, aren't you?"

Quickly, too quickly, Rebecca denied the man's allegation.

"Certainly not! I would never—How could you think— Surely you can't believe..." Her words trailed off, and the man's statement was confirmed. They were silent for a few minutes while Rebecca desperately tried to think what she should do next. The man continued to absently tap his shoe with his cane, not revealing his thoughts, which would have been all but incomprehensible to the girl, anyway.

"So," the man said at last. "What are you going to do now?" He didn't turn his head, but watched the youngster slyly out of the corner of his eye. There was three-quarters of a moon lighting the scene; in its soft glow the man saw the glimmer of two more tears sliding down the boy's face and smiled to himself.

The boy was frightened and alone.

Perfect.

Rebecca couldn't believe that she had been so miserable only two hours before. Then she had been sitting on a sidewalk curb, crying and hopeless, alone in the world. Now she was sitting in a cozy (her mother would have called it dark and crowded) comfortable (her mother would have called it run-down) restaurant (her mother would have called it many things besides a restaurant, but the name her father would have given the place, though not repeatable in polite society, would have been nearer the truth). And instead of being alone in the world, she was with a companion: the kind man from the train, who had brought her here and bought her something to eat (and even Rebecca wouldn't have called it very good, whatever that gray greasy mass had been) had cheered her with his stories, and now was encouraging her to drink a little something to, as he phrased it, "raise her spirits and keep the chill off."

Her mother had allowed her one small glass of claret on the last two New Year's Eves, but absolutely forbade her a single drop at any other time.

"You certainly may not!" she had said the first and only time Rebecca had asked if she could have a small tumbler of wine such as her father was taking with his meal.

"Why not?" she had asked, trying to sound innocent and naive, although she hadn't really expected any wine and now knew what her mother's argument would be, more or less. But she had been prepared for considerably less of an explanation than the thirty-minute lecture Mrs. Westover launched into describing the evils of drink and the levels to which a young woman sank by the imbibing of it.

"Rebecca, a young lady, especially of a respectable class, but any woman who would be or remain respectable, does not drink liquor," she had said, winding down at last. "Not strong liquor ever—whiskey, brandy, Scotch, and I am sure your father could enlarge that list—and a white or light pink glassful only on special occasions. *Very* special occasions. The one drink we have allowed you on the past several New Year's Eves . . ."

Sip! Rebecca had mentally interjected. And last year was the first time.

" . . . is more than sufficient for a girl of your years and station. Now I hope that nothing more need be said on this subject." Mrs. Westover had closed her lips firmly to emphasize the point, and Rebecca couldn't help but be relieved. Not only did she hope that nothing more would need to be said on the subject, but she really didn't see how anything more possibly could be said.

She had wisely since that day never mentioned wine or spirits, but she continued to look forward to New Year's Eve and to view the small glass of sherry her mother intermittently enjoyed with a covetous gaze.

And now here she was with her convivial host practically forcing the drinks down her. It didn't take much pressure, and after the first sour unpleasant taste (the wine served in this nameless little den was vastly inferior to the wine in Squire Westover's cellars; the wine served here was only marginally superior to bile and simply acted as an encouragement to the clientele to advance to the reliable anesthesia of the stronger and more expensive liquors) she found herself enjoying the glasses being set in front of her in an apparently unending stream. She was also enjoying the freedom to indulge, enjoying the heady feeling that was encompassing her, enjoying herself. She laughed a good deal at everything the man told her, although she wasn't really sure of what he was saying anymore.

Her hat had fallen back against her shoulder, and her red curls bounced around her head in a tumultuous riot when she giggled. The man reached for the hat to save it from falling onto the filthy soggy floor, and seemingly by accident brushed the boy's cheek with his fingers.

"Where'd you get that head of hair?" the man asked, twisting one of the curls around his finger.

Rebecca shook her head and giggled, but looking up, the man caught sight of the bartender, who was not laughing. Money was money, of course, and the man was paying out good silver for the swill he was pouring down the boy. And morals were quite obviously something else that did not concern the owner of this den or any of the customers. There had been an immediate understanding by all as to the man's intent, and not one of the patrons raised so much as an eyebrow to help the boy. The bartender's disapproval was not for the man's predilections, but only for the possible legal action that could be taken against his place of business if the man proceeded any further with his design in here.

"Take it somewhere else, mate," that worthy gentleman said as he came to take away the several empty glasses in front of Rebecca.

"I don't think our company's wanted here anymore, son," the man said. He clapped the bedraggled skimmer back on top of her head and raised her up by the elbows.

"Where're we goin'?" Rebecca slurred back over her shoulder, wafting her liquor-drenched breath, which was foul even by the standard of the air in this sewer, into the man's face.

Putting his fingers against her cheek, he turned her to face forward, away from him, before he answered.

"Guess we'll have to find someplace else. Come on. I know a nice private little place where we can be alone. Maybe get some sleep. How does that sound?"

"Souns real good to me. I am just a tittle lired." She seemed to find the antics of her numb tongue hilarious and burst into a gale of drunken laughter.

The man walked her out of the door, trying to look inconspicuous. The few weary glances that were afforded him were not deceived, though, and one sympathetic soul even sighed and went so far as to order another drink in commemoration of the poor lost lad.

Chapter Thirty-seven

It was close to, probably past, midnight by now. Derek had left the little town of Hinckley two hours ago, and it would be at least another two hours before he got to the even smaller town of Melbourne. But even if the quiet hamlets he was passing through had been large, luxurious cities whose beckoning inns and hostels seemed to reach out and grab a man right off the street, Derek would have clung just as grimly to his saddle.

Gallant Rider was holding up remarkably well for a horse that had never been seriously ridden. Derek was forced to admit that his own Verity could not have done better. Gallant was a strong clean-limbed animal with a vast reservoir of energy. Even after five hours on the road, his gait was still steady and, in fact, he seemed to be coming into his second wind. Which was just as well, since they were only to the halfway mark now.

Derek was embarrassed to note that his own endurance was not equal to that of this gelded horse. But Gallant Rider was no longer concerned with the things that were driving the young

Mr. Westover to rage and despair and stealthily draining a good
deal of his energy from him. That was something Derek did not
stop to consider. Then, too, it was damp and the night air was
chill against his moist clothing and skin. He had been on
horseback on and off for almost eighteen hours now, and his
muscles were relentlessly ticking off each mile they were covering. He was extremely tired. Another man would have called
it utter exhaustion and thrown himself from the saddle to the
soft undulating ground rolling past the horse's hooves. But not
Derek. He was much too angry, hurt, determined—and, as the
night wore on and Gallant Rider's pace gently slowed, he was
quite often much too asleep—to consider abandoning his quest.

So once again we will leave Derek on the road to Derby. He
still is not doing anything very interesting. By contrast, we can
even see that the picture of Derek fuming was a good deal more
entertaining than that of Derek dozing in his saddle.

Every hour is bringing him closer to Derby, however, and
whatever awaits him there.

It was now also midnight in the home of Fred Trolley
(somehow one never thought to refer to the place as the home
of Fred and Darcy Trolley). Mrs. Trolley had thoughtfully
prepared sleeping arrangements in the closet behind the pantry. In the wintertime this place would have been like an ice
cave, but in the summer it was only refreshingly cool and had
the sweet breath of a comfortably stocked larder. The accommodations were a little Spartan, but comfortable enough for the
hardworking owner of a farm or a farm laborer. Fred viewed
the sleeping arrangements with satisfaction, then he and Will
returned to the bedroom, leaving the two women to share these
quarters.

A month earlier Phyllis would have been at a total loss if
faced with this same situation. And though she might not have
known exactly what to do, she would have tried many things,
starting with ranting and raving, tearing this room apart,
breaking dishes in the kitchen, throwing furniture in the living
room and finally attacking the men's bedroom, which she
would have totally demolished.

The past weeks, though, had made a new woman of Phyllis
Forrester. She had learned patience, awareness of other peo-

ple, and as much long-suffering as she had any intention of ever acquiring. Now, after Fred Trolley's pronouncement that the women would sleep here, and after seeing Darcy Trolley's fatalistic acceptance of the arrangement, she merely looked around her with an eye to making things a little more comfortable.

She did, however, afford the men a withering look before they left. It was a look that Fred missed, but Will did not; a look that was rife with the message, "All right. This is your brother's home and he is entitled to make what asinine decrees as please him within the confines of these walls. But you, Mr. Will Trolley, need not think I would ever accept this sort of boorish behavior from you!" Will understood, and it was with relief that he left the little chamber with his brother. The temperature in there had become uncomfortably chill. He did not particularly admire his brother or his ways, nor did he want to be like him, but at times Fred's thick skin did seem to be a definite advantage.

By midnight, then, the Trolley farmhouse is shrouded in slumber, with the menfolk comfortably ensconced in the only bedroom on the premises, and the two delicate females engaged in quiet warfare as they contested for room on the thin mattress and a portion of the gauze-thin blanket.

Which brings us to midnight at Westover Manor.

It will be remembered that when Derek returned to the Manor at six o'clock that evening from Ettington, the several absences from the household had been as yet undetected. Undetected, that is, by the general populace of the manor, though several different individuals were aware of one or two of the gaps. Derek galloped away in vengeful haste at about seven o'clock, and it was shortly after that that preparations were completed for the arrival of Gregory and Ulanda Forrester the next morning, and Perseus and Catherine Westover were able to turn their attention once again to their guest and family members.

They were surprised and then alarmed to find that there was no guest, no children, nor several (two, to be exact) staff members anywhere around to whom to direct their attention.

Mrs. Westover made a gallant attempt to get some information from her servants about the missing persons, but she was unable to get a clear answer to her questions, or even any two pieces of information that seemed to match. And what made it all the more confusing was that quite obviously everyone was telling her the truth as they knew it.

Little Matty knew that Rebecca and Miss Forrester had both gone to, and presumably departed from, Ettington railway station. But Alex said that Miss Forrester had not departed the house at the time Matt said she had, but had rather left with Will Trolley some time later. Alex also said that Derek had left in pursuit of these two. Nell was sure that the governess had left, and was equally sure that *she* had been the one to leave with Will Trolley. No, Nell didn't know anything about either Miss Becky or Mr. Derek, and she couldn't think of any reason why Miss Forrester might have left, but she stuck with her story that it was Miss Foster who had run off with Will. Upon that verdict she closed her lips firmly and would not deviate.

There was one point—to Mrs. Westover's great relief—upon which they all seemed to agree: *everyone* had gone to Derby. They may have left anytime between three o'clock in the afternoon and sometime after six-thirty this evening, and the various parties and traveling companions were thoroughly scrambled by the several reports received, but the final destination was unquestionably and uniformly Derby.

Even with Matt's testimony as to what Miss Forrester learned at the railway station, Rebecca's parents would have quickly deduced that their daughter must have sought refuge with their only available relative, her Aunt Minerva Twitchell.

Minerva was Perseus Westover's only living sibling, his older brother, Troyan, having gamely joined the regiments on their way to the Crimean War when a young man. A number of young bloods in the neighborhood had enlisted together as a sort of showy display to their respective belles. Troyan was not the only one of that little band who did not return, and many maidenly tears were shed for the lost heroes. Betsy Walker, the girl Troyan had especially wanted to impress by his courage, had worn the kerchief he had given her under her belt at her wedding that same year. In remembrance. A touching gesture.

Unlike her husband, Catherine Bainbridge Westover had three brothers and two sisters, all living. The Bainbridges were a more volatile family than the Westovers, though, and Sidney and Clarice had quarreled irreconcilably with the family. Jessamyn had eloped with a Romanian prince, and they were eking out their meager existence in his drafty run-down castle in Ploesti. And Martin and Rodney were in partnership together on a farm near Aberdeen, Scotland, where, judging from their spotty correspondence, they would at any moment become unimaginably rich, which must have been a happy prospect for them to contemplate these past twelve years.

Whatever friendships among the Westover and Bainbridge cousins the elder Westovers might have enjoyed were not passed along to their children, and so, practically speaking, Rebecca's Aunt Minerva was the only relative she might have recourse to if seeking asylum.

Of course, the obvious person for Becky to take refuge with was Tilly Baxter, but if that had been the case, Mrs. Baxter would have escorted her back by now. Her Aunt Minerva would send her back just as surely, but it would take longer from Derby.

Therefore, the most easily located of the several missing persons from Meadowview was their youngest daughter at Perseus's sister's home. And perhaps Minerva's house would be as good a center of operations as any there in Derby, since presumably Derek would find his way there eventually, and perhaps also Miss Forrester, if she had indeed left in search of Becky.

It occurs to the Author that such a logical cool listing of the facts and motivations does not convey to the reader Mrs. Westover's feeling that her world was crumbling down around her ears. This morning she had been pleased to learn that the Forresters were on their way to finalize the engagement between their lovely daughter and her idolized son. Her daughter Rebecca was getting along remarkably well in her studies with their recently engaged governess, whose methods, it had been hinted, were unorthodox but who was succeeding where countless before her had failed. This morning, Catherine

Westover's family and staff had all been satisfied, had all been happy.

Had all been here.

Tonight they were all gone.

Well, five were gone out of a household of fourteen, but Mrs. Westover felt like the Good Shepherd in the Bible, who, with his ninety and nine safely in tow, contentedly baaing, no doubt crowding around his weary legs, looked over his flock, saw that his prize lamb was missing and thought, just as Mrs. Westover now did, "Where did they all go?"

Mrs. Westover only knew what she had been able to learn from her remaining staff. In other words, she was floundering in ignorance.

"Perseus, I see only one recourse for you. You must go to Minerva's house in Derby and find our children, our servants and our guest. When the Forresters get here tomorrow, I shall invent some story about you taking a party of the young people on an adventure of some kind and that we didn't receive their cable in time to stop you. I shall tell them you plan to be back the day after tomorrow. You and everyone else." Mrs. Westover ended her statement on a warning note that immediately put the squire on the defensive and made him feel that he was somehow responsible for this rift in the even tenor of their lives.

"You want me to go to Derby, Mrs. Westover? Surely Broderick could deal with this matter more easily than I?" The pleading in his voice and helpless look in his eye had been carefully developed to extract the squire from unpleasant situations, but this time his good wife was not to be swayed.

"Broderick!" she cried in fine scorn. "Certainly not. I couldn't do a thing without Broderick here. The very idea, to suggest that I send the most valuable member of this household away right at the advent of the Forresters' visitation. Really, Mr. Westover."

Far from being offended by his wife's naming the butler as being more important than the squire in his own house, Squire Westover couldn't help but agree. Of course it had been foolish of him to nominate Broderick to undertake this mission, and he couldn't send Derek, since Derek was one of the young people who needed to be located. Therefore, descending through the order of hierarchy at the manor, after Broderick and his son, Squire Westover was the next in authority here. It was, inescapably, his duty to make the uncomfortable trip to Derby, find and convince his prodigal children, guest and servants to return.

"When is the next train to Derby then, m'love?"

"I don't know, Perseus. I suppose you will just have to go into Ettington and inquire. May as well take whatever baggage you are going to need with you now, so you won't have to make another trip back here."

And that is why, at midnight in Ettington, we find Catherine Westover in fitful slumber alone at the manor, while Squire Westover dozes in discomfort at Ettington station, waiting for the train that won't be through here for another four hours.

Chapter Thirty-eight

This story, just in case the Gentle Reader is not completely clear on the subject, is about Derek Bainbridge Westover and Josephine Maria Foster, and the serpentine events that brought them together, then tore them apart, and which may or may not bring about a happy ending between the leading actors in our little drama. However, in the course of our story, to account fully for what might, on the surface, appear to be completely haphazard and chaotic action, it has been necessary to explain the background and motives of some of our other characters.

Of many of our other characters.

The Author mentions this at this time in the hopes that the Reader will understand why we are now diverted to a character study of Minerva Twitchell's Pomeranian.

Mrs. Twitchell had been a widow for these past ten years, ever since that dreadful morning when Clyde Twitchell, her dear departed husband, failed to bring her her morning tea, as he had done every morning of the fifteen years of their—well, if not idyllic, certainly satisfactory—marriage. The reason he did not bring her her tea was that he had toppled over, face-down, into his shaving bowl and died.

Heart attack, the doctor said.

Mrs. Twitchell took to widowhood with great gusto, purchasing a complete new wardrobe in somber colors, which seemed to suit her, and elevating the memory of Mr. Twitchell from the cold and distant individual who had shared a home and polite respect with his wife, to the pedestal of religious adoration. In her faulty memory, Clyde Twitchell could do, and never had done, anything wrong. He had been the most attentive of husbands, the most successful of businessmen, and, to a close circle of very personal friends, she disclosed that he had been the most proficient of lovers (which proves the flights of fancy she allowed herself to take).

"Having been married to a Clyde Twitchell, how could I ever again look at another man?" was her indignant reply to the occasional matchmaker who hated to see her so lonely, and the occasional suitor who grieved to see the healthy legacy Mr. Twitchell had left her in the same deplorable condition. But she never remarried.

Instead, she got herself a dog.

Upon the dog, whom she named Anstopholes, a name of which her mother would have heartily approved, she lavished all the genuine love and affection she professed to have been Mr. Twitchell's before his unfortunate demise.

Now, to resolve the conflict that was left undecided at the Dresin Playhouse: Mrs. Twitchell *had* been in the south of France, but she had returned, unannounced, a fortnight before. Before she had a chance to resume her social rounds, however, she had noticed one morning—as she took her little dog Stoffy's breakfast in to him—that the tender skin inside one little pointed ear, skin that was usually a pearly pink, was flaming red and swollen. So she packed a valise for herself, two for Stoffy, had her maid, Maggie, pack a small carryall, told the butler and housekeeper that they might have another week and should board the house up again, and caught the next train to Liverpool and the best veterinarian Great Britain boasted at the time.

Dr. Michaels inspected Stoffy's ear and prescribed a complicated routine of baths, tonics and ointments, which included two additional visits to Dr. Michaels's office during the course of the week. However, despite Mrs. Twitchell's fussy ministrations and Michaels's prodigious outpouring of prescriptions, Stoffy's ear was back to its pale pink luminescence by the end of the week. Two more days of this frightful compassion might have killed him, but fortunately for him, his ear was pronounced well and whole on Friday morning, and he and his mistress were given leave to return to Derby.

Minerva Twitchell herded her party onto the train only to find after almost thirty miles that it was going to Lancaster, not Derby. Well, she had been overwrought and weak with relief that not only would her little Stoffy live, but with his ear back to normal, he was as beautiful as ever. She may be excused for believing that if she arrived at a railway station on time and saw a train lying in wait, smoking and straining at the bit, that train must be the one she was to board.

However justified she might have been in her error, it did not change the fact that when she finally disembarked at Lancaster, she had to purchase return tickets for herself and entourage and wait for several hours until the next train for Derby and points south passed through the Lancaster station. It finally departed sometime after ten o'clock that night on the return trip that wouldn't get them back to Derby until six o'clock the next morning. Stoffy was a darling, but even Minerva saw occasionally that he could be a bother.

Chapter Thirty-Nine

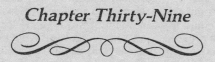

It is so much simpler, in the recounting of a story, for everyone to have names. It eliminates repeated description. And it makes the finished book appear so much neater and assists flash reading or skimming. Therefore, while neither Rebecca nor any of the other characters in our story were ever to know the name of the man who bought her dinner and escorted her to the rat hole in which we find them in this chapter, his name was Malcolm. Malcolm Connelly, originally of Horsham, in the south of England. He ran away to London while still a youth.

Fresh, almost pretty boys were his favorite, and to have ridden in the same train carriage with this helpless, lonely, lovely little boy seemed like a personal gift from whatever god Malcolm worshipped.

The youngster had clutched at the proffered help and had clung to him as his sole support in the swirling sea that surrounded him. Perhaps at some time in his life, Malcolm would have been touched by such guileless faith, but having been first a student and then a teacher in that great school of London for so many years, every vestige of conscience he may once have had was long since stamped out. Now trust like this only made him mentally rub his hands together. And plan.

The boy had inhaled the noxious brew at the den they had just quitted. Malcolm himself would never touch the vile stuff, but it seemed to work wonders on the very young. The boy was practically unconscious by the time they left the tavern, but he was very light, lighter than expected, and quite easy to maneuver down the street, into a cab and then out of the cab a little later.

It let them off in a place many people would believe could exist only in some fevered nightmare. It was so black that one could not tell when one went into or left any building. Outside there was not a hint of the sky to be seen overhead through the smoke and steam and overhanging rooftops that sometimes leaned into each other. Inside the smoke and stench were the same, just more dense, the darkness only accentuated, never relieved, by the dim lights flickering here or there along the walls.

In every city Malcolm had visited, there had been a place like this. They were all the same, like a filthy string unraveling from the same dark tangle through the back streets of all the cities and all the towns. Not just here in England, but in all the cities in all the world. A dark silent shadow under the bright glitter and happy noise of the lighted streets.

There was always this doorway and a hand held out. Sometimes words were spoken and sometimes the money, any money, was simply put into the hand, and it was withdrawn as anonymously as it had appeared. Then after the door there was always a passage with the curtained holes cut along the wall. There were never voices behind the curtains, but they were always drawn, and there were occasionally shuffling noises behind them. With almost a sixth sense, Malcolm always knew which hole to stop in front of and which withdrawn curtain would reveal only a deeper darkness and a fouler stench.

The child he was half leading and half dragging had begun to protest weakly now, but when they entered that doorway they had passed the point where his protests had any meaning.

"Come on, now. That's a good boy. You mustn't be afraid. I just thought you could come here and get some rest. Must be tired after your big day."

"S'dark," Rebecca murmured.

"Has to be dark so you can sleep," was Malcolm's preoccupied response. He had found the room and now was drawing the curtain back.

"In there?" the girl asked uncertainly as the man beside her applied pressure to her arm. In answer he pressed her back firmly, and she stumbled into the nook.

There was space enough to turn and pull the curtain again, but the rest of the floor space was filled with a bed. But no, a bed has a frame and legs and sometimes a mattress on it; this was a pile of rags, simply bunched together on the floor, but it would serve the same purpose.

Malcolm smiled in appreciation and anticipation as he sat next to the boy and turned him around. There was a greasy light in the far corner, up high enough on the wall to prevent its being kicked or knocked over by the loving, and sometimes not so loving, combatants on the floor. The light reflected off Rebecca's face as she was turned toward the man, and once again he congratulated himself on his extraordinary luck. The boy was pretty enough to be a girl, without any of a girl's nasty accoutrements. The man ran an exploratory hand lightly over the boy's body and thought he detected something made conspicuous by its absence. Malcolm withdrew his hand and studied the face under the dim light. Very closely.

"Pretty enough to be a girl," he murmured. Once more he made a search of her body, this time insinuating his groping fingers inside the clothing that hung loosely on the slight frame. And just as his hand encountered incontrovertible proof of the horrid trick that fate had played on him, Rebecca's eyes popped open and in their alarm registered near sobriety.

"My gawd! You're a girl!" Malcolm exclaimed, drawing away in disgust.

Rebecca drew back herself, then stood, then turned around several times in confusion.

"How do I get out of here?" she gasped. As if in a stupor, Malcolm pointed to the curtain that blended into the uniform gray of the walls almost imperceptibly. The girl tore aside the cloth and stumbled out into the passage. After several false starts and pulling the curtain back on various and sundry assorted couples, she finally found the fateful doorway and at last emerged, miraculously unscathed, from the hovel.

Rebecca was luckier than countless before her and countless since, but very few have been more surprised and disappointed than Malcolm.

Chapter Forty

Constable Anthony Simmons led the young lady carefully along the sidewalks and boardwalks that lined Derby's thoroughfares.

"It's quite a piece, miss," he apologized before they started. "I'm sorry, but I just don't have the fare for both of us." Spoken like a true gentleman, without the faintest hint that perhaps she would like to pay their way. Nevertheless, Josephine felt called upon to explain that she couldn't provide a ride for them, either.

"I am afraid I find myself in the same state, Constable. A lady doesn't come to the theater in the company of friends and bring with her a great deal of money." She smiled at him. "But the evening is quite warm, the streets are well lighted, and a pleasant stroll with an agreeable companion sounds positively charming." She slipped her hand naturally into the crook of his elbow, and he gamely returned her smile. In twenty minutes these two had struck up a bully friendship. Both of them had been the sole offspring in their homes, and it was as if they had each found their long-lost brother or sister at last. As Simmons guided her across a muddy intersection, he had to admit she was a very nice-looking girl, and somehow the thought made him feel very proud, as if her attractiveness reflected favorably on his family name. He no more thought of her in a romantic sense than he would a flesh-and-blood sister. Besides, with his Jenny waiting for him at home, why would he need any more romance in his life?

Josephine, too, felt warmly drawn to this happy homely man. She was not acting the coquette. Instead, her actions and sentiments flowed freely. She felt like smiling, so she smiled. Simmons said something she found amusing, so she laughed a little. And somehow she knew that this man would do all he could to help her in her quest, so she put her hand in his arm and her fate in his hands. Which was why, after several blocks, she even went so far as to tell him the truth.

"In the strictest interpretation of the facts, Simmons, you wouldn't actually say I went to the theater tonight with friends."

"Oh?" was his response, delivered as if she had told him her middle name was Maria and not as if she were revealing a mortifying betrayal of his trust. Josephine was encouraged to continue.

"No. Actually, I went there alone."

"To meet someone?" The dear man was still willing to give her the benefit of the doubt, and Josephine sighed.

"Well, not exactly. You see...I came with the intent of learning the address of the house to which you are escorting me." He looked at her, still without blame, only with interest to learn more. So, by backward stages, Josephine rehearsed to him the entire catalog of events that had placed her here alone, in Derby, at midnight, on this Friday night. First she had to explain that she was looking for a young girl who was supposed to be her charge. Then, of course, she needed to clarify what she meant by "supposed to be," which entailed a somewhat condensed version of the mix-up between guest and governess. Which took her back to the beginning of the whole adventure and her initial introduction to and dealings with Mr. Derek Westover.

Like any fond brother, Simmons recognized the soft note that crept into her voice, and under the street lamps they passed at regular intervals, he saw the light in her eyes.

"So you believe this Westover had designs on your imagined wealth and no other motive for the interest he showed in you?"

"I think so," she said with hopeful doubt in her voice. "I don't know of any other reason he would have shown such marked interest in me."

Simmons grinned at her.

"Don't you, then? I guess you haven't got a looking glass?" Josephine giggled a bit, and Simmons patted her hand.

"Look here," Simmons said after a brief pause. "If we're trying to catch up with the girl, we'd better do something about getting there a little faster. We're closer to Beauford Lane now, and we neither one have enough money to ride both of us, but maybe we could each ride one, if you see what I'm getting at." That was said like a true brother, and the idea, though a novel one to Josephine, seemed quite sensible.

"Of course," she said. "How clever of you. Let us see...." She had stopped in the middle of the sidewalk to extract her purse, so Simmons left her to hail a passing hansom cab. The few bob he had and whatever the young lady would be able to find in that purse should cover the hire of a cab.

While still waiting for a likely conveyance, Josephine came up behind Simmons and pressed a few coins into his hands. He didn't have to stop and count it to see that between them they had more than enough to make the rest of their trip in style.

Finally a driver drew his horse up alongside the walk and nodded to the door of his cab.

"You got me just in time, mate," he said. "I was about to take 'er in for the night. But I suppose there's room in this old box for one more fare.'' He laughed at his own wit and was pleased to see the young policeman smile. He didn't want any trouble tonight, no rushing to stop some thieves or the finding of a dead body at the end of this trip, but judging by the man's easy manner and companionable grin, it had been safe for him to stop.

''Where to?'' he asked, taking up the reins.

''Beauford Lane, my good man,'' then turning to Josephine, ''What number did you say?''

''The woman at the theater said 1519 Beauford Lane—I think.''

''That'll be 1519, driver.''

''Right, ho!'' he shook the lines, and the horse plodded into the street. Simmons had hoped this would get them there sooner than walking, but not at this rate, it wouldn't. It did give the young lady a chance to rest, though, and from her story and the general sag about her person, Simmons knew that she was much in need of a rest. And a longer rest than even this tar-slow nag was going to give them.

As the street lamps began to thin out, and they entered the quiet residential area of the city, the driver called back over his shoulder. ''It can happen that I don't come out this way three times in a year, and then just tonight this is the second trip to Beauford Lane I've made.''

Josephine and Constable Simmons were so busy watching the sides of the road for a young girl (a young girl dressed as a boy, that is) that they paid little attention to this comment. As they neared Beauford Lane and there was still no sign of Rebecca, Josephine became more hopeful. Surely if Minerva Twitchell were *not* home, they would have seen Rebecca by now. By the time they reached Beauford Lane she was absolutely convinced that they would find the Twitchell home open and occupied and Rebecca heedlessly asleep in a guest bedroom. She trusted that her aunt had scolded her soundly, insisted that she return to Westover Manor tomorrow, and perhaps had dispatched a telegram earlier this evening that would have put the several minds in turmoil at ease back in Ettington.

The coach came to a standstill, and the driver passed the information back over his shoulder. ''Fifteen-nineteen Beauford Lane.''

As it was past midnight, most of the houses along this street were dark and silent, so Josephine refused to allow her lovely fantasy to be disturbed. A sleepy little maid would answer the door and no doubt be frightened speechless by the sight of a uniformed policeman standing on the doorstep. From upstairs they would hear the aunt call down.

"Who's there, Nan?" (Or "Jane" or perhaps "Percy" if it was a man servant instead of a maid.)

Nan would hardly know what to say, but Simmons would tell her calmly, in an effort to reassure her, that this young lady (indicating Josephine herself) was in search of a Miss Rebecca Westover, whom they believed to be at this address, and whose family were all very worried.

Then Nan (or Jane or Percy) would call up the stairs to say that it was someone sent to fetch Miss Becky, and Mrs. Twitchell would come fussing down the stairs, tying her dressing gown as she came, complaining that she had warned Rebecca that a telegram wouldn't get to Ettington in time and that someone would be here after her before morning.

Josephine hadn't gotten all the way to the end of her story, but it was taking the direction of her becoming something of a heroine in the Westover household, with all of the misconceptions cleared up and Mr. Derek heartbroken to learn the truth and realize he could never marry her now, now that he had really fallen in love with her.

Simmons helped her from the cab, and together they went in search of the Twitchell house, though before they left the cab, Simmons instructed the driver to wait. They finally deciphered the number by the dim light of the moon and approached the house, but even as they drew closer, Josephine could see the boards across the door and windows. Her lovely fairy tale crumbled, and she turned with a stricken look to a very sympathetic Simmons.

"We can ask the neighbors," he said comfortingly, offering her what crumbs of solace he could. "Maybe one of them saw the girl, or she might even have sought some help along the street here, being without money or means to get home."

"Ask now?" Josephine said, but with no real eagerness in her voice. She was too tired, worried and disappointed to be hopeful anymore.

Simmons shook his head. "It's too late now," he said. "We'll go back into town and try tomorrow."

Josephine looked at him in alarm. "But I don't have any-place..." she started.

"You can spend the night with me and Jenny," Simmons said matter-of-factly, as if there could be no question in the matter.

"Is your wife used to you bringing home stray puppies, then?"

"Puppies or people, makes no difference to my Jenny. She's got a heart big enough to fit them all in." Simmons smiled fondly, and the glow of love in his face almost made him handsome. They were back to the cab now, and Simmons opened the door for her.

"The house is boarded up," he told the cab driver. "Take us back into town. I'll give you my address." Josephine looked at him quizzically, and in an undertone he explained to her, "Jenny's got a little sewing money we can pay the cab with."

The driver shook his head as Simmons was giving Josephine a hand into the coach.

"I thought that place looked locked up tight as a drum when I brought that boy here."

"You mean the other fare you brought to Beauford Lane you delivered to this very same number?" Simmons asked.

Josephine had stopped in her climb into the cab during this exchange, and when the driver nodded, she asked quickly, "What color hair did he have?"

"Miss?" the driver asked, momentarily taken off guard.

"The lad you brought out here. What color hair did he have?"

"Well, red, miss. Red as a tomato. I don't usually pay that much attention to my fares, but a fellow'd have to be blind not to 've noticed that head of blazing curls."

Josephine stepped back down onto the sidewalk and grabbed Simmons's arm.

"It's her." The policeman studied her face for a moment.

"The boy? He was your young lady?"

Josephine nodded, but the coachman snorted.

"A girl? You think I can't tell the difference between a boy and a girl?"

"I think if the girl was young and had short hair and put on male clothing and told a stranger she was a boy, that almost anyone would not know the difference."

The driver still looked dubious, but Simmons obviously accepted her story on faith.

"Where'd he—she—the youngster you brought out here earlier, where'd he get to?"

"Well, I don't really—"

"You mean you left a child at a deserted house and didn't offer any help at all?" Josephine was outraged.

"He didn't—"

"You have no idea where we can look, then? You didn't see anything that might help us?" Simmons was trying to remain calm, though the driver could tell by the set to his jaw that the constable didn't approve of his actions, either. Josephine was not trying at all to be calm, and was letting him know in no uncertain terms that she found his neglect criminal. Between the two of them, the driver of the cab felt his collar getting very tight.

"I wasn't worried—"

"You weren't worried!" Josephine cried. "A little girl—"

"Boy," Simmons reminded her, willing to give the driver what little justification he deserved.

"Either. A child! You abandoned a child!"

"Not exactly." The driver was making nervous placating gestures with his hands. "See, a friend came along for him just a few minutes later."

"A friend?" Josephine sounded mystified.

"The boy didn't want to go anyplace else." This explanation was going to be difficult, since Josephine's outcry had made even that rascal feel a little guilty, so now he must try to modify his totally reprehensible actions. But as he was to tell himself later, when the young woman before him was no longer shouting her raucous accusations into his face, he had believed his passenger to be a boy, and was he to be held responsible for every waif on the Derby streets? The little ragamuffin hadn't even paid the full fare.

"I assumed someone would be there soon to meet him—er, her—and he, that is she, seemed content to wait," he continued. He had thought no such thing, but it fit in well with the rest of his story and put a dab of whitewash on his heavily soiled character.

"You said a friend came for the youngster?"

"Well, yes, you see, I did a spot more hacking and then I stopped at the P&P—that'd be Parley's Pub, miss—for a bit of the grog to keep me warm and awake for the rest of the night. Now the P&P is a popular stopover for me mates in the cabbie business, and a feller can usually pass the time with one or two other drivers. So just my luck, I'd sat down and been handed a mug, when who should come in but Jones, and when he seen me he comes over to crow. He says I missed a fare tonight. Said it was mine by rights, but he wasn't a one to say no to money what was put straight into his hand. Said he passed me leavin' Beauford and Fleming, dropped off his own ride, and by the time he got turned around, here comes this fellow leading a young lad. The same redheaded boy he'd seen me pick up outside the Derby depot."

Although the man's style was hardly that of a refined orator, Josephine hung on eagerly to every word he said. At this point, however, she made an impatient noise, which was echoed by the constable, alerting the driver to the fact that his audience was getting restless and would like him to get to the point.

"Yes, well." He cleared his throat nervously and proceeded. If only these two understood how beastly hard it was to put his actions in a good light; a fellow had to have a chance to organize his thoughts. "Jones said these two acted real chummy." What Richard Jones had actually said was that the bloke was being a real pal to the kid, if you know what I mean. "Said he dropped them off together, so you can see that my mind was put at ease over the poor young fellow I'd been forced to leave alone."

"Did this Jones say where he took them?" Simmons asked.

"Well...uh, er, that is, yes, I think he mentioned the place."

"And?"

"Said it was a friendly lookin' place. No name above the door, but a place where you could get a good hot bowl of soup."

"What was the address, man?" Simmons sounded exasperated, but the driver didn't really want to hear what he would sound like when he provided the required information.

"Well, now, he didn't tell me the *exact* address." Simmons made an impatient gesture, and the driver hurried on, almost as if he hoped they wouldn't hear his next words. "He said it was some place on Delancey Street." Beads of sweat had popped out on the driver's forehead, and he could tell they were justified as he saw Simmons's jaw drop open.

"Delancey Street!" he cried.

"What? What is it?" Josephine was instantly alarmed by the note of dismay and disbelief in Simmons's voice.

"You hear a young boy lost in the city is taken to Delancey Street by a strange man, and your mind was put at ease?"

"Simmons! What's the matter?"

He turned to her with a wild look in his eyes that did nothing to calm her frantically beating heart.

"Delancey Street is the first street this side of hell. No, no, I take that back. It's a place straight out of hell, put smack in the middle of Derby, England, by the devil himself. Every sort of degradation, disgrace, villainy and immorality goes on there. We would clean it out, but half the force is afraid to go in there for fear of what they might catch, and the other half keeps asking what would we do with the human trash we found there if we did clean it out? It's not safe for *me* to go down there, with my stick and whistle and waving a loaded gun, but to take a child—boy or girl—is like throwing raw meat to a pack of starving wolves." He actually shuddered, and Josephine burst into tears.

The cab driver sat stock-still during Simmons's explanation, afraid to move, and now the young policeman bounded up into the driver's box and grabbed the other man by his lapels.

"I want you to take me to Delancey Street, to whatever rat hole the girl was left at and wait while I try to find her."

"J-Jones could take you right there. Wouldn't take a minute to find him."

"No time, and you know that," Simmons snarled into the frightened face that was only inches from his own. "The best and only hope the girl has is that we get there as fast as possible."

"I want to go with you," Josephine said.

"You can't go down there," Simmons told her. "A beautiful woman is as much bait as a child."

"I'll stay in the cab, but I have to go. You don't know Rebecca. I cannot let you go alone."

Josephine sounded definite and Simmons tried to see into her eyes by the dim light here. Finally he acquiesced, though obviously against his better judgment. Once again he turned to the driver.

"The young lady will go with us, and you will guard her with your life!" These words were said with no more than normal volume, but the steel behind them made the driver quite certain that they should be taken literally. His life was absolutely forfeit if anything happened to this girl. Thoroughly intimidated, the driver nodded dumbly, and his two passengers got back into the hansom buggy. He couldn't help but imagine what poor old Jones's fate would have been had he been within reach of the young policeman's grip.

Chapter Forty-one

Being on Delancey Street in Derby, England, in the late 1800s, in the wee hours of the morning, was like being on an alien and unfriendly planet. Not only was the landscape distorted and misshapen, the wooden and brick buildings that faced the street seeming to form the boundary between life on earth and wherever this dreary place was, but lining the sidewalks and leaning out of the openings in that solid facade were poor creatures that were only grotesque mockeries of the human beings on our happy planet.

This had started out as a slum, housing the starving families and laborers forced to work for a mere pittance in the silk or cotton mills. The weekly wage was barely enough to buy two loaves of bread and a few potatoes. Their money would buy nothing else, certainly not building materials, and yet these structures had grown, filthy dough leavened by human misery.

In time the laborers fighting for their existence had left this place, and the land and buildings had seemed to topple into each other without their support. All that remained were these awful structures that had no shape, the separate buildings no distinctions, and at two o'clock in the morning, to young eyes blurred by cheap wine, the whole scene looked like nothing so much as the clumsy little mud houses children build and then abandon to the rain.

Rebecca, stumbling out of the cave in which she had been incarcerated, was out of the frying pan, but it remained to be seen if she could clear the fire. Even as she emerged from the doorway, she ran into a bundle of upright rags. From the muffled protests that emanated from it as she tried to disengage herself, she realized there was a living being in the center of that mass. The outer layer of clothing seemed to blend into and become an inner layer of clothing, which eventually congealed into living flesh when one reached the center, with no real differentiation in those central recesses between the dirty smelly material and the dirty smelly flesh.

That person seemed too far gone down the road to oblivion to grasp for a reality any longer and rolled away from the girl like water down a tarry hill.

Not so the next person with whom Rebecca collided. She was completely disoriented in this world gone askew. Pushing away from the ragman had thrown her balance off even further, and she staggered down the broken sidewalk until she fell into another opening. There was a woman crouched there, though barely recognizable as such.

When a small child, Becky had had little patience with dolls or playthings or anything that was a distraction from her darling ponies. But one day her mother had coerced her into her room with an illustrated storybook and entrapped, her mother told her the story of a little boy and girl, brother and sister, who had been abandoned by their parents in the wood. They made their way through the wood together, and eventually came upon a cottage made entirely of gingerbread. At that point Rebecca sat up with interest as her mother turned the page to reveal an illustration. The gingerbread house was there, all right, with flat colorless icing on the roof and windows, but the only thing in the picture Rebecca could see, was a horrible woman coming out of the door. Her hair was frazzled and yellowish white, her eyes were squinty and her nose huge and bent. The lips were indrawn so as to be almost invisible. She was clutching a cane in one hand and with the other bony claw she was grasping for the children.

Catherine Westover had meant to amuse and quiet her young daughter, not scar her for life, but for years after that, Rebecca had nightmares of that horrible old woman clutching at her, pulling her hair, dragging her with those awful hands. They were nightmares from which, often, Rebecca woke up screaming, unable to make her parents feel the terror of being touched by those skeletal fingers.

The storybook illustration was the woman Rebecca stumbled over in the doorway. Just as in her dreams she was grasped by one clawlike hand. But this woman added another dimension to Rebecca's childhood dream by having a hair-raising cackle, which she wailed into the girl's ear.

In blind panic at this nightmare come to life, Rebecca flailed her arms wildly. She twisted and fought, and though the old hag seemed determined not to let her go, Rebecca was driven by panic to get away. Any way she could. The girl finally won, leaving the hag screeching behind her.

Although frightened and confused, she had learned her lesson and picked her way through the debris, both inanimate and animate, with more care now; not slowing to a walk precisely, but to something less than a mindless dash. She had no idea where she was going, but something in the back of her mind kept her headed in the same direction, guided by the thought, more intuitive than deductive, that if she kept going in the same direction she would eventually emerge from this place; that surely the whole world had not turned into this savage refuse heap.

She was no longer blindly stumbling over people, and she had passed several derelicts who paid her no attention, but a few minutes later she was stopped by one more person: a relatively nice-looking woman of a more or less indeterminate age. Rebecca would have classified her as a "grown-up," which put her roughly between forty and sixty-five. She was not well dressed, but she was better dressed by far than anyone else Becky had seen on this street, so one can understand why the girl's first reaction would be one of relief at finally finding someone of sanity and substance to help her in this world gone mad.

The woman was not a walking bundle of rags or a wicked fairy-tale witch, but of all of the people she had encountered since escaping the cavern-inn, this woman presented by far the greatest danger to the girl.

"Oh, ma'am," Rebecca gasped. "Can you help me?"

"I beg your pardon?" the woman asked. Her words sounded wonderfully civilized to Rebecca.

"I am lost and in serious trouble, ma'am." The woman gave her a look that Rebecca mistook for sympathy. "I'm not really a boy," she said with a laugh, suddenly remembering the blasted attire that got her into this situation in the first place. She ran her fingers through her hair in a nervous attempt to make her hair look fluffier and more feminine. "I dressed like this as a sort of prank," she ended lamely.

"I would never mistake you for a boy, dearie," was the woman's surprising response.

"Oh," Rebecca was momentarily nonplussed. "Well, someone else did...I think." As she attempted to tell her story, she suddenly realized that she didn't really remember what had happened too well at all. It had been so dark in there, wherever it was, and so disorienting to suddenly wake up and find oneself in blackness with something frightfully unpleasant going on...she thought. But she had only been half-awake when she stumbled out the door, if she was even awake now. It was very difficult for her to be sure, because this place was like nothing she'd ever imagined before, and if it was real, where could she possibly be?

But the woman seemed to understand. "There, there, pet," she replied. She put an arm protectively, almost possessively, around the girl's shoulders. "I understand everything."

Rebecca looked into her eyes in disbelief. How could this woman, this complete stranger, understand the terror and the trauma that had transpired tonight? But her eyes confirmed what her words had avowed: this woman did indeed understand that the girl was in grave danger.

Rebecca was so utterly relieved that she almost fainted into the arm that was supporting her.

"Oh, thank you!" she breathed, the tears springing to her eyes.

"Now, pet, let me help you. I know a place where you can rest."

That was exactly what Malcolm had told her before they left the tavern, which was the last thing she could remember clearly... or almost clearly. In alarm, Rebecca stiffened and tried to pull away. It was then that she realized that the woman's arm wasn't just supporting her, it was holding her tightly. The woman had a solid frame that Rebecca had mistaken for comfortable. It wasn't comfortable at all; it was rock hard, and the embrace she held the girl in was like a carpenter's vise.

This bouncing from relief to panic was telling on Becky's nerves. Once again she had dropped all of her defenses preparatory to relinquishing her fate into the hands of someone she could trust, and now, in an instant, had to build them all up again. But the practice was making the girl adept, and she was getting much better at early detection of dangerous waters.

"Let me go!" she cried, squirming as best she could in the woman's grasp, which was not very well.

The woman really had remarkable strength, which is not surprising as she had developed it doing exactly what she was doing now, holding people who didn't want to be held, taking them places they didn't want to go. And quite a number of them had been girls, about Rebecca's age, who had somehow wandered into Delancey Street and were never heard of again. The woman had access to a supply of vile drugs that destroyed the minds and wills of even strong men, to say nothing of innocent young girls. Without the mind and will, there is nothing left but flesh, and that suited the woman and her business instincts and her degraded clientele just fine.

"Now, now, luv, don't you be fussing about. You asked for my help, and my help you shall have now, whether you will or no," the woman said, tightening her arm even more, which Rebecca would have thought impossible. She chuckled softly into the girl's ear, a chuckle that raised the hair on the back of Rebecca's neck with its triumphant evil.

"No, let me go! Help! Help me!"

It does no good to call for help on Delancey Street, Derby, England. Like all of the dankest slums the world over, men and women come to Delancey Street when there is no help for them, and they have no help to give. It is the last stop before death; most inhabitants of the street, if they can still think at all, would call it the stop after death. And in truth, death is seldom as ugly as life on Delancey Street.

There were people on the street, some in doorways or sitting on the curb, a few passersby. The cry they heard was from a young innocent, too weak to save herself, imploring aid and mercy. No heads even turned in her direction. There was no help to give, and after a while even human curiosity died here, from horrible satiation.

Rebecca was kicking and screaming and would have bit and scratched anything that came within reach, but besides gaining strength, the woman had also gained expertise in avoiding personal injury and in confining and jerking a person along so that all offenses were rendered more or less ineffective.

"No! No!" Rebecca was sobbing by now. She knew instinctively that where this woman took her, it would be a good deal harder to escape than the dark inn and the stunned Malcolm. As any number of girls could have told her, it would have been impossible.

"I believe this young person would rather not go with you."

A hand was placed on the woman's muscular arm. A man's hand that brooked no nonsense and stopped her in her tracks. The woman swung around to give battle to this foolhardy usurper—she had broken male bones before and could do so again. But when she saw the stick and the uniform, she thought it the better part of valor to abandon her prey. This time.

"Rebecca?" a soft voice called from behind the man's shoulder. At the sight of the form that came around the constable's bulky frame, not only did Rebecca drop her defenses once again, but she also dropped her entire body onto the sidewalk in a gratefully relieved dead faint.

Chapter Forty-two

To tell how Josephine and Constable Simmons had found Rebecca, we must step back in time a little. The driver had nervously directed his horse into the dark and broken streets of the city, afraid of this part of town and what lay ahead, but more afraid of the policeman and his stick sitting behind him in the cab.

"But I don't understand," Josephine was saying. "What is so awful about a gentleman offering to help a young boy who is lost and alone?"

"Miss Foster, some things cannot be put delicately, and perhaps you wouldn't even believe me if I did tell you, so you must simply trust me when I say that any man who would take a young person onto Delancey Street is not a gentleman, and for that same reason he would not be offering help. You can believe me when I tell you that your young friend is in a great deal of danger. Possibly mortal danger—definitely moral danger."

His words seemed to remind him of the urgency of the situation, and he banged loudly on the floor of the carriage to encourage the hansom driver to more speed.

In a short while they left the lights of the city and civilization behind them. There were no streetlights here, and the towering and crowded buildings blocked out any natural light that might have come from the night sky. After Josephine's fearful inquiry and Simmons's far from reassuring reply, it had been silent in the cab. Josephine strained her eyes to distinguish something out of her window, unable to tell if the forms they occasionally passed were people or darkened lampposts. Simmons wished the young lady would talk, so he wouldn't have to dwell on the probable fate of the girl they were trying to rescue. He shouldn't have allowed Josephine to come, he thought. Judging from the driver's reports and estimation of the time, they would probably be too late to prevent harm from befalling Rebecca, but at least they had a chance of saving her life. He wished Miss Foster was not going to be exposed to this.

Miss Foster was with him, though, and there was no use in shutting the barn door after the horse had escaped. He certainly couldn't put her out of the cab here; he was beginning to detect the distinctive odor of Delancey Street. And he couldn't possibly try to take her back to safety and still hope to ever hear of the girl again.

Still mulling his dark thoughts—and one could have no other kind of thought on Delancey—he realized that they had come to a standstill.

"What is it?" he asked sharply, putting his head out of the window.

"This is the place," the driver called back to him, indicating the establishment in front of them.

Simmons grimaced.

"You wait right here," he warned them both as he climbed from the cab. But it was only at the driver that he threateningly shook his stick.

The proprietor of the establishment was reading a greasy newspaper as Simmons walked through the door.

"I'm looking for a man and a boy," Simmons said abruptly, without the courtesy of a preamble.

The proprietor dropped the newspaper. Simmons spared a glance at it and recognized headlines from two weeks ago. Some news can travel incredibly fast in a ghetto, like the waters of a flash flood through a canyon; then again, items like this newspaper can be caught in an eddy and swirled away from the current to lie unnoticed in a stagnant pond for weeks on end.

"We don't have the customers sign in here." The owner's tone was tired and sarcastic, as if he would love to skewer the young constable with his rapier wit but couldn't generate enough energy to make the attempt. He did not sound intimidated. People from the outside world, like the cab driver, were still impressed by vested authority, but in this place there was no authority, and death itself was only slightly intimidating anymore. A policeman, though an unusual and infrequent visitor, was not going to threaten anyone with death, and anything less hardly warranted notice.

"The boy's in danger."

"We're all in danger, mister. This beautiful world of ours is not a safe place to live, or hadn't you noticed that?"

"He has curly red hair." Simmons made one last halfhearted attempt. It was just as he feared; he was going to get no help here. To his surprise, though, a light of recognition sprang to the man's eyes, and Simmons detected the first glimmer of interest he had shown since their interview began.

"Red hair?" the man asked.

"That's right."

"Came in here with a man, you say?"

"That's what I said," Simmons agreed, hardly daring to breathe for fear of destroying the man's sudden communicative spirit.

"I don't know...." His voice faded and Simmons's heart sank.

"Look," he said. "I have no money to pay for the information, and you know as well as I do that if I take time to go back uptown for some more muscle, it would be too late for the boy, even if we were able to find him. But the lad is just an innocent boy brought down here by mistake. Help me get him out."

There was no longer any help for the owner of this little eatery cum villains' den, just as there could be no help for the rest of the adults who existed here. But the man lived near enough to the perimeter of the daylight world to still have the merest shred of decency left, or at least remember that such a thing existed. He could not expect any help for himself here, but there might be a chance that the boy could be saved. Would it kill him to point a direction for this policeman? The man wavered; it was a toss of a coin.

Heads, he didn't care and wouldn't say anything; tails, he still didn't care, but he would mention that they had turned left.

It came up tails.

The man jerked his thumb. "The man bought a few drinks for the boy and then they left, that way," he said, turning back to his paper.

He would never know if the policeman found the boy he was looking for; he never saw or heard of any of these people ever again. But the next day, as he was opening his eatery, his eye was attracted to some kind of stone sparkling on the floor in front of his chair, in the same spot where the policeman had been standing the night before. Picking it up to study it, the owner could see that it was of some value and had most likely been dropped there by one of the countless thieves or pickpockets who frequented his place of business. He took the stone to a pawnshop on the next street but one (one does not pawn possibly stolen articles on home turf). Even at a pawnshop's ruinous rate of exchange, the amount of cash he received was startling.

He had passed a small restaurant advertising for a buyer or partner on this same street, and he stopped in there for a cup of tea on his way back to his place. The man who served him was the owner, and after exchanging a few pleasantries, he asked about the advertisement. They discussed it at length, and when he left, the owner of the tea shop was dumbfounded to be holding enough money in his hands to save his struggling business, and the Delancey Street man went back to his shop to pack his belongings and lock the doors.

He and his new partner, between them, knew all there was to know about creating a casual inexpensive eating atmosphere, and in less than a year's time they were able to close the original little shop and open two new businesses, one for each to manage, a few blocks closer to town, a few blocks farther from Delancey.

The owner, who had lost a young wife years before without having any children, was feeling very chipper one morning and stuck a perky little carnation in his buttonhole on the way to open his shop. Shortly after opening, a comely widow lady entered his shop, ordered some tea and biscuits and made an admiring remark about the flower in his lapel. They talked for a while; they met later that evening. He found she had three children by her first marriage, bright little children, two boys and a girl, who struck up an immediate affection for their mama's new beau.

Six months later, this man married the widow lady, who brought to the marriage a very handsome settlement that allowed her husband to invest in the wholesale of foods at a time when the market was booming.

The two sons were sixteen and twelve and boon companions to the by now well-to-do restaurateur. The little girl, though, was just eight years old and still young enough to be gleefully bounced on her fond Papa's knee. She had long flaming red ringlets, which her brothers teased her about unmercifully. Her new Papa would soothe her, and taking one of the ringlets in his hand, would wind it thoughtfully around his finger.

"Never you mind those young scalawags," he would say, smiling. "I love red hair the very best of all."

"Better even than Mama's?" the child would say wonderingly. Her mother had raven-black hair and the little girl could imagine nothing more beautiful.

"Better even than Mama's," the man would say.

"Why?" the little girl would ask, not because she didn't know, but because she loved the fairy-tale-like story that would follow.

"Because I really believe that it is because of red curls like these that I am your Papa today."

The man had, understandably, become very religious during the past several years, and he believed in divine rewards for acts of kindness. The little girl believed in fairy godmothers in disguise.

And who is to say that one of them was not right?

Simmons hurried back to the waiting cab.

"Where is she?" Josephine called out of the window as soon as he emerged from the shop.

"That way," Simmons directed the driver before he got in the cab.

"Where is she?" Josephine repeated as the carriage started to move again. "Where are we going?"

Simmons was still slightly out of breath. "The man in the pub," he breathed, "said they were there . . . but left. He said they came this way."

Josephine looked out of the window in desperation. The sights that met her eyes sickened her. They were in the very heart of the sewer now, and the dim light that issued from the occasional door opening cast a good deal more illumination on the scene than she would have wished for. The people were filthy, and the gestures they made and the things they called out when they saw her face in the cab window could not be misinterpreted. Not even by a very civilized young woman, who in all her twenty-three years had never witnessed such vulgarity.

"Ignore them," Simmons said, sorrier than ever that the young woman was here to complicate this situation. "And sit back from that window, will you! It's been an hour or more since the girl was out there, anyway. How could we have ever thought there was any hope in this? I doubt if your little charge will ever be found. Just don't make yourself another number in the station-house books!"

It was only his worry and concern for her that was making him sound so pessimistic, Josephine knew that, but she was so undone by fatigue and worry herself that she was turning to him with a sharp retort when she caught sight of the warm glow of a head of red curls out of the corner of her eye.

"Stop!" she breathed sharply, grabbing the policeman's arm. "That's her!"

"Where?" Simmons asked, already pounding the floor of the cab to get the driver to stop.

"There." Josephine pointed to a couple struggling on the sidewalk, a taller woman and a red-haired boy several inches shorter. By now Simmons was out of the cab, though it hadn't yet come to a complete stop. As soon as it did, Josephine followed him, much to the cab driver's consternation, who noticed several vagabonds on the street noticing her. If one of them grabbed her, he was going to whip his horse sharply and get out of here before anybody could stop him. But he would wait until somebody grabbed her.

Simmons had reached the tangled pair, and seizing the woman's arm, he said, "I believe this young person would rather not go with you." The woman turned threateningly. She was a good-size mass of muscles, and Simmons raised his billy, ready to defend himself against a dangerous foe. At sight of the stick, the woman dropped her arm from around the child and hurried away. Before Simmons could decide whether to go after her or not, he was startled to hear Miss Foster behind him.

"Rebecca?" she said. He turned to scold her for leaving the cab, when she gasped and rushed past him to save the girl from falling onto the ground. His scolding forgotten, he lent a supporting arm to get her young charge back to the cab.

"Is this the girl?" he asked over the top of her head.

"This is the one," Josephine acknowledged their hard-won victory.

Between them, clumsily, they got the girl into the cab, and Simmons gave the driver another address. The cabbie was relieved to hear he was to drive now to a quiet inoffensive little residential section of town. It was nowhere near as ostentatious as Beauford Lane, but at least it was civilization. It was also almost directly across town. If he was able to get his fare for tonight, he would have quite a little bundle. However, feeling again those thick fingers at his coat collar, he decided he wouldn't press the matter, but would feel himself lucky to come out of this with his skin intact and a bob or two.

"Where are we going?" Josephine asked, distracted by her ministrations to the girl.

"Thought we'd better go to my house and see what my Jenny can do for the girl. My Jenny's a wonder, she is, and with a little poultice and a lot of hot soup, she can fix whatever is ailing a body."

He sat back in happy anticipation as Josephine continued to flutter ineffectually over the girl.

She needn't have fussed. Simmons's Jenny was a wonder.

Chapter Forty-three

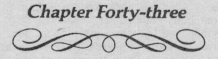

The good Lord help us, what have you brought home with you tonight, Anthony Simmons?" the pretty little woman cried, springing from her chair, where she had been mending some and dozing some, to open the door and bustle her burdened husband to their own bedside.

"Papa? Is that you?" a young voice, or maybe two, called from overhead. Immediately thereafter a little flaxen head appeared at the top of the staircase.

"Back to bed with both of you, now," Jenny Simmons called sharply.

"Is Papa home?" another little voice called.

"Yes, I'm home," Simmons boomed out. "Now get to bed like your mama said. I'll tell you all about it in the morning." The head disappeared and the little voices quieted, satisfied now that Papa was home. And, of course, Simmons would not tell them all about it in the morning. They probably wouldn't remember, but if they did, he would just tell them he had helped a little girl who was lost, which would certainly satisfy his children and fit in nicely with the image they had of him.

Anthony Simmons was a quiet, hard-working, simple-pleasures kind of man. He would never rise to great heights in the force or accomplish any particularly amazing feat in his lifetime. He would live and die in this peaceful little cottage and never be the hero of a great adventure. But he would spend his life in an effort to keep his children from ever knowing Delancey Street; his children and a good many others he would never know.

"She's had a mishap, Jen," he explained to his wife.

"Hurt?" she asked, concerned but not panicked.

"I think she's only fainted, but I haven't been able to rouse her," said the nice-looking girl who had come in with Anthony.

"Whoo! And you won't soon, either, I'll warrant," Mrs. Simmons said, drawing back sharply as the unconscious girl turned her head toward Jenny and exhaled.

"What is it?" Simmons asked.

"Take a whiff," his wife answered.

"Whoo!" Simmons said.

"What is it?" Josephine asked, thoroughly alarmed by now.

"It's drink, luv," Jenny said. "And a bad brew."

"Drink? Do you mean that horrible woman . . . ?"

"Her or the man who first picked her up," Simmons said.

"That woman? What woman? What man?" Mrs. Simmons looked for an explanation, first from her husband, then from the young woman, then back to her husband again.

Anthony Simmons recognized the look in her eyes and knew she would go no further until she had some answers. Besides his children, he also endeavored to protect his dear wife from the harsher realities of life, but Jenny Simmons was a very bright little woman who knew a lot more about the world than her husband had ever intended she should. It took no more explanation than, "She was lost and some man took her to Delancey Street," for Jenny to have a pretty fair idea of the danger the girl had faced.

"Did he . . . ?"

"We don't know. She was fighting with a lot of spunk when we found her, and with a woman, so she may have escaped, though I don't know how."

"Well, now, Anthony Simmons, you just hurry yourself out of here and me and the young lady—"

"Josephine," she supplied, embarrassed that her hostess was giving aid and comfort to someone whose name she didn't even know.

"Me and Josephine will change the child out of those very unsuitable clothes and check to see if she is all right."

Mrs. Simmons felt a great surge of fondness for her husband as she saw the blush of embarrassment mount his cheeks. He had witnessed more vileness in his job than their entire church congregation had ever imagined, and yet, like a shy young boy, his cheeks would flame if his wife even mentioned indecency.

"Out of here, out now." She pushed him toward the door, and, standing on tiptoe, she kissed him on the cheek before she shut the door.

Thirty minutes later she emerged from the room, laden with a great armful of Rebecca's soiled and odoriferous clothing, looking very pleased.

"All is well, Mr. Simmons," she said. "She must have gotten away from the first man, and you and Josephine came upon her before anything else could happen."

Simmons sighed, relieved.

Thirty minutes after that, Rebecca Westover opened her eyes on a sight she had not been sure she would ever see again: a clean bed, a tidy room and herself in a soft, comfortable, white flannel nightgown.

"Hullo," she called softly, less to attract attention than to test the reality of the place. If she could hear her own voice, she would know this wasn't a dream, though if it was and the nightmare she had escaped from was the reality, she didn't want to ever wake up.

"Rebecca? Are you awake?" Josephine was immediately bending over her.

Even as Josephine's worried face and fretful blue eyes came into focus for Rebecca, visions of that other place began to fade. She had drunk a lot of cheap but potent alcohol, and as it evaporated from her brain, it lifted away the recollection of her ordeal.

"Well, hello, Miss Forrester," the girl murmured weakly. So she hadn't been mistaken; she had seen this nice young lady before she lost consciousness, though she was at something of a loss to explain her presence here. But then, she was considerably at a loss to explain her own presence here, wherever here was.

"How are you feeling?"

"I think I have a headache," Rebecca said softly. At that moment Mrs. Simmons, believing she heard talking in this room, opened the door. A beam of light from the kitchen fell across the bed, directly into Rebecca's eyes, and then she was absolutely certain she had a headache.

Jenny had been about to ask if Rebecca was awake, but the groan issuing from the bed answered her question.

"She says she has a headache," Josephine explained softly.

"And I shouldn't wonder." Jenny clicked her tongue sympathetically as she bent over the girl. "Now I want you to drink this."

Rebecca grimaced. "It smells awful," she said.

"And it'll taste worse, but if you can hold it down it will make you feel better." People in the throes of agony will do things that they could never accomplish in healthier times. Rebecca took a breath of air, held it and swallowed the vile concoction that smelled a little like tar and tasted a lot like sewer water.

"There! I drank it!" gasped Rebecca, collapsing back onto the pillows.

"Drinking it was the easy part," Mrs. Simmons said. "The trick is to keep it down. Now you just lie here and sleep while me and my husband and Miss Josephine decide what's to be done next."

Josephine looked up sharply and realized that she had forgotten that the episode was not completely over yet. Quietly, the two women left the room and joined Simmons at the kitchen table.

"You sit down and let me fix you a bite to eat. You may not know it, but you look about ready to collapse."

Josephine knew it, all right, but she felt embarrassed by all that this gallant little soul had done for her and the girl already.

"No, no, please. Don't put yourself to any trouble." She didn't see how ridiculous her protest was. Jenny Simmons had waited up until two o'clock in the morning for a husband who should have been home at eleven. When he finally did arrive with a strange woman, suspicion had never even crossed her mind. Without question she had consigned their marriage bed to an unknown girl, dressing her in her own best nightgown, serving, cleaning, clucking and caring ever since they had come through that door. And now Josephine did not want to put her to any trouble.

"No trouble, dearie," Jenny said, and honestly did not feel that it was. "Let me just boil you a nice egg while Simmons toasts some bread. I have the tea steeping, and we'll have a cozy little picnic." As she was speaking, she was putting the eggs on to boil and cutting the bread for her husband to start his toasting operations at the fire. Josephine said nothing more, but allowed the good woman to provide the food for which she was actually famished.

"Now then," Jenny said as she placed the steaming kettle on the board between them. "What's to be done next?"

The question evidently took them by surprise, because her husband and guest just looked blankly at each other for a moment.

"Well... I... uh..." Simmons began.

"Becky and I had better return, I suppose," Josephine said.

"Return where?"

"To Ettington. Westover Manor in Ettington is where the girl ran away from and where I was staying and supposedly supervising her. It was due to my negligence that she left, and I felt it my duty to find her before any harm came to her."

"Which you did only just," Mrs. Simmons said. There was a brief pause while the thought passed through all their minds as to what a close call the child had had this night.

Then Josephine continued. "But now we need to return as quickly as possible. Tonight, that is, this morning, if there's a train."

"There's always a train from Derby," Simmons said, but not loud enough to be heard over his wife's exclamation.

"This morning! Laws, you don't mean to pack yourself and that child off into a train now, do you?"

"Mrs. Simmons, well, you see . . ." Josephine was reluctant to confess this. "They don't know we've gone."

"They know by now."

"Yes, but I'm the only one who knew Rebecca was going, and I didn't tell anyone I was leaving." Josephine wasn't forgetting little Matty Clark, she just reckoned correctly that he would not volunteer the information to anyone. "So they may know we're gone, but no one knows where we are, and I am particularly concerned for dear Mrs. Westover, who must be worried sick over her daughter." She was, strictly speaking, most particularly concerned about the younger Mr. Westover and whether or not he was worried at all about her. Her concern for Mrs. Westover was genuine but secondary.

"Why didn't you tell someone where you were going?" was Simmons's very logical question.

It was a question to which Josephine did not have a good answer. "I wanted to find Becky myself, so I wouldn't be in as much trouble," she sort of mumbled. Vocalized like that, it sounded a little self-interested. As a matter of fact, it sounded quite self-interested to the Simmonses, but they had the good grace not to mention it. After all, Josephine *had* rescued Becky, even if her motives had not been completely pure.

Instead, looking nervously at his wife, Simmons thought of another delicate subject to be broached. "Ahem." He cleared his throat. "Ah . . . Miss Foster, how are you going to purchase your return tickets? The girl didn't have any money on her, and you didn't have any, and while my wife and I would be more than willing to help, if we could—"

"Please do not concern yourselves about that. I am afraid I was not totally frank with you, Constable Simmons, for I have been careful to reserve enough money to pay for the fares back to Ettington, but I dared not hire a cab or make any other purchases. You understand?"

More than understanding, Simmons was obviously greatly relieved. He and his little family lived sparsely from payday to payday, and he really did not have the resources to be as generous as his nature inclined him. Paying the driver of the cab tonight had almost cleared out what little extra money they had been able to save this entire month.

"And I plan on sending you the money for the cab as soon as I get back," Josephine said, as if reading his thoughts. Feeling as though he had been found out in a stingy intention, Simmons made the proper protests, but they did not change Josephine's determination. Totaling all of the debts she had incurred since she first arrived in Ettington, she had several years' worth of payments to make from her modest wage to several people.

"Anyway, Mrs. Simmons, Constable Simmons, surely you can see that it is important that we get back as soon as we can. I am afraid I don't even have enough surplus funds to pay for a cable to the Westovers and can only relieve their minds by bringing Rebecca to them in person."

Jenny Simmons still did not wholly approve of sending the young girl, so recently victimized, off so soon, but Simmons had one last telling argument.

"What if it were little Teresa, wife? And you didn't know where she was at and worried nigh to death? What then?"

So finally, Jenny Simmons agreed, although she insisted the girl get a couple of hours of sleep.

"Nothing will be happening at the station until six o'clock, anyway," she said.

And she was right.

Chapter Forty-four

Derek Westover is finally drawing near to Derby. His sister and the woman he loves are safe. Will Trolley and the person he believes is the woman he loves are sleeping, more or less comfortably. His father is bound for Derby from Ettington, and his aunt is en route to Derby from Lancaster. And it occurs to the Author that the hero of a romance ought to be allowed a few pages, particularly if he is finally doing something more engrossing than falling asleep on horseback.

Fortunately, Derek caught his second wind outside of Loughborough and has been awake and riding furiously ever since then, with the scent of blood in his nostrils.

Derek had been with his former friend and farmhand to visit his brother before, so he was pretty certain as to where he would find the faithless pair. The Trolley farm was on the outskirts of Derby. From Midland station it had been necessary to hire a coach for the considerable trip back to the farm, but on horseback, coming from Ettington, one came to the farm first without entering the city at all.

There! He could see a farmhouse. If he was not mistaken, the Trolleys lived at the end of this road right here.

He was not mistaken.

It was a little past four in the morning now, and though the sky was a trifle paler, it still could not be called anything but dark outside. Guiding Gallant Rider to the rear of the house, they disturbed a few cows and sheep, but Derek was relieved to note that Fred Trolley had no dog, or if he did it wasn't worth its salt as a watchdog.

Tiptoeing up to the door, he tested the handle gingerly. Just as he had hoped, this being a neighborly agricultural community, the inhabitants did not bother to secure their doors at night. He opened the door and entered, closing it quietly behind him and taking a moment for his eyes to adjust to this darker interior. When he had been here before, he had not taken an inspection tour of the house, but he had seen the three downstairs rooms, so the bedroom or bedrooms had to be on the second story.

He climbed the stairs as silently as he was able. Even still, the occasional creak he could not avoid was heard in the little room at the back of the pantry, which was directly under these stairs.

Almost simultaneously the two women opened their eyes, startled into instant wakefulness.

"A prowler!" Phyllis whispered. Her bed companion did not say anything, and Phyllis was unable to see her, but she felt the motion on the pillow and knew she had nodded.

"What are we going to do?" she whispered again, fearfully.

In reply, Darcy Trolley threw back the blankets and stood up. She seemed to be groping on the floor and against the wall for a few moments and then Phyllis could see her stand up again, holding a large stick in her silhouetted hand.

"Come on!" she whispered, and reluctantly Phyllis stood, too.

Meanwhile, Derek had reached the top of the stairs and was studying the two closed doors in front of him. Rather than risk prematurely waking the occupants in the bedroom by throwing open the wrong door first, he decided to quietly inch open one of the doors to check. He hoped it would not spoil the drama he had planned.

It was well he did, because the room he went to first was a crowded storage room. Before closing that door again, the thought crossed Derek's mind that Fred Trolley must never have thrown away a single possession since the day he was born. The room was packed solid, practically to the ceiling, and judging from the few items he could distinguish, with things Trolley could not possibly ever use again, if he had used them at all in the first place. There were disintegrating harnesses, pots with holes—large gaping holes—in them, a wooden stool or two with one or more legs missing, and other useless mementos of an active farmer's life. The whole room was littered with scraps of paper. The window faced the east, so this room was getting light, and Derek was able to make out the paper at his foot to be a crop sale receipt from ten years ago.

Turning from that door, he approached the sleepers' room with fire in his eyes and vengeance in his heart, though he was not really clear on how he was going to achieve the latter, except through humiliation.

He grasped the handle and threw the door open.

"Aha!" he cried, leaping into the room. "So, I have caught you out!"

Will sat up immediately, throwing the blanket over his brother's head.

"Mr. Derek?" he asked, not trusting the evidence of his own sleep-bleared eyes. "What in heaven's name are you doing here? And at this hour?"

"Your cries of innocence will not avail you, Mr. Trolley. And as for you, you, you . . . *trollop*! Come out of there!"

Fred Trolley was doing his best to oblige the young man, but less to meet the demand than to find out what was happening. He clawed furiously at the blanket and finally tore it off his head.

Derek, of course, was surprised to find Will sleeping with his brother, but not nearly as surprised as he was going to be in a moment, as Fred and Will could both plainly see by looking past his shoulder.

"Take that, you villain!" Darcy Trolley cried, raising the stout stick in her hands. "Don't you dare hurt my Fred!" And with that she lowered the stick, sharply, onto Mr. Westover's head.

Derek was rendered unconscious.

He came to a few minutes later, with a pillow under his head, placed there by Darcy, of course. Everyone was standing around him waiting for an explanation. When Derek sensed his brain stop quivering in aftershocks, he felt it safe to open his eyes. The first person his gaze fell upon was Phyllis.

"Miss Foster!" he cried incredulously.

"That's Miss Forrester, Mr. Derek. The young lady who has been impersonating Miss Forrester in your house is actually Miss Foster."

"Not impersonating me, exactly," Phyllis said in an honorable attempt to be fair.

"Well, all right. As Phyll told it to me, they didn't really mean to mislead your family; that is, Miss Foster didn't."

"You?" Derek asked, uncertainly, totally confused.

"No, the other Miss Foster. The real Miss Foster."

"It's pretty complicated, Derek, old boy. See, when the girls arrived, they were mistaken for each other, then before things could get straightened out, why, me and Phyll..." His voice died away, and Phyllis supplied a delicate ending to his sentence.

"Will and I met and became involved."

Derek looked from Phyllis to Will to make sure he was understanding the full import of her words.

"You mean you and...?" he said.

Will nodded.

"Became involved," Phyllis said firmly.

Suddenly a thought occurred to Derek that should have been his first after the foregoing startling revelation.

"Was it you that night in the barn?" he asked Phyllis urgently.

Her cheeks began to glow, and she replied in embarrassment, "Which night was that?"

"The night you stumbled over me. That is, did you fall on top of me, there on the barn floor one night?"

"Oh, yes, that night." Will looked puzzled and Phyllis reassured him. "He was lying on the floor one night when I came down." She turned back to Derek. "I thought you had forgotten that, with the drink and everything. I thought if you remembered you would have said something."

"I did not remember very much, only that the girl who came giggling down after embracing Will and fell into my arms said she was Miss Forrester."

"Oh. That's right, I did, didn't I?" Phyllis giggled again. "You took me by surprise, Mr. Westover."

"I may not have said anything to you, but I said a number of things to Miss Forrester, er, that is, Miss Foster. Things that may take me a while for which to apologize."

"So. What are your intentions toward me and Phyll?" Will asked, redirecting the conversation to the topic that most interested him.

"What about you two?" Derek asked, still in a daze, still concentrating on the topic of his interest.

"Well, I mean, she *is* supposed to be marrying you. I suppose you could make some sort of demand, and I suspect your mother would want you to make an effort to reclaim her. But I'd have to give you a fight, old friend. I don't intend on giving her up too easy. Course, when we started I thought she was Miss Foster and fair game, and it looked like you was fond of Miss Foster—Miss Forrester . . . the real Miss Foster. I didn't mean to tread on toes, mate, but the truth of the matter is, Phyll and me are planning on getting married. That is, unless you try to step in. But I wish you wouldn't.''

There was wonder in Will's voice as he suddenly realized that he really did hope his good friend Derek wouldn't try to stop the marriage. Not just because of the money, either. This was the first time in his countless dips in the romantic pool that he could feel the water close in above him. He was really in over his head this time and he was not putting forth any great effort to get out of the water. He slipped his arm comfortably around Phyllis's familiar waist and thought of how natural it seemed for them to be together.

''What? Try and stop you two? I wouldn't dream of it. In fact, I wish you all the luck in the world and will even stand up at the wedding for you.''

''That's generous of you, Mr. Derek, but will you stand up for us to her folks?''

''Mr. and Mrs. Forrester? Oh, that's right, they are coming to visit us, aren't they?''

''Exactly, Mr. Westover,'' Phyllis said. ''That's why we had to leave. My parents would have absolutely forbidden it and packed me off to Sheffield or Sunderland or the Sandwich Islands, if necessary, to prevent it.''

''This way, though, I figured we could give them a few months to miss their lovely daughter and then we'd make some kind of overture, me with my best foot forward, as they say.'' Will grinned winningly, and Derek joined Miss Forrester in her belief that Mr. Trolley could go about as far as he wanted on his charm.

''I'm hopeful of eventual reconciliation,'' Phyllis said. ''But perhaps it would smooth the way a little for us if we had an advocate at court.''

''I see. Well, yes, it will be to all of our advantage for me to lay the foundations of peace. For you and your parents, and me and mine. I don't suppose Mr. and Mrs. Foster will raise any great objection, if only I can justify myself to their daughter and convince her to look favorably on my suit." Which brought Derek handily back to the topic that most interested *him.* "Miss Foster! I'd almost forgot. Where is she?" With that exclamation Derek finally stood up and only had to grab Will's arm for a moment before his vision cleared and his balance was reestablished.

"What hit me?" he finally thought to ask.

Will pointed to a formidable-looking bludgeon lying at his feet.

"*Who* hit me?"

"Darcy," Fred said.

The Reader may be interested to learn what Mr. and Mrs. Fred Trolley have been doing during this lengthy exchange. Were they silently following it, or was something else involving them? Well, as a matter of fact, and without diminishing the import of these last few pages, it must be admitted that it was something else.

Fred Trolley, seeing his fierce little wife flatten a great hulking man whom she believed to be her husband's assailant, was struck for the first time in years, perhaps for the first time ever, by what a capable woman he had married. And he also suddenly realized that she was fond of him. For some inexplicable reason, she was still fond of him. He was touched, and for the first time in a good many years the two of them were exchanging tender words. They were gently touching each other. He brushed her cheek with his hand; she put her fingers timidly on his arm. It was a totally unfamiliar sensation for both of them, and they were quite caught up in the wonder of it. They were, nevertheless, paying intermittent attention to the other conversation taking place in the room.

Therefore, when Derek asked who hit him, Fred supplied, "Darcy," with glowing pride.

At the unfamiliar note in his brother's voice, Will studied the two of them carefully and was pleased by what he saw. He loved Darcy and had thought for years that his brother ought to be horsewhipped for the way he treated her and spoke about her. He wouldn't have blamed her if she had left him, but the woman clung to the man she had married and gave every appearance of still putting some value on him and that marriage. Maybe this would mark the beginning of a better life for her.

"As I was saying," Derek said, when his vision had cleared again. "Where is Miss Foster? I thought I was following her here. Or rather, I believed I was following Miss Forrester, who I thought was...well, you understand my confusion. Especially since you are responsible for it. But Miss Foster, *my* Miss Foster, was not at the manor when I left. I am certain of that. I made careful inquiries and was told that she took the same 6:00 o'clock train to Derby. That must have been the one you two took. Didn't you see her?"

Will and Phyllis looked at each other. Phyllis blushed a bit and Will smirked.

"Truth to tell, Mr. Derek, we didn't see much of anybody else."

"Oh, Will, I think a steward brought us some tea once."

"He did? Oh, yes, right you are, luvvy. I remember now. But I'm pretty sure that was all we saw. Wasn't it, Phyll?"

"Yes. Yes, he was the only one."

"I don't understand this. I was so sure I would find her here—she isn't here, is she?" Derek looked suspiciously at the two of them, but it was evident that even if she was here these two would be as oblivious to her presence as they had been on the train. "I just never considered any other possibility," he ended with a puzzled expression.

"Maybe you better check at the station," Fred said. His words were, as usual, few but pithy.

Suddenly that seemed like a very logical idea to Derek, but he enlarged upon it. "Maybe we had all better check at the station," he said. "That is, Will and Miss Foster, excuse me, Miss Forrester, and myself. No need for you two to go."

Fred Trolley was glad Mr. Derek had thought of that, because if he hadn't, Fred was certainly going to point it out to him.

"What do you mean, we had all better go?" Phyllis asked.

"What do you need me and the lass for, anyway?" Will echoed.

"The Midland terminal is a large and busy place. Three of us can look through it faster and much more efficiently than one. There is also the slight chance you may recognize one of the crew from your train, whom we could then question.'' He paused for a moment to see if any further objections would be forthcoming. ''Come along then, get dressed.'' He began making motions and noises like a mother hen, shooing them into action.

''Now?'' Phyllis shrieked.

''It's five o'clock in the morning, man,'' Will protested.

''The station is open all night, and who knows what has happened to Josephine? The sooner we start looking for her, the better. Let's go!''

The other two could see that Derek was not to be dissuaded, and since any chance for further sleep was gone by now, they agreed that they might as well accompany him.

''But we're not going back to Ettington with you,'' Will grumbled as the ladies left the room and he began to dress.

''Of course not,'' Derek agreed impatiently.

''Well, I just wanted that understood before we headed for the station.''

''Will, my old friend. I only want you and Phyllis to come with me so that we can avoid confusion here in Derby.''

Chapter Forty-five

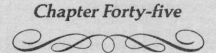

Derby station was also the headquarters of the Midland Railway company and as such was a very busy place. Activity commenced early in the morning and quieted down only very late at night, but never really ceased.

At midday the station resembled a riot in full flight (or whatever it is riots do when they get under way) but each of our characters about to converge on the station at six o'clock in the morning (and there do seem to be quite a number of them) assumed that things would not be quite as hectic at that hour.

The station was located on a rise of ground, allowing a clear view of the surrounding countryside. Whether placed there with the intent or not, it had provided numberless passengers coming to Derby by train the opportunity of turning in excitement to a traveling companion and crying, "I see it! There's the station!"

It was a steepish climb to the station on foot from the town, but the younger Simmonses, out for an early-morning romp, didn't notice it much, climbing it as effortlessly as a swirling cloud of smoke from a smoldering fire. The elder Simmonses, though, and their two companions, were painfully aware of the extra effort their sore, twisted, abused and deathly weary muscles were called upon to exert in order to lift their legs to climb the hill. After looking at the incline, Josephine honestly wondered if she was going to be able to make it. And once there, how could she possibly board another train for the fifty-mile jounce back to Ettington?

Rebecca didn't even look.

Jenny Simmons thought it was criminal to have the girl out and traipsing to the train depot at six o'clock in the morning, but nobody had any money to hire a cab, and Josephine had already rehearsed the necessity of leaving immediately. As soon as Rebecca woke she, too, joined the argument. "I am fine—I really am, and though I can't remember much of what happened last night, I have a feeling I should be surprised that I feel so well."

Josephine smiled and patted her hand, Mrs. Simmons was suddenly busy pulling the bedclothes and fluffing her pillow, and Constable Simmons turned away from the doorway, from which he made occasional surveys, with a gruff clearing of his throat. But nobody offered the girl any enlightenment, other than explaining to her who Josephine really was.

"You could stay with us for a few days while Miss Foster returns to Ettington, assures your parents of your well-being and makes some kind of arrangement for your return," Jenny suggested.

But Rebecca seemed quite as eager as Josephine to return to Ettington. A two-day "running away forever" statement was quite sufficient for her, especially with firsthand experience of the alternatives to having a somewhat high-handed mother overseeing one's life. Since she was rebounding from her ordeal with the phenomenal recuperation of youth, Jenny Simmons really had no choice but to allow the journey.

Jenny, too, felt the drag of gravity as she tried to lift her feet—feet that had enjoyed no sleep all night, and had been raised from the floor for only a very brief hour and a half while their owner planned and tossed and fretted and fumed.

She's a brick, Anthony Simmons thought, watching his wife gallantly putting one foot in front of the other, keeping one eye on Rebecca and the other on their children, who were scampering ahead of the adults or lagging behind. He was not a man who took his wife for granted and realized what he had been asking of her when he brought the two young strays home with him. That she would work all night long and mother them both didn't surprise him—it was the way she was—but it reminded him how much he loved her. He never considered that he was the one who had traveled all over Derby the night before with a young lady who had simply asked him directions to Beauford Lane, guiding her, advising her, listening to her, joining her quest, and in the end personally rescuing the girl for whom they were looking. There was a reason why Simmons and Jenny made such a compatible pair.

Simmons, as the man in the group, assumed he couldn't possibly be tired and refused to listen to his own creaking bones as he climbed the hill with his brave little company.

To all of them, except the children, it was a very long climb.

The squire really shouldn't have minded the train ride. He was able to sleep all the way, so it was just like being home. It was probably getting to the train in the first place that he hated so much. In fact, it had to be, since he didn't know anything about the rest of the trip.

It had been almost four o'clock when the old man who stayed in the station nights shook him awake, saying, "Derby?"

"Wha . . . ? No, the name's Westover."

"Didn't you say you wanted to get to Derby?"

"Oh. Oh, yes," the squire said, getting his thoughts in order. "Is the train here?"

"She'll be pullin' in in about two minutes, sir. You best be ready. She don't hardly stop at all and won't be expecting to take on any passengers this time of night."

"Righto. Now where did my hat get to?"

"There."

"Of course. Thank you. Now my—"

"Umbrella?"

"Where is it?"

"Under the bench."

Finally Westover had both his person and his thoughts in order, and only just in time. He was pulling his coat around him and trying to fasten the button over his indulged middle as the engine came stampeding into the station, evidently unaware that it was the wee hours of the morning and some people in Ettington were trying to sleep.

"Hold off a minute, boys," the station man called to the engine crew, who were already set to start out again. "Got a passenger for you tonight."

The men looked up, surprised, as the squire came through the station house doors and headed for the passenger car.

"Is this train going to Derby?" he called.

"That she is, cap'n," one of the grimy crew called back. Westover nodded and touched his hat, then clambered up into the waiting car. He had no more than found himself an empty seat, when the engine gave a snort, pawed the ground, and the restless herd was off again.

In the seats before and behind him were passengers in assorted states of semirecline and all indulging in the comic sport of "public sleeping." Before the train started up, a snorer or two could be heard throughout the car, but the noise of the engine soon reduced their efforts to insignificance. Squire Westover lost no time in joining them.

Although the train passed through several more towns that night, it picked up no other passengers, arriving at its destination squarely on schedule. By then it was nearly six o'clock, and most of the passengers were awake, some of them for more than an hour. As ladies straightened their skirts and attempted to smooth their hair, the gentlemen were pulling down trouser legs and pulling up stockings. Squire Westover was one of the last to relinquish his stranglehold on sleep, but was finally roused when the woman sitting across the aisle from him turned to another woman next to her and exclaimed, "I see it! There's the station!"

This gave the squire time to sit up, do his pulling, recover his hat and remind himself that he hated to ride on trains. He really hoped it wasn't going to take too long once he got into Derby to meet Minerva and find the young people.

There are different ideas on the subject of family traits. Some people believe that the same ability or characteristic is often passed from the parents to each one of their children.

Minerva Twitchell was of the group who claimed that only one member of any family can inherit a trait from his or her parents. Her brother Perseus was the one in her family who could sleep anywhere, anytime, in any circumstance. Mrs. Twitchell had been unable to sleep at all that night and saw the Derby station on its little rise through red-rimmed eyes. If she had known anyone in Lancaster, she would have been taken to their house and announced herself arrived for a visit. Of some duration. It was not uncharacteristic of her, and friends and family had come to accept it. Unfortunately, none of them lived in Lancaster, forcing her to make this exhausting trip. If she was going to make the same transportation mistake often in these, her declining years, she would have to recommend Lancaster as a likely place for relocation to some of her acquaintances.

"Wake up, Maggie. We are coming into Derby."

"Are we there already?" the girl said, yawning and rubbing her eyes. Her mistress gave her a sour look. She saw no reason for the girl to flaunt her sound night's sleep in her face.

"Check on Anstopholes," she said crossly. "And you had better start gathering our things. We will be there in just a minute."

Maggie busied herself in fulfilling her mistress's instructions. She was used to Mrs. Twitchell's unaccountable temper, and it was easy to overlook when one had just enjoyed a good night's sleep.

"Thank heavens the station will be reasonably calm at this hour of the day. I only hope we have no trouble getting a cab this early. All I want is to be driven quietly to my home and rest in solitude for many days,'' Mrs. Twitchell said as the train pulled into the station.

Derek had tried to rush them, but Phyllis and Will were in no particular hurry and tended to hang back. The result was that they traveled at an average speed. They arrived at the station at the same time two trains, one from the south and one from the north, pulled in simultaneously. Derek was sorry to see that. If they had hurried just a bit faster, the station would have been practically empty, they could have searched it and made their inquiries and been out of there by the time these trains disgorged their passengers, who would only complicate his search. At that thought he darted an unfriendly look at his two companions, additionally irritated by the fact that they were impervious to any outside ill humor.

Dismounting his horse, he left the two lovers behind him and hurried into the large building, unwilling to wait for them any longer. They knew why they were there; let them begin their search as soon as they would.

Derek entered the large doors on the east side of the building. Glancing over the passengers who had just disembarked from the trains, his first reaction was one of dismay at all of the strangers he must sift through before he could hope to get any information. His second reaction was one of happy surprise as he recognized his Aunt Minerva as one of that sleepy-looking throng.

''Aunt Minerva! Mrs. Twitchell!'' he hailed, raising his hand. But with the noise of the trains and the passengers and the hawkers out in full force even this early in the morning, he doubted that she had heard him. To his surprise, though, a look of delighted recognition lighted her face, and she waved in his direction. Derek started toward his aunt, and she toward him, but before they met she veered, and he realized she had not waved at, or been coming to meet, him at all. It was someone behind him she was greeting and, curious, he turned himself to find her friend.

The Simmons party entered the station through the west doors, which were the closest to them, because none of them, by now not even the children, wanted to go another step farther than they had to.

"Oh, blast the luck!" Simmons said. "Looks like we should have stopped to have breakfast."

"I told you so," said Mrs. Simmons, shaking her head at their folly.

"Why? What do you mean?" asked Josephine.

"It looks like a couple of trains just pulled in," Simmons explained. "There will be a great crowd there now. If we had waited just half an hour longer, as my wife suggested we do, they would have all been cleared out and you would have had an easier time at the ticket counter."

"Now there will be long lines and people shoving and no doubt a number of surly passengers this time of the morning, who will not appreciate my little brood playing at hide-and-seek among their legs."

They were there now, though, and while there may have been advantages to coming at a later time, no one suggested they leave and come back up that hill again.

The Simmons parents were busy keeping eyes and hands on the Simmons children. Rebecca, heavy with fatigue, was lagging behind a bit. Josephine was in front and leading the group when she saw the squire.

"It's Squire Westover!" she exclaimed. The strangers passing on either side of her looked surprised at her outburst, but not nearly as delighted as she was. Looking around at their faces, she immediately dropped back to share the information with people who would appreciate it more.

"Look," she said, grabbing Simmons's arm, thereby forcing him to release one of his charges, and pointing. "It's Squire Westover."

"One of your Westovers?" Constable Simmons asked incredulously.

"The very ones. That's Becky's father."

"Dear!" Simmons said, calling to his wife and diverting her attention from her children, thereby releasing another of them into the mainstream. "Miss Foster says she can see Miss Westover's father."

"Where?" Jenny asked.

"There!" said Josephine, pointing again. Miss Crawford had told her that a young lady never points in public; it is not considered good manners. But then, Miss Crawford had told her many things that one should certainly abide by while living in a girls' school that Josephine had found to be impractical, impossible, or perhaps just inconvenient in the outside world.

"Are you sure that's him?" Jenny Simmons asked uncertainly at the distant figure.

"I am. No one but the dear squire would wear such unsuitable apparel on a day like today." The squire labored under the impression that a heavy woolen tweed was an appropriate fabric for all climates and seasons, even a steaming railway carriage in August.

"Well, if it is, dear, you had better catch him. It looks like he is in a hurry to get someplace."

Looking up again, Josephine saw that Squire Westover was indeed moving rapidly through the crowd, and she would have to hurry if she hoped to intercept him. She looked uncertainly from the retreating figure before her to the preoccupied figure behind.

"You go ahead," Jenny said. "Me and Anthony will bring Miss Becky along after you stop her father. Go. Go now." She waved encouragingly, so Josephine scurried away from her into the crowd.

Phyllis Forrester and Will Trolley meandered into the train depot at a very leisurely pace. They were not worried about anybody, they did not have to find anybody, and they certainly did not feel as if they wanted to spend time with anybody else. It is one of the injustices of life that so often it is the ones with the least pressing motivation who succeed first. Perhaps it was because those two were not rushing about, losing time, turning around, dodging people, backtracking. Because they were not reacting to any pressure, even after entering the station sometime after Derek did, they were right beside him in the throng he was furiously trying to buck, while they were peacefully slipping through it like a hot knife through butter. In fact, they were the first ones to see Rebecca.

Rebecca, the poor child, was dead on her feet. In addition to as much traveling, as little sleep and even more trauma than Josephine had gone through the night before, she had an additional quart of very inferior wine with which she was still contending. Jenny was walking next to her, leading her through the milling passengers in the direction Josephine had gone.

"Hurry along. I think I see her."

"And you say she saw my father? Here?"

"That's what she said. I wouldn't have thought she could make out a face from that distance, but she swore she recognized him and his clothes. She said she would hold him if we would catch up with her. Oh, there she is now."

The crowds in Midland station could easily be likened to a strong wind, or even a hurricane. They seemed to swirl and twist around in chaos, with a lost and panic-stricken look in their eyes. People ran and bumped into each other, rebounding and then hurling themselves forward again. No one could be seen. No one could be heard. The effect was very distressing to anybody trying to find another person. And then suddenly, without warning, one might find oneself in the eye of the storm.

Just as Jenny Simmons said, "Oh, there she is now," two people moved away, and Rebecca and Jenny found themselves in the calm of the eye.

"Rebecca?" Phyllis said.

"Phyllis!" Josephine said.

"Josephine?" Will said.

"Will?" Rebecca said.

"Rebecca?" Minerva said.

"Minerva!" the squire cried.

"Papa?" Rebecca said.

"Perseus?" Minerva asked.

"Derek!" the squire, Rebecca and Aunt Minerva all cried at once.

"Derek?" Josephine asked.

"Josephine!" Derek exclaimed.

The reader must be aware that there was a great deal of head turning, jaw dropping and incredulous gasping going on during this staggered exchange.

Phyllis was surprised to see Rebecca there, but Josephine was absolutely stunned to see Phyllis, whom she had secretly hoped was at the manor and would have by now made all the very difficult explanations. Will, of course, was startled to see Josephine there, while Rebecca was very pleased to see Will. Then it became extremely confusing, with the Westovers all discovering each other simultaneously. Last of all, even though it is often said that people in love can be aware of each other's presence by the subtle shifting in the atmosphere alone, Josephine and Derek saw each other, and suddenly for the two of them there was no one else in the depot.

Josephine, in her strange assortment of clothes, with her hair disheveled, her cheeks aglow after the climb up the Midland hill, was quite the loveliest picture Derek had ever set eyes on. As he gazed at the clear countenance, that dear form, he could not imagine how he had ever believed her to be anything but as pure as the driven snow.

Derek, as he stood before her, breathing heavily, his dark eyes piercing her to her very soul, was like some passionate Greek god come down from Mount Olympus to wed a mortal maiden. Herself, perhaps? Dared she hope? Well, of course. He didn't want to lose such a valuable source of revenue.

The thought heightened her color, making her appear even more adorable to Derek, who already believed she was the very epitome of adorableness. As they stood facing each other, a shaft of the morning light entered the long eastern windows and sought them out in the very center of the depot. It sparkled in their hair and reflected brilliantly off their eyes and faces. To each it seemed that the other was standing in an ethereal nimbus of light that set them apart from and above the common herd in the train station.

Squire Westover and his sister, turning from their happy reunion, saw only two young people, both appearing to be somewhat travel-stained obviously in love with each other and looking slightly ridiculous. Derek wore a look of idiotic adoration, and there was pathos and longing swimming in Miss Forrester's eyes.

"What are you doing here, Mr. Westover?" Josephine asked, the awkward huskiness in her voice endowing the question with greater seriousness than the words alone warranted.

"I came after you and Will Trolley."

"Will Trolley? Me and Will Trolley? Why in the world would you think I would be with Mr. Trolley?"

"What else was I to think when Will told Alex, and Alex told me, that he was running off with Miss Forrester...Miss Forrester?"

Finally something other than blind devotion could be seen in Derek's eyes: a twinkle of mischievous teasing. Josephine didn't see it. She had ducked her head in embarrassment.

"And after the way I saw you two carrying on in the hayloft, my honor needed some sort of satisfaction. Mr. Trolley is lucky to be standing here before us alive and unmaimed."

Josephine looked up in surprise at Derek's speech.

"What do you mean, 'carrying on in the hayloft'? I assure you, Mr. Westover, such unseemly behavior would never occur to me in my wildest dreams."

Will, who was within hearing distance of Josephine's insulted disclaimer, looked across at the two of them.

"Miss?" he asked.

"No offense to you, Mr. Trolley," Josephine told him. Will and Derek both thought she was blushing because of her unfriendly tone concerning Trolley. She was actually blushing because, as a matter of fact, behavior at least that unseemly *had* occurred in some of her dreams, and those were not even her wildest dreams.

"I know that . . . now," Derek said softly, with the huskiness now in his voice.

"What?" Josephine's question was but a soft breath of sound.

"I said, I know now that you were not with Will in the hayloft."

"Why would you think I ever was?" she asked, still very confused by Derek's accusation.

"Because the young woman who stumbled over my drunken form that night told me she was Miss Forrester."

"Oh. Derek . . . Mr. Westover . . . I . . . well, you see, I must tell you . . . that is, you should know . . . yes, you certainly need to know . . ." Josephine paused and took a deep breath. "The truth is, Mr. Westover, that I am not Miss Forrester."

"I know."

"I am Miss Foster."

"I know."

"Josephine Foster. I am a governess. Or at least, I meant to be a governess."

"I know."

She stopped and looked into his eyes hopefully, still not completely convinced that he knew what he said he knew. He couldn't; not with that curve to his lips and that dimple in his cheek.

"It was never my intention to deceive you. Not in the beginning, anyway."

"I know that, too. I know everything about your changing places and Will and Miss Forrester's . . . friendship."

"Well, if you know so much, Mr. Westover," Josephine said, managing, at last, a little spunk, "then you know that you have been pursuing nothing but phantom wealth. So you see, your charm has been wasted, and you must go fortune hunting elsewhere."

"Miss Foster," Derek began with exasperation. If the girl would only shut up so he could finish with this irksome explanation, he could get on with the business of folding her desirable little body in his arms and kissing those ruby-red lips! Her body was, on the contrary, quite bulky and lumpy, owing to her layered ensemble, and her lips were decidedly pale.

But before Derek could say anything else, the squire clapped his son on his back, laughing heartily.

"I must say, m'boy, when your mother sent me off on this little mission, I feared it was going to mean a lot more work than this. Who was to know that all I had to do was step off that train and I'd find my son, my daughter, my guest, my daughter's governess and my farmhand all waiting on the platform? And my sister," he finished warmly, giving Minerva another hug.

"Father, perhaps we had better go to quieter surroundings. I think you deserve a full accounting."

"Of course, you're all coming to my house," Minerva said. Her brother's hearty personality tended to rub off on Mrs. Twitchell and, though she usually preferred the role of pampered guest, under his tutelage she cheerfully assumed that of lavish hostess. "I have already sent Maggie ahead, with Stoffy, to alert the staff that I will be arriving with guests in tow. They will have the house open and lighted by the time we arrive."

"Oh, really, Mrs. Twitchell, I am afraid that will be a terrible inconvenience," Josephine said.

Before Minerva had a chance to reflect and conclude that the girl was right, the squire boomed forth his approval of the plan, the paltriness of the objection and seemed to encircle them all with his arms and guide them to the line of hansom cabs that were by now waiting outside the station.

The Simmons family, on the periphery of the reunion, hung back, sure that the invitation couldn't have included them. But the squire beckoned them, as well, and stopped them in their retreat.

"No you don't," he called. "Any friends of Rebecca's and Miss Forrester's are friends of ours. Isn't that right, Minnie? The more the merrier, that's what I always say."

Caught up in his father's infectious magnanimity, Derek grabbed Anthony Simmons by the arm and offered the crook of his elbow to Mrs. Simmons.

Even Minerva smiled warmly at them and murmured, "Of course, of course."

The ride to Beauford Lane was certainly different from the trip to the Twitchell house a number of them had made the night before. For one thing, the great relief to all of their minds at finding everyone else well and happy was like reviving tonic for many of them. In almost drunken good-fellowship, they divided into three different cabs, mixing and matching the party, so that Jenny Simmons was riding with two of her five children, Will Trolley and Minerva Twitchell. Constable Simmons was in another cab with Phyllis and Derek and two more of the Simmons children. The squire counted himself lucky indeed to be sharing his coach with the lovely Miss Forrester—that is, Josephine Foster; nobody had explained matters to him yet—his beautiful daughter, wearing a simple but becoming dress he couldn't remember ever seeing before (one Jenny Simmons had lent her) and a very pretty little girl introduced to him as Teresa Simmons. Her mother had been worried to see Teresa put into a cab with strangers, because she was the shyest of her children. But long before they reached Beauford Lane, she was perched gaily on the squire's lap, recounting a hair-raising experience her dog, Bowser, had gone through just last week. The story had something to do with the neighbor's cat and an evidently lethal bat the neighbor wielded, though because of the child's pronounced lisp, it was difficult to grasp all the finer details of the story. Nevertheless, she charmed her audience, and even with Derek in another cab, Josephine was sorry to see the ride come to an end.

She was especially sorry, because now came the explanations, and she was fearful of the effects those explanations would have on many of their lives.

Chapter Forty-six

What've you got to eat, Minnie, m'dear?'' the squire bawled as they entered the house. "We have some famished people to take care of here, I'll wager. What d'you say, little Teresa? Doesn't toast and crumpets with strawberry jam and hot chocolate and scrambled eggs and jam tarts sound good to you?'' With every menu item the squire recited, the little girl's eyes got bigger and bigger, until by the time he got to the jam tarts, there was little else of her face to be seen.

"Perseus!" Minerva hissed. "I've been gone for a week! I don't know that we have any of those things."

"Well, you must have something, Minnie. Check it out." Having sent his sister on her way, the squire turned to direct other traffic. "Miss Foster, why don't you and Will go see if you can help my sister dredge up something to eat, while Miss Forrester and Rebecca come here into the dining room, and we'll see if we can't make things a little cozier."

The Misses Forrester and Foster looked uncertainly at each other, and Derek could tell that it was time his father learned the truth, or at least as much of it as Derek was aware of himself.

"Father, before we do anything else here, there are some things you need to be told and some misconceptions that need to be cleared up."

"Of course, dear boy, just let me get things settled."

"No, Father. Now. Please sit down." At the sound of his son's voice, the squire looked quizzically at him. This command he had been wielding was unfamiliar to him after thirty-four years with Catherine Westover. The sleepless night must have gone to his head, and he realized his son was probably right: he did need to sit down, and he sank into one of the hall chairs.

"Miss Forrester, Miss Foster, I believe I will need your help with this." Again the two young ladies looked at each other and then stepped forward to stand on either side of Derek, who stood looking down at his father. "You first, Miss Foster." The squire looked expectantly at Phyllis, but it was Josephine who cleared her throat and began.

"I am Miss Foster, sir. Josephine Foster. It was I your wife engaged as governess for your daughter, Rebecca."

"Now you," Derek prompted the other girl.

"And I am Phyllis Forrester. Ulanda and Gregory Forrester are my parents. Of course I don't remember you, and you've seen me before only as a small child. So you couldn't recognize me, but I am the person your wife invited to Westover Manor."

The squire looked in confusion at the two girls and then addressed his son in injured tones.

"Why didn't you tell me?"

"I didn't know!" Derek exclaimed. "I was deceived along with everyone else. I thought it was Miss Forrester we welcomed as our guest, and much to my chagrin, I thought it was Miss Forrester with whom I found myself reluctantly falling in love." Josephine drew in her breath and looked up at the tall man at her side. The squire looked to her for help, but seeing the adoration in her eyes, could tell that no help would be forthcoming from that quarter. He turned his attention next to the other young woman.

"Why didn't you say anything, young lady?" he asked.

"Squire Westover, I do not know what you know about the power of love, but until I came to your home, I can guarantee that it was more than I knew about it." Will had come up to join the line by now, and here he put his arm around Phyllis's shoulders, lending her some badly needed support. "William and I...struck up a friendship. More than that, really. In short, sir, we fell in love. And since knowing Will, I have come to the realization that money, position, prestige, all of the things I had so valued up until now, are no longer the most important things in my life." Will squeezed her affectionately, and she turned to smile at him.

"That isn't to say that me and Phyll don't want any of those things, guvnor," Will added.

"No, no, the privileges of my birth have certainly cheered my existence to this point, and I believe they would make any life I chose more pleasant. But if the choice is given me of my former possessions and the love I have found, there is no choice. I am going to marry Will."

"Will Trolley? My farmhand?" Of all the startling disclosures the squire had heard so far this morning, Phyllis's devotion to Mr. Trolley seemed the hardest for him to accept. Will had never considered the squire a legitimate target for his charms, so Perseus Westover had never personally felt their power, although he had witnessed their devastating effect on some of the female members of his household staff and even his youngest daughter. And now old Gregory Forrester's daughter? Well, did you ever? The more he thought about it, the more tickled he was by the idea.

To any inquiries the squire had always replied that he and Gregory Forrester were the best of friends, thick as thieves, cheek by jowl, that sort of thing. But Forrester's confounded superiority would tax the patience of Job! Whenever Mr. Westover had the misfortune to spend some time alone with Mr. Forrester, the conversation was heavily one-sided, dealing largely with how much money Forrester was making, how successful his business dealings were and what a glittering gem in Sheffield society his wife was.

This spirit of competition had in fact begun in their college days, when young Forrester had constantly practiced his one-upmanship on his older, shier, clumsier and quieter schoolmate.

Perseus had always felt the one area where he had bested Forrester was in his choice of marriage partner, and since then Forrester had been trying to make up lost ground. His latest boast had been what a valuable asset in the marriage market his daughter was going to be.

"She'll make some lucky blighter damned happy, Westover old boy. Prettiest thing in Sheffield, I'll warrant." That last was always accompanied by a painful jab in the squire's ribs. "Yes, sir, that girl has been raised to be worth something to her family name."

Now here was that very girl, the finest filly in Forrester's stables, vowing her everlasting and unchangeable love for a rude farm laborer who was actually employed on the Westover estates, and her willingness to be parted from all her wealth and position before she was parted from him.

"When I overheard the telegram my father sent about coming down to Ettington, I knew that Will and I had to elope. For the time being, I must not see my parents, though I, that is we, have hopes of being reconciled to them in time."

The squire could see that the desire was sincere and decided he would dispense with the gloating, at least to Forrester's face. For the inner satisfaction it would give him to see Phyllis Forrester marry a farmhand, he would forgo pouring any salt on the wound and would hope it could heal naturally.

"Don't you understand, Squire Westover?" Phyllis pleaded.

"You're not going to make this hard for us, are you, sir?" Will added.

"What? No, no, children. I know that true love is not something you can choose beforehand or fight against after the fact. I would never think of standing in your way."

"I am delighted to hear you say that, Father." From the sound of his son's voice, the squire realized that he had put his foot in it now and that he was more or less committed.

Oh well, he thought, looking at the pretty girl at Derek's side, of whom he was genuinely fond. Forrester's getting a fine lad as a son-in-law under that cheek of Will's, and I don't know how money could make Derek's little love one whit more precious. So he smiled at Josephine in a kindly fashion, which showed Derek that his father, at least, was reconciled to the match.

"And what have you to say for yourself, young lady?" the squire said, sternly addressing his youngest daughter, who had come up to sigh over the romance.

"Me?" she asked innocently, stalling for time.

"Yes, you. What are you doing in Derby? I hope you're not going to tell me that you're in love with the Midland station-master?" Despite her father's gruff voice, Rebecca at last felt herself upon safe ground. The Midland stationmaster was nearly seventy years old and was a confirmed misogynist. She grinned, a little, then joined the inner circle here to add her defense.

"I was running away to Aunt Minerva's because you ruined my horse," she said, trying to make it sound justifiable.

"Gallant Rider?" Derek asked in surprise.

"Yes." Rebecca used her most injured inflection.

"Ruined?"

"Yes, ruined. He can't do anything now except wander around in that pasture all day, because you had him gelded!" She said the last word boldly and was pleased to see the shocked color mount Miss Foster's cheeks.

"He's far from ruined, Becky," Derek said. "He only wanders around in the pasture because no one will take him out. But I just rode him from Ettington to Derby in less than ten hours, and I'll wager he'd be able to go back again today, although I don't think I could."

"My Gallant Rider?"

"Your Gallant Rider."

"He's all right?"

"Better than all right. He is a magnificent animal, little sister. He will be a worthy steed for some fine horsewoman."

"Oh, Derek!" Rebecca cried, hugging her brother in a rapture of joy. Then turning to her father, she squeezed his neck and planted a happy kiss on his cheek. "Did you hear, Father? Gallant Rider is all right!"

"I heard, I heard," the squire protested, as, chuckling, he struggled to loosen the hold his daughter had around his neck, and forgetting, in the process, how angry he was supposed to be with her.

"Phyllis," Will said, taking the lass in both of his arms and giving her a resounding kiss. "You won't ever regret staying with me."

"I don't ever plan on it," Phyllis said with determination, as if she was quite aware that Will had the ability to make her regret her decision if she gave him the chance, but had no intention of him ever having that chance. No, she had decided never to be sorry about this. Which, incidentally, she was not.

"Am I to understand, Mr. Westover, that you rode that poor horse all night to Derby from Ettington just to catch up with me?" At last it was Josephine's chance to talk to Derek.

"You and Trolley, yes."

"Because you thought I was Miss Forrester and now you know that I am not?"

Derek found himself entranced by the tilt of her chin, the length of her white throat, the soft slope of her shoulders. Distractedly he nodded in answer to her question.

"I have no money, Mr. Westover."

By now his attention was focused on the rise and fall of her breasts under the layers of material covering them, the waist that simply begged for his arms, the seductive swell of her hip. He forgot to answer her altogether this time.

"My parents have no money."

Reluctantly he pulled his eyes back to her face and his mind back to the subject at hand.

"We are poor."

"Is that significant?" he asked.

"Is that significant!" she fairly shrieked.

Suddenly every eye in the room was on them. Everyone had been preoccupied with his or her own interests and ignoring Derek and Josephine's exchange, but Josephine's outburst made them the uncomfortable center of attention.

"Mightn't we speak someplace privately?" she hissed.

"Of course. Aunt Minerva's garden. Aunt Minnie, do you still have the old swing in the garden?" he called to Minerva.

"Straight out the kitchen door," Minerva called back.

Derek offered his arm to Miss Foster, and the squire watched the two of them leave the room with a look of fondness, approval and sweet reminiscence in his eyes.

"Is that significant!" Josephine exclaimed again. Not as harshly this time, or perhaps it just seemed softer because they were alone in the little garden, sitting quite close on the swing, of which Derek had insisted they take advantage. "My imagined wealth was the only reason you showed any interest in me at all."

"Now Josephine . . ."

"You said yourself you were reluctant to fall in love with me," she said, purposely misquoting him.

"I said I *had* fallen in love with you. I was reluctant only because my mother had arranged the match, and . . ." His voice died away.

"And . . . ?" she prompted.

"And because I thought you were something less than—" Derek groped clumsily for a delicate phrase "—an unsoiled flower."

To his surprise, Josephine laughed merrily at him and the picture his phrase called up. And then, most surprisingly of all, she kissed him. It was a very short kiss before she realized her audacity and drew away.

"Then you were not trying to marry me for my money. And I was not having an affair with Will. And yet, despite my very understandable misgivings, I fell in love with you, though I thought you were a perfect cad, and you fell in love with me, who, on the other hand, you thought was not perfect at all."

Josephine, though possessing a vivid imagination, was very inexperienced in the theater of love, and nervously kept chattering as Derek put his arm around her, drew her *very* close and started softly kissing her cheek, ear, neck and shoulder. He already had arrived at the conclusions Josephine was drawing and was not interested in them at all now. But the girl kept talking until, at last, he was forced to shut her up by covering her lips with his own.

The two of them sat together on the garden swing, tentatively exploring their long-delayed, mutually proclaimed love, for a long time. Sometimes they spoke in quiet tones to each other, silly little phrases that would mean nothing to anyone but them. But more often, no words were spoken at all. They would kiss and part and gaze into each other's eyes and then kiss again. It was a gloriously drawn-out forenoon, which neither of them felt the least compulsion to end.

Their stay in the garden lasted all the time it took to prepare a very passable picnic for fourteen people, the consumption of the same and a strained period of polite chitchat in the drawing room between the Simmonses and Mrs. Twitchell, while the squire napped and Will and Phyllis looked at one of Mrs. Twitchell's old albums, which under any other circumstance,

in any other company, would have been as drearily boring as
the grave.

In fact, Derek and Josephine weren't prompted to leave their
little nest until the sun threatened to banish the shadows under
the tree that the swing hung from.

"I suppose we had better go in. My aunt will wonder what
has become of us," Derek said.

"I suppose you are right," Josephine said lazily. He stood
and drew her to her feet, directly in front of him, their arms
coincidentally wrapped around each other.

"And do you mean to tell me, Mr. Westover," she said,
smiling up at him, "that, even believing what you did about
me, you rode all the way to Derby for me?"

The playful light in his eyes vanished and was replaced by one
of perfect seriousness.

"Miss Foster," he said, with something very like a catch in
his voice, "I would ride around the world and back again for
you."

Epilogue

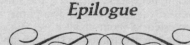

Now, traditionally, this is the point at which love stories come
to a conclusion. The curtain is discreetly drawn on the man and
woman who have, after agonizing doubt and delay, discovered
each other and their love. The reader closes the book with a sigh
and the reassuring phrase "they lived happily ever after"
echoes in that sigh.

But things are not so simple in our little romance. There are
still a number of characters who have not yet been disabused of
their mistaken impressions or enlightened as to the young people's intentions, none of which were at all in accordance with
what had been carefully planned for them. And these are not
weak personalities, willing to accept whatever fate throws in

their way. These people are accustomed to seizing life by the horns and twisting it to meet their pleasure.

We can hardly end the story without assuring the reader that Squire Westover was, in fact, able to masterfully maneuver his wife into not only approving of the idea of her son marrying a penniless governess, but into actually believing it was she who thought of it in the first place.

And Phyllis's fortune is still hanging in the balance. Before the story ends and the book is closed, it must be reported that when Gregory and Ulanda Forrester first received news of their daughter's marriage, Gregory Forrester was outraged.

"A farmhand!" he'd shouted, tromping about the room, looking for something on which to vent his wrath. A sofa pillow that had innocently fallen to the floor was kicked savagely aside. "Westover will never let me hear the end of it."

"I understand, dear, that his own son did not make an advantageous marriage, either. She is a simple teacher, or a secretary or some such. She didn't bring a penny with her."

Ulanda Forrester was not as concerned about the Westover fortunes as her husband, but she wanted to calm Gregory's temper.

"I will disown her, of course," Forrester said. "They will never see a penny of my money!"

"Now, dear." Mrs. Forrester was not pleased, either, to see added fortune and prestige evaporate before her eyes. But Phyllis had enclosed a little note for her mother in the letter Forrester had crumpled and thrown into the grate. Her daughter sounded blissfully happy. It brought tears to Mrs. Forrester's eyes when she read it.

A few months later, she was able to get to Derby and see her daughter, with a grandchild on the way. There was a glow in Phyllis's cheeks and a sparkle in her eye; Ulanda saw her daughter's new assurance and confidence in herself and felt the warmth of love that emanated from her for her husband. And, well, then Mrs. Forrester met Will Trolley. He was absolutely charming. He said the most delightful things and could seem to do no wrong—in a woman's eyes he seldom did—and the change this marriage had wrought in Phyllis was little short of miraculous.

Mrs. Forrester returned to Sheffield with a new light in her own eye.

"Well?" Gregory had demanded belligerently.

"They are very happy."

"What about him?"

"I like him."

"What? That good-for-nothing, money-grubbing—"

"He did not marry our daughter for her money," his wife said.

"It's a good thing, because she is not going to get any of it."

"We'll see," Mrs. Forrester said quietly.

Mr. Forrester looked up sharply at his wife. Ulanda's family was very rich. His father-in-law had fared even better than Forrester in the Sheffield cutlery market and had invested his profits more wisely. His wife, therefore, wielded a certain amount of influence over Gregory Forrester when she got determined about something. From the tone of her voice when she said, "We'll see," Forrester had the sinking feeling that she was determined about welcoming her daughter and her husband back into the family.

She was.

In time, they did.

And as to Broderick, that virtual paragon of butlers. If we end the story now, the Reader is left with the mistaken impression that his infallibility has been shattered, that he is the object of scorn, having been duped by a simple little governess and having acted wholly out of place to the daughter of the wealthy Sheffield Forresters. But if, in fact, the Reader believes that, how little has the Reader come to know our Broderick.

When the young master returned to Westover Manor with his newly betrothed, the butler treated pretty Miss Foster with a certain familiar deference that conveyed to the Westovers and the Westover staff that they all may have been surprised by Mr. Derek's choice of partners, but Broderick was not. He had obviously known from the moment he met her that Josephine would be mistress here eventually, and that he didn't need to waste his time with Miss Forrester—that is to say, Mrs. Trolley. It was really an amazing thing to witness, the way he turned every surprising development to his advantage, never missing a beat and elevating the respect in which he was held to something approaching awe.

The Simmonses were such a deserving family, surely the Reader would be interested to learn that every year, without fail, Josephine and Derek sent them a generous Christmas box, packed with toys and games and beautiful fabrics and canister upon canister of toothsome exotic delicacies. In a separate envelope, tucked in the box, was always a fifty-pound note and a little message from Josephine that said, "Please apply this against our account." Anthony and Jenny carefully invested that money and with it were able to send each of their five children to school, two of their sons to university, and provide a handsome dowry for their daughters' marriages.

In the course of their marriage, Derek and Josephine bore and raised four children, which cannot be done without a certain amount of heartache and grief. They had occasional disagreements. Derek's mother was never easy to live with, and Mary Foster, Josephine's mother, drove Derek to distraction.

In short, they did not live happily ever after. But they were happy most of the time.

Josephine loved Derek so much that morning in Aunt Minerva's garden that she didn't know it was possible to love him any more. And yet, as each year passed, she saw that the years before had only been a shadow of the love that grew between them. Perhaps Derek had sensed the joy life with this woman would bring him, though, as he held her in his arms and murmured fiercely, "I would ride around the world and back again for you."

* * * * *

Harlequin Historicals®

COMING NEXT MONTH

#37 THE FOREVER ROSE—
Curtiss Ann Matlock

When beautiful Quaker Maggie Holland saved Jake
Cordell from three desperadoes by holding them at
gunpoint, her peaceful ways were jeopardized. But as
violence entered her life, so did passion. Would the
embittered Jake see—before it was too late—that Maggie's
love could overcome the ghosts of his past?

#38 RECKLESS LOVE—Elizabeth Lowell

Janna Wayland led a gypsy's life in the canyons of Utah
Territory, taming the legendary mustangs for which men
paid dearly. But Virginian Ty Mackenzie entered her
recluse existence and vowed to capture the wild beauty for
his own.

AVAILABLE NOW:

#35 CHASE THE
THUNDER
Patricia Potter

#36 GAME OF HEARTS
Sally Cheney

CHRISTMAS IS FOR KIDS

Spend this holiday season with nine very special children. Children whose wishes come true at the magical time of Christmas.

Read American Romance's CHRISTMAS IS FOR KIDS—heartwarming holiday stories in which children bring together four couples who fall in love. Meet:

Frank, Dorcas, Kathy, Candy and Nicky—They become friends at St. Christopher's orphanage, but they really want to be adopted and become part of a real family, in #321 *A Carol Christmas* by Muriel Jensen.

Patty—She's a ten-year-old certified genius, but she wants what every little girl wishes for: a daddy of her own, in #322 *Mrs. Scrooge* by Barbara Bretton.

Amy and Flash—Their mom is about to deliver their newest sibling any day, but Christmas just isn't the same now—not without their dad. More than anything they want their family reunited for Christmas, in #323 *Dear Santa* by Margaret St. George.

Spencer—Living with his dad and grandpa in an all-male household has its advantages, but Spence wants Santa to bring him a mommy to love, in #324 *The Best Gift of All* by Andrea Davidson.

These children will win your hearts as they entice—and matchmake—the adults into a true romance. This holiday, invite them—and the four couples they bring together—into your home.

Look for all four CHRISTMAS IS FOR KIDS books available now from Harlequin American Romance. And happy holidays!

XMAS-KIDS-1R

Especially for you, Christmas from
HARLEQUIN HISTORICALS

An enchanting collection of three Christmas
stories by some of your favorite authors captures
the spirit of the season in the 1800s

TUMBLEWEED CHRISTMAS by Kristin James

A "Bah, humbug" Texas rancher meets his match in his
new housekeeper, a woman determined to bring the spirit
of a Tumbleweed Christmas into his life—and love into
his heart.

A CINDERELLA CHRISTMAS by Lucy Elliot

The perfect granddaughter, sister and aunt, Mary Hillyer
seemed destined for spinsterhood until Jack Gates arrived
to discover a woman with dreams and passions that were
meant to be shared during a Cinderella Christmas.

HOME FOR CHRISTMAS
by Heather Graham Pozzessere

The magic of the season brings peace Home For
Christmas when a Yankee captain and a Southern heiress
fall in love during the Civil War.

Look for HARLEQUIN HISTORICALS CHRISTMAS
STORIES wherever Harlequin books are sold.

HIST-XMAS-1R

Wonderful, luxurious gifts can be yours with proofs-of-purchase from any specially marked "Indulge A Little" Harlequin or Silhouette book with the Offer Certificate properly completed, plus a check or money order (do not send cash) to cover postage and handling payable to Harlequin/Silhouette "Indulge A Little, Give A Lot" Offer. We will send you the specified gift.

Mail-in-Offer

OFFER CERTIFICATE

Item	A Collector's Doll	B Soaps in a Basket	C Potpourri Sachet	D Scented Hangers
# of Proofs-of-Purchase	18	12	6	4
Postage & Handling	$3.25	$2.75	$2.25	$2.00
Check One				

Name _____

Address _____ Apt # _____

City _____ State _____ Zip _____

ONE PROOF OF PURCHASE

To collect your free gift by mail you must include the necessary number of proofs-of-purchase plus postage and handling with offer certificate

HH-3

Harlequin®/Silhouette®

Mail this certificate, designated number of proofs-of-purchase and check or money order for postage and handling to:

INDULGE A LITTLE
P.O. Box 9055
Buffalo, N.Y. 14269-9055